Signs of the Soul

Suzie Parker

Signs of the Soul was edited by Tonya Bluston

Thanks you Em.

What is a pleasant feeling?

What is an unpleasant feeling?

What is the place in between these?

Buddhist Wisdom

ACKNOWLEDGMENTS

Signs of the Soul is a story that is deep in my heart, I fall in love with this book every time I read it. This book has taken a long time to finish and I would like to thank my children for putting up with my endless hours at my laptop.

Thank you all.

Baby,

What happened to you on the wire while trying to help me, I shouldn't have asked you to help me it was wrong. I asked you to leave your life for me. I'm not worth that to anyone. The day that I first saw you my soul came alive, I couldn't help myself I wanted you in my life. All I wanted to know was who you were, you intoxicated me. Playing that game with you was my way to see if you belonged in my life.

I have never been that lucky, but you came into my life, the time that we spent was worth a lifetime of luck. The love that we have for each other will never die. It will last longer than us being man and wife. I'm sorry that I'm not there to wipe away your tears and hold you to tell you everything is ok. Please don't forget to dream because that is the special part of you.

I'm selfish and I'm sorry for leaving you.

PS

I will always love you.

CHAPTER 1

My office keys fell from my hand, making a loud crashing sound on the wooden floor in the hall outside my office door. The noise reverberated down the vacant hall; thankfully, it was early and no one was in the Sydney Museum offices at this time.

"Good one, Laura," I groaned to myself.

I tried to bend over to retrieve the keys without dropping my research papers and morning coffee. I paused for a moment to readjust myself in an effort to not lose my paperwork. On my second attempt, I managed to make a strange yoga move to pick the keys up while holding onto everything. I had a lot of work to get through that day and I didn't need to add putting all my papers back in order to it.

The north side offices of the Museum always had a chill to them. My office was on the ground floor of the north side offices. The hallway was part of the hundred year old section of the building. The top portion of the walls and the roof of the inside hallway were lined with pressed green tin, and brown wooden panels wrapped the bottom part of the walls. When the offices were built in the seventies, the century old windows that faced outward had been rotated. Now they ran along the top of the offices to let the outside light into the hallway. The six panelled glass windows could not be opened since they were too high up and heavily painted. It always bothered me that the designers did that to the windows; I wanted to turn them back the right way up and strip off the brown paint to show the wood.

Placing the key into the lock, I made another yoga move to grip the contents of my arms tightly, as I turned the key to open the door. A rush of chilly air swirled up to meet me, giving me goose bumps as the door swung open. My body shivered as I flicked on the light switch - this was my usual physical reaction to entering my office so I thought nothing of it.

My office was a decent size, and was painted white to match the coloured shelves lining the walls, like all the offices on this floor. My shelves were filled with books and artefacts that I had collected from house auctions and junk shops over the years. A large brown and green wooden art deco desk and an old office chair the same colour of my desk stood near the door. The desk and chair were prized finds of mine from a second-hand shop that I had bought the desk just after starting work at the Museum eight years ago.

In the corner of the office was a large, white-topped table that was used for photographing and examining artefacts. I loved my work as a Research Assistant at the Museum, but my passion and the area in which I revelled was Egyptian history. The research I carried out at the Museum covered all areas of history. Mostly this didn't bother me, but now and then I found myself wishing I could focus on Egyptian history full-time. While I understood Egyptian Hieroglyphs, Cuneiform script was my main strength. I could read it like a newspaper.

I was twenty-six years old and unmarried. I did not mind being single; after all, this was the nineties and the pressure of being married was not like it once was. I felt strongly that the right guy would come along when he was ready. I was tall for a woman, about five foot eight, and of average build. My hair was reddish brown. And my eyes - people would often tell me that they were very blue - "the colour of the soul", as a woman put it to me once.

Placing the papers down on the desk, I reached over and turned on the PC. Computers were the newest thing in the work place, they were slow to start up only being the nineties, not thinking much of it I gave it time to do its thing. I turned my attention to my newest acquisitions. It was a stack of six old pine boxes which stood in the middle of the room. A clipboard poked out of the top box. I glanced at the paperwork, I shivered again. I turned to shut the door hoping that this would help with the chill as well as deter anyone who wanted to interrupt me. Music always helped me think as I worked, I pressed play on the CD player, to help me think. A purple cardigan hung on the back of the desk chair I slipped it on to help with the chill.

Janis Joplin's voice cried out as I blew into the lid of my coffee and glanced down at the list attached to the clipboard. The boxes had come from a deceased estate; the items had been bequeathed to the Museum by an old gentleman. I didn't know him. I had been given the job of photographing and recording every item. Dr Colman, my boss, also

2

wanted me to complete some ancient translations before the weekend. Today was Wednesday, and that's why I had arrived early. As the only person in the museum - and in fact in all of Sydney - capable of reading Cuneiform, Dr Colman liked to show off. I did not really have the time to go through these items, but I would nonetheless ensure they were categorised correctly, as I always did.

I took a tentative sip of coffee and tried not to scold my tongue as I studied the list of items that were in the boxes. Nothing stood out to me. Once more, I skimmed down the list.

The top box reached my eye level, opening it, I saw that every item was wrapped in newspaper, and tied up with brown string. Some of the newspapers dated back to the forties.

Not wanting to waste any more time, I carefully picked up one of the parcels and took it over to the artefact table. The items in the boxes could have been anything, from any time and any country. The list of items did not tell me much: *Old wooden boxes, clay pots, plates, wine glasses...* I was confused about why they had been sent here; they should have gone to a charity shop, not a Museum.

This collection was not from anyone famous in Australia's history or world history. Dr Colman had been persistent that I go through these items but had not told me why he wanted these boxes.

I went through most of the first box, and most of it had just been plates and teacups - nothing that should be in the museum. As I laid the last item from the box onto the table, some of the paper fell away from the parcel. I frowned as I slowly moved a part of the paper to one side. "What the - ?" My heart skipped a beat.

Swiftly, I slipped on my hands the cotton gloves that we use to handle artefacts, before I moved back more of the paper. My jaw popped open at what was laying before me. It was a beautiful white alabaster Egyptian Shabti; it was about twenty centimetres long with what seemed like a gold inlay. Its eyes glazed up at me. Shabties were servants to their owners - they were a very significant part of the burial process in ancient Egypt.

In ancient Egypt, they were placed in their owner's tombs; these little statues and the spells from the Book of the Dead were vital. Their owner would call upon their Shabties to help them in the afterlife. China's Entombed Warriors are the same thing, just on a larger scale.

When the owner needed them, a magic spell was spoken - this was the sixth chapter of the Book of the Dead, Illumine the Osiris. The Shabties would come to life and assist their owners by saying, "I'm here." This Shabti had its *Nemes*, or cloth headdress, with a carved face and crossed arms. Its legs and feet were covered with what resembled cloth-type carving; this is typical for Shabties. It had a deep gash down the front but its wakening spell was still there. However, its owner's name had been cut out. Someone did not want the Shabti's owners name spoken. An Egyptian's name is important; if they cannot speak their name to Osiris after their last trial into the Underworld, they would not be able to enter into the afterlife. One of the trials was to weigh your heart against an ostrich feather. If your heart is lighter than the feather, you can go into the afterlife. Your family and friends need to be able to speak your name to keep you alive. However, if you fail, your mummy is place into eternal sleep. If you passed, then every night Osiris will come to get you to take you to the Underworld. Then, the next morning, you come back to your body, to sleep. Most of the Shabties we had in the Museum were only ten centimetres long. This was much bigger and of better quality than I had ever seen. It did not seem to be a fake and the age and patina were there.

The office door burst open. "Damn it!" I jumped and spun around almost dropping the Shabti to the floor.

Chester erupted into the office. Out of breath and holding his chest, he glanced around the room for me. The boxes was concealing me from anyone who entered the room. I waited for him to end his performance before I acknowledged that he was in the office.

"You need to work out more, Chester. Or maybe… do some work." I giggled at him as I restored the Shabti back to the safety of the table. "Look at what I found."

Chester stopped his over-acting to inspect the Shabti. He raised one eyebrow and nodded. "Wow, nice. Did it come with the boxes?" Chester asked.

"Yes." I answered him.

"Cool. Its name is missing." He pointed to the Shabti's legs.

"Yes, I know," I answered him as if I was sixteen.

Chester understood my banter immediately. He answered me by brushing me off, prior to taking a breath and beginning to ham it up once more. He waved his hand at me while he tried to get his breath back. I was not in the mood for his theatrics now. I crossed my arms and sighed. For a moment, I watched him putting it on, hoping he would go back to work. That was Chester, always wanting to be in the limelight. I knew it was not going to end anytime soon.

"Laura... did you... see..." Chester breathed.

"Did I see what?" I asked, while shaking my head at him. I needed to be short with him or this would go on longer than it should.

He stamped his foot at me. "Laura Sinclair, not *what*... but *who*... did I just see?" Chester stated, still catching his breath and fanning himself as he fell into the desk chair. He took my coffee, sipped it, then pulled a face and put it back, disliking the taste due to there being no sugar in it. Plus, it was now cold.

"Oh sorry, *who* did you see?" I replied trying to act as if I cared.

Chester was an archaeologist. His passions were Roman and South American cultures. He loved that men in Roman and South American times could parade around in skirts and all that gold. Back then, it was seen as masculine, but in our times, it is looked upon as feminine. He did not do any more digging; he loved working at the Museum because he did not have to get his hands dirty in a pit.

"Guess." Chester jumped to his feet and studied the Shabti again before nodding. "Nice," he stated once more. He began to fan himself once more while trying to act as if he was still out of breath.

"Thank you. Do you want a glass of water, or an asthma pump? I'm sure I have one around here somewhere." I began lifting up papers, acting as if I was searching for an asthma pump, hoping of all hopes he would go back to work soon.

"Laura," Chester slapped me.

"Did we get someone new on staff?" I asked with a sigh, while slapping him back in return. He pulled a face at me.

"No, you're hopeless sometimes. *The builders* are here. I tell you, I'm in love. I have to help them today, I'm so lucky."

Chester slipped his hand under his shirt, and moved it back and forth. Once more, I sighed at him, I loved Chester and he was one of my best friends but sometimes, he had bad timing. I found myself rolling my eyes and shaking my head at him, willing this will be over soon. He slumped down once more in the desk chair, grinning at me. His white teeth glinted in the light of the office. His long pointed shoes flipped back and forth making a clicking sound.

"Chester, you were in love with the guy who made your coffee yesterday. I'm busy now go away, I'll see you at lunch."

I endeavoured to heave Chester out of the chair, and out of the office, but he begun whacking at me to stop me once more. "Chester I have work to do. Go away." I growled at him.

He pushed his weight down in the chair not wanting to move. "There is one who resembles... one of the Village People. I mean, they are all like the builder in the Village People. They are all young and well built, but there is one. Oh, Laura I'm in love." Chester put his hands to his face and made his eyes go wide.

"I'm happy for you, good luck... Now go away, I'll see you at lunch." Once more I tried to shove him out of the door, Chester pushed me back. He was stronger than me.

He made a clicking sound at me. "Oh, Laura, you know, sometimes you need to live a little."

Chester clutched my arm and yanked me out of the office and down the hallway. His office was in the other direction. I did not even have time to take my cotton gloves off. He dragged me to the end of the hall to the elevator. Impatiently, he rattled the button of the elevator a few times. After a couple of moments the number had not moved. It seemed like it was taking its time. Chester groaned.

"Chester, Dr Colman wants me to go through the boxes and he wants me to also to finish the translations. I can't play now - can we do this later?"

"Shh. No." Chester waved me off, not wanting to hear it.

He let out another impatient grunt. He had a firm grip on me; his hand was wrapped around my wrist firmly. Chester was well built; his clothes sat on him just right, and he was always dressed in the latest fashion. Chester had history and reference books in his office like most people who worked in the Museum. However, Chester also had a good collection of fashion and gossip magazines. They were research as he put it. I would find him reading them more than anything else.

Without a word Chester changed direction, hastily, he towed me to the stairwell, it led down into the North Basement. The stairwell is part of the old building. The steps were wooden and narrow, and some of them moved. I hated going down them, in fact, no one used these stairs; it was easier to use the elevator. There was one small window in the stairwell that cast the only light; it was surrounded in blue tin, which lined the walls. The old green carpet stirred as I tread down on the steps, I clutched onto the rail with my gloved hand as we descended. My stomach flipped out of fear of Chester pulling me over. I held on tighter.

"You know, my life is fine." My voice was hitched from the fear of falling.

Chester stopped, turned on the stairs, and shook his head at me. "Oh Laura, I'm in your life and you're not normal, baby. You read Cuneiform for God's sake, before university even. That's not normal. You can be closed down as well - no guy is going to like that."

"You're an Archaeologist, you like that stuff too, remember. I'm not closed down.... I'm just a deep thinker... I live a lot in my head there is nothing wrong with that."

"I get to talk about Archaeology now. I get to watch over other people

7

doing the dirty work. It's bad on the nails all that digging. I go out, I meet people and go on dates, Laura." Chester said as if he was trying to teach me.

"I sang with The Band the other night and I had a date..." I paused for a moment to think the last time I had a date. "And it's not my fault that I am not an Archaeologist, you know that." I said the last part in a hushed voice.

"I know that... but when?" Chester broke into my train of thought.

"When, what?" I sucked on my bottom lip. I did that when I was stressed. Chester was pushing my buttons. He knew he would get this reaction from me.

"When... did... you... last... go on a date?" Chester put his hand on his hip, not caring that we could plummet to our death any moment.

"I don't remember..." Answering him as if I was a naughty schoolgirl, I pulled my hand out of his grip, then turned on the stairs to try to go back to work.

"That's my point." Chester grasped hold of my arm again and dragged me firmly down the stairs. I let out a yelp while clutching onto the railing once more. At the bottom of the stairs stood a heavily painted wooden dark brown door that led to the North Basement hallway. Chester released his grasp on me as he pushed hard on the door to open it. When he popped it open, I spun around to try to escape once more. Chester was too swift. His hand flung out like a serpent and seized my arm.

"They say never let your attacker take you to a second site," I said trying to pull away.

"Ha Ha. I'm not letting you go. Take your medicine like a good girl."

We made our way along a small passageway with besser brick walls. It was always colder and darker down here. We came to a halt at some large yellow metal doors. Chester motioned at me to peer through the little window high up in the door.

8

Valuable artefacts were stored down here. The basement was out of date and needed restoring; over time water from rain had been leaking into the basement. Many of the larger artefacts that had been stored in here had been damaged and the smell of mould could be overwhelming sometimes. The Museum had just acquired the money to update the basement - it had been a long time coming. We had spent months fundraising, walking around with tin cans, collecting money in the Museum. We had done antique appraisal days, long hours of putting prices to other people's treasurers. Finally, after a car boot sale and the trustees meeting, with what we had raised, we could fix the problems in the basement.

Chester kept nudging me as we peered through the little window. Most of the basement was underground. A large roller door opened out to the loading dock on William Street. Chester pointed from behind his hand to one of the builders. The builder had a red flannel shirt, with jeans and work boots. He seemed about my height. His hair was dark, thick, and curly. He was tanned, and his forearms were wide - he looked like he should be on a farm. He was attractive, I would give Chester that. I noticed that a tattoo poked out from under the sleeve of his shirt. I could not quite see what it was. He and the other men were carrying work gear into the loading dock.

"See *man meat*. Who can't love that?" Chester ran his hands through his hair, his dark eyes running over the builder's body. His mouth pulled together making a humming noise.

"Oh yes," I answered.

I was impressed the builder was handsome. His mates were dressed the same: ripped shorts, old shirts and work boots - what girl would not like that?

Right now I did not care. I wanted to go back to my office and find out what was in the rest of the boxes. In addition, why was there a Shabti alongside all these worthless things? The guy Chester had pointed out was not in my league. He was sporty and I was not. I would never date anyone like that. He was good for a quick glance over the shoulder and that was all.

"Well, Laura I'm going. I'll see you at lunch. Dr Colman wants me to help the boys." Chester grinned at me, flicking his eyebrows as he spoke. He kissed me on the cheek as he pushed open the yellow door.

"Have fun. Behave yourself." I gave Chester a playful slap on the shoulder. He waved me off as he danced away from me. Thankfully, this was over for now. I knew I was going to hear more of it later, I had no time to worry about it at the moment. I spun on my toes and hurried back up the stairs.

I met Marisa in the hallway as I made my way through the door to the office level. She stopped when she saw me, Marisa glanced at the door that led down to the basement. "You left early," Marisa said.

Marisa Cress was my childhood friend and flatmate. I hurried to help her with her books as she unlocked her office door a few doors away from mine. She was a thin build, a little shorter than I was, with thick dark hair and high cheekbones.

"I wanted to know what's in the boxes," I informed her.

"Oh, did you find anything good?" she asked.

We had gone to university together she also was an archaeologist like Chester. I was never able to obtain my doctorate due to funding problems.

"Possibly. I haven't had a chance to finish sorting through the boxes yet. Chester had me go down to view *man meat* in the basement." I made a face as I told her about Chester's latest obsession.

"Anything good?" Marisa raised an eyebrow at what we had been up to as she unlocked her door.

"Maybe, the one with dark hair, but he's not my type. Too sporty." I shook it all off, trying not to think of him and I together in anyway.

"See you at lunch?" I nodded in answer to Marisa's question as I placed her books on her desk.

~

"Hello, we're going to be lifelong friends. I'm Chester Reed. I'll try to remember your names but I have a lifetime to remember them. So what class is this?" He asked glancing around the room then grinned back at us.

That was our first day at university, he had sat down next to us in our first Ancient History class. We had no choice; Marisa and I could not resist him, he was like a lost puppy. Most people Chester met ended up being putty in his hands. He had a knack of talking his way out of trouble. If we had any class practices, Chester gave the professors a smile and a tilt of his head, and he would be able to just sit and watch. He also had a gift of getting them to do what he wanted. He would ask the professors to show him, and by the time they had finished they would be out of time for him to do it.

Marisa and I both had a love of history and had wanted to work in this field since high school. Dr Dean was one of our professors. On our first class at university, he entered the classroom without a word and began to hand out papers to the class. Marisa's eyes softened as soon as she saw him; he was handsome, and most girls, including me, enjoyed his classes. He always had a good enrolment in his units. He was knowledgeable and a respectable teacher. I felt you always learn more from people like that.

Marisa's hair went down to her waist back then. I always thought she had classic dark features, which made her pretty. However, Marisa's thoughts were not the same as mine. As Dr Dean passed her, he flipped the paper down in front of her. Marisa, catlike, brushed her hair aside before smiling sweetly at him. His head twitched as if she had cast an invisible fishing hook at him. She was eighteen; it didn't matter if he was ten years older than her now that we were all adults. She had never done this before but for some reason, Dr Dean had brought forth another side of her. Dr Dean was tall and thin, and his eyes would wrinkle when he smiled. He had an accent that would drift from Australian to American. All of us girls and Chester would talk extra sweetly to him - he seemed

11

to enjoy the fuss that we gave him. He was a black and white type and did not like being messed around. He kept all the girls at arm's length, but on the first meeting he seemed to soften towards Marisa. It was the closest to infatuation at first sight I had ever seen.

He was taking pleasure in the fact that Marisa was batting her eyes at him; the rest of the class seemed not to matter anymore. Marisa wet her lips and fluttered her eyes at him once more. Dr Dean gave her another double take before swallowing hard.

"Thanks, Dr Dean," she purred.

"Um..." he cleared his throat, trying to break her spell. As he moved away from Marisa, shaking his head, she side-glanced at me, pleased with herself at what she had done. I was trying not to laugh.

"Now I don't expect any of you to be able to read this," he stated as he begun the class, out of a box he took a small clay tablet he handed it to one student for it to be passed around. His voice was still unsteady as he spoke.

The students studied it for a moment before passing it on to the next person. The clay tablet nestled in the palm of your hand. It had what seemed like little triangles forming patterns in it, which made words.

"In ancient times, this was the best form of portable information. One person can carry quite a few of them over long distances. There aren't a lot of people who can read these now or who want to read them," he added while watching the tablet being passed around the room. "Clay back then was used in the way we use paper and plastic today. When it was not needed or broken, they would throw them away. When you start digging, this will come old hat with clay, but they are important. At any site, you are more likely to come across mountains of clay pots than anything else. They are not worth anything so thieves leave them. It is good for us now because we can read what was happening back then. It is also a good dating tool and sites are dated by pots."

When the tablet was passed to me, I ran my finger along, mumbling to myself as I read it. It was my first time holding a clay tablet, I had read about, I felt a thrill as it nestled in my hand.

12

Dr Dean stopped talking to the class. "Do you understand this?" he asked me.

Turning red I peered up at Dr Dean, who came and stood over me. I slumped down a little before handing it on. "Yes," I said quietly so the class could not hear.

"Really? What's your name?" Dr Dean waved his hand at Chester to hand it back to me.

"Laura." I slowly took the clay tablet back from Chester, wanting to fall into a dark hole.

"Laura, please," Dr Dean said kindly, urging me to read it out.

"Oh.., um.,. It's talking about the boarders between Egypt and Nubia. They're not being guarded. The King is not sending forces to keep the boarders safe and they are being slowly taken over by Nubians, um, rebels. Also... they need more money to protect the town... um... a tribe stole the gold delivery. The end part is broken off - I can't read what tribe it was." The entire class was watching me; they all seemed amazed.

Dr Dean, impressed, nodded his head slowly. "Very good, I'll have to keep my eye on you. I'll be out of a job with you around."

"Sorry," I squeaked out handing the tablet to Chester once more.

Dr Dean smiled kindly. He chuckled at me as he spoke. "No, don't be, kid. You did well."

After class, Chester and I waited for Marisa. She had gone back into the classroom because she had forgotten her book. Chester had stated that he was having lunch with us. Marisa came out of the classroom with all smiles.

"I have a date," she said, wiggling her shoulders at us.

~

Once left alone, I managed to finish going through the boxes before

13

lunch. The rest of the items were mostly old household pieces and some of them needed to go to the tip. I did find more Egyptian figures, however, they could have been purchased at any street stall or tourist shop in Egypt. Laying out the better items from the boxes, I photographed and recorded them, and then placed tags on the artefacts before they went into storage. I had recorded the alabaster Shabti; it needed more research so I kept it to one side. I wrapped it and placed it in my desk draw under lock and key.

The day was so nice; the sun felt good on my skin as I ambled down the sand stone stairs of the Museum at lunchtime. Chester, Marisa, and I made our way over to one of Hyde Park's lawn areas just over the road from the Museum to have something to eat. Marisa and I sat on the grass however Chester had a small blanket to sit on so that he would not get grass stains on himself. While nibbling on my sandwich, I read down the list once more hoping that the ancient owner of the Shabti would jump out at me. Chester endlessly chatted at Marisa about the builders. I was only half listening and really did not care. If I could pin point a time frame then it could help me date the artefact.

"Chester, how are you still employed?" Marisa asked.

I glanced up from the list, Chester pulled a face at Marisa. I giggled at them both before going back to the list.

"*Because*, Marisa, *I* know how to work the people to my will. Unlike *everyone* who works around me, *I* have my ways." Chester wiggled his fingers at her before blowing her a kiss.

Marisa rolled her eyes at Chester then gave me a glance. I knew the expression too well, she used it a lot when Chester was on a 'Chester roll', as she called it. Chester leapt up and forced his way between us. He sat half on my lap, almost knocking my drink over. He put his arms around my neck then peered at Marisa from behind my clipboard.

"Stop it, Chester," I scolded him. "Is he upsetting you again, Marisa? Do you want me to mummify him for you? I'm sure Dr Colman will not notice a new mummy in storage." I pulled my clipboard away from him. "Then you can watch your builders without pretending you are working," I added, mocking him.

"I think I remember," Marisa stated, glaring at him. Chester hid his head on my shoulder as he waved her off. "You tie him down and I'll get the coat hanger for his brain," Marisa added.

Chester sat up on my lap. He crossed his arms and glared back at Marisa. "That's not nice, Miss... be nice! Anyway... when you two have stopped putting all the attention on yourselves I'll finish telling you what happen today," Chester said like a little child.

He paused for a moment, like a teacher waiting for the class to quieten down. He tapped his finger on his arm while he waited. Some people were jogging on the many wide paths in the park, while others contentedly strolled passed us. No one cared how we were acting. Chester was still waiting, his fingers shifting back and forth rapidly. Marisa and I moaned.

"Sorry, Miss, we're ready to listen now," I said smirking at Marisa.

Chester took a deep breath before carrying on. "Well, he is a country boy from Wagga." Chester paused, seeming pleased that he had our attention again. He went on, "I don't like the country, too many animals, but he is living in the city now, so I don't have to worry about that. He's into football, and also his friends are teaching him how to surf. I'll have to start watching football so I know what I'm talking about. His uncle owns the business. The other men Paul is working with... well, I don't really care." He smiled contentedly, pleased with himself that he had found out all of this before lunch.

"Are you going to do any work while he is here?" Marisa queried, trying not to laugh.

"We work in a museum with old things, remember. They're not going anywhere soon, *Marisa*. You should know that." Chester waved Marisa off with his hand.

"Why do you work at the Museum, Chester?" I asked, trying to shove him off my lap.

Chester put his arms around me and pulled me to the ground. He rolled me around with him. "Because, I love history... and the Museum and... I love you, Laura... baby." Chester kissed me on the cheek and

15

rocked me back and forth. "I love my Laura. And you love me... I'm your best friend. I'm going to have sex with Paul because he is the man for me."

"Get off me Chester or I'll French kiss you." I threatened him pressing my lips together trying to kiss him. Chester let out a squeak before swiftly letting me go. "What about Marisa?" I said pulling a face at him, while picking blades of grass off my clothes and smoothing my hair back down.

"I'm not going to sleep with Marisa, she's a girl." Marisa pulled a sad face. "Oh, you know, I love her too, Marisa, baby." He spoke it as if Marisa was not there.

Marisa lent over me to poke Chester sharply with her finger in the shoulder. "Thanks a lot. Nice to know you care so much about me, Chester."

CHAPTER 2

The next morning I needed to go to the basement at the museum. I wanted to compare the Shabties in our collection with the new one. I knew that a tray of them was somewhere in the museum. I had gone to the Ancient Room in the main part of the museum to search for them, but for some reason they had been taken off display.

The museum always had a feeling to it. Parts of the main museum had been added to throughout the years, and the feeling was in the newer parts as well. It wasn't as strong as it was in the older rooms. Dark brown wooden cabinets that reached from floor to ceiling adorned the old rooms. The Bone Room had always fascinated me. *The Rocking Man* was still rocking in his rocking chair, just as he had done when I was a child. In the older rooms the floors were covered in woollen green carpet that was overdue for replacement.

One room we used for our special exhibitions. There the walls were covered with black curtains. It was always gloomy in that room. Chester loved nothing better than to hide behind the curtains and jump out at the Uni students who helped with exhibitions. The south-side rooms of the museum were where we kept the Australian artefacts. The Ancient Room was not a big space; its layout was similar to the Bone Room.

I could never put my finger on the mood of the museum. I enjoyed the feeling of its structure, a feeling that I got from most old buildings. The only words I could use to describe it were "antiquated, but forthcoming."

Because the Shabties had been moved from the Ancient Room, the only place they could be was in storage. To my delight, the builders had not started for the day. The basement was empty and I had it to myself. Taking my time, I searched in a few drawers for the Shabties, hoping they hadn't been loaned out. The paperwork stated that the Shabties had been loaned out for student study, but now should be back. I never trusted the paperwork. The north basement had five rows of lockable cabinets on the far wall. They were of the same type of wood found everywhere in the building— wood that was slowly being replaced by stronger metal cabinets.

The cabinets held drawers of bugs, birds and small mammals, artefacts that needed to be under lock and key. There were gold nuggets locked in a stronghold in one of the rows. There were clay pipes from the convict times of Sydney's history. I came across a pipe with an owl carved into it; I thought the pipe was one of the nicest in our collection. In a locked room behind the wooden drawers were larger pieces of our ancient collection. The first mummy I ever saw was in that locked room. When I was a child, the mummy sat in the main front room, which is now the museum's café. The paintings on her coffin fascinated me. Back then, I couldn't read the inscriptions on the side of the coffin. However, now I knew that she had been a priestess of Horus during the Roman era. Her name meant *The One Who Loved Ra*. As it had done when I was a child, her raven hair still spun around her head. Some of her face had fallen away, but she looked like she had simply fallen asleep, forever frozen in time.

On the other side of the basement, where the builders were working, the shelves were packed with large mammals, old bikes, clay pots, record players, stuffed birds and old toys. Anything that showed the history of Australia and the world sat on those shelves. This part could sometimes be unsettling, with the eyes of all the stuffed animals watching as I moved down the aisles. This is where most of the contents of my boxes would end up, with students and professors using them for research.

I pushed the wooden finds trolley along the rows of drawers. We used the trolleys when transporting artefacts from one place to another so that we didn't drop them. It reminded me of a tea trolley.

I pointed my finger at the labels as I strolled along. "Miniature Bat of Kenya, Butterflies of Madagascar," I mumbled to myself.

Halfway down the third aisle was the drawer I was searching for. With two hands, I slowly opened it. On one of the trays was an almost complete set of Shabties. They were green in colour. They had Egyptian headdresses, little engraved faces, crossed arms and carved legs and feet. They lay soundly in four rows. These were smaller than the alabaster Shabti, and were of poorer quality. If you could afford the best for your afterlife, you would have the best of the best. These green Shabties were from a nobleman's crypt. The note left in the drawer by the doctor who found them stated, *"Trying to be better than the Joneses. I think not as good as they could be."* It was written in the thirties.

"Sorry to upset your rest, but I need your help," I said, apologising to the Shabties as I took them out and placed them on the trolley. Like the mummy in storage, I had seen these little statues as a child and been amazed by their magnificence.

Carefully, I wheeled the trolley to the elevator so that I could return to my office. My mind was mulling over facts about Shabties, trying to remember anything that might help me find the ancient Egyptian owner.

"Is your friend here today?" A man's voice came from behind me, making me jump a little as I prepared to press the button once more.

I turned around with my hand on my heart to find Chester's friend standing there. Maybe I was wrong about him; maybe he *was* gay. Chester was going to be happy.

"Yes, he's helping out with a new display that we acquired from South America. He'll be busy for a few days," I said, trying to be

19

helpful.

"Great." The way he answered was not how I would expect him to answer. I did not understand the expression on his face. In the background his workmates were hovering, trying not to be obvious that they were eavesdropping.

"I can tell him you…asked after him if you want. He'll be happy to know." I heard a snigger from one of Paul's workmates. I glanced past him.

"Oh." Paul's face went red and his workmates chuckled once more. His eyes widened. "Oh…no, no…shit...no. I'm not…I'm not like that."

Another one of his mates snorted. Paul spun around to glare at them before turning back to me.

"Oh…I'm sorry." I had misunderstood him.

"This isn't going very well. I'm…I'm Paul Gibson," he told me, rubbing the back of his neck. He was still red in the face.

"I'm Laura Sinclair. It's nice to meet you."

I pushed the button again to hurry the elevator. Paul grasped my hand to stop me. The texture of his skin was rough. He towed me out of sight of his workmates, and I assumed that he wanted to talk to me in private. Glancing down, I could see the tattoo on his arm closer. It was a snarling goblin.

"Would you like to go to dinner with me tonight?" Paul asked me once we were away from his friends.

His eyes were a warm chocolate brown in colour. I needed to shake my head to clear it and understand what he had just asked me. 'Is this some sort of joke?' I thought to myself. To better comprehend what was going on, I glanced over at the other men, who seemed to have gone back to work. However, they were still

20

listening.

"Would you like to go out with me tonight?" Paul asked once more.

There was no hint of a joke on his face. He flashed a smile at me, which made my knees go a little weak. There was something about him I couldn't say no to.

"Yes." The word left my lips before I could let my brain work.

"What time do you get off work?"

"Um…five thirty?" I already knew what time he finished work due to Chester's carry on yesterday.

"Should I pick you up here?" Paul asked.

My brain didn't want to function. Guys like this didn't normally ask me out. However, what Chester had said to me on the stairs rang in my ears. *I have to live a little*. It was one date, it wouldn't hurt.

"Yes…that'll be good," I told him. "I'll meet you at the museum's entrance tonight after work."

"I'll see you then." Paul smiled at me.

"Okay," I squeaked out, half realising what I had just done.

Once in the safety of my office, I stood staring into space. *"What are you doing?"* I said to myself. *"He's not your type. Chester wanted to date him. What the hell am I doing?"*

I wanted to go back to work, as I had a lot to do. Instead I picked up my phone and dialled a few numbers. *"Hello."* I heard Marisa's voice come over the line.

"Help." Fell from my lips, it was the only word I could say.

As soon as I hung up, the sound of Marisa's high heels resounded down the hallway. The clicks bounced off the walls until they came to a stop at my door.

"What did you do?" Marisa asked as she rushed into my office. She examined the trolley, likely thinking that I had broken something.

"No, not that. Chester is going to kill me."

"What did you do? Did you go outside in your purple cardigan?" Marisa sniggered.

"No, I wish I had…. Paul asked me out on a date."

"Really," Marisa said in surprise, holding herself as support.

"Don't act so astonished. Yes, he asked me on a date," I scolded her, feeling a little hurt.

"I'm sorry, but he's not your type." Marisa came into the room and sat down, frowning at me.

"I know, this could be a new leaf for me. Or maybe he's making a complete fool of me," I said, trying to sound hopeful and doubtful at the same time.

Marisa sighed. "Laura, don't say that. There's nothing wrong with you. Who knows, you two could be made for each other. You're going on a date and you need my assistance." Marisa grinned at me, trying to act as though everything would be all right.

"This isn't the first time I've been on a date." I frowned at her.

"I know, I know. But it has been a long time," Marisa reminded me. It had been six months, and my last date was nothing to crow about.

In frustration, I plonked myself down on the high chair at the finds table. "Thanks, I know it has been a long time. He was a lot of fun, but he kept going on about how he could do my job better. He was an accountant." I giggled.

"I did meet your last date. What time are you meeting Paul?" Marisa asked, trying to sound upbeat.

"Five thirty here."

"Here?" Marisa asked, shaking her head at me. "Sometimes, Laura, you can be such a scatterbrain."

"I had a brain fart, okay?" I put my head on the table.

"A brain fart?" Marisa repeated.

"Are you going to help me or are you going to do your parrot impressions? I can't leave because Dr Colman wants me to finish more cuneiform translations before the weekend. I'm still working on authenticating the Shabti."

Marisa let out a breath. "He needs to get *you* an assistant. Dr Colman gives you too much work. You should tell him."

"Okay, when I have my doctorate I'll tell him. Till then, I like and need my job." I waved my finger in the air.

"He won't sack you, Laura, he needs you to do his dirty work. How else can he show off?" she grumbled.

Dr Colman gave me cuneiform writing in the form of images from the British museum. I translated them and put them into the database for him. Dr Colman liked to double my workload near the weekends. He also liked to show off the fact that he had someone on staff who could translate the tablets.

"Paul could have asked me to shave my head and wear yellow and I still would have said yes. He had cornered me. I had to say

23

yes," I said, still not sure why I was going on a date with him. It must have been a joke.

"Yellow doesn't suit you. I couldn't see you shaving your head, either. You have a nice-shaped head, but you couldn't shave all your hair off. Maybe at the back." Marisa made a face at me, trying to lighten the mood.

"Marisa, I know that. Help me. *Please*," I begged.

"Okay, okay. Don't worry. I'll go home and get something for you to wear."

I let out a breath in relief. "Thank you. You're a life saver." I leapt up to hug Marisa. "You remember when I covered for you when you were dating John?" I asked, releasing her from my grip.

"Yes." She smiled sweetly when I said the name of our former professor, Dr John Dean.

"When I took your notes, finished your assessments? When you needed to sleep in after a wild night out?" I added.

"Yes." Marisa smiled wider. I think her memory of John was getting away with her.

Marisa and John should have been married with ten kids by now. I never understood why they hadn't taken things further.

Marisa snapped out of her fantasy and held up a finger to stop me. "I have only half paid you back. I still owe you for the assessments. This pays you back for the note taking and for covering for me in class."

"Okay. Thanks."

"You're welcome," she replied cheerfully.

After work, I stood on the sandstone stairs of the museum. I had a few minutes until Paul would arrive for our date. Marisa had returned with one of my blue cotton dresses, makeup and even an electric shaver.

It was late summer and the nights were still pleasant. I had finished the translations and was feeling triumphant that I had completed them with time to spare. I leaned against the sandstone wall, watching an ant on the footpath in front of me. It had a butterfly wing that it was dragging into the museum's garden. In paintings, artists used butterflies as images of the soul. Maybe this was a sign, as Marisa had said. Paul and I could be made for each other. But then again, it was just a date.

"Laura!" I jumped a little, the call of my name stirring me out of my daydream. Chester scuttled out the main door, his arms waving in the air.

"Laura, baby! Ooh, you're pretty." He took hold of me in one of his bear hugs as he waltzed me around. "The coffee boy asked me out." He let go and began bouncing on his toes as he stepped away to examine me.

"Ricky, that's his name," Chester said. "He's taking me to that movie. You know, that one we were talking about, the one we were going to see the other night."

I nodded, peering at him sheepishly. "Chester…Paul asked me out."

"Oh, I already know that. Good luck to him. He's too straight for me anyway. I gave up on him hours ago." Chester kissed me, then looked me up and down once more. "You're gorgeous. Go get him, you hussy. I have to go. Me, I'm always handsome."

Chester blew me a kiss. I knew Ricky by sight from the coffee shop on the other side of the park. He was attractive, his hair cut short and bleached at the tips. He had the same sense of fashion that Chester did. Ricky's shirt was tight and showed off the

25

contours of his body. He must work out, he had a thin build and a bright smile. He seemed happy about life.

Once Ricky reached Chester's side, Chester waved his hand through the air, introducing us. "Ricky, Laura. Laura, Ricky."

"Hi," we both said.

I was happy for Chester. He hadn't been on a real date for a while and he seemed more eager about this date than any he had been on before. Chester bowed to Ricky and Ricky returned the bow. Ricky held out an arm for Chester to take, like a well-rehearsed dance. "Ciao, Laura." Chester gave me one last wave as they headed to Hyde Park.

Once alone, I glanced at my watch. It was almost a quarter to. This may have been a joke after all, as Paul was late. I decided to give him ten more minutes before I gave up and went home.

The time ticked slowly. Just as I was about to give up on him, the high-pitched beeping sound of the crossing made me glance down the street. Paul jogged up to me. "I'm sorry…I misjudged the buses," he said, out of breath. He must have run most of the way here.

"That's all right." He grinned as I met him at the bottom of the stairs. "You look good," I said.

"So do you," Paul replied.

He was wearing jeans and a white collared shirt that wasn't buttoned all the way. I got a sneak peek of what was under that shirt as he tried to cool himself down. He shook it a few times in an effort to pass fresh air over his tanned skin. His aftershave drifted up. It smelled nice.

I hated first dates. I never knew what to say. They say that you have to sell yourself, to make yourself sound attractive to the other person.

Without a word, Paul turned and began striding down the street. "Where are we going?" I asked as I hurried after him.

"Chinatown. I have to go to footy prac tomorrow morning, so I can't be out too late." He slowed his pace so that I could catch up.

Dating a footballer. Is that what it's like? Oh well, it's Friday night and I'm out, not sitting at home watching a video. Paul didn't talk as we made our way to the other side of the city. Sydney's Chinatown is not very big. It has a few nice restaurants and some quick eateries, as well as a few shops.

"Have you been in Sydney long?" I finally asked, trying to break the silence.

"No. How long have you worked at the museum?"

"About seven years. Do you like what you do?" I needed to get Paul talking so that I could understand him a little better.

"I don't like working inside. I like it better outside. All those things in the museum storeroom are kinda creepy. There's one, the lion. It's been watching me."

I giggled at him. "Oh, that's Wallace. He was a famous lion in his day. He got out of his cage in Melbourne and scared a lot of theatregoers in 1911. He's been in the museum for about fifty years. Be nice to him."

Paul glanced at me. I think he was trying to work me out. "That's what I mean. You're working around dead things; how can you do that?" We had made our way through the Chinatown gates. The two red lions greeted us.

"It's easy," I said brightly. "You like working outdoors, I like mysteries and old things."

27

Paul stopped as he studied me for a moment. His eyes ran over my face. I could see his mind ticking. In a split second, his face became still, then his eyes fixated on a spot over my shoulder.

"In here." He pointed at a glass door behind me. I was confused; it seemed that he had been about to say something, but thought better of it.

I knew this restaurant. Paul opened the door and the aroma of Chinese herbs and spices filled my nostrils. Stairs led down to a ground-floor restaurant. Once I had stepped into the stairwell and down a few steps, Paul followed me. The restaurant was packed with Chinese families. It was noisy and crowded. I liked this place, but not for a first date. The walls were painted red, the floor contained white tiles, and green pillars stood in the corners. A painting of two dragons fighting over the ball of wisdom covered the back wall. Rows of bench seats and long tables filled the room. I felt a little deflated by his choice. Why did he ask me to go here?

Just above the chatter from the diners was the sound of woks banging. The room was hot and steamy. A glass buffet stood to one side, near the kitchen, its cabinets filled with food. Two women stood behind the buffet waring miserable expressions as they dished food onto plates. Paul passed me a tray, chopsticks and a plate. "Thanks," I said politely.

Paul filled his plate with noodles and sweet 'n sour chicken. I decided to give him a break after he paid for my meal. He did say he had footy training in the morning. I wanted to enjoy my meal, so I let it go. It seemed as though I would be getting a rental video tonight after all. I'm sure there was something I hadn't seen yet.

Paul paused as he studied the room. His hands full, he nudged his head toward one of the less-packed bench tables. Without questioning his selection, I followed him. We sat facing each other at the end of a table.

28

A Chinese family was sitting near us. I nodded at them. "Ni hao," I said to the woman next to me.

She bowed her head at me, then turned her attention to Paul. She gave me a remorseful glance I didn't understand why she had done that.

She spoke to me in Chinese, I didn't speak Chinese so I couldn't understand what she was saying. I just smiled and nodded to be polite. The woman turned to the man next to her and began speaking to him in their language. She pointed at me, then at Paul. It was a good thing he was busy with his food. The couple's reaction was strange; they seemed to know him. I was about to ask Paul about it, but he spoke first.

"Have you lived in Sydney all your life?" he asked after slurping down a mouthful of noodles.

"Yes, I grew up in Chatswood," I said slowly, concerned about the way the couple was reacting.

They moved away from us, speaking quickly to each other. They seemed to be pointing at Paul's tattoo. He gave them a quick glance before returning to his meal. Their reaction hadn't fazed him.

"We did a job there the other week. It's very leafy," Paul said, waving his chopsticks around.

"Yes it is. Chester said you come from Wagga." The couple had hurried over to another table. I kept my composure as I spoke, trying not to make an issue of what had just occurred.

Paul frowned when I said Chester's name. It was the first real reaction he had given all night. "My family has lived in Wagga forever. That guy hung around a lot yesterday; he gives me the creeps. I think he thought we were going to nick stuff or something."

"Chester is a good friend. He wouldn't think that. He's really nice once you get to know him. He's a little out there, but he has a big heart." I was trying to sound light-hearted and to convince Paul that Chester was okay. Paul was a blokey bloke, and men like Chester challenged his manhood.

I reached over and took the soy sauce off the table. I poured it into my short soup, giving Paul a moment to process what I had just said. I didn't want to tell him that Chester had a date tonight and was somewhere in town. I could feel Paul watching me as I mixed the sauce into my food, swirling the noodles in the broth.

"You seem very relaxed with Chester," Paul said. The way he spoke Chester's name was strange. My thoughts were right about Paul's attitude towards Chester.

"We…I mean, Marisa and I…we have known him since University," I said. Paul didn't say anything, but just nodded. "Why did you come to Sydney to work?" I asked, trying to change the subject.

Paul dug his fork into his sweet 'n sour and shovelled a big portion into his mouth. He looked happy to talk about something else, but didn't seem pleased that I had asked him about Wagga. He took his time answering my question. I gave Paul a moment by taking a mouthful of soup. It was still warm, but not the finest I had ever eaten. The dumplings had sat in the water too long. They were falling apart and one of the meatballs was about to float to the top of the broth. It was like this date; I was hoping it would end soon.

My question lingered in the air while Paul wiped his mouth with a paper towel. He studied me with his brown eyes, reminding me of a teacher I once had. It seemed as though Paul was judging me just as this teacher had done; no matter how much I studied, I would always fail. Paul's eyes skimmed my face. His mouth slid to one side before he spoke.

"There's more work here than in Wagga. Uncle George needed help to keep his business going. The beach was calling. That's what pushed me into coming. I've always wanted to learn to surf." Paul bent over his plate once more.

"Are you any good at surfing?" I asked. I think I was talking louder than normal; it was noisy in the restaurant.

"I'm getting there," he said between bites.

"You'll have to teach me some day."

Paul stabbed his plate and took another mouthful of food. "Sure," he said.

I had said the wrong thing. *"You have to sit and watch on the beach while your man surfs; girls don't surf."* I had heard it all the time in high school. At least Paul wasn't telling me how to do my job. I glanced up at a wall clock; it was only seven o'clock.

Based on his reactions throughout our date, I didn't know why Paul had asked me out. He was a fast eater. He kept shovelling it in as though he were late for something. It seemed that he could be nice, and he *was* handsome. I didn't understand what he was about. I wanted to ask him about the couple's reaction, but thought better of it.

"Do you live near the beach?" I asked, trying to keep him talking.

"Yes, I have a house in Dee Why. What about your family?" Paul asked, seeming a little calmer.

I knew Dee Why well; it was on the Northern Beaches of Sydney and had a good bus route to it.

"Mum and Dad still live in Chatswood, and I have a sister, Bess, who is in London. She works as a chef in a fancy hotel. What about your family? Have you got any brothers or sisters?"

31

"Me, Mum and Dad are still around, and I have four brothers. Me brothers are in Wagga. Me older brother, Brett, helps Dad on the farm. Dad is getting on a bit. He needs the help."

Once he had finished eating, as I expected, Paul wanted to leave. To my surprise, he started escorting me home. He was quiet; maybe this was just him. That was okay; I understood quiet.

"What's that song?" Paul asked as we made our way back to my unit.

"What?" I asked, not knowing what he was talking about.

"The song you keep humming. You were humming it this morning in the basement as well."

I thought back to the morning. "Um," I started. I hadn't realised I had been humming. "How did you know I was humming this morning?" I asked.

"It was a bit loud," he answered. His mood had changed.

"Was it?" I blushed.

"Yeah," Paul said.

I stared off into space, thinking. I knew very well what song I was humming.

Paul clicked his fingers in front of my eyes, trying to get my attention. "What's the song?" he asked again.

"It's called 'Summertime,'" I answered snapping out. "I sing it sometimes. I'm not sure why. Sorry if you don't like it."

"No, it's all right. You're not a bad singer. You should join a band or something."

"I sing in a cover band sometimes. They play stuff like The

Doors. They like me to sing Janis Joplin or The Pretenders, that sort of stuff."

"Cool." Paul seemed impressed. It was the first bit of positive emotion he had shown all night. This Paul I didn't mind. If he kept acting like this, I would be happy to go on a second date.

"There's a pub at the Rocks called The Blue Raven. The band plays there most weekends. You should come one night."

"Yeah, I should do that," Paul said. We were close to my flat. The aroma of pizza filled the air.

"What sort of farm does your father have?" I asked.

"Cattle, mainly. A little wheat, but there's more money in beef." Paul's answer was short; apparently, he didn't want to add more.

"Do you own your house?" I asked.

"Hey, Laura." A familiar voice rang out from the pizza shop. The owner, also my landlord, waved at me from behind the counter.

"Hey, Perry." I waved back. He was busy tonight and nodded as he went back to work. The smell of pizza would be filling my flat.

I stopped at the step that led to my place. A locked door stood at street level and a flight of stairs travelled over the shop, to my front door.

"A few more payments and it's mine. What about you?" Paul puffed out his chest a little, seeming proud that he almost owned his home.

"No, still renting and I'm sharing." I grinned.

"Who do you live with?" Paul seemed a little worried; maybe he thought Chester would leap out at him.

33

"My friend Marisa. We work together at the museum."

Paul stood a few feet away from me. I knew that he was not coming up. I took a few steps closer to where he was standing. He hadn't tried to hold my hand all night, nor had he tried to touch me. I wouldn't have been happy if he'd made an advance. Until now.

"Thanks for tonight. It was pleasant," I said, still confused about why he had asked me out.

To my surprise, Paul leaned in and kissed me quickly on the cheek. "I'll see you soon. I'm glad you had a good time. I did, too."

It astonished me at his statement. I was under the impression that, after tonight, I would never see him again. To go along with the protocol of dating, I dug into my bag for a pen and paper so that I could write down my phone number. It was the 90s, the days before everyone had mobile phones. Paul pocketed the paper and gave me another kiss on the cheek. I wasn't holding my breath that he would call me.

"Good night. Thanks for tonight," Paul said, nodding.

"Nice to meet you, Paul." At that moment I came to a theory that because Chester had hit on him, Paul had asked me out to prove to his mates that he was straight. That theory fit my comprehension of what had happened on our date a little better.

Once Paul had disappeared around the corner, I went upstairs to the flat. When I walked through the door, I found the lounge room and the kitchen empty. The kitchen light had been left on, which was normal. A glow of light came from underneath the door to Marisa's room. Our bedrooms were located on either side of the bathroom. We respected each other's space from day one. In terms of a flat mate, I could not have asked for anyone better than Marisa.

We kept a statue of King Tut on a table near our bedrooms. We turned the statue to the wall if either of us had a date staying the night. The front door bore a smiling sun that we also turned around if we brought a date home. Last year, I had to sit in the hallway most of the night waiting until Marisa and her date moved to the bedroom. They had gotten a little carried away on the couch. The front door opened into the lounge room, and there had been no way of sneaking past them. I was about to give up and go to Mum and Dad's house when finally, at two in the morning, they moved to the bedroom.

However, tonight Tut was staring up at me. I knocked before going into Marisa's bedroom.

"How did your night go?" Marisa asked as she took off her headphones and paused her movie.

"Not bad," I answered as I let out a sigh.

Marisa studied my face for a moment, then frowned. "Not that good, either."

"He took me to Chinatown."

Marisa's face lit up slightly. "There are some good restaurants in Chinatown. Which one did you go to?"

I slumped against the doorframe. "The one we went to for lunch the other week."

"Oh, okay." Marisa patted the bed. I sat down and told her about my date. "At least you went out," she said after I had finished.

"True. I'm not holding my breath, though. I don't think he'll be phoning me back," I said.

"I wouldn't be holding my breath, either." Marisa crumpled her face as she spoke.

35

Monday morning Marisa and I met up with Chester after we got off our train. The museum train station had not changed since it was first built. It still had its original mosaic sign. The walls of the platform were tiled in green and white. Marisa and I climbed the stairs of the station and entered the street as we did every morning. Chester was waiting up another flight of stairs near the coffee shop at the end of Hyde Park. We didn't even have a chance to say good morning before Chester dragged us into the shop. He didn't have to pay for his coffee that morning. Ricky lit up like a Christmas tree when he saw Chester approaching the counter.

During our walk to the museum, Chester told us all about his weekend with Ricky. I finally manage to tell Chester about my date with Paul on Friday night. Chester strolled beside me with his hands behind his back, nodding his head as I spoke. He raised his hand to his chin and stroked it a few times before putting his hand behind his back once more.

"Yes, yes. You didn't talk too much about that Egyptian madness again, did you?" Chester asked as he went to a tree near the ANZAC Memorial and began spinning around the tree.

"No, I'm not that silly," I growled.

"Well, that's them football types for you. All muscles and no talky. They're good for a romp and to show off in the nightclubs, but that's all. I have Ricky now. He's my soul mate. I'm in love." Chester batted his eyes at me.

"You don't care, do you?" I asked. Chester shrugged his shoulders. I tried to slap at him, but he ducked away. He waved us off before he began dancing along the path to the museum.

He flung his arms into the air and began yelling. "Anyway….Cooky! Here I am, I'm coming. I've always loved your tights, Cooky!" Chester was yelling at the statue of Captain Cook that stood at the end of the path. Chester did a bizarre dance

36

as he chanted. "Ricky and I are going to do some shopping tonight. He needs a new bed!" Chester was too happy to listen to me this morning. He bounced down the path.

"Chester, did you break his bed, you animal?" I giggled at him even louder.

"Did you put weight on, Chester?" Marisa said just as loud. "I think you have a few pounds on your hips. You'll have to stop eating."

He paused in mid skip, spun around to poke his tongue out at us and flung his hands to his hips. "No, damn you. No, when I'm hot, I'm hot. Ricky has a stuffed dog. It died years ago and he didn't want to…well, you know. So he got it stuffed." He said this before spinning back around to skip down the path once more.

Passers-by stopped to watch Chester. The man was batty, but happy.

CHAPTER 3

~

My sister Bess was born when I was six years old. When Bess first came home, Mum would push me away from her if I got too close. I didn't understand why. All I remembered was that I wanted to know who she was. Early one morning I slipped into the bedroom that once had been mine. The light was low and the morning sun drifted in softly through the window. The bedroom's walls had not changed since I was a baby. This was the room closest to Mum and Dad's room. The room was taken away from me two weeks before Bess was born. Nothing was told to me about her arrival.

My old baby furniture that had stood in the garage for years had been repaired, repainted and cleaned. Now it stood in my old room. For months my father had worked on the pieces during his days off. I had cried the first night in my new room, missing my old surroundings, my comfort, my safety. I was fond of the blue and white rabbit wallpaper, of my old room. I had drawn an eye on one of the rabbits near my bed. I would talk to the rabbit before I went to sleep, telling it all my troubles. My new bedroom was smaller. It had basic furniture and wallpaper with yellow daisies. It was a more grown-up room, but I still missed what once was mine.

I didn't hate the little intruder, and I knew better than to talk back to Mum. However, I felt left out of the changes that were happening in the house. I felt an overwhelming need to know who this new person was. I crept softly to her cot. Bess lay wrapped in her pink fluffy blanket. She was small, with a tuft of blond curls sitting softly on her forehead. The cot was positioned in the middle of the room. I treaded silently closer. Like a stalking animal, I paced around the cot to see her better. I was hoping that she would wake up and play with me.

"Bess, this is my doll. Her name is Dolly. If you want to play with her you need to ask, okay?"

Bess's little hand moved as I spoke and came to rest on her cheek as her lips made a sucking movement. I waited for her to do more, but she just lay there in her blanket. She reminded me of a caterpillar. I thought that maybe if I reached through the white bars of the cot to touch her cheek, she might wake up and play with me.

I reached out to her. "My name is Laura and I am your sister. If you don't cry at me, I'll play with you if you want. It's nice to meet you." Her cheek was soft.

"Laura, you're going to wake the baby." Mum startled me as she entered the room and ushered me out. I felt as though I had been caught up in a windstorm of flannel and hands, as I was hurtled out of the room.

From then on, my time with Bess was filtered. I knew it was an act on my mother's part. It was only a matter of time before things went back to the way they had been before Bess arrived.

The days before I went to school and the arrival of Bess, I spent a lot of time alone. Dad would go to work each morning and Mum would pack a lunch for me before leaving. She would be gone most of the day. I thought that was what parents did. We lived in an average red brick home. It had three bedrooms and a full-sized back yard with a mulberry tree in the middle. The wallpaper in the lounge room had big red and yellow flowers. The carpet was beige and the kitchen was post-war green. To this day, I can't stand that colour.

Every morning I would go into the kitchen and Mum would have breakfast waiting for me. A small seventies-style table sat in the corner. Mum would be perched on a stool at the sink, drinking coffee. Dad would have left for work well before I had woken up. Eve, my mother, was curvy, her hair was straight and red-brown. We had the same complexion and she was stubborn. Mum would not bend on anything unless it suited her. Dan, my dad, was a fair man who would try to see both sides of things. He had a dark beard back then, with little bits of grey in his hair. He was of average height and weight, with a round face. There were never any sparks between Mum and Dad. They seemed to just exist, and were always polite to each other. It was never like what I saw on TV, but I had no other couple to compare them to. I thought that if you found a man and you liked him more than others, you married him. That was my conception of love and the world around me.

Mum would sip from her brown striped coffee cup as she watched me eat my breakfast. The dishes sat drying on the dish rack. Mum's brown shoe would sway back and forth as she watched for nine thirty to tick over on the clock. This was before I had begun school.

"Don't forget to put the dishes away. Please, get dressed today. I have set your clothes out on your bed. The neighbours may see you and we don't want that, do we? There's a load of washing in the washing machine to go out as well."

"Yes, Mum," I answered as I wiped milk off my chin with my hand.

"Don't do that, Laura. Here." Mum handed me a paper napkin. "Don't forget, don't tell anyone you're alone. I'll be back before your father comes home."

"Yes, Mum. I know not to say anything." I answered robotically as I wiped my already dry chin with the napkin, just to please Mum. This was a well-rehearsed conversation; we had it most mornings. The other afternoon she had come home to find me still in pyjamas and the house a mess. It did not go down well.

"That's a good girl." She nodded, content that she had gotten her point across and that her little secret from Dad was still a secret.

When Bess was born, at first I worried about who was going to care for her. I was by then at school and I didn't think she should come to school with me. The other kids didn't bring their brothers or sisters with them. I asked a classmate because her mum had just had a baby. She laughed at me and said her mum cared for the baby.

Mum stayed home with Bess for a while, things were different after school. She was there and had afternoon tea ready for me when I got home. However, a year later I came home from school one afternoon to find Mum waiting for me in the lounge room. She rose to her feet, placing Bess on the floor before smoothing her hair. My heart skipped a beat as she brushed down her brown and red dress. Mum had only one good dress and this was it. Bess had just started walking. She came up to me with her arms out, pleased to see me. I held onto Bess's heavy weight as Mum moved across the room to the door.

She didn't meet my eyes as she spoke. "Dinner is in the oven and in an hour you need to take it out. I've set the timer." Without a sideways glance, Mum left the lounge room.

"Yes, Mum," I down heartily said as Bess was trying to kiss me. I didn't want her touching me Mum was leaving again. I stood there holding back tears as she readied herself to leave.

"That's a girl. Mind your sister for me. Don't let her go outside."

As Mum picked up her handbag a car horn sounded in the drive. From where I stood, I could see the taxi driver's blue shirt outside the window.

"Yes, Mum," I said. Mum applied her last-minute lipstick before leaving.

This was the late seventies and if I was home alone with my baby sister, no one would question it. From that day forward, every afternoon after school Mum would wait just inside the door for me to return. She had it timed to the second. The taxi would pull up just as I came home. I could not be late; once she left Bess alone because I was a few minutes late. I was grounded for a week because of it.

If a neighbour saw her, Mum would wave and smile at me. "Just off to the shops, be back soon." It would be for the neighbours to hear, not for me.

In the winter, she would wear her beige fur-collared coat. In the summer, Mum wore her brown and red dress with yellow beads, and her brown shoes. They were set aside for special occasions and for when she went to *the shops*.

I turned on Bess that day, I was blaming her for Mum leaving. As my little sister tried to cling to me, I pushed her over. Bess let out an ear-piercing scream as she hit the floor. This frightened me and shocked me back to the realisation that I was the only one who could protect my sister.

I scooped her up and held onto her as I began crying. "I'm sorry. Come on Bess, come and help me with my homework." She was fine, but I never forgave myself for it.

Bess would cry, when she realised Mum was about to leave. It was hard to calm her down. She learned quickly that when I came home, Mum would go away. A few times Bess tried to run after Mum, but she was always shoved back inside and the door slammed in her face.

At ten to six, the taxi would pull up out front. Mum would spring out and hurry inside. She would change into her housedress,

42

then head into the kitchen to serve dinner. Mum would have it on the table by the time Dad came through the door. Where she would go or what she did, at that age I never knew.

~

Monday morning I laid the smaller Shabtis on a leather mat on my finds table. I positioned the alabaster Shabti next to them. The alabaster Shabti was older then the museum's statues; it made ours appear feeble in comparison. If the alabaster Shabti had been made in the last ninety years, it would stand out in contrast to the museum's Shabtis. This morning I had discovered that, just near the Shabti's feet, was the symbol for *wife*. I needed to record my results, then submit a report to Dr Colman who was eager to know my findings. Many thoughts about the Shabti swam in my mind. I sat back and swung around on the high chair to ponder my evidence. Janis was playing at medium volume in the background. I'm sure I drove everyone crazy as I sang along.

This was a real artefact. The Shabti had once belonged to a wife and was of good quality. It must have had a royal or noble owner. The documents that came with the Shabti stated that it had been bought in Cairo in the forties while the owner was stationed there during the war. The documents included a photo of the owner holding the Shabti with his officer mates. I went back to examine it under my magnifying glass, hoping to find more clues on it.

A knock sounded at the door. "Come in," I called.

The door slowly opened. I stood up and turned Janis off, thinking it might be Dr Colman trying to hurry me up.

"I thought you might need a coffee."

In astonishment, I spun around. Paul was standing there, trying not to spill a large coffee. I was taken aback, as I had not heard from him all weekend. Paul tried to prop the door open with his foot. As it swung back on him I hurried over to assist.

"Thanks, that's really nice," I said, taking the coffee off him. I held the door open to let him in.

"I asked your flatmate how you had it. I saw her in the café." Paul strolled in and began glancing around the room as he sipped his coffee. He inspected the contents of my shelves.

"Marisa?" I asked, sitting down at my desk.

He was wearing a blue flannel shirt with baggy shorts and work boots. I noticed that his calf muscles showed when he walked. "Yeah." Paul nodded at me, then moved an old brown ink bottle around with his finger.

"Thanks," I said again.

Taking a sip from my coffee, I watched him roam around the office. I was confused about what he was doing here. After Friday night, I didn't think I'd see him again. I was sure he didn't act as though he had a good time. I was going to avoid him while he was here. It wouldn't be that hard. Maybe he thought differently, or maybe I had misunderstood him, now I was confused.

Paul ran his finger along my books and pulled a face at an old copy of Tutankhamen's tomb catalogue. He made another face when he started pulling out my Book of the Dead. Paul pushed the book back into the shelf and turned his attention to the finds table. His hand reached out to pick up the alabaster Shabti.

"What are...?" he was about to ask.

"Don't!" I squeaked as I jumped to my feet. "Not without cotton gloves…I don't drink or eat over there, either. Please." I pulled the stool out and away from the table for him to sit on. The last thing I wanted to do was explain to Dr Colman why the Shabtis had coffee on them.

"Sorry." He seemed surprised at the way I was acting and sat down on the stool.

"It's all right. Sorry, I shouldn't have jumped at you like that."

Paul put up his hand. "It's okay, that's your work. I get it. Are they worth anything?" He glanced over at them once more.

I nodded uneasily. "On the black market maybe, they're worth more. If you could pass off fakes, they can be just as much." An uneasy feeling come over me, I shouldn't have told him that.

"I like the alabaster one." He pointed at it with his little finger. "What's the difference?"

"The alabaster one is…it…I don't know yet. I do know that alabaster is found near gold. It's easy to carve because it's soft." I stopped. I wasn't sure how much he was going to listen to and the feeling could I trust him came over me. Most people glaze over when you talk history. On the other hand, Paul seemed like he was interested, so I went on. "Gold is the skin of the gods. That's why there is so much gold in Egypt. Alabaster is seen as we see silver today." I stopped. "Why are you here?" I blurted out. Paul frowned and opened his mouth to answer me, but I didn't let him speak. "Friday night, if that was some sort of bet, then it's all right, joke's over, I get it. You don't have to try anymore. I'll keep out of your way until you've gone, no harm done."

"Laura, I asked you out because I like you. I like your smile, this is no joke. I just wanted to get to know you more. I'm sorry if the date wasn't as good as it could have been. Why would you think it was a joke?" He seemed hurt at what I had said.

"Crap. I'm sorry. I put my foot in it, please forgive me. I don't know why I thought it was a joke."

"I like you, really I do." Paul slid to the edge of the stool and took my hand.

I let out a breath and felt a little foolish about the way I had acted. "I'm sorry. How about we try this again? I'm singing tonight at The Blue Raven, at the Rocks."

I was fond of The Rocks; it stood on the city side of Sydney Harbour Bridge and was part of the city's oldest settlement. It has a dark past of overcrowding, poverty, Cyprians, drunkenness and even the plague. All the good stuff that makes Sydney history more interesting to read and study. Some streets are said to be haunted by a ghost in a rag coat. Old sandstone buildings still stand, along with art galleries, pubs, shops and old homes.

"I would love to hear you sing tonight," Paul said, sounding a little happier.

"I'm singing until nine and I can meet you after that for a few drinks, if you want."

"No, I'm coming to hear you sing. What time do you start?" Paul asked.

"Um…eight."

"I'll be there."

It was a Monday and the band wanted to practice. This was the quietest night for the pub. The stage was small and stood in the corner made of thick black plywood. The Pub's two large lead windows hid the goings-on from the street. They still had shutters from the forties when pubs had to close at 9 p.m. Two large, thick green wooden doors led into The Blue Raven. The walls were made from a mixture of coloured bricks. Names were carved into the bricks in one wall, some of them bearing dates that went back to the eighteen hundreds. Another wall was made from sandstone that belonged to the building next door. The carpet was torn and of a different colour that it had begun life with. The bar came out of the back wall. Stools perched around it, with chairs and tables scatted around. A few groupies sat at one of the tables near the

46

stage, waiting for Dylan.

Dylan was the guitarist and lead singer. He worked in a bank. Sean, who played keyboard, worked at Taronga Zoo. Ben, the bass player, worked with Sean. The drummer, Connor was an artist who had made a good name for himself with his paintings. We were friends from University. They had their own lives now, but we still got together to play. Dylan thought of himself as God's gift; he had dated both Marisa and myself at different times. He was a nice guy besides that, he would never lead anyone on, he would make it clear what you were getting into with him. He was the type of guy you couldn't stay mad at.

Dylan would ask me to sing with them from time to time. They liked to play Janis's songs, or some of The Pretenders or Blondie. They would cover The Doors, AC/DC, The Eagles and Daddy Cool. Dylan sounded like Jim Morrison when he sang. His voice was deep and rich. In some ways, he resembled Morrison as well. He enjoyed the groupies and would encourage them to attend these types of nights.

Marisa, Chester and Ricky sat near the stage. Chester found out that Paul was coming and kept a chair next to him. He had placed a bottle on the seat to stop anyone from taking it, even though the pub was mostly empty. I was worried that Paul would act the same way he had on our date.

By just after eight, Paul had not arrived. I was half worried and kind of pleased that he might not come. I sat on the edge of the stage, waiting for the band to tune up. My mind floated away. I was thinking about dogs fighting. I don't know why.

"Laura, what are you doing?" Dylan touched my shoulder.

"What?" Flinching at his touch, I snapped out of my thoughts.

The boys had finished tuning and were ready to begin the show. I was holding the microphone tightly in my hands, which hurt from

47

my firm grasp.

"What's with you tonight? You're jumpy as a rabbit." Dylan leaned over me and gave me a nudge with his shoulder.

"Nothing. It's okay." I jumped to my feet and jammed the microphone into the stand. The sound made everyone recoil.

"Never changed," Sean mumbled as he hit a few keys.

"She has a hot date!" Chester yelled a lot louder than he should have.

"Shut up, Chester." I bent down, picked up a coaster and threw it at him. It flew through the air before bouncing off his shoulder.

"Hey, that hurt. Ricky, did you see what she did to me? She's trying to dent me." Ricky rubbed Chester's shoulder and kissed it.

"Laura, don't hurt my baby," Ricky scolded, still rubbing Chester's shoulder.

"It's okay, you big baby," Marisa murmured, rolling her eyes at Chester, who, with crumpled face, snuggled closer to Ricky.

"Marisa, you're always on her side." Chester threw the coaster at Marisa. "Laura has a date, Laura has a date," Chester chanted as he began dancing in a circle.

"Ohh," the band heckled me.

"I'm going home. I don't need this." I turned the microphone off and tried to leave the stage.

Dylan seized my arm to stop me. "Get back here, Laura, and sing. So sensitive. Shut up, Chester. Leave her alone or we'll be singing The Doors all night."

"I know what side you're on, *Dylan*." Chester pulled a face at

48

him. Dylan stuck his finger up at Chester. Chester tried to act hurt and threw his hands to his face to simulate being scared. Dylan glanced at the bartender, who had been watching our carry on. The bartender was tapping his fingers on the bar, not happy with the way we were acting. Dylan turned away from Chester and began to play a few chords. The band jumped in after Dylan egged them on.

I had sung a few lines before Paul finally arrived. He went to the bar and ordered a drink. My heart began to flutter when I saw him. Paul spoke to the bartender and pointed at me. The bartender nodded before pouring a lemonade, then turned and took a bottle of wine from the bar's back wall.

Paul gave me a quick nod as he came over to the table where Marisa, Chester and Ricky were sitting. He greeted them as though he had no problem with Chester or Ricky. Chester, on the other hand, wiggled his fingers at Paul. Ricky quickly pulled his hand down to stop Chester.

Once the song was over, Paul came to the stage with my drink. Dylan's groupies were clapping and screaming, pleading with him to talk with them.

"Hey," Paul said, a big smile crossing his lips. I crouched down to his eye level. "You sound good."

"Thanks. I didn't think you were going to make it," I said. Paul handed me the drink. "Thanks," I added.

"You're *very* welcome. We don't want you to get thirsty, now. I said I was coming," Paul replied smoothly.

I took a sip, not wanting to drink too much. It would make me burp through the next number.

Paul reached out his hand and nestled it on the back of my neck. His thumb moved gently on my skin. It felt nice.

49

His dark eyes studied me, but I could not read anything in them. He drew his lips to mine, he begun to kiss me. His lips were soft. Enjoying the sensation of the moment, I forgot where I was. A few cat whistles and howls from the people around us made me snap back. Maybe I had been wrong about him.

"Hey you two, come on. They're going to kick us out if you don't stop." Dylan began to play again.

Paul kept my eye contact for a moment before I began to sing. I shook my head a few times to clear my mind and concentrate on the song. I think I sang a few wrong lines.

After the gig, we sat around drinking while the band played on. Paul seemed to get on with everyone. He didn't talk to Chester or Ricky much, but seemed polite when they spoke to him. Paul acted like anyone who had just joined a group. It made me think that the way he had acted on our first date was not the "real" him.

Later that night Paul and I strolled down to the wharf. Paul wanted to catch the last ferry to the North Shore; it was only a short walk from The Rocks. One of the many trains rattled past us in the above-ground train station. It sounded its horn as the metal wheels roared on the tracks. The sound of the wharf was that of metal and the sea. We had paused near one of the railings that overlooked the water. People hurried past, as one of the ferries docked, in one of the Quays' many portals. Circular Quay is one of many links to the North Shore and other docks on the harbour. It was always the nicest way to get anywhere in Sydney. The wharf and the foreshore were always busy, lined with buskers in the daytime and the homeless at night. It was always sad to see. In one corner near a high-end café was a cardboard lean-to where a homeless man had made his home. He had been there for as long as I could remember.

Paul had a few minutes before he had to go. The water lapped on the concrete wall just below us. Paul leaned in once more to

50

kiss me. It was just as enjoyable as it had been earlier that night. He ran his finger on my lips before kissing me once more, then stopped. "I have to go away for the rest of the week," he said softly.

I placed my hand on his chest. Paul was only a little taller than I was. "I think I'm going to miss you. Where are you going?" I asked.

Paul studied me for a moment before answering. It appeared as though he was thinking about what to tell me. "I'm glad you're going to miss me. I think I'm going to miss you, too. It's just a work thing, don't worry yourself about it. When I get back I have a preseason game. Do you want to come?"

"Yes, that would be good." He hadn't answered me about where he was going. I was about to ask again when a large green and yellow ferry entered the dock. Its engines roared loudly as it came to a halt. Water thrashed against the wall, making the walkway move under our feet.

"I'll call you when I get back." Paul kissed me on the cheek before dashing away.

"See you then." I don't think he heard me; he was out of sight too quickly.

I didn't hear anything from him while he was away. By mid-week I found myself checking my phone to make sure it was still working. I was confused about why he had not called. I didn't know where he was and there was no way of contacting him.

To pass the time, I busied myself with the alabaster Shabti. The Internet was still a new thing, so finding online photos of Shabtis to which I could compare ours was a lot harder. I had pored over endless images in the books in our collection, but had encountered nothing but dead ends. I ended up sending emails to a few museums. Along with the emails I included a photo of the Shabti. I asked whether anyone had one like it in their collections. I was a little disillusioned by the end of the week, as no one had seen one like it or had one in their collection. I had more questions than answers, but that's normal. Sometimes with an artefact you never find answers in your lifetime—or any answers at all.

"Laura? Wake up." I felt someone pushing on my shoulder. The side of my body was stiff. I opened my eyes to find Marisa standing over me.

"You fell asleep." Marisa knelt beside me. I was in the lounge room of our flat, it felt as if it was late.

I sat up a little, still half asleep. I didn't know what was going on, papers slipped to the floor, from my lap. "I'm all right," I said, wiping my cheek. It was wet, as though I had been crying.

"You should give it a rest. It's two in the morning." Marisa seemed concerned.

My eyes fixed onto the darkest part of the room. I tried to remember what I had been dreaming about. It felt important. I thought about it, but no images came to my mind.

"You were singing. That's what woke me up. It seemed like you were singing to someone. It was weird," Marisa said. She frowned at me as she gently placed her hand on my shoulder.

"The same song?" I asked.

"Yes. Is it because you haven't heard from Paul all week?"

I wiped the water from my eyes. "No, it's okay. Thanks. I'm sorry for waking you. I'll go to bed now." I didn't want to say anything. The matter was private and no one needed to know.

"Do you want to talk about it?" Marisa asked, watching me with concern.

"No, I just want to go to sleep. It's all right." I tried to reassure her that I was fine. I was still a little confused and half asleep.

This was not the first time I had these dreams. They were usually flashes, nothing more. I felt upset, hurt and angry. My heart was racing. I didn't want Marisa or anyone else to know about them, as they were person

CHAPTER 4

~

My primary school fete was the biggest event of the year. The school seemed to revolve around it. My headmaster kept track of the families that had attended and would make a point of speaking to the families that had not been there. It was as though the world itself would fall apart if one family missed out without good cause.

My headmaster was grey-haired and balding. He wore cheap suits, brown squared shoes and bright ties. He peered down through his glasses when he spoke to me.

One morning while I sat in the lunch shed before school, reading one of the many books that weighed down my bag, the headmaster flew out of the office doors and across the bitumen playground to stop one of the mothers. She and her family were new to the country and the school. The mother was Italian and spoke broken English. The headmaster began pointing at her and trying to tell her how important the school fete was, that her family had missed. I smiled as the headmaster pointed his finger at the mother, trying to explain why her family needed to go to the fete. The mother smiled and nodded while glancing sideways at her son. Her son, who understood English well, stood next to her with a smug expression on his face. He was a hot head in class and would get in trouble for lying to teachers.

The mother, confused about what the headmaster was saying, began speaking quickly to her son, who was in my class and was translating the headmaster's words. Through fits of giggles he flung his hands around, pointing and making big gestures, copying what the headmaster was doing. He listened to the headmaster, nodding and placing his hand on his chin, then spoke to his mother in Italian. His mother appeared confused. The headmaster, on the other hand, was confident that he had gotten his point across.

Without another word, the headmaster marched away to speak to another mother.

The mother spoke rapidly in Italian to her son. I don't think he had told her everything the headmaster said.

The school fete was the same every year with pony rides, go-carts, face painting and dunk the teachers. All the mothers had to cook something. They made sure to use their best recipes for chocolate crackles, sponges, lamingtons and toffees.

Mum always cooked her sponge with mock cream and strawberries on top. The sponge was Dad's favourite. He would hurry off to the cake table so that he could buy it back, but one of the teachers always bought it before the fete began. This drove Dad crazy, and every year he tried to outwit the teacher. However, every year the teacher beat Dad to the cake. Once again, Dad came wandering back, muttering under his breath that he wasn't happy. He had missed out again.

"Don't worry Dan, I'll make you another one," Mum tried to reassure him.

Bess was now three years old. I was nine. We were dressed in the same outfit—blue blouses, tan skirts, white knee-high socks, black buckled patent leather shoes and red purses. I wanted to wear jeans, but Mum would not allow it. Dad was in blue dress pants with a matching blue tie and a light blue short-sleeved shirt. We were all over dressed for the fete, but Mum had made a fuss over our clothing. Outwardly, Mum wanted us to look normal, but I felt that her attempt didn't work. It was just embarrassing.

Dad, still miffed about the cake, reached around to his back pocket and took out his wallet. He began thumbing through the different coloured notes. Mum glanced at the money as Dad's fingers flicked along to find the right amount.

Mum's new dusty pink dress and white shoes suited her well. She became twitchy as Dad licked his thumb. He retrieved two green notes—two two-dollar bills.

Mum breathed through her teeth, it sounded like a hiss. "Dan, don't give Laura that much."

"Eve, it's all right. Here, make sure you care for your sister." Dad winked at Bess as he handed me the dollar notes. It being the seventies, four dollars was a fortune for a kid.

"Yes, Dad." My mind began racing at the thought of what I could buy. I considered putting some of it aside and spending it elsewhere.

"That's the girl. We'll see you at twelve." He pushed my hair down and gave me a kiss on the cheek. Dad was a good guy, smart. He was always a straight thinker.

"Laura." Mum was standing stiff, not pleased that I had that much money.

"Yes, Mum." I quickly glanced at her.

"Don't eat too much, and watch your sister," she said coldly.

"Yes, Mum."

She nodded. I knew she wanted to add more, but had thought twice about it, in front of Dad.

There was always a lot going on at the fete. I wanted to see as much as I could before Bess tired and wanted to go back. The other kids were in t-shirts and jeans. A few of my classmates laughed at me because I was dressed like Bess. I kept my eyes straight ahead, trying not to hear the heckling. This was a Catholic private school, my family didn't go to church. It was the closest private school to our home.

The sports oval was the only patch of green at the school. Bitumen and concrete covered the rest of the grounds. Houses had been built up around the school, closing everything in. The school buildings were a mixture of weatherboard and brick.

The fete spread out over the sports oval. It was busy, Mum and Dad were helping with the kids' art show. Bess's eyes lit up when

56

we came across the ponies. She tried to drag me to the fence. I let go of her hand.

"Laura, please, I like the black and white one. Can I have a ride? It's only twenty cents."

Three women dressed in cowgirl outfits led small ponies around a fenced-off area. A woman wearing a red cowboy hat was leading the pony Bess wanted to ride. A few kids stood in line, waiting their turn. A man stood at the gate, taking money for the ride. The other children's parents stood to one side, smiling and waving at their children as they waited.

I didn't see why I had to hold Bess's hand. "Go and line up Bess." I pointed sharply to the line.

Bess put her hand out and wiggled her fingers at me. "Come with me," she pleaded. I crossed my arms and rolled my eyes at her.

"No, I'll stand here and watch you. If you want to go you don't need me," I grumbled at her, leaning back on the fence. I shook my head, standing my ground.

Bess made a face at me, then stormed over to the line, stamping her feet as she went.

"You're a drama queen, Bess," I grumbled under my breath, she heard me and poked out her tongue in response.

After a few moments Bess had forgotten that she was mad. She began to bounce on her feet, smiling at me. She kept a watchful eye on the pony she wanted to ride. Rolling my eyes again, I turned to watch the woman leading the ponies around.

"Hey, Weirdo." The voice came from behind me. I knew the tone well.

Jennifer Jenkins was short and tanned, with straight blond hair. She was pretty, but had a cold heart. On hot summer days she enjoyed telling everyone about her in-ground backyard pool. Her father was a bank manager. My father had worked for him for a while. Dad could not stand Mr Jenkins. The headmaster and some of the teachers would fuss over Jennifer. I think they had housing loans with her father's bank.

Jennifer flicked her hair back before she spoke; she had seen a TV star do it once. I overheard her saying this in the girl's toilet after she chased me in there last year. I hid in there all lunch time, she had carried on about how much she resembled a Brady. She was like a cruel Brady sister.

"Get lost, Jennifer," I snapped, keeping my back to her. I tried to act as though I didn't care. However, my heart was pounding and my throat was about to close over. There was no way I would let her know that.

"Oh, see, girls. It's Weirdo's little baby sister. A baby Weirdo." Jennifer had spotted Bess.

Jennifer flicked her hair over one shoulder as she turned in Bess's direction. Kimberly and Heather were twins and not very smart. Jennifer had them eating out of her hand. The twins were a little taller than Jennifer was, and were thin. They hovered just behind her with blank expressions. They acted only when Jennifer said or did something, it was unhealthy to watch. Jennifer seemed to draw power from them, she also took pleasure in making little kids cry. Her eyes would go cold it was like watching a soul freeze over.

I hurried over to Bess, cutting Jennifer off from her assault on my little sister. Bess was only a baby and didn't need to know this type of person yet. Jennifer made my life hell at school; she wasn't going to do it to Bess. I'm sure Jennifer was making it her life's mission to upset me as much as she could.

"Are you going to ride on the pony too, Weirdo? They're a little small for you. You're a big girl now, you need a big horse to ride." Jennifer tried to push herself close to me as she spoke loudly in my ear. She shoved her shoulder into my back. Kimberly and

Heather laughed, egging her on.

"Hey Weirdo, do you have your TV back? You missed a great show last night. Too bad you'll never see it." Kimberly and Heather giggled harder at what Jennifer was saying.

Bess was getting upset. She kept peering around me, trying to get a glimpse at Jennifer. Each time, I moved her away. Bess was about to say something to Jennifer, but I put my hand over Bess's mouth to stop her.

One afternoon Bess and I had been watching TV when two men came to the house to take our set away. Mum let them inside and pointed at the TV. Without missing a step, the men, dressed in suits, unplugged it, hoisted the heavy set off the floor and carried it out. The fatter man groaned as he walked backwards out of the lounge room with the TV. When Dad came home to find his TV was gone, he was furious. He and Mum fought that night, Bess and I fled to my room to hide from them.

My teacher had wanted us to watch a documentary on Ned Kelly that night. The next day in class, the teacher asked questions about the documentary. When my turn to answer came I told her that our TV had been taken away. Jennifer jumped on this; her enjoyment of my embarrassment was downright cruel. The teacher, on the other hand, didn't believe me. I had to write lines on the blackboard over lunch for punishment.

Jennifer pushed against me once more, almost knocking Bess and me over. "I have two TVs. When I go home, I'm going to watch my portable TV while I'm swimming. Nice dress, Weirdo." She flicked the fabric of my dress while making a sound of disgust.

"You can't do that at the same time. There's too much water in the way, Jennifer," I answered, pushing her back.

The pony that Bess wanted to ride was ready. To get away from the girls, I hurried Bess into the round yard. Bess was upset and had gone quite white. My hands were shaking a little as I helped

59

her onto the dusty black and white pony. Jennifer tried to push her way into the line, but one of the mothers stopped her. Jennifer's eyes went icy as she sized up the mother, but she must have thought better about making a scene.

Instead, Jennifer flicked her hair back over her shoulder and began to press against the fence. She rocked on it, trying to intimidate me. The owner of the ride was having none of it. "Young lady, you're too big to ride my ponies," the woman growled. "I think you better leave."

Jennifer tossed her hair with her hands again and glared at the woman. "My father can buy me one at any time. I don't need *your* nags." She scowled at the owner before leaving.

A few steps from the pony and Bess was content. By the time she finished her ride, she had forgotten about Jennifer. Bess was endlessly chatting about her pony. I, on the other hand, was still upset about Jennifer and was not listening to Bess.

We stopped to play the games on the sideshow. I kept a watch out in case Jennifer returned.

"This is the last game," I informed Bess. We were almost out of money and had nothing to show for it. At the far end of the oval, tables had been set up for people to sell bric-a-brac. I wanted to buy something for myself. Bess put the last ball into the clown, then we strolled down to the tables.

I had a hard time keeping hold of Bess's hand as we wandered down the lines of tables. She kept pulling away from me. I finally gave up on holding onto her, when Bess once more jerked her hand out of mine. She spied a large pink teddy sitting next to a table.

"Laura, I want this," Bess pleaded, waving the ratty teddy in the air before hugging it. She planted herself on the ground and began talking to it.

"My name is Bess. What's yours? I like you. Do you like me? I'm sorry your eyes are all funny, but I think I can fix you so that you'll feel better."

The bear was old and falling apart. Its stuffing fell out as she hugged it. With Bess rooted to one spot, I used the opportunity to explore the other tables, hopping she would stay put. A few tables down, some shell jewellery caught my eye. However, after turning the price tag over, I thought better of it. Bess had her heart set on the teddy. There was no way I could buy anything for myself, as we had only sixty cent left.

I checked to see if Bess was okay before I moved away from the table. She was pushing stuffing back into the bear. "I'm sorry if this hurts, but it's for your own good." Bess kissed the bear on the ear.

Content that she was all right, I wandered down the next row of tables. My foot hit something hard. It was a box containing cancelled library books. Most of them were romance novels, with men and women kissing on the covers. I had never seen men with muscles like that. When dad wore his swimmers, he didn't resemble these men. Disappointed that I hadn't found anything, I started putting the books back in the box so that I could head back and buy Bess's teddy.

However, a book at the bottom of the box caught my eye. On its cover was a watercolour painting of a man with a strange beard and clothes. He had the skin of a leopard wrapped around his neck. The cover said, *A Day in the Life of a King of Egypt*. The book's plastic cover was stuck to the bottom. With a tug, I ripped it from the base of the box. A smell of must hit my nose as I flipped through the book. It had a water stain on each page.

The images in the book sparked something in my soul. My mind began to race. My eyes hurriedly scanned the pages. I wanted to know everything about the images. Who were these people? Question after question…I needed to know more.

It was the story of a boy king. One of the watercolour pictures showed him sitting down and watching a man who was talking to him. I flipped through more pages. There were black and white photos. I stopped for a moment at a picture of boats with triangular sails. I flicked a few more pages to find what seemed like little wooden fat men. On the other page was a chair made from gold with a man and a woman facing each other. Under the photo was the caption, "*A chair found in Tutankhamen's Tomb, maybe a gift from his wife.*"

In the back of the book were two types of funny writing. One was hieroglyph and the other I didn't know. Underneath was the caption, "*Ancient cuneiform. Dead form of ancient writing.*" I wanted to know what this writing meant. Something told me to find out more.

"Are you going to buy that?" The sun blocked the man's features. I smelled smoke; a ring of it drifted over his head. "If you're going to buy it, then buy it."

I staggered to my feet. "How much is it?"

"Two dollars for the box," the man barked.

"I…I just want this book. How much for this book?" I stammered.

"I'm only selling the box. Put it back if you can't buy it."

"Sorry," I answered, gradually placing the book back in the box. My heart sank. I really wanted just the book, not the box. Bess wanted the teddy and that was all I could afford.

Miserably I made my way back to where I had left my sister. "Bess?" I glanced around for her. She was nowhere to be seen.

She had disappeared and the teddy was gone as well. My heart began hammering fast. I couldn't see her anywhere.

"Bess?" I flicked back the tablecloth she wasn't under there.

"Can I help you?" asked the woman who was running the stall.

"Sorry, I've lost my sister. Have you seen her? She's four years old and blond, carrying a pink teddy."

"No," she answered swiftly before turning back to serve a customer.

"Bess!" I called as I hurried away from the stall, rising up on my toes to search for her. "Bess, where are you?"

Mum and Dad were going to kill me. Maybe Jennifer and the twins had taken her. Bess was only a baby; Jennifer could do anything to her. I hurried back down the sideshow, my mind and eyes searching for her blond hair and ratty old teddy. The sideshow was crowded with people playing games, making it hard to see.

I pushed my way through the crowd, stopping a few times to call for her. "Bess!"

It was less crowded by the ponies. I thought Bess might have gone there to show her teddy to the pony. I glanced at someone's watch. Time had run out. I had twenty minutes before we had to meet Mum and Dad. As I hurried to the ponies, something hit my leg hard. I fell rigidly to the ground, flat on the grass. My face scraped severely on the surface.

"Oh, Weirdo, you fell over. You have dirtied your ugly dress." Jennifer stood over me, laughing.

My knee was grazed, and so were my hands. I wiped my cheek with the tips of my fingers. I could feel something wet running down my face. The tips of my finger were covered in blood.

Kimberly and Heather laughed so hard they fell over each other. "Weirdo, she fell over."

Recovering a little, I turned over to see that my skirt was above my hips for all to see. I shoved it down. My clothing and hands had grass and blood stains on them.

"Are you all right?" asked a woman who had come to assist me.

A crowd gathered around me as blood poured down my face. The woman tried to help me up, but I resisted.

"I'm okay. I need to find my sister. Thank you," I said to the woman. Her hand hovered in the air as I rose to my feet. For a moment it seemed as though the woman wouldn't let me go.

"I'm fine," I insisted, putting my hand to my bloody head. She took hold of my arm as I swayed on my feet. "I'm fine," I repeated. This time the woman slowly let me move. The crowd parted as I staggered towards the ponies, which were now standing to one side and eating. The lady who had led Bess around was sitting in the shade. Bess was nowhere to be seen. My hands and knee were still stinging from my fall. Jennifer was not giving up; she and the twins blocked my way as I headed to the stalls. I was not in the mood for this anymore. Jennifer's fun was over.

"Get away from me, Jennifer," I said.

A grin slid across her mouth and her eyes went cold. "What are you going to do, Weirdo?"

All that was on my mind was finding Bess and going home. I pushed past Jennifer and the twins. "Weirdo lost her sister," Jennifer chanted.

I paused and turned around. "What did you do to my sister? If you hurt her…"

"I didn't do anything to her. I'd get something from her if I did."

Jennifer laughed again. She glanced at the twins, who were pretending their heads were bleeding. While Jennifer was watching the twins' performance, I pushed her over. The expression on her face was priceless. It was one of shock and hurt. While the twins helped her up, I hurried back to the stalls.

Out of breath, I began searching for Bess among the rows of

tables. Down the first row from behind me, I heard a familiar giggle.

"That's my sister. Hello, Laura," a voice said. Bess was sitting on a woman's lap the woman resembled Cher. Her hair shimmered in the sun just like Cher's.

Bess had a big smile for me, not understanding the stress I was in. "My sister, she looks after me when Mummy goes down to the shops. Mummy goes down to the shops a lot."

"Does she?" asked the woman. Then she realised that I was injured. "Are you all right?" she asked in shock. She took Bess off her lap and approached me.

"I'm okay."

A girl with thick dark hair, big glasses and a yellow t-shirt leaned on the table she seemed curious about what was happening. I had never seen her before. The lady gently clutched my hands, turning them around as she inspected them.

"Laura likes to play hide and seek. Don't you?" Bess giggled but stopped when she saw my expression.

"Come and sit down." The lady guided me to the chair she had been sitting on.

"What happened, Laura?" Bess asked, now upset.

"Don't worry, Bess, your sister is going to be okay. My name is May," the woman gently introduced herself. May softly lifted my head, turning it to one side. "Who did this to you?"

I glanced away not wanting to answer, May tilted her head at me. She smiled, seeming to understand that I was not going to answer her. She had large white teeth and an herbal smell. I didn't know what it was, as I had never smelt it before.

"One day, life will turn on her," May continued, then changed the subject. "This is my niece, Marisa. She's going to your school on Monday. I think you two are going to be good friends."

Marisa waved at me and smiled.

"Hi, Marisa," I said. "Bess, where have you been? I've been searching for you." My head was spinning a little.

"Did you hide from your sister? May asked.

"Yes, I was playing a trick on her," Bess answered playfully.

May made a clicking sound at Bess. "That's not a nice thing to do."

May pulled over a large leather handbag. Images of butterflies were pressed into the leather on its flap. She placed her hand inside the bag and moved it around as though she were searching for something. Stopping a few times to see what was in her hand, May finally dragged out two cloth hankies.

"Marisa, could you please pour out a cup of water?" May asked. Without a word, Marisa went over to a cooler and took out a glass bottle of water. She poured the water into a cup before coming back.

"Thanks, Marisa," May said. She dabbed the cloth hanky into the water and gently pressed it onto my face. It felt warm.

"Laura, are you alright?" Mum's voice seemed to come from nowhere. Bess ran up to her, wrapping her arms around Mum. "What happened?" Mum asked.

"She's not telling," May said. "She'll be alright; it's not deep.

I'm May and this is my niece, Marisa."

Mum nodded at May. "I think we'd better go. Thank you for helping my daughter."

Mum helped me up and began to lead me away. "Thank you, May, Marisa," I said.

"You're welcome, Laura. Come and see me any time. See you soon, Bess. No more playing tricks." May waved goodbye.

Once we were out of sight, Mum stopped. "What happened?" She sounded a little mad.

"Laura?" Marisa called from behind us. She handed the teddy to Bess. "You forgot these." Marisa had the Egyptian book in her other hand.

"I didn't…" I sputtered. My hand hovered over the book, then drew back.

Marisa shook her head and smiled, pushing the book at me. "Aunt May said you need this book. She said something about a Soul Path she talks like that sometimes. Don't worry, I still don't understand it." Marisa put the book into my hand before going back to her aunt.

That afternoon, after Mum had bandaged and cleaned my hands and knee, Dad wanted to know who had tripped me. He was going back to the school to give the headmaster a piece of his mind. However, when I revealed who it was, he backed down. Dad screwed up his face before going off to his garage, mumbling as he went. This was where Dad went to think.

When Mum was finished bandaging me, I locked myself in my room. I had a record player and a small assortment of records.

Janis Joplin was my favourite. I played her records more than any others. I lay on my bed reading my new book, eating up every word. It was like my music; the pages of the book spoke to my soul, which was asking to learn more. I wanted to know more about Egypt and cuneiform. I wanted to know how to read this writing. This, maybe, is what May had meant by a Soul Path.

The next Monday, Marisa entered my class. She sat down next to me. We became friends that day, real kindred spirits. I had never had a close friend before. It was nice that we were on the same page.

CHAPTER 5

After the night that Marisa found me on the floor of the lounge room, she tried to talk to me about it. However, I wasn't in the mood. I never understood why I had these dreams they didn't happen all the time. They had begun in my twenties, but now were happening again. The next time it happened, I was stunned when the cold of the bathroom tiles woke me. I lay there, trying to think about what I had been dreaming. All I could see were flashes. The dreams felt private; I couldn't tell anyone about them. To Marisa's credit, she never told anyone about my foolish dreams, either. Marisa wasn't that type of person.

"Hey." Saturday, a week later, Paul called me. It was good to hear his voice.

"How did you go?" I was in the kitchen of my apartment, talking to him over the phone.

"What?"

"You were working away?"

"Oh yeah, no, it was good. Tomorrow you're coming to the footy. I'll meet you at the change rooms, okay? I got to go. I'll see ya. Bye. It's good to hear your voice."

"Bye."

The phone went dead before I could say more. I slowly hung up. Standing there for a moment, I felt confused. Paul's mood had changed once again. Sighing, I picked up some glasses and headed into the lounge room. Marisa watched me as I returned. I was sucking my bottom lip, deep in thought.

"What's up?" Marisa asked.

I didn't answer, I just shook my head at her then grinned. Two pizza boxes lay on the coffee table. Marisa slapped at Chester's hand as he tried to put a piece of anchovy onto her slice.

"Did Pauly finally come home? Did you miss him? Do you want to have straight sex with him?" Chester said, mocking me as he slapped back at Marisa.

"Yes, yes and we've only been out twice." I sat down on the floor next to the coffee table and handed out the glasses. I looked down at my pizza; someone had piled anchovies and olives on it.

"Come on, Laura, tell us what's wrong," Ricky said as he poured wine for everyone.

Chester watched me as I took a bite of pizza, he always did it, thinking I didn't like them. I began humming loudly as I chewed, he pulled a face as I ate, it was in annoyance of my musical performance.

We were about to watch *The King and I* on TV. It was Chester's favourite movie. Since University, we would order pizza and wine and watch *The King and I.* We could see it on video, but it was more fun to wait for it to air on Saturday Night Movies. Chester made another face at me as I munched loudly on another bite of my pizza.

"Ricky, do you see what she's doing to me? Make her go away." Chester waved at me.

Marisa took a bite of her pizza. She opened her mouth at Chester and showed the contents to him. Chester let out a high-pitched squeal and ducked his head behind Ricky.

"Ricky, make them stop, quick, make them stop. I want to watch my movie," Chester said into Ricky's shoulder.

"How can you eat that?" Ricky asked Marisa and me.

I finished my mouthful. "I like olives and anchovies," I said, then added, in answer to Marisa's question from before, "I'm going to a football game tomorrow to watch Paul."

"So? Don't you like Paul anymore?" Ricky asked.

Chester fell on the floor, fanning himself at what Marisa and I were doing. Ricky tried to pull Chester back up.

"Yes, I have to sit there and watch him play by myself." I made a face. Chester glanced at me from the floor, then I added. "Don't get me wrong, I like watching a bunch of sweaty men running around a field."

Chester grinned at the mention of sweaty men. The movie was about to start and he began twisting on the floor. Chester seemed like he would keel over if I didn't stop talking.

"Why don't we all go tomorrow? We can make a day of it. You and Paul can do whatever after," Marisa said. She ignored Chester, who was now pointing at the TV and bouncing up and down on his knees. He put his finger to his lips to hush us.

The music for the movie had started. Chester would soon be puffing out his chest as Yul Brynner did in the movie.

"Yeah, that would be good. I'll make lunch." Ricky answered, holding onto Chester and trying to calm him down.

"Fine, we're going to a football game tomorrow. Now, shhh." Chester took the remote and turned up the volume on the TV.

The next day we spent an hour riding a bus to the North Shore of Sydney. Paul had been too tired to speak on the phone last night; that was what I told myself. It was what I had told myself the week Paul was away. He was working, he was busy, he was tired. It had almost become a mantra by the end of the week. I didn't want to think he didn't care.

Outside the oval, the bus stopped near the entrance it was full of fans for the other team they had sung all the way there. We paid before we walked through the gates the crowd was in a good mood. A few men were still singing chants as we entered the grounds, Ricky and Chester begun singing chants of their own.

"We're going to war to watch, to watch the straight men kick some balls," Ricky and Chester chanted.

71

A young boy was struggling through the crowd, selling pies. He yelled in a high-pitched voice over the other voices. Paul came to watch me sing, I told myself; I would have been a fool if I had told him I didn't want to watch him play.

"Is that Paul over there?" Marisa asked.

I peered over the heads of the people to see where Marisa was pointing. Paul and his teammates were standing around, talking to a group of girls.

"That's him." My heart leapt a little as I said it.

I moved closer. Paul grinned when he saw me. He pushed away from the girls he was talking with and came over to me. He was wearing a maroon football jumper with white shorts, the other team was dressed in blue. His football boots made a clopping sound on the path as he moved towards me.

"Hey, glad you made it." Paul quickly ran his finger on my lip, then leaned in and kissed me.

"I made it." I smiled.

My friends were standing behind me. I think Paul frowned when he saw them, but it was quick and I wasn't sure.

"Hi Paul. Did you miss us?" Chester grinned.

"Hey Chester. It's good to see you all again. I have to go. I'll see you after the game, okay?" He was only speaking to me he ran his finger on my lip once more.

"I didn't want to watch the game by myself," I blurted out quickly.

"It's all right, just thought it would be you and me tonight, that's all. It's been a long week." Paul rubbed my shoulder before going back to his team.

"Don't worry, they aren't going to stay after the game."

Paul glanced back and nodded. The look on my friends' faces

said it all. I didn't know why I had said that; it fell out of my mouth and I wasn't able to stop it.

"Sorry, I shouldn't have said that," I apologised to them.

"Well, it's the truth. We aren't staying after the game and you didn't tell him we were coming," Marisa said, trying not to sound funny about it.

"Still, I shouldn't have said that. I'm sorry," I repeated.

Chester grabbed hold of me and kissed my cheek. "I'll forgive you this once. I don't know about Marisa. She may stab you in your sleep. Unless you get lucky tonight. Then Marisa will have to do it another night." Chester grinned at me.

"Shut it, Chester." I slapped at him.

The weather was warm, there wasn't a cloud in the sky, it was the last days of summer. The grandstand had wooden benches. Chester and Ricky walked ahead to find the best seats.

The other night at The Blue Raven, Paul and my friends had acted as though they had known each other for years. I didn't understand why Paul had been cold to them today. I tried to reassure myself about his behaviour, yet again.

On the other side of the field, groups of men sat on benches, wearing the other team's colours. We had dressed in Paul's team colours. From where we were sitting, I could see the change rooms. A few members of Paul's team stood near them, still speaking to the group of girls. I didn't know what worried me more about these girls—the extremely low-cut, tight dresses they were wearing or the way they kept brushing their bodies on the footballers.

"Football hags." I felt something cold on my arm. Ricky had pressed a cold drink against my skin.

"What?" I asked, taking the drink from him.

"Football hags. They hang around footballers so they can date

73

or marry them." Ricky nodded his head toward the girls.

"Oh, right. I've heard of them."

Finally Paul came running out with his team. When the crowd saw them, they clapped and cheered. It reminded me of Roman times, with people watching the gladiators. Paul glanced up at me and gave me a nod. From his bag Chester dragged out sets of pom poms in the colour of Paul's team. He handed them around.

"What are you doing?" I asked.

"Having some fun. You remember that, or doesn't your Pauly let you have fun?"

"Ha ha, Chester." I snatched a set of pom poms from him.

"You know, Chester, it's the Americans who use pom poms," Marisa said, shaking her pom poms in his face.

"Marisa, shut it," Chester said, shaking them back in her face.

Ricky knew more about the game than I did. He talked me through every move. We sang a chant whenever Paul's team kicked or made a goal. Paul's team was up by two points when the whistle blew for half time.

Paul's face was covered in dirt; he was playing hard. I flinched quite a few times when he slammed himself into another player.

"He has to kick after they tackle five times," Ricky explained.

Paul was running with the ball. A man from the other team ran hard at him, throwing him to the ground. I flinched again. It was hard seeing someone you knew being handled like this. He seemed fine he just shook it off and continued playing.

"After the game you can give your Pauly compliments where he needs them." Ricky gave me a kiss on the forehead.

"Thanks for the help," I told Ricky, then flinched once more when Paul ran into another man with his shoulder.

"Ricky, don't kiss Laura. Her man goes a greenie colour when

74

you do that," Chester said, making a sickly face.

"Which green is that, Chester, the one when we're around or another type of green?"

"What are you two talking about? He was okay the other night."

"Please, Laura, wake up, will you? Mr. Beefcake. He doesn't like *us*," Chester said from behind his hand.

"It'll be all right, don't worry." I waved it off.

Marisa listened to what Chester and Ricky were saying, but didn't say anything herself. She had gone quiet since we met up with Paul.

After the game Ricky and I had to hold Chester back when he found out there were naked men in the change room.

"How come they can run around naked and I can't help them?" Chester asked as Ricky took hold of him around the waist. I stood in front of Chester to stop him from running into the change room.

"Unhand me, man, let me go. I need to be in there. They need me to wash them, wipe them and rub them in oil." He announced trying to pull away.

People were walking past us, giving Chester sideways glances because of the way he was acting.

"Chester, stop it, please." Ricky said something in his ear. Chester jerked his head at Ricky, then raised an eyebrow in question. Ricky nodded, a large smile glided across his face.

Chester stopped and crossed his arms. "I'll be good."

I sighed. I didn't know what Ricky had said to Chester, but whatever it was, it worked. I rolled my eyes at Chester.

As soon as they had blown the whistle, Marisa had said her goodbyes, then gone off to give her number to a player from the other team.

Paul's team had won. Fans walked past us, singing chants. Paul pushed his way through the crowd as people slapped him on the back, congratulating him and his teammates.

"You played well," I said as I kissed Paul hello. He smelled like a public shower.

"Thanks." He kissed me back, then glanced over at Chester and Ricky.

"Congratulations," Chester said. "Well done, Paul. We're going. Good to see your team won. We'll see you later, Laura." Chester's eyes narrowed, then he grinned at Paul, tilting his head to one side.

"I'll see you tomorrow," I told Chester and Ricky. I sucked my bottom lip as they walked away.

"You okay?" Paul asked.

I glanced back at him. "Yes, I'm fine. Where are we going?" Chester and Ricky had disappeared into the wall of people.

"The football club. It's not far, we can walk. You sure you're all right?"

"Yeah, let's go."

Paul was quiet as we walked to the football club. He didn't seem like the kind of person to hold hands.

"What does that tattoo mean?" I asked.

Paul glanced down at his arm. The goblin glared out with a forbidding stare. "I had to earn it," Paul said.

"Earn it?"

Paul appeared smug about what he had just said. "Yeah, um, I needed to, I needed to spend ten seconds with a mad bull to get it. It's just a thing a group of us did in Wagga."

"Ten seconds with a mad bull, wow. Okay. It must be a country thing."

76

Paul shrugged his shoulders and half smiled as we made our way to the bottom of the football club's stairs. "That's what you do in the country," he mumbled.

The football club was filling with people who had been at the game. We made our way through the front door. I had never been to this club. It seemed as though the owners had spent a lot of money to make it first-rate. It was a two-storey building with the team's logo in lights on the front. The foyer's floor had burgundy carpet. Photos of players in action lined the walls. To one side, large glass doors led into another room. I followed Paul as he pushed open the doors.

"You played a good game, mate. Good on you, mate." A man took hold of Paul's hand and shook it eagerly. Paul smiled and nodded at him.

"Hey, Pauly." A voice rose over the crowd. Members of his team waved at Paul. They were also the guys he worked with at the museum.

The room was set with tables and chairs. A dance floor filled one side of the room. In the back corner stood pool tables. On the other side stood a bar.

Paul took hold of my arm and pulled me over to his mates, who were sitting near the pool tables. So much for just him and me.

"Laura, this is Dick, Sid and Dale."

Paul pointed to the girls sitting at the same table. I took in a breath. I knew by their dresses that they were the ones who had been outside the football change room. But that wasn't why I had taken a breath.

"This is Heather, Kimberly and ...... Jennifer."

It felt like my heart had stopped, then started at a full gallop. The day I left high school, I was happy that I would never see them again. Now they were all blonde, and looked like they had nose jobs as well. Their breasts were bigger than they were the last time

77

I had seen them.

"It's about time we met you. He's been hiding you away from us," Dick said, shaking my hand.

"Here I am." I smiled back at Dick. He seemed nice. Dale gave me a nod. As he stood, he pointed at the others, wobbling his glass at them.

"Beer, beer," Sid, Dick and Paul chanted at Dale.

"What do you want to drink, Laura?" Paul asked, taking me around the waist.

"Beer will be fine," I said quickly. I needed something to numb the feeling of Jennifer wanting to kill me. The feeling that I was about to die washed over me. A little bit of alcohol in my bloodstream would make this easier.

"I can get you a wine if you want," he said.

"Whatever is easy, wine or beer, doesn't matter," I replied, shrugging my shoulders at him.

Paul smiled. "I'll get you a wine." He kissed me quickly, then went over to the bar with his friends.

I stood a bit away from Jennifer and the twins, not wanting to get too close in case they charged. I took in another breath and blew it out slowly.

"So, who's dating who?" I asked, trying to be nice.

Jennifer glared at me as though she had been sucking a sour lemon. The twins mirrored her expression. Jennifer's eyes were just as cold as they had ever been.

"Does it matter who we're dating? We go to all the parties and all the games. Weirdos like you don't belong here," Jennifer replied dryly.

"Oh. I'll remember that," I answered.

"Yes," Kimberly added.

"For your information, Paul is hot property, and when he has finished sleeping with you, he'll see the light and come back to where he belongs. I don't understand what he's doing with you." Jennifer said the last part under her breath. "I'll give you some advice. Get the hell out of here now."

"Oh, okay, I'll keep that in mind. I'll let you know when we break up. Then you can sleep with him." I should have left right there and then, I wanted to get out. However, the fact that I wanted to stand my ground and show Jennifer that I was better than her was getting in the way.

Jennifer flicked her hair with her hand. "Do you remember that crazy thing she always did at school?" she asked the twins. "She would fade out in class. Where do you go, Weirdo? Oh, did your mummy and daddy get their TV back?"

"You girls getting on?" Dick asked. He came up, kissed Jennifer on the lips and put her drink down in front of her. She brushed him off.

"We're going to be best of friends in no time," Jennifer said calculatingly.

I managed to sit far away from Jennifer and the twins, using the men as a buffer. The men became lighter as they began to drink. To keep away from Jennifer's eye contact, I watched Paul and Dale playing pool. I sat back and watched a few games. After Paul had finished his game with Dale, he gave me the cue stick to hold, then went to the bar to buy more drinks. Paul went to help him carry the drinks back.

"Who wants to play me?" I asked, studying Dick and Dale.

They acted as though I had asked them to go to church with me. Dick was red headed with bushy eyebrows, and had a kind smile. He had a stocky build and seemed easy-going. Dale was blonde and shorter than I was. He had a boyish appearance and seemed to be dating one of the twins. Sid had long hair and was scruffy; his clothes hung off him. Dick seemed to be the better

79

friend to Paul, but Sid hung onto Paul's every move. Sid also had a tattoo that was a smaller version of Paul's goblin. 'Sid must be from the country as well,' I thought. However it seemed he couldn't hold onto a bull for that long.

"Will you play for money?" Dale asked slowly.

I studied him for a second. Jennifer let out a loud giggle from behind me. "I'll play for money," I said. Paul came back as I put twenty dollars on the pool table.

"Laura, what are you doing?" Paul snatched my money off the table. With his other hand he tried to take the cue off me.

"I'm playing pool," I answered, taking back the cue stick and my money. I threw the money back on the table.

"You're playing for money?" Paul said in surprise.

"Yes." I grinned.

"Are you sure?" Paul asked as though he was trying to get me to back out.

"It's okay, it's only twenty dollars," I said, twisting the cue in my hand and making out that I was worried.

"All right." Paul took some money out of his pocket and put it next to my twenty dollars. He was betting against me. His friends put more money on his pile. They were betting against me as well.

"Okay then. Dale?" I stood there with the stick upside down, trying to look like a fool.

Jennifer and the twins must never have asked the boys to play. Jennifer leaned over to whisper to the twins. She was smiling at me in a very sly way.

"Let Laura play with you; it'll be fun," Jennifer said to Dale.

"I'll play you," Dale piped up, acting a little eager.

Dick handed the stick to Dale. Paul racked the balls, watching me as I kept a straight face.

"Ladies first." Dale waved his hand over the table.

"Thank you," I said, grinning sweetly and tilting my head slightly at him.

On the break, I didn't hit the balls too hard. This was so they would stay on the table. Dale went for the lower-number ball lying near the side pocket.

"You get higher numbers," Dale said after his turn.

"The higher number, okay, I got that." My first ball rolled down to the end of the table and rested on the cushion. Dale's next ball went in. He missed the next. I hit my next ball. It rolled down beside my first ball. Dale stalked around the table to line up his ball, but it didn't go in. I gave it a few moments, pretending to study my next move in a girly way. Then I leaned over to hit my ball, which also went down to the end of the table, resting adjacent to the other balls. Dale gave me a few glances, then looked at Paul. Dale had three shots left.

Paul came up to speak to me. "You sure you know how to play?"

I kissed him on the lips. It was a little more passionate than it should have been. For the first time tonight, I was having fun. I wasn't going to have a chance to do this again.

"Hey you two, I'm winning a game here," Dale sang out.

"Are you sure you know how to play?" Paul asked once more. I didn't reply.

Jennifer and the twins were giggling at me in the background. At my next turn the white ball was at an odd angle to the other balls.

"She doesn't know how to play," Heather said a little louder. Jennifer hit her with her elbow.

My balls lay on the table in a line. Dale had one more to go. On an angle I firmly hit the white one. It rolled to the top of the table away from the others and bounced off the cushion, then raced down to the coloured balls. The white ball hit the coloured balls at just the right speed, splitting them and sending them into the side pockets. Then the white ball rolled back up, hitting the black ball into the other side pocket. The white ball rested alone on the table.

I glanced over to see, Jennifer was sucking lemons again.

"I win. Sorry, Dale," I said as I scooped up the money.

The guys stood with frozen expressions. I hated doing that to Dale; he seemed like a nice guy.

"Thanks for the game, Dale. Double or nothing?" I asked as I counted my money.

Dale let out a belly laugh. "No thanks, Laura. I know when I've been hustled."

"I think she has just taken us for a ride, boys. Where did you learn to play like that?" Paul hugged me.

"We didn't have a TV for six months when I was growing up." I said this to Jennifer, not to Paul. "I would play my dad's pool table. It's amazing what happens when you don't have a lot of TV to distract you." It was cold of me to say this, but it felt good. I saw it as a little payback on Jennifer.

"Well," I said, counting my winnings. "How about we go to a nightclub and I'll buy you hurt men some drinks?"

Paul seized me around the waist and walked me out of the football club. "The girl wants to party. Let's show her a good time, boys."

It was early and the nightclubs weren't open, but a pub close to Paul's home in Dee Why was open. The pub was quiet, with only a few drinkers. It smelled like any pub—stale beer and cigarettes.

There were two large windows in the front, and the back was dark and gloomy. A few men stood playing pool, while a couple of other men sat at the bar, which took up most of the side wall. It contained every spirit you could think of. Dale and Dick went over to the bar. The sound of card machines whizzed in the background. The nightclub was next door, and wouldn't be open until later.

Paul hadn't let go of me since we left the football club, the fact that I had won the game seemed to have turned Paul on. Dick and Heather pushed two tables together. When Dale returned with the drinks Jennifer seemed delighted at what he was carrying on the tray. Her ice-cold eyes gleamed with frozen delight.

"Hey, good idea, Dale. Do you know this game, Laura? If you don't, I'm happy to show you how real people can drink." Jennifer spoke to me as though I were a kid.

"No, Jennifer, I don't need you to show me."

Dale placed a glass in front of me. "Laura, are you going to be okay with this?"

"She'll be fine," Paul said, rubbing my arm.

Jennifer's unsympathetic eyes glared at me, watching and waiting for me to slip up. Paul drew me closer. It seemed to upset Jennifer even more that he was showing me affection.

"You up for this?" Paul asked

"Try and stop me."

"That's my girl."

Dale lined up small glasses in front of us. I reached over and picked up a plate with a lime wedge on it. Jennifer salted her hand, licked it and drank down the tequila. She turned as I did the same, the boys clapping and egging me on.

Later that night the pub was busier. My head was feeling a little light. I wasn't too drunk, it was just the sense that everything was okay with the world. I could smell the alcohol on Paul's breath as his lips moved gently on the skin of my neck. We had done more tequila shots in between beers.

"Do you want to go?" Paul asked against my neck. I nodded.

83

Paul stood and took hold of my hand to help me to my feet. We said our goodbyes and were almost out the door.

"Paul?" Sid hurried after us and said something in Paul's ear. I couldn't hear what he said.

Paul glanced over at the pool tables. He frowned, then turned to me. "Laura, can you meet me outside?" He ran his hand on my neck.

"I have to go to the little girl's room," I replied.

Paul smiled and kissed me. "Okay."

Paul and Sid went over to the pool tables, I waited before going into the ladies. Paul had his back to me, as I watched for a moment. A group of guys in their twenties greeted him, at first I thought it maybe a work thing. Paul nodded at them with crossed arms, listening to what the man had to say. Sid stood just behind Paul. I couldn't see what they were doing. I could only see the men Paul was talking to. One of the men pulled a ten-dollar note out of his pocket and handed it to Paul. *'He must have owed Paul money,'* I thought before I continued into the ladies.

The ladies' toilets stunk of bleach. Three cubicles lined one wall. A tap dripped slowly into one of the three sinks along the other wall. I gave myself a quick glance in the mirror. I ran my fingers through my hair and took a deep breath, trying to clear my head. I had hurt my friends today. I needed to make it up to them. I was too intoxicated for any deep thinking now, but the expressions on their faces had been too much.

I slowly pushed air past my lips, my cheeks were flushed from alcohol and Paul's lips. Paul should be ready by now, I needed to hurry. I quickly splashed a bit of water on my face after I came out of one of the cubicles.

As I was about to leave, someone clutched my shoulders and pulled me backwards.

"If you think you're going to be in my life, I'm going to make

84

your life hell." The hands clutched hard on my skin. I could feel the nails digging in. It was Jennifer.

I reached around and took hold of Jennifer's hands to get them off me. Her fingers dug harder into my shoulders. I spun around in pain. Jennifer's eyes were wild as her hand tried to grasp my neck.

"Get off me, bitch," I snarled at her, trying to grab at her hands.

"Why should I?" she replied, her voice wild.

We struggled in circles, I could hear the scuffle of our feet on the floor. After a few moments somehow I managed to shove Jennifer off me. She stumbled backwards. I tried to leave, but Kimberly was blocking the door. Heather leaned against the other wall with an elated expression on her face. Jennifer and I commenced a bizarre side step; I went one way, she went the other.

"You're going to walk out of here, Laura, and you're not coming back. Get your hands off Paul. He's mine." Jennifer spat out as she grasped my arm. She was about to fling me around.

The door of the ladies opened and Kimberly fell forward. Paul's face appeared in the doorway. His eyes turned to Jennifer. She and the twins backed away without a word.

"Come on Laura, I'm ready to go."

Paul pushed the door open wide and held out his hand. He was still watching Jennifer, and he seemed to know what had happened. Paul didn't say anything as we walked to the main road. I came to a stop and pulled my arm out of Paul's.

"I'm going home." I started storming off to the nearest bus stop.

"Laura, come back." Paul hurried after me. "Jennifer is a little hot headed at times. I'll tell her to leave you alone. Please, Laura, don't go." I stopped. Paul put his arms around me. "I'll look after her. Don't worry."

CHAPTER 6

~

The school bus pulled up in front of the three-storey sandstone museum on College Street in Sydney. I had never been here before. My eyes stared out the window of the bus and ran along the bricks of the building, then up the sandstone stairs, trying to take it all in. I had been waiting for this since my teacher had announced the excursion to my fifth-grade class.

"Come on." Marisa stood in the bus aisle. We were the last ones left. She pushed up her glasses and smiled at me, understanding my excitement.

"Sorry," I told her. She seemed just as eager as I was.

"Come on, Laura, this is going to be great."

Our teacher counted the students as we left the bus. "Could everyone wait at the stairs, please?" She repeated every fourth student. We had to wait for another bus to pull up and unload other students from our school; it was a little late.

Ever since I had found the Egyptian book at the school fete, I had read everything I could about Egypt and cuneiform. My school library and our local library didn't have much. Inside the Museum was all this information rolled into one and more. I had never been to the Museum before and I couldn't wait to find out what was inside. I was in hope to find out more of Egypt and cuneiform, I didn't know why this was so important but it was.

I leaned against the sandstone wall, running my hand over it as we waited. I could hear the air coming out of the vent that recessed into the wall. It seemed as though the museum was breathing. I tilted my head up to see how tall the building was. The sky was blue the clouds seemed to fly off the roof, from where I was standing. The museum felt like an Egyptian temple that I had read about, holding its precious treasures.

Our teacher cleared her throat as she waited for the class to quiet down. I snapped out of my trance, noticing that the other students had joined us. The teacher stood in front of us in her woollen green tartan skirt and poly cotton puff blouse. She tucked her clipboard under one arm, then adjusted her handbag.

She was a good teacher, she seemed to understand me. Mrs. Clanton's hair was blond and thick, the curl of it set in an afro. She enjoyed listening to me talk about Egypt, and she cherished Marisa's love of Roman history. To impress her, Marisa and I would search for old National Geographic magazines, Marisa looking for articles about Rome, and me searching for information on Egypt.

"I can't stand this place. Miss, why can't we go shopping? My mother was happy to take us. We can leave Weirdo and Weirder here. They seem to like it," Jennifer said as she flicked her hair over her shoulder.

"Jennifer Jenkins, would you be quiet, please. If you stop your comments, you just may learn something. As for addressing your classmates in that manner, if I hear it again you'll be walking with me at lunch for a week. Do you understand?" Mrs. Clanton scolded her. "Come on, class, stay together." Once my teacher was happy that Jennifer had settled, she began to move. My class marched up the stairs, the other class following us.

The front part of the museum was bathed in dusty light that entered through large windows running along the front of the building. The dust danced in the light, down to shadows that lay on the wooden floor. To the left of the heavy front doors, wooden display cases divided off an area. I couldn't see what was over there. However, something was pulling me to that space. I wanted to go and explore, but we needed to stay together.

"Good morning, children. My name is Judith. I'll be your guide today. I would like you all to stay together while on the tour of the museum." Judith spoke quickly. She was dressed in a bright red woollen suit, high black boots and a red woollen hat. Her teeth were white; when she smiled all you could see was their brightness. They dazzled my eyes. She had a pointy nose and her mousey hair was rolled into a bun.

"Come this way." Judith waved her hand in the air to show us down to the first room on the right. She walked ahead of us with her hands behind her back.

Tingles covered my skin, I rubbed my arm as we moved into the museum. I felt that I belonged here or needed to be here. Judith's boots made a clinking noise on the old wooden floor as she stepped quickly along the corridor to the first room.

A few glass and wooden cases stood along the wall of the corridor filled with artefacts. Marisa and I slowed our pace at the back of the class so that we could see into the cases. Stone axes of all sizes lay in one of them, while little birds called finches perched in the next.

Judith came to a stop at the doors to the first room. She pushed on them, the large doors opened with a low grown. Back then the room that is now the Australian Room was a long space that ran down the side of the museum. The room was full of freestanding wooden cases in three rows. It was amazing. I turned around, trying to take it all in. The roof was lined with pressed tin and the lights hung on what looked like brown ropes. Dark brown floorboards ran the length of the room. The walls were white and lined with large display cases. The windows were high above the floor and sat in their own cavities. The light in the room was gloomy. An old car sat on one side, while at the far end was an old house.

"Good morning, Dr Colman." Judith smiled at a round man with a bushy black beard. Dr Colman was the only person in the room.

His unlit pipe hung out the side of his mouth. He was about to open a case containing a collection of silver mugs. He stopped and took his pipe out of his mouth. Dr Colman's eyes glided up and down Judith's suit. A smirk came across his face as he tapped his pipe on the only shaved part of his chin.

"Morning, Judith. Nice to see the new uniform fits you just right. Good. Good idea of mine, I think."

Judith wiggled her body a little. "Thank you, Dr Colman."

Mrs Clanton cleared her throat at them, Judith backed away realising what she was doing. Dr Colman took a breath as he glanced around to see thirty children watching them.

"Yes, yes," Dr Colman said, nodding and returning to the wooden case.

Judith brushed down her dress as she giggled. Mrs Clanton stared at her. Judith let out a breath before pointing to one of the long cases. "Now children, this coat belonged to a *convict* who was on the First Fleet. Can anyone tell us what the arrows mean?" She said the word "convict" in a funny way.

In the case hung a red and white high-collared coat, a red cap and pants that came out from the bottom of the coat. The outfit was hung in the same way that Dad hung his suits in the cupboard. The convict suit was dirty and had holes in it. Black arrows were on one of the shoulders. On the other side of the suit were two more arrows. None of my classmates had put their hands up. Marisa and I both knew the answer to the question.

"You say it, Laura." Marisa pushed my arm into the air.

"Yes." Judith pointed at me. Jennifer pulled a face when she saw who Judith had called on. I slowly put my hand down, thinking again about answering. "Go on, young lady."

My face went red. "Um, it means that the coat belonged to the English government. The convict uniform is government issued. Also, the man who owned the uniform was right handed; his right side is all worn."

Jennifer let out a laugh. "She doesn't know."

Dr Colman stopped what he was doing and walked over to the coat. He studied it for a moment and slowly nodded his head. He seemed impressed.

"Young lady, you're right about the arrows, but you can't say if he was right handed," Judith scolded me. Embarrassed, I put my head down and backed away.

Dr Colman put his hand up to Judith and pointed at me. "She's right. I wish I'd seen that. Want a job, kid?"

I grinned. "Yes, please. Can Marisa have one as well?"

Dr Colman let out a belly laugh. "Finish school, go to University and I'll see you then, kid." He left the room, not waiting for my answer.

"Okay now, children, follow me." Judith continued her tour of the room.

After Judith's tour, we were left to explore the museum. Marisa and I didn't stay together. We wanted to see different things across the three floors. Marisa wanted to spend more time with certain artefacts, while I wanted to spend more time with others. Judith had given each of us a paper that asked us to find different artefacts in the museum. Jennifer and the twins bullied another kid to fill them out; first, they had tried to get me to do it. However, our teacher saw what they were doing and stopped them. Jennifer lingered a bit at the gold bar in the Minerals Room, but that was the only interest she showed all day.

Marisa and I met back at the Ancient Room, which was the best room of all. In a large case at the back was a display of Roman artefacts. Marisa's eyes lit up as she made her way to the Roman legionnaire's armour.

In the case on one of the walls were green Shabtis, about ten of them. Next to them was a poem. The description stated that it was a magic spell to awaken Shabtis.

"Oh, these Shabtis, if one counts and one reckons the Osiris to do all the work that are wont to be done there in the God's lands, now indeed obstacles that are implanted therewith, as a man at his duties, 'Here I am' you shall say when you are counted off, at any time to serve thee. To cultivate the field, to irrigate riparian the land, to transport by boat the sand of the east to the west and vice-versa."

The lights in the room had gotten brighter for a moment while I read the incantation aloud, then they dimmed. I thought it was cool, the idea that these little statues would come to life and help a person out.

The scarabs in the next cabinet took my attention away from the Shabties. They were no bigger than my fingernail. Under them, I could see writing in a mirror. I didn't know what it said.

"How did they do that? It's so small." A voice came from behind me.

I jumped a little. An old woman a little shorter than I was moved closer to the case. Her olive skin was wrinkled and her eyes were like dark pools, with a tone of calmness. She was dressed in black, very much like the Italian grandmothers who came to my school. A tuft of black and grey hair peeked out from under the black headscarf wrapped around her head. She smiled kindly at me. Her little finger almost touched the glass as she spoke. She paused to lean back on her walking stick.

"I don't know how they did that," I answered.

There was a warm feeling about her, as though she was a kind soul. "Do you know about these things? What are they for?" she asked, pointing at the case again. Her accent wasn't Australian. I didn't know what it was.

"The scarabs?" I asked.

"Yes."

91

"They're used to protect the heart. They were wrapped in your bandages when you died and placed over your heart."

She smiled. "That's right. The heart, to the ancient Egyptians, was part of your soul and your mind. You feel everything with your heart. Love, anger and hurt," she informed me. I studied the case for a moment, then turned back to ask the old woman a question. She was nowhere to be seen.

Marisa was waiting at the door, I hurried to catch up to her. "Did an old woman come past you?"

"No, there are no old people here. Unless you want to count Jennifer and the twins." Marisa grinned at me.

I stood on my tiptoes to scan the room. I couldn't see the old woman.

"Come on, I want to see *The Riding Man* in the Bone Room. Aunt May told me that I needed to see it. I don't know why." Marisa let out a long breath.

The Bone Room was a little unsettling, with all the death it contained. It held the largest collection of bones in the Southern Hemisphere. As we wandered around the room, I kept a watchful eye for the old woman, but she had vanished. I felt sorry for the skeleton of the horse; it was up on its hind legs and had been there for a long time. *The Rocking Man* sat in his rocker, keeping *The Riding Man* company as he always had. I wondered to myself, 'If they could talk, what would they say after we all left?'

"Are you alright?" Marisa asked as we entered the Main Room, once we had finished the Bone Room.

"Yeah, I'm fine." Marisa had said a few things to me and I hadn't heard her.

Judith stood waiting for our papers as we entered the Main Room, which was on the left side of the museum. It was the same as all the other rooms, with large glass wooden cases lining it. In the middle of the room was the only flat case. Sunlight from the windows high up on the wall shone down on it, dust drifted down in the sunlight. I approached the case. For a moment I didn't realise what I was seeing. In front of me was a white wooden coffin. It sat low on the ground, its broken lid hovering above it and revealing a mummy inside. The paint had faded over time to show some of the grey wood underneath. My heart pounded and my mind began to race. I wished I had a camera. I felt like Howard Carter peering into that little hole in Tutankhamen's tomb, when he relayed to Lord Carnarvon, *"I see wounderest things."*

My hand went over my mouth and I knelt to see the face under the lid. The ancient mummy's hair was a mess around its head. It was the blackest hair I had ever seen. The mummy's face seemed at peace under that madness of hair. Still, I was sad to see the mummy in such a condition. Its small hands had been placed together and its protective magical amulets had been taken away. My eyes danced along the side of the coffin to see whether I could read any of the hieroglyphs.

I knew some of the symbols. A zig-zag line meant "water." A sharp oval meant "mouth." An arm meant "give," and a circle meant "Ra" or "the Aton." I couldn't find the mummy's name on the information plate. I knew that she was the Priestess of Horus. Horus was the son of Ra, and Ra saw through Horus's eyes. This was so Ra could watch his people.

"Weirdo is doing it again. Look at her. She's so weird."

I snapped out of my reverie. I had been feeling calm, like I was meditating. Jennifer stood on the other side of the case, laughing at me. I no longer felt at peace with the world. In fact, I could have slapped her. I had been so caught up in my moment, I hadn't realised that my classmates were watching. Red-faced, I pushed myself off the floor. Marisa had come to stand beside me.

"You know, Jennifer, if you found your inner peace, then maybe you'd be a nicer person." Marisa pushed her big round glasses up her nose. It was the first time I had heard her speak like that to anyone.

Jennifer had managed to rope in our classmates. They were laughing and making jokes about how I had been acting.

"What's going on?" Mrs Clanton pushed her way through the class. "We have a few minutes until we go back on the bus. If you're going to buy anything from the gift shop, you need to hurry. If not, I want you to stand near the exit door. Jennifer Jenkins, it seems you can't control yourself. You'll need to walk with me at lunch for the rest of the week. Or maybe a caning will improve your manners." Being the seventies, it was okay to hit children.

Jennifer stood up to Mrs Clanton, her soulless eyes fixed on the teacher. "The headmaster won't like you talking to me like that," she announced coldly.

Mrs Clanton let out a throaty laugh and crossed her arms. "Unlike the headmaster, my husband has our home loan with another bank. Also, Jennifer Jenkins, I have quite a few good friends on the school board. You can't intimidate me, Missy, like you think you can with the rest of the school. This week you can walk with me at lunch. Now go and stand at the exit door and wait for me."

Jennifer backed down, Marisa and I giggled quietly to each other. Jennifer tried to wait for the twins, but Mrs Clanton pointed to the exit door and made Jennifer move. The twins hurried off to the gift shop, not caring that their leader wasn't there.

"Did your mum give you money for the gift shop?" Marisa asked.

"No, but Dad did. I asked him. Did your aunt give you money?" Marisa was the only one who knew about Mum and the shops.

Marisa nodded. "Cool. Yes she did." Marisa's mother and father travelled a lot and Marisa often stayed with her Aunt May.

I paused before we hurried to the gift shop. "Thank you, Mrs Clanton."

"You're welcome, Laura, Marisa. Off you go, you two." Mrs

94

Clanton seemed pleased that she had scolded Jennifer.

The gift shop had the usual gift shop things—plastic toys, fridge magnets, lunch boxes and the like. I wanted a book that could help me with cuneiform. We didn't have much time, and Dad had given me only two dollars. After a few minutes of searching, I hadn't found what I was looking for. Marisa had found a book about Roman history that she seemed contented with. In the clearance bin, I found a book on Amarna, which had been Tutankhamen's father's kingdom. The book was only a dollar. Downhearted, I went to pay for my purchase, standing behind Marisa.

"It's time to go, children, please pay for your things." Mrs Clanton announced.."

Once finished my class hurried out of the museum, I slowly ran my hand over the sandstone bricks outside. I tapped my finger on them a couple of times. The gesture wasn't meant as a goodbye, but as "I'll see you soon." The bus was waiting for us out front, we lined up before boarding it.

"Did you find what you were looking for?" The old woman was standing at the bottom of the stairs. Marisa seemed not to notice her, she was ahead of me about to get on the bus. I stopped quickly and turned around to see if I would get in trouble for stopping.

"Where did you go before?" I asked.

"I had to go. Here I am, now," she said softly.

"Oh, okay."

The woman opened her handbag. It was made from a red Persian carpet and had a carved silver handle. The woman's hand moved inside her bag and pulled out a brown-batted book.

"I think this is what you are looking for." She handed the book to me. I opened it and saw that it contained information about reading cuneiform. "This will get you started."

I looked down in surprise at what was in my hands. "How did

95

you know that's what I was searching for?"

"Laura, could you please hurry? We're waiting for you," my teacher called out.

Everyone was on the bus. "You need to go, I'm happy to be of service, Laura." the old lady said kindly. "Goodbye for now. We will meet again."

"What's your name?" I asked.

"I'm Cleo."

"I'm Laura. Thank you."

"You're welcome, Laura. Happy to serve." She bowed at me.

I waved goodbye to Cleo and hurried to the bus. As I sat down next to Marisa, the old woman waved at me. "Do you see that lady?" I asked, pointing at Cleo.

"Yes."

"She just gave me this book." I opened it. It contained images of Amarna letters. The book had translations about how to read cuneiform—just what I needed.

CHAPTER 7

High school came and went. Marisa and I wanted to study archaeology at University. Nothing changed with Mum, she would go to the shops as she always did. Each time, she arrived home just before Dad did. Dad seemed not to notice what she was doing.

I was eighteen when the mail carrier delivered my final results. I ran all the way to Marisa's house a few streets away so that we could open them together.

"Hi, Mr Cress," I said, out of breath. He was working in the garden with his wife. I clutched the fence post as I spoke, trying to get my breath back.

"Hey, Laura. She's waiting in the kitchen for you."

"Thanks, Mr Cress. Nice to see you back, Mrs Cress."

Mrs Cress smiled sweetly at me. "Good to see you too, Laura," she called.

I hurried toward the house, Marisa's mother always had the latest of everything. They were nice people and made me feel at home. However, when Marisa and I were at Aunt May's house, we could flop on the couch and she wouldn't mind. Here, behaviour like that wasn't allowed.

I stopped at the front door, took off my shoes, placed them on the rack and wiped my feet on the doormat before hurrying inside. The house had highly polished floorboards, and to keep them in good shape, Mrs Cress insisted on no shoes in the house.

Marisa had grown into herself. She no longer wore glasses. She had high cheekbones and her eyes radiated a pretty hazel colour in the right light. Marisa sat at the kitchen table with her hands on a large white envelope. She had no expression on her face; it was white from her dread of what lay inside.

"You okay? Did you look? Didn't you get the marks?" I asked, seeing how pale she was.

"I haven't...oh, Laura, what if I didn't get the marks? I'm sure I got trig wrong." She held the envelope tighter.

"Marisa Cress." I sat down in front of her and took hold of her hands. "We both study together. It's all right. We're going to University next year and it's going to be great." I let go of her hands and took hold of my envelope. Marisa slowly took hold of hers. "On the count of three," I said. "One, two, three. Go."

We put out thumbs under the flaps to open our envelopes. I held my breath, my heart was beating hard. I closed my eyes as I quickly pulled out the piece of thick paper. Marisa did the same. I let out a breath slowly as I processed my marks. After a moment, we both looked at each other and smiled.

I loved University. It was different from high school, as everyone wanted to be there. I had a part-time job to help cover my fees. I was still living at home. It was just as cheap, and I didn't have far to travel to the University of Sydney every day. It was only an hour trip by train. The University was on the other side of the city. The campus had its own museum, and the library was to die for. I spent hours poring over old books.

By our second year Marisa and I were doing well at our studies. We found that hustling pool was a good way to make extra money. We were due to go to Egypt that year, any extra money was good. It was part of our end-of-year marks, and Dr John Dean was heading the trip. I was excited and couldn't wait, it would be my first time going overseas. I felt as though my life couldn't get better.

One afternoon, Marisa, Chester and I were hanging out in the student recreation room. Dylan's band was playing onstage. The room had pool tables, vending machines, a coffee bar, tables and chairs. A large notice board spread across the back wall. Dark blue carpet covered the floor. The room was always dark, with thick

98

blue curtains covering the windows. The large room opened to a canteen and one of the many passageways to the lecture rooms.

Marisa had just won three games of pool in a row and was taking a break. It was always fun watching young male egos. The first-year guys were the easiest to hustle. It never went over well that a girl could win. On this day, both Marisa and I had played a guy who eventually was ready to bet his father's car. At that point we stopped, as we had a limit on the amount of money we took students for. Chester was flipping through a fashion magazine and sitting on a table next to me.

"I'll play you again, Laura. You can't win. I'm ready for you." The first-year student danced a little in front of me, trying to get me to play.

"Come on, man, give it up. They've already won a hundred dollars off you." The guy's friend took hold of his shoulders to pull him away.

"A fool and his money," Chester mumbled as his face lit up. Whether the gesture was over a jacket or the guy who was wearing it in the magazine, I wasn't sure.

"No, I don't like losing to girls." The first-year student yanked away from his friend.

"Don't play them, then," I said.

The guy was about to get in my face, but his friend took hold of him and dragged him out.

"This isn't over. I want another game to get my money back."

"Not happening," Marisa said. She began reading Chester's magazine over his shoulder. "I'm done. You keep losing and you're no fun. I have a date tonight and now I can buy that dress."

Chester slammed his magazine on the table. "Have you got a date with Dr Dean again?"

"Yes." Marisa grinned. She had been dating John on and off

that year. I had been sworn to secrecy.

Suddenly I noticed that the music had stopped. Dylan had been playing a few bars of a song, but his lead singer stood with his arms crossed, refusing to sing. Connor was sitting behind the drums, swinging his drumsticks in the air as Dylan and the lead singer began arguing. Sean sat on a speaker, looked over to Connor and rolled his eyes.

"I'm not singing that hippy shit," the lead singer said, standing his ground.

Dylan threw his hands up. The lead singer jumped off the stage and stormed away. "Hey! We have a concert tonight," Dylan called after him.

The lead singer flipped the finger at Dylan as he left the room. Marisa and Chester were slapping at each other over her date with John.

I knew the song they had been trying to play. Dylan had his back to me. We had dated in the first year but had parted as friends. We wanted different things; he wanted every girl he could get his hands on, and I didn't.

I picked up the microphone and climbed onstage. "I'll sing the hippy shit."

Dylan looked at me and put his hands on his hips. "Yeah?"

"Yeah, come on."

"Okay." Dylan began to play. The others quickly caught up with him. I knew the song; it was "Summertime."

"Summertime and living is so easy fish are jumping and the cotton is high.

Oh your daddy is rich and you mama is good looking.

So hush little baby don't you cry.

One of these mornings, you're going to rise up singing then you

100

will spread your wings and you'll take to the sky

Oh until that morning nothing will harm you with dad and mama standing by

Oh, one of these mornings, you're going to rise up sing then you'll spread your wings and you'll take to the sky

But till that morning nothing going to harm you with daddy and your mama standing by"

It was a song that had, at one time, been sung by both Billie Holiday and Janis Joplin. Dylan and the band played it the way Janis had, with heavy guitar licks and droning sounds. I knew the song well, as it was in my dreams. It was the song I hummed when my mind was elsewhere. By the time I finished singing, a small crowd was standing and clapping. It felt good.

Chester ran over to me, pushing his way through the crowd.

"Out of my way, the star needs protecting. My baby, you did good!" Chester pulled me off the stage and helped me out of the room.

"Laura, meet us at The Blue Raven at The Rocks tonight! Nine thirty," Dylan yelled. I nodded as Chester pulled me out of the room.

"Told you," Marisa said to me. Over the years, she had told me that I should sing more.

"Laura?" Out of the blue, a student handed me a note. We were on our way to the next class. Chester let me go so I could open the note to read it.

"Who's that from?" Marisa asked.

"I have to go to admin."

"Do you want us to go with you?" Chester asked. He was still protecting me as though I were a real pop star.

"No, it's okay."

101

"That's good. I have to get Marisa ready for her date."

"No you don't, Chester." Once again, Marisa slapped at Chester.

"I'll see you later." I didn't understand why I had to go to admin, but thought it must have been some sort of paperwork issue. I was still on a high from singing and felt good about myself.

It was hot outside and students were enjoying the sun. It had been a cold winter. This was one of the nicest days we'd had since last summer.

I pushed open the big glass doors to the administration building. The room was warm and uncomfortable, as though the heater had been left on. The office was busy, I looked down at the paper again. *Laura Sinclair, please report to admin.*

One of the ladies looked up from her desk on the other side of the room. "Can I help you?"

"I'm Laura Sinclair. Someone in admin wanted to see me."

"Oh, yes." She began moving papers around her desk. Once she had found a computer printout, she came over to me at the large counter.

"Now, last year, when you started payments for your course and your trip to Egypt, you and your father signed a contract for payment. This contract states that you need to keep up the payments. According to our statements, you have only paid the deposit for last year."

She showed me the paper in her hands. It stated that no monthly payments had been received, either for this year or last year.

"I had been ensuring that I put money into the account every month," I said. "It should have been paid." I didn't understand. The woman showed me another computer printout to back up her claims. The information wasn't sinking in.

"What does this mean?" I asked in shock, I could feel my throat closing.

"Well, you can't go to Egypt, and because the trip is part of your grade, you can't finish this course. You owe the University money for the bounced payments. That's extra on top of your last year's and this year's payments. You need to pay the University back before you can carry on your studies. We have to crack down on this. People are not paying the University back. I'm sorry."

I stood there, feeling as though I had just fallen through the floor. My stomach turned. I felt sick. "I can't finish my studies?"

"Not while you're this far behind in your payments." She said it softly, trying to be nice.

"Can't I catch up?" I asked hopelessly.

She sighed. "Laura, you haven't paid since last year. There is also a late fee on these payments as well. The University will not let you carry on without a full payment. For last year and this year."

"Crap." The word slipped out of my mouth. "How much?" I asked in a hush.

"Ten thousand dollars. I would advise that you not go to any more of your classes. You may want to pick up your studies another time, once you've paid us back. I'm sorry, Laura. You need to pay this back soon."

I stood outside the office and watched everyone pass, but I wasn't taking in what they were doing. My mind moved slowly. With the papers in my hands, the numbers stood out. I owed ten thousand dollars, I needed to process what had happened. My feet began to move, I felt like I was in a tunnel. My dreams had been taken from me. What I had worked for was no longer in my grasp.

When I finally realised where I was, I was sitting in the back of Dr Dean's class. It had taken me a while to come around to where I was and listen what he was telling his class.

"The modern thinking about the soul is that, before you are born, your reason for being here—being a doctor or even a homeless man—has already been mapped out for you. It's classified as a *soul contract*. You have one main contract, but the people who come into your life may have a contract with you, or you may have one with them. This could be to help you or them on your life paths. Objects can also help you along your path—a coin found on the ground that pays for a paper that gets you a dream job. We see that our eyes are the windows to our souls..."

A girl raised her hand. "Dr Dean, what about soul mates?"

Dr Dean rolled his eyes and smiled. "Soul mates. There could be more than one in your lifetime. However, a *true soul mate,* they are very rare. How do you know you have met one? They say you have a feeling that you have met the person before—like a person you knew in your past life or a kindred spirit."

Dr Dean glanced at the clock, then at his watch. "Okay, I want to know about *rw nw prt m hrw*. Also, Ba, Ka, Ren, Sheut and Ib." Dr Dean wrote the words on the blackboard. "I want to know what they are and what their relationship is. I'll see you next time with your answers."

The class hurried out of the room. Once it was empty, Dr Dean approached me and sat on the table in front of me.

"Book of Coming Forth by Day, or the Book of the Dead," I said. "The book was first used in Egypt in 1700 BC. It was found on the coffin of Queen Mentuhotep of the 13th dynasty. Ka is the spirit. When you died, your Ka left your body. Ba is what we think of as the soul. Ren is the name; you could remain living so long as people spoke your name. Sheut is the shadow. You can't exist unless you have your shadow in life or the afterlife. Ib is your heart. Your heart is made by one drop of blood from your mother. Your heart is the brain you feel from your heart with every deed. Everything needs to be intact. You need the Book of the Dead to get through the twelve hours of night, or the twelve trials. Then you need to have your heart weighed to see how light it is. Then

104

you need to speak your name to Osiris so that you can pass into the afterlife."

Dr Dean smiled, the corners of his eyes wrinkling. "A+. You're always one of my number-one students."

"I hear you have a date with your soul mate tonight."

He blushed a little. "You don't mind?"

"I'm not Marisa's keeper, but I think Chester is trying to help her out."

Dr Dean rolled his eyes and sighed, shaking his head. "They broke the mould when they made him."

"Do you know?" I asked.

"About your debt?" I nodded, answering him. "Yes, I know. Do you mind me asking what happened?"

I sighed. "I have a good idea what happened, but it's better that I don't say anything. I have to pay it back, that's the main thing."

Dr Dean looked at the floor, his eyes began to move back and forth as he processed his thoughts. "I can get you a job at the Sydney Museum. Your translation skills are valuable and I'm not going to let them waste away."

Before I could say anything, students began streaming into the classroom. I hugged him and gave him a kiss on the cheek. "Thank you."

"No worries." He touched his cheek. "Marisa might get jealous."

"Could you not tell Marisa or Chester? I want to say it in my own time."

"Sure. But it was just a kiss on the cheek." I slapped a playful slap on his shoulder. "I won't." he added.

The ride home was tough my dreams had been whipped away from me. I watched out the train window. I needed time to calm down before walking through the front door of Mum and Dad's house.

At first I thought no one was home. It was mid-afternoon. I stood quietly in the front hall for a moment. The sound of dishes clinking in the kitchen confirmed that someone was there. I took a deep breath and let it out slowly. My heart was beating a funny rhythm and my stomach was turning over. I felt like I was in trouble. I had been trying not to cry all the way home but now it was hard to hold the feeling.

Mum was washing up in the kitchen. She turned around when I let out a breath behind her.

"You're home early. You feeling okay? You look sick," she said as she took off her gloves and put her hand to my forehead.

I pulled away from her and went to the table, setting down my book bag.

"Laura, don't put your bag on the table."

"Mum, do you know what this is?" I pulled out the paperwork.

She studied the papers for a moment. Her hand flew up and smoothed stray hairs into her bun. "No," she answered slowly.

"This is how much debt I'm in."

"Laura, what have you done?"

"Mum, I can't go to University anymore because I owe them ten thousand dollars. All the cheques that were posted to pay for University have bounced. I owe for *all* of last year and the rest of the half of this year. I can't finish my course until this is paid off."

"Oh. We can work this out don't tell your father. Everything is fine. I'll talk to the bank; there must be a mistake. Don't worry, it's nothing." Her expression hadn't changed. I couldn't read her.

"Mum, not 'we.' I'm paying this off with my own money. Next time I *will* tell Dad. And it's not *nothing*, this is my life." I was so angry she had taken that money. I wanted to shake her and make

106

her react in some way. However, I just stood there.

"Oh well, I've got to go down to the shops. I'll see you tonight. Bye."

Mum hurried out the door I didn't want to yell after her. I just watched her through the window. Mum had been doing this for years and covering it up. The words, "don't tell Dad" had been leaving her mouth for as long as I could remember. It was a pitiful way to live. Her mind must have been a mess. Mum had almost made it to the garage when she reached one hand to the wall, steadying herself. Her other hand went to her face. I think she was crying. The child in me wanted to run to her, hug her and tell her that everything would be okay. However, I didn't do this. I was pleased to finally see some emotion in her.

That night I sang my heart out. By the end of the evening, I was drunk. I could hardly see when I went home with Dylan. That Sunday I met Marisa and Chester in the city for coffee and told them about my situation. It was harder telling Marisa than Chester, as we had the same dream. The expression on her face said it all.

Three weeks later I started working in research at the museum. Because I had finished my first year, I was qualified to do this job.

CHAPTER 8

~

The night I stood in the street ready to go home, Paul pleaded with me not to leave. He wanted me to stay.

"Laura, it's been a long week." He took my face into his hands, kissed me once, and gazed into my eyes. "Come home with me, Laura. I'll deal with Jennifer, don't worry."

The next morning, Paul's arm lay under my neck. His goblin tattoo stared back at me. Most of the night I lay listening to the ocean. We were only a few streets away. In the quiet of the night, I could hear it. Quietly, without Paul knowing, I slipped out of his bed. His snoring reassured me that he was still asleep. I needed to get to work. It was still dark as I left Paul's home on the Northern Beaches. The salt air filled my lungs it felt invigorating as I stepped out in the morning air.

The bus stop was a good 20-minute walk from Paul's place. The trip gave me time to think. Last night had been pleasant. It was our first time together, and it seemed he was trying to make up for Jennifer's actions. Nothing could make up for Jennifer or the twins. If they ever said they were sorry, it would be a soulless act.

I quietly let myself into my apartment, then smiled. Marisa's jeans and male clothing lay on the floor. The statue of Tut faced the wall. Marisa must have done well with her footballer. It seemed as though she wouldn't be going into work. Chester was working at Sydney University for the day, while Paul had finished his work at the museum. After I finished creeping around the apartment, I left for work alone.

In my office I found a pile of old papers in the middle of my desk. I flicked through them. A note was attached.

Laura, could you please go over these papers and write a report on them? Thanks. Dr Colman.

Dr Colman wanted me to write a paper about his latest find for some magazine.

"Great." I grumbled a few other things to myself as I stormed out of my office.

Judith glanced at me when I reached the last step behind the museum's main desk. She was a lot rounder and greyer these days and would no longer fit into the woollen dress she had worn the first day I met her. She was the eyes and ears of the museum. Somehow, Judith knew everyone's business.

"Good morning, Laura. How was your date on Sunday? Did you make the game on time?"

"It was good and, yes, thank you. Have you seen Dr Colman?" I hadn't told her who I was dating or that I was going to a football match, but somehow she knew. I didn't act surprised; I just smiled, not wanting to be on the tail end of her gossip.

Judith looked down at her monitors, which showed images from the cameras that covered the museum as well as the offices and hallways. She could see everything.

"He's in with the dinosaurs," she replied, waving her hand grandly over the monitors.

"Thanks."

He was on the upper floor at the back of the museum. I didn't take the elevator, and I could feel Judith's eyes on my back as I hurried up the stairs.

I found Dr Colman on scaffolding. He was holding the thighbone of a giant wombat. This long-dead creature was the size of a small ton truck. It came from an era when Australia was home to many large animals. The wombat was called a Diprotodon, which means "two front teeth." It carried its babies in a pouch, just

109

as its small cousins did today. The Diprotodon died out about 46,000 years ago. The creature's bones had just arrived; Dr Colman had been talking about them for months. He had found the remains during his last trip to the middle of Australia. This was what he wanted me to research and write about for the magazine. I wanted to keep researching the Shabti. Dr Colman had an assistant to help him with the Diprotodon; he didn't need me.

He looked down. "Good morning, Laura."

I leant against the rail and crossed my arms. "Good morning, Dr Colman."

Dr Colman handed the thighbone to his assistant before climbing down. "Laura, I'm glad you came to see me."

"I haven't finished my report on the Shabti. I need some more information from other museums. I was thinking on phoning John at The Met in New York."

"Who?" He frowned.

"Dr John Dean."

"Oh yeah." Dr Colman's eyes moved up and down my body. He did this to most women, and it was creepy. He nodded and lifted his hand in the air to stop me from talking. "Laura, I'm taking over the rest of this research on the Shabti. It's something I would like to take on myself."

"Dr Colman, I'm to pick up my studies next year and this Shabti will be good for extra points on my finals."

Dr Colman's eyes drifted down to my chest before he answered. I wanted to slap him. "I'm sorry, Laura. I need you to start on my papers."

I didn't want to leave the museum and putting Dr Colman off side was a bad idea. I had almost paid off what I owed to the University, and the institute was happy for me to study part time in pursuit of my doctorate. I needed to pay for it. If I upset Dr

Colman now I would be out on the street. I had to back down. He liked to run the museum as though it were his own kingdom. An argument wasn't worth it. There was something special about the Shabti. Dr Colman's eyes had said it all when they fell on the Shabti for the first time; they had lit up like Christmas lights. His mouth had dried, just like it did when he watched the high-school girls in their short skirts from his office window.

After returning to my office, I turned on Janis and raised the volume. Dr Colman's papers lay on my desk like a slap in the face. I flipped through his incomplete paperwork, grumbling to myself as I did.

Twelve months later, Paul and I were still together, but now I was living in his house. His house was cold with not a thing out of place. It had once maintained the same red brick exterior that Mum and Dad's house did, but was highly renovated. The exterior was white, while the interior floorboards were highly polished. Paul didn't allow shoes in the house. I could see my face in the floorboards that covered almost every room. When I was alone in the house, I would breathe on the floor and run my finger on it to make a mark. Then I would repolish the board with my sleeve. Paul never knew I did this. It was childish, I know.

The kitchen's bench tops were black marble with white cupboards. The bathroom had the same colour palate. All the furniture was black and had hard lines. The house was not one in which you could just flop around. Paul was also anal about mess; he would carry on until it was cleaned up.

"You know, Chester has moved in with Marisa," I said while Paul and I watched TV one night not long after he had returned from another out-of-town job. Throughout the past year, I had tried to get Paul to accept Chester and Ricky. It wasn't working. This was my next attempt.

"Oh." Paul kept his eyes on the TV. His lips didn't even move.

111

"Yeah, Ricky and he thought it would be a better way to save money." I tried to sound upbeat.

"Ricky is there as well?" Paul sounded surprised and a little angry.

"Yes," I said softly.

"That's nice for Marisa," Paul said, a little miffed as he drank from his beer. He let out a loud burp after it went down.

"I know Marisa has been lonely since I moved out, but she won't say it." I was rambling, trying to sound positive.

"Poor Marisa."

Now was the time to let out the last blow. "I haven't had my friends here since they helped me move in. I thought I could have them over tomorrow night for dinner. I've already told them," I said quickly.

Paul's body stiffened. He shut off the TV and walked out of the room. I sat on his hard black leather lounge and watched the glowing screen as the picture faded. Tilting my head toward the ceiling, I let out a breath. The bedroom door opened, then slammed shut.

Marisa, Chester, and Ricky arrived at Paul's house on time the next night, at 7:30. It was good to see them outside of work, like old times. Paul was nowhere to be seen. Chester walked around the house. Every now and then he picked up something, pulled a face, and set it down.

"The kitchen is this way," I said to the others as Chester scurried off to the main bedroom. I needed a drink and when Chester had finished going through the bedroom drawers, I knew he would want one as well. I poured five glasses, one for everyone. I had been nervous all day; this wouldn't be my first glass.

Chester came screaming into the kitchen and made a beeline to his wine glass. He drank the liquid in one gulp, then wiggled the glass at me, indicating that he wanted it filled again.

"You shouldn't look in straight peoples' drawers, Chester, you know it gets you drunk," Ricky said, smirking at Marisa.

Throughout the next two hours, we consumed two more bottles as we waited for Paul to come home. I spun my fork on the table, fuming as we waited.

"You know, we could eat. Every time you do, people show up," Marisa said. She seemed more sober then I was.

I took another sip of wine. Ricky was trying to throw bread into Chester's mouth; a few bits had fallen to the floor. I had uncaringly spilled wine on Paul's glass-top table, knowing this would drive him crazy.

"You're right, Marisa, let's eat," Chester said, missing the next bit of bread.

"Yes, this is my dinner party. Let's eat," I agreed.

I stabbed at the chicken that now lay cold and dry on my plate. Marisa leant over and filled my glass, once more.

"Marisa, you shouldn't get her too drunk." Chester wiggled his finger at her.

"If I want to drink, Chester, then I'm having a goddamn drink." I took a big mouthful of the red liquid and sucked it through my teeth.

"I was about to say, 'If you get too drunk, then you can't yell too loudly at Pauly.'" Chester blew me a kiss. I grinned a drunken smile at him. In my stupor, I could see my friends rushing through their dinners.

Once everyone had finished, I scraped the leftovers onto the black marble benches, then left the unwashed plates in the sink. Happy with my disorder, I escorted my friends to the front door.

113

Chester turned and put his arms around me. "See you at work, Laura. Thanks for dinner."

Marisa pushed Chester out of the way; he slapped at her as she pushed back. "See you tomorrow, Marisa," I said. "Thanks for coming." I hugged and kissed her goodbye.

Chester returned, pulled Marisa out of the way, he put his arms around me tightly. He let me go and kissed me on the forehead then he pulled me back to look at me. "They don't all love us," Chester said. "We upset their manhood, Laura. Don't worry, we still love you. He mustn't be good in bed." Chester grinned at me.

"I'm sorry, I'm not in the mood. Thanks for coming. I'm sorry." I gave Chester another kiss on the lips.

"Good, you're just the right amount of drunk. So, he isn't that good in bed?" Chester asked, grinning at me again.

"Chester." I took hold of his cheeks, trying not to be mad at him.

Ricky pushed between Chester and me. Chester wiggled his fingers as Ricky hugged me, trying to make me smile.

"I'm sorry he's not that good in bed, Laura, but he must have something that keeps you going," Ricky said. "Do you need more batteries?" He patted his pockets as though he were searching for something, then threw his hands in the air and shrugged his shoulders. "I'm all out, I can't help you." Ricky smiled, enjoying his joke. Chester seemed proud of his boyfriend's teasing.

I frowned; nothing could change the way I was feeling. "Not in the mood, Ricky, but thanks for coming."

"Okay, sweetie. See you soon." He gave me a big bear hug. Chester hugged Ricky and me. Almost in tears, I watched my friends walk down the cement path and onto the street.

Once they were gone, I went back into the kitchen and began flicking the light on and off. I wanted so badly for Paul and my friends to get along. He didn't want it; I'm not sure if he wanted me. I was angry. He had no right to do this, to act this way towards my friends. If he really cared about me, he would have shown up. Throughout the months I had put up with endless hateful glares from Jennifer. I didn't belong, I didn't know what I was doing anymore. When Paul was around he threw endless parties over the weekends. Most of the time I sat alone and watched as he drank himself legless with his mates. Paul went on his trips every two months and would be gone for three or four days at a time. He never called while he was gone and I never knew where he was going. It seemed that I didn't matter.

A little later, the sound of Paul's truck hit my ears as I sat in the dark of the dining room. A light flicked on in the kitchen. It shone out from under the dining room door.

"What the?" Paul said. He had found my mess.

I heard plates being moved around on the marble bench top. I waited, my heart pounded. The door opened, I crossed my arms as Paul flicked on the light.

"You shouldn't sit in the dark, it's not good for your eyes. How was your night?" Paul asked in an off-handed manner. His eyes flew to the mess on the table before they narrowed.

"I had fun with my friends, but dinner was a bit dry." I was just the right amount of drunk to do this.

"Why?" he asked absently.

"Because we were waiting for *you*!" I snapped.

Without a word, he just stood there with an unconcerned look in his eyes.

"You know, I have to put up with all your friends," I said. "I sit there watching you run around kicking a ball. I don't like football. The endless parties, you're always going away, you don't phone me or tell me where you're going." I paused, as my voice broke.

"I'm sorry," he said, coming over to me.

"Don't!" I shouted. "If you cared about me you would have been here. You're not sorry."

Paul stopped and crossed his arms, then let out a little laugh. "You're right, I'm not sorry! Laura, you're friends with two fags!"

"So it's okay to have Marisa as a friend, is it?" I snapped back. I jumped to my feet, threw my hands in the air, and stormed off into the bedroom, locking the door behind me. With tears running down my face, I paused to slump against the door as I wiped them away.

Paul tried to open the door. When he couldn't, he pounded on it. "Open the door, Laura. Stop this!" he roared.

"Piss off!"

Paul crashed on the door. The noise was deafening, as though the door would break. I could feel the force on my back as I slid to the floor.

"Open the door you bitch, you're not locking me out of my bedroom!"

I ran to the bed and put my hands over my ears Paul kept pounding heavily on the door. He had never been this mad, my heart was now beating out of my chest. He finally went quiet after a few moments. I hadn't stopped shaking, uneasily I slipped off the bed and crossed the cold floor. I peered underneath the door in an effort to determine where he was, but I couldn't see him.

All of a sudden, he began pounding on the door again. I hurried back to the bed and curled into a ball, willing his anger to be over.

The next morning when I silently exited the bedroom, everything was clean. To my relief, Paul had left for the day. I had convinced myself that we were both drunk the night before, a fact that explained the way we had acted. I had University in the morning and the museum in the afternoon, I needed to focus on that.

Dr Colman had come up with a bright idea; he wanted the minerals in the Chapman collection to be updated. It was the biggest collection in the museum and had its own room. He wanted information about the minerals' condition, and also wanted new photographs taken and written information placed in our computer database. Dr Colman's nose was put out, because I was at University for three half-days per week, I had less time to do his lackey work.

After lunch, Chester found me on the second floor of the museum, where we held the Chapman display. Albert Chapman had been a well-known Sydney mineral collector who, in the 1960s, sold his collection to the New South Wales government. The museum had displayed the minerals—one of the largest collections in Australia—ever since. When Chapman died, he had only one mineral left—a large gold nugget. He had sold everything else.

I was trying to take crystal quartz out of a display cabinet and place it onto a tray without dropping it. Every time I opened a cabinet, a visitor stuck his or her head in the display. I had to wait until the visitor had finished before I could remove the rock.

"Did you get home okay?" I asked Chester.

Chester smiled, but his look quickly turned to a frown as he watched me set the tray on a finds trolley. "What happened?" he asked with concern in his voice.

"Nothing." I frowned, giving Chester a quick glance as I pulled off my cotton gloves. I bent over and pulled a file from under the trolley.

Where I was working, rows of white wooden cabinets lined the walls. They ran around the square room, while three large floor cabinets filled with gemstones sat in the middle. I worked near the large stairs that led down to the Bones room. I kept my eyes down as Chester tried to make eye contact while I filled out the condition

117

form. Chester took a deep breath and loudly let it out through his nose.

"Don't lie to me, missy. Something happened last night, I can tell. You look like you haven't slept and you've been crying." He took hold of my face and stared deep into my eyes.

A woman walked past us, listening. Without a word, I pulled my face out of his hands. I set down the file, picked up the camera, and took a photo of the gemstone. The woman stood just behind Chester, looking into one of the cabinets and eavesdropping.

"I'm fine, Chester. We had a few harsh words, that's all." I stared over at the woman to let her know that I realized she was listening. Chester glanced over his shoulder. She gave up and left.

Chester took hold of my hand and kissed it. "Sweetie? Tell me. He didn't hurt you, did he?" I didn't want to answer him, but Chester was waiting. I began sucking my bottom lip. "Tell me, Laura," Chester continued. "What did he do to you?"

"Nothing. He doesn't like, *who I'm friends with*," I said. I breathed out the last part.

Chester let go of my hand. I placed it on Chester's cheek. "You're my friends and he has to live with it. I love you and Ricky. You are like my family and no one can tell me I can't be friends with you."

"Is that all that happened?"

"Yes." I lied too quickly.

Chester studied me for a moment. To his credit, he left things alone, I hated hurting Chester. He was crazy sometimes, but that's what we all loved about him. His family wanted nothing to do with him. He had to work his way through University to pay for it. The day after we had met in class I found him asleep on a park bench with a bag of his clothes. My heart sank when I saw him there. I never understood why he became homeless. For a few months, he stayed at my place. Mum and Bess loved him, and while Dad never

118

understood him, he enjoyed having Chester around. By the end of the month, Aunt May had rented out her granny flat to him so that he would have his own place. Chester never talked about his family, but was happy to treat us like a new, mixed-up family.

The afternoon dragged on. Part of me didn't want to talk to Paul. The other half wanted to run away. I took my time walking to Paul's place from the main road, ensuring that with every step my feet touched down on the path's cracks. Tree roots had lifted some of the paths, and I placed my feet on the highest parts so that I could balance on them before stepping down. A few people hurried by on their way back from the beach.

I smiled at them as they passed. The sound of approaching bare feet on the pavement made me step to one side. A guy carrying a surfboard hurried up the road towards the bus. I think I had been humming "Summertime" again. I noticed dried sand covered his bare feet and the tang of salt water hit my nose as he passed. I watched him jog away from me. His thongs were lashed to the surfboard with a leg strap. Part of the strap swung in time with the white shirt that hung from the back pocket of his jean shorts.

I flicked my head to one side. An image came to mind and my eyes fixed onto the glow of the setting sun. My heart raced. I could see only shadows in my mind; they were moving quickly. I felt troubled, angry, as though I was in a half-dream state that had nothing to do with my feelings towards Paul. I reached out my hand. I could almost feel the shadows. I wasn't sure where I was. Suddenly I found myself standing in a classroom with a lot of swift movement around me. I couldn't fix my eyes on what was happening.

"Hey, miss, are you okay, love?"

I shook my head. An old man stood in front of me, holding onto my arm. My eyes fixed on him for a moment. His voice was muffled and I couldn't really hear it. I took in a breath and let it out, blinking my eyes before focusing on him.

"You okay, miss?" he asked again as he rubbed my arm, trying to wake me.

"Yes," I said, a little breathlessly. I smiled at him. "I'm all right. It's been a long day. Thank you." I smiled again and hurried away.

Once I reached Paul's house I placed my hand slowly on the gate I was still a little dizzy. That was the strongest imagery I had been through. The tiny front yard was covered with white pebbles. To one side stood a shrub that had been landscaped into the shape of a ball. Small lights ran along the front of the house, highlighting the accent render.

Paul was home; I could smell food cooking. I took a breath and opened the gate. Sheepishly, I walked into the kitchen and stopped, my heart pounded. Paul smiled at me, as if nothing had happened. He stopped cooking, rushed over, took hold of me, and kissed me.

"You go have a bath and I'll finish dinner," he said softly.

"Um," I began.

Paul placed his finger on my lips. "Don't say anything. I'm doing everything tonight."

"Okay. But…"

Paul turned me around and led me down the hallway to the bathroom door.

"Paul."

"Shh, no, not now." Again, he put his finger to my lips, then leant in and kissed me passionately. He stopped and led me into the bathroom.

The room smelt nice, as it was lit by scented candles. Paul pushed me in and closed the door behind me. I sat on the side of the bath and turned on the silver taps. Water rushed out. My mind was still feeling strange after what had happened in the street. Paul was softening me up and trying to say sorry for having upset me. I slowly poured bubble bath into the water.

"What am I doing? Am I going to give in a little and let it slide?" I mumbled the words to myself as I undressed. Chester's face came to my mind, I didn't know what I was doing.

My clothes dropped to the floor and I slipped into the bath. It was just the right temperature. My fingers weaved through the bubbles. Letting out a groan, I slid my body under the water. I lay there with just my mouth and nose above the water's surface. The sound of the popping bubbles and the smell of the fragrant candles wrapped me in the unrealistic safety of a cocoon. I had been trying to think all day. 'What the hell am I going to do?" This was my time to think. I had to. 'What am I doing?'

Paul had a problem with Chester and Ricky, not with Marisa. I wasn't going to stop being friends with them. I would have to see Ricky and Chester at work and when I went out without Paul. However, I didn't know about my feelings for Paul. I wasn't ready to let him go yet. He could be a pig, but he could also be loving and caring. It was the latter traits that I was in love with, but last night had scared me. It was the first time he had ever acted violently, but I had pushed him to react. The situation was just as much my fault as Paul's.

I let my hands float in the large white bath. My body felt warm. The sound of humming came to my ears. In my mind, I could see a room, clearer than what I had seen during my walk home. I stopped humming for a second. I felt as though I was there in the room. It was a small room with a single door, padded walls, and a padded floor. I was lying on the floor. I glanced over to see a dark figure on the floor beside me. I reached out my fingers to touch the figure's hand. I knew this figure; he had called to me in my dreams. He needed me. The feeling around him was heart-rending and my soul ached for the sadness inside him. I began humming to soothe his pain. Our hands entwined for the longest time. I couldn't see his face. Suddenly, my mind was torn from the room.

Someone was touching my lips. I lifted the rest of my face from the water. Paul sat on the side of the bath, watching me. He

121

touched my bottom lip again. I waited for him to say something, I could still remember the feel of my dream state and I wanted to go back.

"I'm truly sorry about last night. I don't know what came over me. I think I just need time to get used to your friends, that's all."

I sat up. "You're not easy with Ricky and Chester, I get it. I can still see them at work or when I go out with them." Paul's face tightened when I said this.

"Are you hungry? Dinner is ready." Paul changed the subject, he picked up a towel and held it out for me.

Late that night, once Paul was asleep, I walked into the backyard and looked at the stars. The city lights blocked some of them. The image that had come to me in the bath played in my mind. The dark figure worried me. He needed me, he was hurting. Why was this happening? How do you find someone when you don't know what he looks like, what his name is, or where he lives? But it *had* been just a dream, *I think.*

From inside the house, Paul's snoring stopped. I sighed, not wanting him to join me. The grass was wet and it was getting cold, so I went back to bed.

CHAPTER 9

Things had calmed down. Paul had been loving and caring, and our relationship was going well. A few weeks after our fight, I woke up to the sound of heavy pounding on the front door. It was about lunchtime on a Sunday. Paul had gone away on one of his working trips and was due back that evening. The previous night I had taken a chance and played a gig with the band. I fell out of bed with a thud as I ran to answer the door. My head was throbbing and the pounding from the door echoed loudly in my head. I stood for a moment, trying to balance my hangover. "Hello, who's there?"

"Laura, open the door."

My hand froze on the handle. "What the?"

I opened the door slowly and peered around it. Jennifer bared her teeth at me in an expression that I think was a smile.

"What do you want?" I asked, a little too loudly. I put my hand to my head.

She wasn't alone. The twins stood behind her. Jennifer pushed on the door and I stumbled back as she and the twins stormed their way into the house.

"Come on, Laura, you need to get ready. I can't believe you're not ready," Jennifer said, flipping my hair in the air in displeasure. They spun around me like predators, my stomach begun turning.

The girls surrounded me and kept talking at me as my head swam. The only word I could understand was "makeover." They kept saying it as they walked around the house.

Jennifer and the twins stormed into the bedroom and threw open my cupboard door. Clothes soared across the room and onto the floor. Jennifer would study a piece of clothing, make a face, and then toss it to one of the twins.

"What were you thinking when you got *this*?" Jennifer asked, pulling a face.

"Here put *this* on. I think *this* will do."

"I'm not going anywhere with you, I'm not insane." I hurried into the bedroom, pushed Jennifer out of the way, and shut the cupboard door.

"Oh no, Laura. You want to be one of us, you need to look like us," she snarled.

Jennifer grabbed my wrists. I tried to pull them out of her grip, but Heather had taken hold of my arms and pulled them behind my back.

"Get your hands off me," I yelled. It was useless; I was outnumbered.

Before I knew what was happening, they had dressed me in the tightest clothes I owned, then dragged me out of the house and into Jennifer's car. When they pulled me out of the car at the mall, I tried to make a run for it, however it was useless. Jennifer strutted ahead and the twins kept hold of me as we walked into a hair salon.

"Hi Misty. This is *the one* we've been talking about. She needs some work."

"*Some* work?" Misty questioned. Her scrutinizing eyes ran over me.

"Oh Misty, okay, she needs a lot." Jennifer smiled at me, then added, "Laura, thank Misty. She's very busy."

"Piss off, Jennifer."

"No Laura, its Misty."

"Oh sorry. Milly, piss off. This is called kidnapping and assault."

Misty snarled at me. "You'd think she would be happy that I'm going to help her."

Misty was as blond as the other three. She was also tiny. I was out of place and outnumbered. She smiled slyly as she ticked off my name.

"This way."

Misty and Jennifer led me to the sink as the twins kept hold of me. The hairdresser clicked at a young girl and pointed to the sink, indicating that the girl should wash my hair. By the time they were finished, I was blond. I had tried to leave a couple of times, but they kept pushing me back into the chair. Finally, I saw my reflection in the mirror. It was shocking. I was too blond for my complexion, my face was washed out and I looked sick. My hangover from the previous night wasn't helping the situation.

I hoped they were finished, but as I stood up to leave, the twins seized my arms and dragged me up the escalator to the top floor of the mall. My arms were hurting from their grip. The twins kept chatting at me, which confused me even more. They took me to one of the high-end clothing stores, with nice clothing and price tags that would make anyone break into hives. Heather and Kimberly sat me on a bench seat and held me down as Jennifer flipped through the clothing rack. The girl who worked in the shop seemed to know them well. She chatted to Kimberly as Jennifer did what she wanted in the store.

"I don't think this will fit you. Oh no, I think your thighs are too big for this, what a pity." Jennifer shoved a dress back on the rack.

I hadn't eaten all day. My mouth was dry and I felt sick. I figured that if I could throw up on the twins, they might let me go. However, no such luck. My stomach was not on my side as Jennifer dumped a pile of clothing onto the counter. She opened her bag and threw her Visa card next to the pile.

125

Our next stop was a unit a few streets away from Paul's house. I managed to slip out of the twins' grip and began running for it, but Heather and Kimberly grabbed me again after I stumbled on a path.

"Come on Laura, you are not going to waste this new look."

The unit was on the building's top floor. It was a typical 1960s-style unit like many others on the North Shore of Sydney. Jennifer opened the door and the twins pushed me in. I had entered a two-bedroom unit with a kitchen, bathroom, and lounge room. My jaw dropped. The place was a mess. It stank and plates were piled high on the kitchen's bench tops. In the lounge room, a leather lounge stuck out from beneath piles of bottles, magazines, TV dinners, and clothes. The same mess covered the rest of the unit. Paths through the mess led to the unit's other rooms.

Heather pushed me into the bathroom and I dry heaved as the smell hit my nose. Rubbish streamed out of the bin next to the toilet, which itself was a completely new vision of horror. Its lid was open, revealing a brown interior. Inside the bath lay a pile of wet clothes onto which a tap dripped water. The smell was terrible. The shower was mouldy and white scum covered the glass. My stomach churned once more as Heather pushed me down on the side of the bath.

Kimberly entered with a bottle of wine and handed me a glass. "Have a drink, Laura. You seem pale."

I took a sip from the glass, hoping that the wine would make me throw up on them. The fluid hit my stomach hard.

Jennifer appeared with one of the new outfits, which she tossed into my lap. "This one will be good for tonight."

"I'm not going anywhere. You've had your fun, now let me go."

Jennifer shook her head. "No, Laura, we're going to party. This is what it's like to be one of *us*. You're such a try-hard, Laura.

Even at school. Now you need to look like you belong with *us*."
She looked down her nose at me as she spoke and her hands
swayed as the words spewed from her mouth. I knew she didn't
mean any of what she was saying. I thought if I could get near a
phone, I could call for help.

Kimberly studied the dress they wanted me to squeeze into. "Oh
Jennifer, you always know just the right thing to wear." I expected
her to fall to the floor and kiss Jennifer's feet.

"Thank you, Kimberly. I know, I'm always the best. Laura,
when we're finished with you…" She stopped in midsentence and
smiled at the other girls.

The lack of food and the wine went right to my head. Every
time I took a sip from my glass, Heather topped it off. I hoped that
I would be sick soon.

When they had finished, heavy makeup covered my face. My
skirt was too high and my top was too low. I looked like a hooker
or a drag queen. I could have passed for both. Jennifer stalked
around me like a sculptor admiring her work, nodding and smiling.

"It's party time," Kimberly said. My shoes were too small and
too high, causing me to stumble as the girls dragged me out of that
cesspool of a place. How anyone could live there was beyond me.

They towed me out of the unit and stuffed me into the back of
Jennifer's car. Kimberly thrust me against the back seat to keep me
from leaving. Jennifer's car was an expensive two-door. Daddy
must still be paying her bills. The mess continued in the car, with
piled-up coffee cups and fast-food wrappers on the backseat floor.

We drove to the same pub we had visited after Paul's football
game. The twins worked as a tag team. The music was loud and
my head pounded along with the beat. I managed to grab a handful
of nuts in the hopes that they would settle my stomach a bit.
Heather dragged me to the bar so that I could buy everyone's first
drinks.

After I finished my second glass of Southern and Coke, I took a deep breath. The game was over; I needed to get out of there. The nightclub was not all that busy, it being a Sunday night. The atmosphere was smoky and dark. Shadows moved around the dance floor as people shifted in front of a spotlight. I sat back. The twins were still talking to me non- stop. Shutting them out, I studied the room. In the corner sat five guys in business suits, this was my way out. I sat forward, stretched out my arms over the table, then pulled them back swiftly. Doing so, I knocked Heather's drink into her lap.

"Bitch, what have you done!?" She jumped to her feet, trying to brush the mess off her dress.

Jennifer let out a breathy laugh and waved us away. She was talking to a guy she knew.

"Sorry Kimberly. I didn't mean to do that," I said, acting as though I cared.

"I'm Heather. I was going to get the money back on this."

"Oh, Kimberly, here, I'll take you to the bathroom." I began directing Heather towards the girls' toilet. Kimberly tried to come with us, but I pushed her back into a chair. "It's alright, Heather, I'll look after Kimberly."

"I'm Heather," Heather repeated, still swiping at her dress.

I waved off the mistake. The twins were easy to tell apart, but I really didn't care who was who. "Come on, let's go to the bathroom and fix this."

The businessmen were sitting near the toilets. I rolled my foot as we passed them. "Oh, I'm sorry, these are the silliest shoes," I said as I fell into the closest man's lap. I pulled up my leg to show him my shoe, then ran my hand all the way up to my hip. "These silly things, they always make me fall."

"That's all right, babe. If you want to fall into my lap, you can do it any time." The man put his hand around my waist and moved me onto his lap a bit more.

"Thank you for saving me." I wiggled a little getting comfortable on him.

The men with him seemed pleased to see me, as well. Heather, began heaving me off his lap in annoyance with what I was doing. The businessman frowned as his arm tightened around my waist.

"Now, now, she's hurt. I'm here to help her out. She looks like she needs a lot of TLC after that bad fall. Isn't that right, sweetie," he cooed at me.

"Kimberly, he wants me to stay. I'm so lonely. I'm having no fun. Let me have some fun please. You haven't let me have fun all night." My new friend was holding onto me tighter, not wanting to let me go.

"Wait your turn, honey." He pushed Heather away as she tried to yank me off his lap, once more.

Heather glared at me. She wasn't pleased. She gave Jennifer a quick look, but I didn't care. Jennifer was busy with her friend, so she was not going to help. "She needs to come with me," Heather said. I glanced across the room.

I smiled at my new friend. "Oh, you're so funny."

I ran my finger over the man's tie and tugged it a little when he grinned. Heather gave up on me and hurried into the bathroom, more concerned about her dress than about me. Jennifer's male friend had left and Jennifer and Kimberly were now talking to each other. My new friend skimmed his finger over my bare shoulder. I giggled.

"My friends over there have been saying that they would love to party with you." I wiggled the man's tie in his face. "We're looking to party, but it's so boring tonight. See, my friend on the end said she was so bored that she wouldn't charge for her first customer tonight. My other friend over there said that she is bored and that she would party for free for the first customer and half price for the second."

The men glanced over at Jennifer and Kimberly. I had told them what they wanted to hear. I leant back on the first guy's lap, running my finger on his friend's face. All five men were listening and ready to stampede across the room. I had to act quickly so that I could get away.

"I have to go to the little girls' room. I know that they would *love* to meet you. I'll see you soon."

I slipped my finger into one of their drinks, then lifted it into my mouth and slowly sucked on it as I stood up.

The guy swallowed hard. "Well…well, babe, you better go to the little girls and come back soon, real soon. I want to know what *you* want to charge." I leant over, ran my tongue along his lips, and then licked my own.

"You just have to wait," I said, teasing him a little more.

"Hurry," he said breathlessly.

I grinned, then stalked over to the bathroom door. I stopped and turned around. The men moved swiftly to Jennifer and Kimberly. Doubling back, I hurried out, pushing my way into the street. I hopped as I slipped off my shoes and ran down the highway. Once I had turned a corner and made my way down another street, I stopped.

Lack of food made my head spin and my stomach began to twist. My knees gave out and I landed on a patch of grass. It was dark except for a streetlight that made a misty glow. I knew how to hold my liquor and could drink when needed, but my stomach had begun moving sharply, rapidly, first one way, then another. The last time I had felt like this was after the first party Marisa and I attended. I threw up all the way home. Since then, I had learnt my lesson.

Now, however, I was feeling it and some poor person's roses were in the way. I didn't know what had happened today. Jennifer must have been planning this for some time. I sucked in a few breaths. The light from the house turned on.

"Hey, get out of here or I'm calling the police!" yelled someone from the front door.

I pulled myself to my feet. "Sorry."

At Paul's house, the front light was on and so was the lounge room's light. Paul must have arrived home. I made my way into the house and then the lounge room. I sat on the couch, my head still spinning and my feet sore from the walk home in my bare feet. A note sat on the table.

Laura,

I didn't bother cooking you dinner, I know how you girls get. Hope you and the girls enjoy your day out.

Paul

"A girls' night out," I said aloud. "Is that what this was meant to be? I wouldn't call it that, you son of a bitch. You knew about it." That night I slept in the guest room.

"You look really good. You should keep your hair like that," Paul said the next morning, smiling at me.

"Like hell I will," I mumbled into my coffee as I sat at the kitchen bench.

"Did you get my note?" Paul seemed too happy.

"Yes."

"Did Marisa find you?"

"No. Was she looking for me?"

"I don't know, she said something about work," Paul answered offhandedly.

131

"No. Why didn't you tell me they were going to do that?" I tried to keep my voice down. I was too angry to worry about what Marisa had wanted. I would find out later. It was the same thing all over again; his friends were more important than I was.

"It's good for you to make new friends. See, Laura, if you just give them a little time, you'll get on. They're a great bunch of girls. Jennifer is nice once you get to know her." Paul tried to kiss me, but I pulled my face away from him. He left for work.

At the museum, a pile of papers waiting for translation sat on my desk. I pushed my sunglasses up on my cap and let out a groan. Now I had to use my alcohol-soaked brain. I had crept into the museum through the back door so that Judith wouldn't see me. Turning on my computer, I set my head on my arms and waited for it to start. Then I pulled the first paper from the pile. It contained cuneiform that Dr Colman wanted me to translate. I slowly lifted my head and rested it on my hand. The sound of my one-fingered typing echoed through the room. The words and symbols began to swim together. I needed water. I flipped my glasses back down over my eyes as I considered standing up.

"Oh my God, what is wrong with you?" Chester entered my office. "No runny nose, you look like the living dead. What happened? Did you have sex with Paul? I told you, honey it's not good for you. You need a real man. This blood-sucking thing is not sex."

"Chester, stop it. Stop yelling," I said, putting my hands to my ears.

He lifted my cap. "Hello, what the hell. Laura, did you know that your hair is a strange colour?" He put his hand to his mouth. "See, I told you that having sex with Paul would do strange things to you."

"Chester, please don't yell at me."

He lifted my glasses. "My God, Laura, did someone kill you last night? Please don't eat me. Do you want me to get the salt so that we can dry you out and mummify you?"

"Chester!" I pulled a face at him, then put my hands to the side of my head. I felt sick as the room spun.

"Okay, okay. You need water and Panadol. Still, honey you shouldn't have sex with Paul. He's not all that good. Bloodsuckers will do that to you."

"Ah, Chester, you're reading too many teen novels. No one killed me last night." I groaned at him.

Chester hurried off. I put my head down on the desk. Every sound echoed through my ears. I reached for the phone, thinking that I should call Paul and ask him to take me home. Then I stopped. I pulled away my hand as Chester returned and set down a glass of water in front of me. I didn't look up as he placed two tablets into my hand.

"Thanks," I croaked.

Marisa entered the room. "What did you do?" she asked, sitting at my desk so that she could meet me at eye level.

"It's not what I did, it's what *they* did."

"They?"

"Yes, the bitches from hell."

"See, I told you they vamped her." A face emerged from behind Marisa. My eyeballs hurt too much to focus on Chester.

"Chester," Marisa scolded. Her face was anxious.

I told them about what had happened the day before. Chester and Marisa looked concerned and glanced at each other as though they were taking part in a secret conversation.

"What did Paul say?" Marisa was the first one to speak when I had finished.

"They're a great bunch of girls," I answered in a mocking tone.

Chester's face turned. His joking had ceased and now he looked sullen, He and Marisa glanced at each other again. Chester nudged Marisa. This wasn't going to be good.

I sat up. "Go on," I said.

They had been keeping something to themselves, but I could see that they were dying to say it now. Marisa took a breath and let it out slowly. "Okay, Laura, listen. This isn't going to change. You know that as well as I do. I came to see you yesterday, just for coffee, and he couldn't tell me where you were."

'So that's what Marisa had wanted,' I thought.

"Laura, we love you," Chester said. "Somehow when you're around Paul you become blind to the way he treats you. Why are you doing this to yourself?"

I wanted to tell them that they were wrong, but in my heart I knew they were right. Paul should be sticking up for me. He should have been mad, not happy, about what Jennifer and the twins had done.

I slowly let out a breath. "I need to leave. I'll have to go to Mum and Dad's place. I can't go back there."

"Laura, you need to leave Paul and pick your life up again. Everything will be alright," Marisa said.

"You're right," I answered. Chester nodded in agreement.

Mum face dropped when she saw me coming through the door of my parents' home. "Where's Paul? What happened?"

I couldn't answer her. I wanted to sleep. I collapsed onto my bed in my old room. I left Marisa to tell Mum and Dad what had happened. I couldn't face Paul tonight. I needed to feel stronger before I did. My mind couldn't face what I needed to say to him.

Dad liked Paul. He enjoyed the fact that Paul played football and he liked having someone to watch football games with.

Sometimes the two of them would fight over a game after Sunday lunch at Mum and Dad's house. Still, later that night, Dad and Marisa went over to Paul's house to get some of my clothes.

I slept a troubled sleep until Dad returned. He set down my bag just inside my door. I opened my eyes, seeing his shadow in the doorway. "He wants to talk to you," Dad said. I still wasn't feeling good.

"Thanks, Dad. Sorry to do this to you and Mum. I'll talk to Paul, but he can wait."

Dad waved it off. "Don't worry, you and Bess can come home any time, you know that. Get yourself back on your feet. We'll worry about it then."

"Thanks, Dad."

He kissed me on my forehead and left me alone in my room. It hadn't changed from when I had moved out. The room felt unused and lonely. It contained a double bed along with rock-star posters that I had hung on the walls. The musicians seemed like strangers to me. My cupboard was empty. The room had no life in it anymore. My toy hawk looked at me; it had remained on my pillow during my absence, waiting for me to return. Its eyes looked like those of Horus. The eyes that Ra used to see all. This toy had seen and heard a lot—every one of my childhood tears, fears and happy moments. I pulled it off my pillow and held onto it as I closed my eyes.

I didn't go to work or to University for the next couple of days. Each day, I felt okay in the afternoon, but by the next morning I was sick again. I had dyed my hair back to its original colour; I did feel better looking like me again.

"She'll call you, Paul, don't worry," I overheard Mum say one night. She didn't know that I was listening. I hadn't heard the phone ring, so she must have rung Paul.

"Like hell I will," I muttered.

135

I couldn't leave the situation hanging too long, but Paul needed to understand that his friends were not the be-all and end-all. If he wanted me in his life, he needed to treat me better. He would have to make it up to me if he wanted me to stay.

"You need to talk to him, Laura," Mum said as I got ready to walk out the door. It was my first morning back at work.

"I will. Just not yet," I called over my shoulder as I hurried out the door. I pretended I was running late. Since that phone call the other day, the only thing I had heard from Mum's mouth was an entreaty to talk to Paul.

"It's not right to leave him this long." She hurried out after me.

"I have to go. I'll see you tonight." I was still feeling rotten, but I had to go back to work and to University. I had missed a week of classes and an assessment that I had to take. I would have to make it up.

As I sat on the train from Chatswood Station to the city, I had time to think. If I was going to leave Paul, I would have to find my own place. Places are not cheap on the North Shore. I might have to find a place on the other side of the city, a bedsit or something like that.

"Laura." Dr Colman met me in the museum's front room as I walked through the door. "How are you?"

"I'm a little better, thanks for asking."

"Good, good, good. We have an exhibition on the queens of Egypt coming up." Dr Colman had just smoked a pipe. Now it hung unlit from his lips. I began breathing through my mouth as my stomach twirled at the odour.

"Yes, I know." I swallowed hard.

Dr Colman looked at my chest. "I want you to set it up. You know the Egyptian collection better than anyone here."

My eyes popped open. "Are you kidding?"

136

"No, Laura, I'm not. Now off you go." Dr Colman waved me away.

"Thanks so much," I said, shocked. My first response had been to hug him, but when his eyes had slid to my chest, I gave up on that thought. He handed over paperwork for the exhibition, and nodded at me before walking away.

The exhibition was to highlight Egyptian artefacts that we had in the museum, as well as other pieces in collections from around Sydney. I ambled into the Special Exhibition room with my head spinning with sickness and excitement. I glanced around to see if anyone was in the room. Spying no one, I did a little dance. This was what I had always wanted to do, and the exhibition was opening in a week. I had to spend the morning on the phone ensuring that all the artefacts were on their way to the museum.

At morning teatime, Marisa, Chester, and I sat in the museum's café, My stomach had begun turning the wrong way again. The only things that helped were a cracker and herbal tea. Marisa read a magazine while Chester chatted with another workmate. I was half listening as Chester told the worker about a movie he and Ricky had just seen. I was trying to determine the setup of the Special Exhibition room. I moved small paper display cabinets around a larger piece of paper in an effort to find the best configuration. Marisa let out a laugh as she read the magazine.

We looked up as she took a sip from her coffee. Then, realising that we were staring at her, she set down her cup and pointed at the magazine.

"There's a questionnaire…*How to know if you're pregnant*," Marisa explained.

Chester smiled and clapped his hands while bouncing in his chair. "Oh, ask me, Marisa. Please, please. I want to tell Ricky if I am."

Marisa sighed and gave him a look. Chester let out a groan before he reached over to take the magazine from her hands. She slapped him and took it back.

"Okay, I'll do it," Marisa said, pulling the magazine out of Chester's reach.

"Marisa, that hurt. I'll tell on you." Chester blew on his hand, then rubbed it.

"Behave or I won't do it," Marisa scolded him.

"I'll be good." Chester sat up and wiggled, banging his chair on the floor. "Come on, Marisa, I'm waiting. I want to know if I'm pregnant. Ricky is going to be so happy. I want a boy, but I know Ricky wants a girl. What am I to do? Go on, go ahead." Chester flipped his hand at her, then crossed his arms before going quiet.

"Question one. Are you having mood swings?" Marisa said the words in a funny voice.

"Yes, when I think of my old roommate. I want a boy. No, a girl. Laura, what do you think?"

"Keep me out of this, Chester." I went back to my room display.

Marisa rolled her eyes before reading on. "Question two. Are you feeling sick in the mornings or throughout the day?"

"Only when I have to come to work. So, yes to that question, but not on the weekends." Chester clapped his hands.

What Marisa had just said put a shock through me. I tried not to react, but I was moving one piece of paper around the same spot repeatedly.

"Question three. Have you missed any periods?"

"I never had one, so yes to that question." Chester was bouncing in one spot.

Marisa sighed again. "This is silly." She closed the magazine.

With a shocked look on my face, I stared into space. I tried to answer the last question for myself, counting back the days.

"Come on, Marisa, more. More. More. I might be having a baby." Chester sounded upset that she had stopped he was about to rip the magazine out of her hands. However, Marisa pulled it away from him and they began fighting like children.

I looked down at my fingers, continuing my count. "What are the other symptoms, Marisa?" I said softly.

She stopped fighting with Chester. "Laura?" She pulled the magazine away from Chester, sounding just as stunned as I felt. Chester feebly grabbed at the magazine as what I had just said registered with him.

"Marisa, can I come back to your house today? Is it okay if I use your place for a while?" Luckily she understood what I needed.

"Yeah, Laura, that's okay," she said softly.

"Thanks."

"Laura, you hussy. Who's the lucky guy, then? Ooh, Paul is going to be pissed." Chester tried to hassle me after he finally cottoned to what was going on.

"Chester, I haven't slept with anyone but Paul."

He waved it off. "Must have been the postman then. Paul is not up to that type of manhood."

"Chester," I growled.

Later that afternoon, after a quick stop at the chemist, Marisa and I went to her place. We didn't say much. Chester insisted that he wanted to help, but backed out when I told him what I was planning to do. In fact, he pulled a face of disgust.

"There are a lot of girly things I can't do and would love to, but this...that's sick," Chester mumbled as he hurried back to work.

I used a few sticks. The double blue lines kept popping up. I was having a baby.

Marisa didn't know what to say. She had never been through this before. However, I knew what I had to do. "I have to talk to Paul."

"Do you have to?" Marisa asked. She didn't want me to see him.

"Marisa, he's the baby's father."

"I've never been pregnant, but I know that a baby will not fix anything," Marisa said.

"I know, but it's the right thing to do."

"Yeah, but *is* it the right thing?" Marisa asked.

CHAPTER 10

"Paul, it's me, Laura. I'll be down at Dee Why beach at 6:30 tonight. I'm ready to talk." Paul wasn't home; I left a message on his answering machine.

Dee Why beach was a long, narrow strip of beach One half was Dee Why, while the other half was Long Reef beach. A large, grassy headland stuck out at the Long Reef side. The sun hadn't gone down yet behind me. Hang gliders flew around on the sea air off the headland a mist was covering the water. I sat on the big cement steps that led down to the sand. I had waited a day before calling him, I hadn't slept much the night before.

It was drizzling rain. I liked going down to the beach when it was like this. I loved the smell of the salt water mixed with the rain. The crashing of the waves had a different sound when it was raining. I sat there watching the waves crash to the shore and the birds flying about. The sun was throwing an orange and blue glow over the clouds. I didn't know how, but somehow it showed my mood.

~

Six months after we talked, it was summer time and I had some time off work. When we got off the plane at Wagga, the heat rose up to hit us. The air was dry and the sun beat down hard on our skin. The plane had stopped on the tarmac which increased the temperature. Sweat poured off my forehead as we went to get our bags near the picket fence.

Paul's parents met us in the airport waiting room. It was a small building, but cooler. Wagga was inland New South Wales; there was no sea air to cool you down when it got hot. When it was hot in this part of the country, it was hot. Wagga was one of the larger towns in this part of the country.

After Paul's mother finished hugging and kissing him, she began to examine me. "Oh Paul, she's really pretty. Nice to meet you, Laura. I'm Fay and this is my husband, Leo."

It's nice to meet you, Mr and Mrs Gibson," I greeted them politely.

I've heard a lot about you. Call us Leo and Fay." I smiled as Fay leant in to hug me, then began fussing around me.

I quickly glanced over to Paul for help, but he was shaking Leo's hand. "Hi, Dad."

"It's nice to see you, Son." The tension between the two men was strange; I couldn't put my finger on it.

It was an hour drive from the airport to their farm, the car was cooler with the air conditioner on. I enjoyed watching the countryside unfold in front of me. Paul's hand moved over to mine and held it as we drove; his mother seemed pleased to see us being affectionate

Finally, the 4WD turned onto a dirt road. I had been daydreaming and hadn't realised that we had arrived. I snapped myself out of it so that I could take in the farm. As we drove along the fence line, Fay began talking to Paul. The thing that struck me was that it was nervous chatter.

aul had seemed to relax when he got off the plane. He began telling his mother about what he was up to in Sydney. I hadn't heard him

142

talk so much; it was weird, but I put it down to him being happy to be home. He was also smiling a lot more than usual.

Paul's family's home came into sight. It was a big house made of sandstone with plum trees on either side of the wrap-around veranda. I had always had loved this type of home.

"Come on, Laura, I want to show you something." Paul began pulling me away from the house as I got out of the car.

"Paul, Laura has only just arrived. Look at her. I'm sure she would love to get out of the heat; I know I need to," Fay said to Paul, holding onto his arm and stopping him.

Paul paused for a moment; he saw the sweat dripping down my face. "Sorry, let's go inside. We have plenty of time." He grinned.

As a showcase, with nothing out of place. The walls were thick, which kept the heat out. As we moved through the rooms I begun feeling cooler. I could hear muttering coming from another room.

"Hey, I'm home!" Paul yelled out, three. Four grown men came flying out of the other room.

"Pauly!"

The three men grabbed their little brother and dragged him into the lounge room, slapping and mock punching him. I stood back in shock, holding my stomach to protect the baby, not sure what to do with this rough play.

"You would think I had a pack of animals, not boys," Fay said as I slowly followed her into the lounge room.

Leo came strolling out of the kitchen; he was pouring a beer into a glass. He gave the boys just one look, a hard look. It was a look of a man who needed to be respected. The boys stopped and backed away from each other.

"Thank you, Leo," Fay said to her husband. She took my hand, then said, "Brett, Leo Jr., Cliff, this is Paul's Laura."

One by one, they politely shook my hand. "It's nice to meet you all," I said as Paul came over to put his arms around me. He kissed me on the cheek.

"It's good to see Paul's taste has improved," Cliff muttered into his hand, but I heard it. His brothers chuckled and I'm sure I heard a growling sound from one of them. Once again, Leo gave another glance at Cliff for speaking out of turn. Paul was glaring just as hard at Cliff. I was unsure what was going on.

Paul shook his head at me and smiled. "So, Mum, what's for lunch?" he asked, changing the subject.

"It's chicken and salad," she answered, smiling.

"Mmm, I've missed your cooking, Mum," he said happily.

The family chattered as they went into the kitchen to eat. They seemed like a close family and they knew how to laugh. I liked that. Paul's father was not as hard as he seemed he could be —just as chatty as everyone, but he knew how to stop the boys when things got too far.

"Would you like some help, Fay?" I asked, a little unsure what to do.

"Thank you. It's so nice to have another woman about the house." She handed me a plate.

144

We were there for two weeks. It was hot most of the time, but the house stayed nice and cool. Once the sun went down, it was a lot nicer outside. After dinner we sat out on the veranda. His family had Queensland chairs that were handmade and leant back at the right angle. A length of wood stuck out so that you could put your feet or your drink on them. During that holiday I laughed more than I had in a long time, since I started dating Paul. He was a different person, not the one I saw in the city.

We didn't stay in the same room. Paul was in his old room and I was in the guest room. That was okay; it was his family's house and I didn't mind playing by their rules.

Late one night a light tapping sounded on my window. I woke with a start. Not sure what I would fine, I crept swiftly over to the window, I found Paul there, grinning at me.

"What are you doing?" I asked.

"Can't sleep."

"Well, you won't be able to sleep if you're standing at the window." I giggled at him.

"Come on, come for a walk."

"I'm not dressed."

"It's okay, the cows don't mind." He took my hand and helped me out of the window.

He led me down to the dam, which was far from the house and well hidden by gum trees and reeds. The night was warm. As soon as Paul got to the edge of the dam, he took his clothes off and dove under the water.

145

"Paul?"

After what felt like forever, Paul still hadn't come up. Concerned and about to yell for help, I approached the water's edge. Without being detected, a hand came out of the reeds and grabbed my leg. With a swift yank, I fell into the water. Paul's arms unseen draw closer around me to pull me up. I came to the surface, gasping for air.

"I hate you," I gasped.

Paul laughed as he held onto me. I tried to swim away from him, but he held onto me tightly. The water was cool. Paul's body pulled closer to mine. He began to kiss me.

"You can't hate me," he breathed as he moved his lips on my skin.

~

That earlier night when I had called Paul to come and see me at the beach, he had quietly sat down beside me. It seemed like he had a bad week without me. I was glad. "How are you?" Paul asked after studying me for a few moments.

I scrunched up my face and moved my head from side to side if to say, *"I could have been better."*

He nodded. "Your hair is back to its normal colour. I did like the blond on you." He reached up and touched my wet hair.

I didn't answer him right away. Paul went quiet; he hadn't changed from work. "That's not me. This colour is my colour, not blond. You know there are two of you?" Once I began, I didn't let him speak. I went on. "There's the Paul who's with his mates. I don't

146

matter to him. Then there's the Paul who's away from his mates. You know, when we first met I was surprised that you had asked me out. I thought it was some sort of trick. When I tried to talk to you about what happened the other night, you didn't want to listen. I can't be like your mates' girlfriends. You want me to be someone I don't want to be. I can't ask you to be someone else. That's not fair on you. So I don't see why you should ask this of me."

Paul still hadn't spoken. He was letting me say what needed to be said. I couldn't tell him about the baby, not yet.

I continued. "I felt that I didn't matter. That's why I haven't spoken to you until now. I still can't understand why we're together. There are a lot of walls in our way. One day we're going to get tired of climbing over them."

Paul took a slow breath in and out. He wasn't mad; his face was blank. I sat quietly to let him say what he needed to say. If Paul didn't want to be with me, I wasn't going to use the baby to force his hand. I knew he would still be in my life, but I could let him go if that's what he wanted.

"Laura." He stopped. I was beginning to think the worst. Paul took another breath before speaking.

"Laura, I need to say I'm sorry. I know I shouldn't have let Jennifer do that to you. It's been a very lonely week without you. I don't know how I can make it up to you. When Dick told me what they did…I shouldn't have let it happen."

We sat quietly for a little longer. Paul reached over and took my hand.

"I know we move in different circles and we don't like the same things…" He stopped and took another breath. "Laura, when you weren't around I understood how much I missed you and how

147

much I care about you. I want you to come home, Laura. I miss you and care deeply about you. He gave me a moment to speak before he kissed my

"Paul." I was going to tell him that it wasn't going to work and that we should just leave it as this. That's what I should have said. He did say he was sorry.

"Please Laura, don't say you can't. I know you may be thinking that you should end this, but don't. I care about you."

I lay my head on his shoulder. He put his arms around me and pulled me close to him.

"Paul." My voice was muffled by his shoulder. "I'm pregnant."

He pulled my head up so that he could look at me. "Are we having a baby?"

"Yes."

Paul's face lit up like a Christmas tree. He was grinning from ear to ear. "You'll have to marry me now, Laura." He placed his hand on my belly. "I'm going to be a dad."

I nodded and half smiled. "I guess you are."

That night, back at Paul's house he left me alone while he went to get dinner. I paced around the house, thinking about what to do. My hand circled round on my belly, sending love through my skin to the little life inside me. I had gone from leaving him to having his baby to marrying him, all in the blink of an eye. I had an uneasy feeling that I had said yes when I should have said no.

When I phoned Mum and Dad to tell them where I was, Dad didn't sound pleased. Mum, on the other hand, sounded overjoyed that I was with Paul. I needed to tell them that Paul and I were having a baby. I worried about how Marisa and Chester were going to react.

After hanging up the phone, I heard a sound in the hallway. The hallway was dark and gloomy. The door of one of the guest bedrooms was moving slowly back and forth. I had never seen it do that before. A cold feeling came over me; it was as if someone was watching. I glanced up and down the hallway before going over to the swinging door. There was no reason for it to be moving as it was. The door squeaked as I pushed on it with one finger. I peered around the door. The room was cold and had the feeling that no one had lived in there for a while. I didn't come into this room much.

The room was a double room with the same black and white colour scheme as the rest of the house. Stepping through the door quietly, I scanned the room. I didn't want to touch anything; it felt like I was in another person's house. Without a reason the cupboard doors were open and swinging back and forth as well. I stood and study them for a moment.

"This room needs to have colour," I told myself.

A large double bed stood in the middle of the room on a white shaggy rug. The curtains were black. Steel furniture was placed in the room to fill it. All the walls were white as well as the skirting boards and cupboards. The way the house looked had always puzzled me. It wasn't what I thought a country boy's house would look like. What did I know? I sighed and went over to the cupboard to open it.

The built -in cupboard was empty. I didn't understand why it was open. I stepped to one side to close one of the doors. A floorboard moved a little under my foot as I stepped on it. I bounced on it and the board flipped up before slapping back down. I bent down and pushed it. It sprang up then lingered in the air before falling back

149

down. I don't know why, but I felt like a naughty kid. I moved up the floorboard to peer inside the space, I could just see an old, square biscuit tin sitting in the dark. I swallowed, then glanced up at the bedroom door, hoping that Paul wouldn't come in and find me here. The door was still open. I quickly went over to quietly close it; a closed door gave me the false hope that I was covering up what I was doing.

Hurrying back to my find and wasting no time, I reached my hands under the floorboard to lift the tin box out of its hiding place. It had a picture of a rosella, which was faded. The paper label looked like snails had chewed at it.

I pushed my fingers into the side of the tin to open it. It wouldn't open; there were no locks, but it was stuck. I tried a few more times to pop it but it wouldn't open. Scurrying over to the bedside tables, I pulled open the drawers. They were empty. I. In search of some sort of aid, I hurried out of the room. Stopping in the hallway in mid stride to listen for the sound of Paul's truck, I found everything to be quiet. I hurried into the kitchen; like everything in Paul's house, his things were too good to use on an old box.

Rushing out of the room down the hall and into the laundry room, I went through the cupboards to find something to help. On the top shelf was a small screwdriver. I let out a breath as I ran back to the spare bedroom. Time was running out. If Paul came back now, I would have to smuggle it out later, and that would kill me. I needed to know what was in that box. It could be Paul's box. It could have anything in it. I didn't know; that was the reason I wanted to open it. A box like this didn't belong and that heated up my desire to open it.

I closed the door behind me once more. I hurried back to the box, sliding a bit across the floorboards to get to it quicker. Hastily I pushed the screwdriver under the lid to pop it open. This was not the thing to do with something this old; at work I would have taken my time opening it. For a moment, I took in what was under the lid. I took a breath as my fingers lifted out the contents of the box.

There were two notebooks and a newspaper clipping lying in my hands. The newspaper cutting was from when Tutankhamen's tombs were found in 1916. I quickly thumbed through the booklets. They talked about Nefertiti's Temple. One notebook belonged to Dr English and the other belonged to a Dr J. Dixson. I knew the name Dixson; Dr John Dean had said that he had worked with a Dr Dixson. It couldn't be the same person, surely. John was in America now so I couldn't ask him. I thought that I could post the books to him.

The sound of Paul's truck pulling into the garage stopped me. I put the books back into the box and something brushed my hand.

"Laura?"

I put my hand into the box. "I'm coming, hang on!" I yelled at Paul. I pulled a necklace out of the box.

"Laura, where are you?"

The necklace seemed like 18-karat gold surrounded with cobalt blue and red stones. In the middle was a greenish-blue scarab. I turned it over. On the bottom of the scarab was the spell thirty B from the Book of the Dead. The chain was gold. I hurriedly slipped the necklace over my head and placed the papers back inside the box. I could hear Paul's footsteps coming down the hall. Instead of putting the box back, I shoved it under the bed, then rushed to put the boards back as Paul opened the door.

"What are you doing?" Paul frowned and glanced around the room.

I tucked the scarab necklace into my shirt. "Nothing. We'll need a baby's room, that's all." I grinned, waving my hand around.

"That's right. Come on, your fish is going to get cold."

Later that night after Paul and I made love, Paul turned over and went to sleep. He didn't notice the necklace. I lay there turning it over in my fingers. My head was spinning with everything that had happened that day. I was going to be a mother. The scarab looked old; it seemed to be a real one. It would protect the soul. To calm myself I read the back of the necklace. It was recorded in the Book of the Dead as the soul protection spell:

"'O my heart which I had from my mother, O my heart of different age, O not stand up witness agents me, do not be opposed to me in tribunal. Do not be hostile to me in the presence of the Keeper of the Balance. For you are my ka which was in my child, the protector who made my members hale. Go forth to the happy place whereto we speed; do not make my name stink to the Entourage who make men. Do not tell lies about me in the presence of the god; it is indeed well that you should hear! I speak my name to Osiris my soul is pure."

Paul rolled over and opened his eyes. "Are you okay?"

"Um yeah, sorry," I answered him before rolling over to go to sleep.

That night I had a strange dream.

I was standing on the banks of the Nile. I was watching the water flow past me. The date palms that grew along the bank were bright green. The water looked cool. I wanted to go in, but something stopped me. I was in Egypt. There was so much I wanted to see; my heart was beating fast, but it was as if I were on a movie set.

Behind me were sand dunes, a mist floated from behind them. I could feel the sun, it was warm on my skin. There were no temples. I wanted to go to the tombs, but I didn't know where they were.

I began to walk down a path. I found myself in the Kings Valley. I couldn't see the entrance to the tombs; there were just rocks. I couldn't find the tombs anywhere. The high sandstone cliffs stood quiet over the top of me. The shadows moved on the brown, yellow and white cliffs as if they swayed in the wind.

The sound of a hawk high in the sky made me turn. It let out a cry as it flew above me. It turned in a circle before it flew ahead of me. Without much thought, I followed it down a trail, the sound of my sandals on the sand bouncing off the walls of the cliffs.

Turning a bend in the path, I came face to face with a large cobalt blue wooden door with black bands that held the door together. Cast iron scrolls decorated the door, which stood alone in the landscape. The hawk landed on the doorframe. I reached out to touch the door; the hawk watched me with a curious eye. The door felt warm from the sun and seemed to be breathing under my touch. I pulled my hand back. I wasn't afraid; I wanted to open it. I needed to see what was on the other side of the door. It was from the reaction of the breathing door.

I reached out once more to the cast iron handle. It was locked. I looked up at the hawk. "It's locked." It puffed out its feathers; it had a key in its beak. The hawk dropped the key onto the sandy path at my feet. It landed heavily.

"Thanks." I picked up the key, which was black with a rose on the end of it.

The bird pecked at the doorframe, egging me on to open it. I put the key into the lock and turned it. The door sounded like a cell door as it swung open. Behind the door everything was dark however, slowly a soft light came from inside. It felt warm and inviting. Without hesitation, I stepped inside.

I found myself at the bottom of the stairs of a little white house. It had a big porch in front. On one side was a porch swing that was falling off. I hurried up the stairs. I noticed a brown rabbit hiding under the swing. It scampered away as I got close. Reaching out to the door, I turned the handle. Without too much trouble the door popped open. The hallway was covered in cobwebs and there was no way to walk down it. A room to the right was the only room I could enter. The house seemed as if it hadn't changed since the 60s. A fireplace with a burning fire stood on the far wall. Everything was in black and white, but the fire was brilliant red. On the mantel stood photos in frames. I couldn't see who was in the photos, it was as if they hadn't decided on what the image was going to be.

The floorboards made a creaking sound from behind me. Turning away from the fire, I saw that a rocking chair had appeared in front of me. It moved back and forth. Three rag dolls watched me; their eyes and heads moved as I came closer to them. I reached out to touch their faces as I knelt in front of them. A feeling of sadness overwhelmed me. I couldn't understand why tears were running down my face. It felt like I had missed something, but I was unsure what it was.

"Why are you crying?" a voice asked me.

"I don't know why," I answered the voice while wiping my eyes.

"Have you lost something?" The voice was a man's voice, it seemed to calm me down somehow. I knew this voice well.

"I may have, but I don't know when or what," I answered.

154

"You still have a piece of what you may have lost. Look in your hand." In my hand was the scarab necklace.

"But this won't bring back what I have lost," I said to the voice. It was too dark to see where the voice was coming from; I couldn't see him.

"I know, but you have to wait longer 'till you find it again," the voice answered me.

I peered harder into the darkness to see where the voice was coming from. A dark figure was sitting and watching me in a wingback chair. I hadn't realised that the figure was sitting so close until I moved over to sit on the floor next to him. He was just a black figure. He reached out and stroked my hair gently. I wasn't scared of this figure; it seemed gentle and warming. My soul knew him well. I trusted this figure. My head rested in the figure's lap. His hand gently touched my face.

"When?" I asked softly.

"It's not the time, but soon. You will know it when you see it."

"I miss you."

"I miss you, but soon, baby, soon."

I jolted awake in the dark, Paul lay next to me, snoring. I lay watching the shadows wishing that I could go back to my dream, but it was gone.

I didn't tell anyone about this dream. For some reason I wanted to keep it to myself. Even weeks later I would find myself drifting back to my dark figure. I didn't know why, but he would be there in my thoughts, waiting for me. He was the same I had been humming to.

155

Marisa and Chester were disappointed that I had gone back to Paul. Chester kept giving me disappointed glances. Marisa was doing it as well. Again, I would have to stop my studies at University. With great pleasure, Dr Colman would put me back onto fulltime. He would be happy that he had his dog's body back.

Paul went away again the week I came back. I was still working on the exhibition. The room looked fantastic. I took the box with the diaries in it to work and put it under my finds table. On my spare time I wanted to research it.

Dr Colman came strolling into the Special Exhibition room after I had finished. He was acting as if he had done all the work in setting it up. With his white cotton gloves, he moved gradually around the room, nodding. Every now and then he would open a case and move a piece to another angle.

"Dr Colman?"

"This is very good, Laura, for your first time."

"Thanks. It would be good if we could have the Alabaster Shabti as a centre peace."

He closed the last glass case before turning to me. His eyes moved up and down. "Yes, it would. However, the Shabti isn't here. I have, um, sent it to a friend to look at."

"Oh." That meant he had put it away somewhere and I would not see it again.

"Okay...I'll use the priestess mummy as a centre peace, maybe." I wanted to ask where the Shabti was and who was examining it, but Dr Colman wasn't the type of man to do that with. He would shut down even more about what he had done with it; he may have had an unknowing student researching it. I had to let it lay where it

156

was; it just proved that it was important. I wished I had kept a photo of it.

The next week during the opening night, the priestess mummy sat in the middle of the room. Soft light shone on her, giving the room a magical feel. Mum and Dad had come to see my first exhibition. I hadn't told her and Dad yet about the baby. Dad walked around beaming with pride as I gave them a tour. Bess was working in London; she had rung me the night before and told me to take lots of photos.

Mum seemed happy at what I had done. There were fans made of gold, jewellery made of coloured stones, statues of gods—Anubis, Osiris, Basset the moon goddess and Nut, the goddess of the sky. They all stood there peering out at us, showing us a moment of their long lives.

After I had finished showing Mum and Dad around, Chester grabbed me and pulled me out of the room. Marisa ambushed me. They were ganging up on me as they pulled me into the hallway of the museum. The hallway was empty. They took me all the way down into my office so that we couldn't be overheard. Judith had been shadowing us all night; she was spying on me. She had an idea that something was happening with me, she always had an uncanny knack of knowing something was up.

They pushed me down into my brown chair. "Have you told your mum and dad yet? About how dumb you're being," Chester said, holding me down. Marisa had turned my lamp on and rotated it into my face.

"No, Paul's not here. I will when he gets back."

The two of them were standing over me. "Why haven't you told your parents?" Marisa asked.

"When he comes back. He'll be back on Monday. No problems," I said, covering my eyes against the light.

"What are you doing, Laura?" Chester sounded worried.

"I'm having Paul's baby. I have to at least try. We're going to get married. It will all right, don't worry." I grinned at them.

Laura, I know I kid around a lot, but this…" Chester let out a sigh. "We love you. We can see what he is going to do to you. I will never say to you to do anything to the baby, but you don't have to marry him, Laura." Chester turned around the photo of Paul on my desk so that it faced the wall.

"Chester's right; Paul will leave you," Marisa stated.

"He's changed; he really loves the baby."

"But does he love you, Laura?" Chester asked, kneeling beside me. "Oh, Laura, we can't stop you and we will stand by you, but don't hurry into anything. Please."

I patted him on the shoulder. "It'll be okay, Chester. Marisa, don't worry. Things will be fine." I knew I hadn't convinced them.

Monday night was when Paul came home. I had asked Mum and Dad to come over for dinner. Paul could be distant when he came back from his working trips, but I would put it down to him being tired. I told him about Mum and Dad coming over. He just nodded, then went off for a shower.

Mum was all smiles as soon as she came into the house.

Dad, on the other hand, felt the same that Marisa and Chester did. As soon as Paul came into the room, he kissed Mum on the cheek. Dad didn't acknowledge Paul; he kept his thoughts to himself.

"What's going on?" Dad asked as Paul sat down next to me.

I decided to just say it. "Mum, Dad …um… Paul and I are having a baby."

Mum's smile became bigger. Dad crossed his arms and glared at Paul.

"What are you going to do?" Dad asked right away, to Paul, not me.

Paul answered, "We're going to get married."

Mum jumped up and hugged Paul. "Oh, Dan, don't worry, it's all good. I'm going to be a grandmother."

A month later, Paul and I were married in Paul's backyard

CHAPTER 11

A few months later, I said goodbye to Marisa, Chester and Ricky. Marisa and Chester had signed up for a massive dig at Stonehenge. Bess was helping Ricky do some work at the hotel where she was working. I wanted to go on the dig, but my stomach was too big.

During my last two months of pregnancy, I stopped working; it was getting harder to move and I needed rest. It was good to sleep in. When Paul left for the day, I would make myself a bowl of ice cream and pickles. He didn't understand the cravings; his mother, Fay, told him that she didn't have them. His mother had six boys; it seemed she knew better than I did. So I would wait until he left and then pig out.

The guest bedroom was now a baby's room. The walls were still white with no baby decorations to adorn them. Paul didn't want it painted. The baby furniture had an antique look to it. Paul hadn't wanted any of the hard furniture. It was the one room in the house that had been softened.

I had taken up going for walks in the mornings. It was relaxing. I wouldn't go far; I just liked to see what people did in their front yards and who was out walking their dogs or jogging. Early morning was the best time.

One morning, a sharp pain consumed my body just as I arrived home. I stopped to grab hold of the gate. At first I didn't know what was wrong. I thought that I had hurt myself while walking. The pain slowly went away, but I didn't feel good. I slowly made my way up the path. I had to stop a few times to take a breath.

Paul had bought me a mobile phone; in the 90s they were big and heavy. I had left it on the kitchen bench. People weren't addicted to phones back then.

160

Making my way slowly into the kitchen, I sat on the floor to dial Paul's number.

"Hello,, Paul speaking."

"Paul I…need…you…to come home."

"Are you okay? Are you having the baby?"

"YES!" I screamed at the phone as another pain ran through my body.

"Okay…I'm coming." He hung up the phone before I could say anything more.

"Fine, I'll just wait here," I said as I lay down on the kitchen floor, trying to breathe through the pain.

I think Paul broke all speed records, as it seemed like he was there in no time. "Laura?" I could see Dick's legs from where I was laying. Paul came hurrying into the room, pushing him out of the way.

"I'm here," I said between breaths.

"Are you alright?" Paul sat me up.

"NO! This hurts." I groaned as I put my face into Paul's shoulder. I hadn't stopped breathing heavily.

"What can I do?" Paul asked.

"Have the baby for me and I'll watch," I joked, cringing with more pain.

Paul lifted my head off his shirt and grinned at me. "How about I get you to the hospital." He helped me to my feet.

"That works." I cringed.

Paul wrapped his arms around me and helped me out of the house.

"I'll drive," Paul said, looking at Dick, who was holding my bag.

"You're not going anywhere," I growled at Paul. I took hold of Paul's shirt and pulled him into the back seat.

"Dick, I think you should drive," Paul said quickly. "Breathe, Laura," Paul kept saying to me. I had never seen him nervous before, but this was doing it.

"Dick, could you call our families please?" I asked in between the pain.

"Don't worry, Paul already asked me,"

Once we arrived at the hospital, a nurse put me into a wheelchair before pushing me off into a room. A small plastic baby bed sat in the corner of the room. The walls were pale grey. A few monitors stood ready for the nurse to hook onto me. My clothes were taken off by the nurses and in one move a white gown was slipped on me like a well-rehearsed performance. I gasped for air a few more times. As pain ran through me, I grabbed hold of Paul's shirt.

"You're doing great, honey," Paul tried to reassure me.

"I don't want to do this anymore!" I breathed.

After a few hours of screaming, the doctor came in when I was close to delivering the baby.

"You're almost done, Laura, you're doing fine. One more push and the baby will be out," the doctor said from under the white sheet that was covering my legs.

All of a sudden, after one more push, my screams of pain stopped. They were replaced by another high-pitched cry. "Do you want to cut the cord?" the doctor asked Paul.

The doctor handed Paul a pink, bloody, little screaming creature. Paul examined the baby for a moment before coming over to me to place this creature into my arms.

"It's a girl," the doctor informed us. The nurses' eyes crinkled at me as they watched the creature move towards me.

162

I didn't know what to say or do when she was put into my arms. This little creature had just given me pain and I should have hated it, but I couldn't; she was worth it. The baby quieted down and made a sound as she moved around in my arms. I couldn't take my eyes off her.

"What are you going to call her?" asked one of the nurses.

"Emily Eve." Paul smiled.

"Hello, Emily," I said quietly.

By the time we came back to my room, Mum and Dad were waiting for us.

Paul placed Emily into Mum's arms while I was settled into my bed. A few flowers had come to my room while I was having Emily. Once I was settled, I was exhausted, but contented. I lay back on my bed to let everyone have a chance to meet Emily. Dad's face became soft as Mum placed Emily into his arms. His voice went strange as he talked to her. Then he started on the coo-cooing. "Dan," Mum scolded him. "You'll give her nightmares."

Mum informed me that Marisa, Chester and Ricky were flying back with Bess in a few days and that Paul's family was on their way. Finally, after a few hours it was just Paul, Emily and myself in the room. We were quiet, watching this little creature as she slept. Everything was there: ten toes and ten fingers. She was the most beautiful thing I had ever seen.

"You did well today," Paul said, kissing me on the cheek.

"Thank you." In the last few months he had been a different man, the Paul I needed him to be.

A nurse came into the room. "I think that Laura needs some sleep now. We're taking the baby to the nursery."

Paul took Emily out of my arms. I was tired but I could have lasted a little longer. He put Emily into the baby bubble. "I'll take her," Paul said quietly.

When I awoke later, I found Paul asleep on a chair with his feet on the bed. In Paul's arms, Emily was also sound asleep. Paul seemed contented. One thing Mum said to me was to never wake a sleeping baby, to sleep as much as I could. I smiled, rolled over and went back to sleep. I couldn't have asked for a happier time.

The next morning Emily woke me for a morning feed I had the hospital room to myself. Paul had gone to work, the once Emily was settled, we went outside onto the balcony, the hospital looked over the water of Sydney Harbour. It's one of the best views for a hospital.

It was still early in the morning, he birds were flying around the trees below us. A familiar sound came to my ears. I looked around to see where it was coming from, a hawk had landed on a tree on the edge of the bushy area beyond the carpark. It resembled the one from my dream.

"I called her Emily," I said gently. The hawk spread out its wings before ruffling its feathers. It let out a cry before it flew high in the air and disappeared. It was as if I was telling my Dark Figure.

Once I came home, it began filling with Paul's family, his three brothers, his mother Fay and his father Leo. Fay was tall and thin with blond hair; Paul had her eyes. Leo was a little taller than Paul was; he had a hard face. His face belonged to a man who had worked hard all of his life. Fay took Emily out of my arms as soon as we came in. Paul's three brothers—Brett, Leo Jr., and Cliff— ambushed Paul as soon as they saw him.

I stood in the hallway trying to understand the madness that had taken over the house. This was the first time since our quick trip to Wagga that I had seen Paul's family. They had taken over and I felt like I was the visitor.

The next week was the same; every time I went to pick up Emily, Fay was there taking her out of my arms. "It's all right, Laura, I'll take her. You go and put up your feet. Have a shower.

I've got this." I smiled and backed away from my baby, hoping that Fay would leave soon.

One morning Emily wasn't in her cot. In a panic I begun looking in every room for her; she was nowhere. From the hall, I could hear someone in the lounge room I hesitated. I stopped just near the door. It sounded like someone was singing.

"Hush little baby, don't say a word. Grandpa's gonna buy you a mockingbird. If that mockingbird don't sing, Grandpa's gonna buy you a diamond ring. If that diamond ring turns brass, Grandpa's gonna buy you a lookin' glass. If that lookin' glass gets broke, Grandpa's gonna buy you a billy goat. If that billy goat don't pull, Grandpa's gonna buy you a cart and bull. If that cart and bull turns over, Grandpa's gonna buy you a dog named Rover. If that dog named Rover don't bark, Grandpa's gonna buy you a horse and cart. If that horse and cart fall down, you'll still be the sweetest little baby in town."

I poked my head into the lounge room. Leo was singing "Mockingbird" to her as he walked up and down the floor, bouncing her on his shoulder.

He paused as he saw me. "Don't let me stop you, Leo." I smiled.

"This should be her song; she likes it." He bounced Emily in his arms. She had melted his heart—a hard man had just become putty in her hands, without a word I backed away.

Bess, Marisa, Chester and Ricky came home at the end of the week. It was good to see friendly faces again. When they came over to see Emily, Paul's face went green, however he held his tongue. Chester and Ricky both went gaga over Emily; she seemed happy with all the fussing.

However, one by one everyone left. Soon after Paul's family went home, he went away to work again for a few weeks. I was left with Emily on my own. I wasn't happy that he was doing that now, but it was work. What could I say or do?

Time flew quickly and before I knew it, Emily was smiling, sitting up and saying her first word: "Dada."

She was daddy's little girl. If there was a football game on, I would find Paul lying on the couch with Emily on his chest, watching the game. If Paul heard her cry, he would stop what he was doing and go to her.

I went back to work full time when Emily was a year old. I had been working part time up until then. When Emily wasn't at day care, she was with Mum while I worked. Dad loved having her; he would listen to Emily's endless chatter. Emily would follow Dad into the yard. She kept chatting about everything that was important to her, and Dad would smile contentedly as he listened. One day I found him playing dolls with her when I came to pick her up after work. The one thing I always ensured was that Dad was home when Mum was caring for Emily.

University now was a distant dream; there was never any time to go back. A month after I returned to work, a memo came around. It was about an upcoming dig that the museum was funding. They wanted extra hands to help with it. It was all paid for—food, lodging, even the airfare was funded. Every year the digs would be in a country like England or Turkey. This year, the dig was in Egypt. My heart sank as I read the details in the email.

"Are you going on the dig, Laura?" Marisa asked later that day at lunch. She had come back to work soon after I had.

"Going where?" I asked, pretending I didn't know.

"To Egypt," Marisa said back, pulling a face.

"No, I can't. I have a family and too many bills. Are you going?"

"No, I'm going back to England for another excavation. Everyone knows how much you love Egyptian history. Why don't you go?"

Ricky and Chester had gone back to England to work. Marisa was doing some teaching before she went back as well. Her work visa had expired and she needed to be home for a while before she could go back to England.

"I can't." I answered while sipping my juice. I couldn't do it to Em; she was too little.

"It may be years until the next one comes along."

"Paul said he was going to be working away again soon and I can't leave Emily for so long." Marisa shook her head. I picked at my sandwich. I wanted to go so badly, but I couldn't. Maybe when Emily was older, but Paul was never interested about Egypt when I talked about it. I knew he wouldn't go with me. When you have a family, you have to put things on the back burner, and that's what I had to do. That's what I kept saying to myself.

More years passed. I was now thirty-four. Emily had turned five and was about to start her first year of school. She was overexcited and she had to tell everyone how big she was and how good school was going to be. She spent the day beforehand with Mum and Dad. She followed her grandfather all day, talking about her first day at school. Then, once at home, Emily was on the phone with Paul's mum and dad that night. Emily ensured that her clothes were sitting on a chair in her room and that her shoes sat on the floor in front of the chair. She was so worked up that I had to sit and rock her and sing her to sleep. When she was upset, I would sing "Mockingbird" to calm her down.

The next morning Mum, Paul and I walked into the school gate with Emily. Dad had to work that day. Emily was so small next to the other kids in the school; without a thought she showed us to her classroom. As soon as Emily walked inside, she took hold of Paul's hand and hid behind him. All of her bravery had left her.

Some of the children played happily in the classroom. The walls stood bare, ready for the 'students' artwork. Some mothers sat on a carpet with their children at the front of the room. Other kids were

167

holding onto their parents, like Emily was. I knelt next to Emily. Her eyes were watery, she was scared and she seemed smaller. My little baby was not as big as she thought, and my heart melted at her fear.

"We can stay until the bell rings," I said to her.

Emily rubbed her eyes on Paul's hand. He was displeased that his little girl was upset.

"We'll come and get you at three p.m. when the bell rings." I picked up her arm. Mum had given Emily a cheap digital watch.

"When the clock reads three, that's the time to come home." I pointed to Emily's watch.

Emily's teacher came over; she was young. She bent down next to me to talk to Emily. "Can you tell me your name?" the teacher asked.

"Yes," Emily croaked from behind Paul's hand.

She smiled. "My name is Miss Grey. What's yours?"

"I'm Emily."

"That's a nice name. Emily, can you read your name?"

"Yes," Emily said, peering around Paul's hand.

"I have everyone's name on their table. Do you think you can find your name?"

Emily nodded.

"Maybe your dad can help."

The small, colourful tables sat in four groups with red plastic chairs. Miss Grey pointed at the tables. This was the primary school I had gone to, and it hadn't changed much. The outer buildings were the same. However, the rooms had been updated throughout the years.

Emily looked up at Paul; he was trying to pull it together. I think he was ready to run with her.

"Do you want my help, Emily?" Paul asked.

"Yes," Emily sheepishly answered.

They both went over to the small tables, with Emily leading the way. She seemed a little braver with Paul there. Emily had her father's eyes, but she resembled me at that age. After a few minutes, Emily stopped at a table and pointed to a tag taped to it. Miss Grey stepped up and looked at the tag. She smiled.

"Very good, Emily. The drawer under the table is for your books. Can you put them in and put your bag on the peg on the wall? Then you can come and sit with us on the mat." Miss Grey smiled at Emily.

Emily gave her a big smile. Her nerves had melted away. She let go of Paul's hand. Emily's chest puffed out a little as she put away her books. When Emily was finished, she came up to Mum, then to me and gave us quick hugs goodbye. Acting like a big girl, she went up to Paul and patted his hand. "It's okay, Daddy, I'm alright now."

He wasn't taking it too well, Paul's face had gone hard. He was trying to hold it in as she said goodbye to him. Emily let Paul go and went over to the mat. She sat down crossed legged without any more fuss. That moment she had grown up; now she was beginning her own path in life, and this put a loneliness in my heart. I was going to slowly become less needed until she become an adult and left home. I would not be there when she fell over or if a child was mean to her. It was hard to think about this, but it was a part of growing up. I smiled as she turned to a boy sitting next to her. He was rubbing his eyes; he had been crying. She placed her hand on his shoulder. "It's okay. You know we'll have fun. My name is Emily and we can be friends if you want."

"Okay." The kid sniffed.

169

My stomach turned a little, I wanted to cry. Mum took Paul by the arm as we walked out, he stopped just by his Ute.

"You alright?" I asked. His mood was still hard.

He seemed put out. "Yeah."

I tried to hug Paul, but he pulled away. Mum frowned a little at the way he acted.

"It's okay. You know she still loves you. You know she'll be dying to tell you all about her day when she gets home," I told him.

"Yeah, I know," Paul answered while opening the door of his Ute. He wasn't in the mood for talking. He left without another word.

As he drove away, I let out a sigh. "Don't worry, he's fine," Mum said, waving to Paul as he drove off. He didn't look back.

"I have some shopping to do," Mum told me, acting a little twitchy. I knew what that meant. "The *shops* don't open until 10:30," I told her.

The house was deadly quiet once I arrived home. Standing in the hallway, I heard the sound of birds outside. Over the years I had slowly softened the look of the house. The house always had to be clean, but right now there was nothing to do. I sighed before going off to make myself a coffee.

Sitting at the sink, the sun shining outside, I let my mind wander. A few tears rolled down my cheek. Paul and I had tried to have another child, but it seemed that I could not fall pregnant again. I had asked Paul if we should have a test, but he kept putting it off.

"Don't worry Laura, we'll have a baby soon." The other one was, "There's nothing wrong with me."

This year was the last year of telling myself, "I'll have another one soon." Time was moving on.

170

I I had taken the day off so that I could be home for Em when she finished school. Mum wanted to come to school with me to pick up Em. I met Mum outside the shopping centre. Behind it was a club with pokies in them. She had been there most of the day and had no shopping bags with her.

"You alright?" I asked her. She seemed frustrated.

"Yes, why shouldn't I be?" Mum thrust her seatbelt buckle into its holder a little harder then she should.

"Is everything okay?" I asked once more.

"Yes, we're going to be late." Mum settled in her seat as a car honked behind us. Without another word, I drove on.

We stopped at a set of lights, her mood had not changed. "Mum?" I didn't wait for her to answer. "You should stop."

"What are you talking about?" She didn't like me talking about her *problem*.

"You know what I mean. You've done something and you're upset. What is it?"

"Nothing. I've done nothing. Could I borrow some money?" Her voice changed from glum to hopeful.

I closed my eyes while shaking my head. "If you need me to pay an overdue bill, then I'll pay it. I'm not giving you any money, Mum. I'm sorry."

"I can pay it," Mum snapped at me as she whipped herself around to look out the window of the car.

"How much and where do I have to pay it?" I groaned, I cared about her problem but I was worn out by it.

Mum kept glancing out the window she reached out to touch it. "You never complained. You were always a good girl."

Mum was buttering me up. I began sucking my bottom lip. This wasn't going to be good. "How much?"

171

"It's the phone bill; they're going to cut it off tomorrow if I don't pay it."

"How much?" We were almost at Emily's school.

"Two thousand dollars," she told me in a rush of breath.

"Mum! How did it get that high?" My voice fell out of my throat.

Mum went quiet. I couldn't back down now; I had said that I would pay for it. I pulled up a little way down from the school. There was a line of cars parked on both sides of the street; there was no way to get any closer.

I turned to Mum in disbelief. "Give me the bill, please."

Mum opened her second-hand purse; it was stuffed full of paper slips and blue Lifesavers wrappers. I had given her a nice bag for her birthday last year. She told me she had lost it. It took her a moment to find the bill. She opened a few papers; I couldn't see what they were, as she closed them too quickly.

"I didn't have enough money to pay for it. After getting a few things, you know how it is?" Mum tried to tell me. She talked to me so steadily, without a hint of a problem in her voice. I was almost convinced, but I knew better.

After a few moments of scratching around, she found the bill. She didn't give me the whole thing, just swiftly ripped off the bottom. On it she wrote the address for where I had to post the bill. It had a code on it; I had never seen anything like it.

"Don't tell your father. Just post it to that address and that's fine. Good." Mum settled in her seat. She began studying what a woman passing by was wearing. "She shouldn't wear that, it's too tight."

"No Mum, I'll not tell Dad." I shouldn't have done it, but she needed my help.

"That's a good girl." Mum grinned, down playing her actions to me or her problem.

Emily was cheerful when she saw us. Mum smiled. Emily chatted endlessly about her day on the way home in the car.

"It sounds like you had a good day," I said, finally getting a word in.

"Yes I did. You know, there was this boy and he kicked a ball at a window and he broke it. He had to walk with a teacher all lunchtime. Can I call Grandma and Grandpa Gibson? They need to know that I'm okay and I survived. What about Daddy? Can I call him? He needs to know as well that I'm okay."

"Can't you wait until he gets home?"

"Please, Mum, he'll be worried. You know, Grandma, we had to line up before we went to class. Some kids were pushing, but I wasn't. Did you have to line up when you were at school, Grandma?"

"Yes we did," Mum answered, smiling at Emily.

"I bet not like us," Em stated from the back seat.

I should have told my dad about the bill. I had told Mum that I would if something like this happened once more. However, yet again I was going to push it under the carpet.

Once we were home, Emily ran into the house to phone Paul's parents. When she finished, she hung up to dial Paul's phone. He was not due home for another two hours. Emily tried quite a few times, but Paul didn't answer his mobile phone. After a few more tries, we heard Paul's Ute pull into the driveway. Emily dropped the phone and ran to the door, jumping up and down as she opened it for him.

Paul was early. I didn't think much of it; he must have wanted to come home to see Em. Emily needed to tell him everything about her day; she almost jumped into his arms as she hugged him.

"Let me have a shower first, Emily, and then you can tell me everything."

Paul put her down before he went into the bathroom and shut the door. Emily sat in front of the closed bathroom door. She was still bouncing, talking quietly to herself. When Paul finished and came out of the bathroom, she leaped into his arms.

The two of them went into the lounge room. He had forgotten to kiss me hello like he always did. I brushed this off because today was Emily's day and she wanted to tell her dad that she was okay. The next day, without telling Paul, I paid Mum's bill out of my money so that he wouldn't know.

Everything had fallen into a new pattern. I would sometimes drop off Emily, or sometimes Paul would. Mum picked up Emily after school. I would get her on the way home. I would also make sure to phone Mum to confirm that she had picked Emily up, and she was not alone.

Another memo had gone around in an email about a second Egyptian digging trip. I still couldn't go, especially after paying for Mum's so-called phone bill. I sighed and deleted the message. Marisa was still in England; she was there for 12 months this time, and she also had a dig in Scotland. For the last six months she had been working at the British Museum. When she had time she would scan tablets with cuneiform on them from the museum's collection. She would then email the scans back to me to translate. She was also working at Oxford University, teaching.

Marisa was spending time with Bess, Chester and Ricky. Chester was working at the British Museum as well. Ricky was still with Bess in the big hotel in London. I smiled when I saw the latest email from Marisa.

Hey, you old Mummy,

Hope Emily enjoyed her first day at school. I'm coming home soon. Chester and Ricky are coming home with me. They must miss the warm weather. It's reallllllly cold here. No, wait, it's snowing

174

again. God, I miss the sun. However, I've enjoyed the Englishmen. "Mind your own business, I'm not telling you anything, so don't ask." Your sister said to say hello. She's sounding more English every day. Have to get her home.

Miss you. Hugs and kisses to you and Em. See you soon.

Marisa

P.S. Chester said to give a sloppy kiss to Paul for him. He said he couldn't wait to see that green colour that Paul gets when he's around. Yes, they are here while I'm typing this. ☺ XXXXO

CHAPTER 12

A few weeks after the email, Emily and I were in the kitchen cooking dinner. Emily loved to help. Mum had made biscuits with her the other week. Mum wasn't a good cook; the biscuits were burnt, but Emily was so proud of them. While cooking, I put on our favourite CD and we sang as we worked.

Emily had developed a taste for Janis Joplin as well as the other bands I listen to. She would sing and dance in the kitchen. She loved fairies and butterflies; her butterfly wings were her latest favourite things to wear.

"Em, could you please hang up your wings if you are helping me cook?" I bent down to her and we put our noses together. "I don't want your wings to burn up."

Em smiled at me before kissing me on the nose. "What if I don't want to cook?"

"Then you need to sit at the bench and do your homework," I replied.

"Can I keep my wings on while I do my homework?" Emily was twisting her head from side to side as she looked in my eyes. She was making me a little seasick.

"As long as the wings don't get in the way of your homework." I quickly kissed her on the nose and she giggled.

Emily stepped back before she turned on the spot and curtsied to me. I did the same back to her. She bounced off into her bedroom to get her homework. I turned off the CD player once Emily came back. The kitchen was still the same, but a few antiques had found their way inside. I thought the house had a decent blend of old and new. Paul did not say anything about the antiques, but he wasn't overly thrilled with them. He would cast

176

his eyes over them and his lips would narrow before he moved away.

That night Paul was nowhere to be seen. He normally would be home at six, or sometimes a little earlier. However, tonight there was no sign of him. I dished out his dinner at our normal time and set our own dinners on the table. Emily finished her homework and started wiggling in her dining room seat in front of the food; she was hungry. It was not fair to make Emily wait, but this was Paul's number-one rule, that we were to eat our night-time meal together. Hoping that he wouldn't be long, I let her sit until it finally got to be too much for me and her.

"If we eat, Daddy may show up." I tried not to show that I was becoming worried. The other part of my mind flashed back to a night when he had done the same thing.

There was no sign of him when we had finished. It was dark outside and Em needed to get ready for bed.

"Go and have a bath, Em," I said when finished eating.

"But Daddy is not here yet."

"I know, but he must not be too much longer. Please Em, go and have a bath."

"Okay." She slid out of her chair but took her time leaving the room. Her expression showed confusion and concern about what was going on. She paused before leaving the room.

"Em please, bath."

"I'm going," she said.

Paul always phoned if he was going to be late unless he was working away. I was having flashbacks of the time Paul hadn't shown up for the dinner with my friends. Since they have been away, he has seemed happier. There was no reason for Paul to be so late. While Emily was in the bath, I rang his mobile phone; it was turned off. I thought maybe he was having a drink with his mates and had forgotten about the time.

I flicked through the list of numbers I had written down until I came to Dick's number. "Hi Dick, this is Laura. Is Paul with you?"

"No, Laura, he's not with me. I'm not sure where he is. Have you tried the pub?"

"No, that's my next call. Thanks, Dick. Sorry to interrupt you and Jennifer."

Jennifer had moved in with Dick a few years ago, and he was talking about marrying her. However, nothing had happened since then.

He went quiet for a moment, then said, "Um, Jennifer and I broke up a few months ago."

"Oh, I'm sorry to hear that." I wasn't sorry about anything to do with Jennifer, but Dick was always nice to me.

"Thanks, Laura. Sorry I couldn't help. Did you call Dale?"

"No, I'll try him before the pub. Thanks."

Dale's phone was turned off as well. I didn't like Dale; like a puppy, he hung off every word Paul said. I knew that wherever Paul was, Dale wouldn't be too far away. It was sick the way he hung around. Emily didn't like him, either. Dale and Heather would show up at the house, hanging around and eating our food, and most of the time I had to push them out. One day I hid when they came to the door. Emily and I sat in the hallway until they left. If I didn't feed them and act as though I were happy to see them, Paul would get stroppy at me. Dale and Paul would work on their cars while Emily and I would have to entertain Heather. Kimberly did not come to the house much; Jennifer never came to the house at all.

I rang the pub next. I could hear them call his name, but Paul didn't answer. I was about to phone the hospital, but Emily was standing in the doorway of the kitchen so I put the phone down. She was in her pyjamas and had a storybook in her hand.

"Can you read my story, Mum?"

"Sure," I answered, trying not to show my worries.

Emily and I made ourselves at home on the couch in the lounge room. The couch was no longer a black leather model; now it was an oversize one that we could sink into.

I knew this story without reading it; Em loved the watercolour pictures. Her long, reddish-brown hair smelt fruity from her shampoo. She couldn't go to sleep with wet hair, so I would dry it while reading to her. I loved these moments.

Em turned to the first page as I ruffled her hair with the towel.

"The yard was overgrown as it always was. The sea breeze blew through the grass, Lolly and Black Bean lived in a little house that was made out of driftwood and glass bottles. It was well hidden in the sand dunes. Lolly and Black Bean were Sea Shore fairies. They would spend springtime helping baby seals find their mothers and chicks that had fallen from their nests.

They would dress themselves in lost fabric that was found on the beach. Lolly's dress was made of blue dots, and Black Bean was dressed in stripes. They lived near a..."

"Holiday Cottage," she read over me.

I stopped drying Em's hair. "Are you going to let me read this?" I asked playfully.

"Yes, but you're ahead of the pictures and the words..." Em closed the book when she heard the sound of Paul's Ute coming up the driveway.

I sighed in relief; I was beginning to think that something bad had happened to him.

Emily bounced to the front door. "Daddy!" she yelled as he came into the house. He acted as though nothing had happened.

"Are you alright?" I asked.

"Yes, why?" Paul stopped for a moment and glanced me up and down. It was as though he didn't understand what I was saying.

"You're late. I was getting worried that something had happened to you." Emily was in Paul's arms, kissing him repeatedly on his cheek.

"I went and had a drink with an old friend. We met up after work. I lost track of time. I didn't mean to worry you."

"Your phone was turned off."

"I must have bumped it. I dropped it the other day and now if I bump it the wrong way, it will turn off. I'm going to have a shower." Paul put down Emily and shrugged his shoulders at me.

"Your dinner is in the microwave," I told him.

"I'm not hungry, we ate at the pub. Sorry." He didn't even kiss me hello.

Later that night, after Emily went to bed, Paul and I watched TV together. He was a lot quieter than he normally was. Usually at night we would talk about our days.

"Which pub did you go to?" I asked.

"Just the pub I normally go to."

I nodded; this was the pub I had rung earlier. "Who was this old friend?"

Paul was quiet for a moment, then slammed the TV remote onto the coffee table. I flinched; I hadn't seen this mood in a long time.

"Why are you asking me so many questions? He was an old friend, that's all. I haven't seen him in years and I ran into him this afternoon, so we went for a few drinks," Paul roared at me. He had pushed his face into mine.

My heart was pounding; it felt as though Paul was about to hit me. "I was worried about you, that's all. Your phone was turned off." My body was shaking and I tried to keep my voice calm before I spoke again. "I was sitting here thinking that something had happened to you. I was about to call the hospitals."

Paul got to his feet and stood over me, trying to intimidate me. "Well, as you see I'm fine. I'm going to bed now, or do you need some more answers about everything I'm doing?"

Paul threw the remote across the room. He stormed off and slammed the bedroom door behind him.

I turned off the TV and sat there, trying to understand Paul's mood. I didn't know what I had said to upset him this time. I went to bed later that night. First I checked on Emily. She was sound asleep, luckily, and hadn't heard any of it. I went to the spare bedroom to sleep. Paul was gone early the next morning; things really hadn't changed with him. He still hated my friends, and at times he treated me like a doormat.

I remembered one time, when Emily was 1 year old, I had stood at the front door holding her. Paul had packed his bags, as he was about to head out the door for one of his trips.

"It would be nice if we could come," I told him. "It would be like a family holiday."

Paul turned to me. I thought he was going to kiss us goodbye, but the expression on his face made me take a step back.

"First, you don't *ask me again to go*. You *got it*? Second, you don't ask me *where* I'm going. Understand?" Then he left. He was gone for a month that time.

We never went away together. He had taken Emily to his family's farm a few times throughout the past five years, but that was it.

The phone rang, snapping me out of my thoughts. I reached over and picked it up. I was making breakfast for Emily and had almost burned her toast.

"Hello."

"Hi Laura how are you?" My heart jumped. I didn't know Marisa was home. Marisa was just the pick-me-up I needed; the day was looking up.

"Hi Marisa, how are you? Are you okay? You don't sound so good. When did you come home?" Something wasn't right, I could feel it.

"I'm fine. We came back yesterday. Um, can you come over today?"

"Sure, I have nothing to do today. I'll finish getting Em ready and come over."

"Okay, I'll see you then. Bye." Marisa hung up.

Marisa was not herself; we usually chatted for a while, but that had been a short conversation. I didn't know what was wrong with Paul, and to top it off there was something with Marisa to add to my worries. I hoped the two weren't connected, or that it was just me.

Just before lunch, Emily and I arrived at Marisa's flat. It had been a long time since I was there. I used my key to let myself in. The mood in the flat said it all. Marisa was standing in the kitchen making sandwiches. Ricky was sitting on the couch, staring off into space. He glanced up and smiled when he saw us, but his face had lost its lustre. Emily rushed up to him and threw her arms around him. Chester and Ricky always made a fuss over Emily. I think they had some bizarre plot to kidnap her and make her their own. It would have been hard to get her back because they would spoil her rotten, more so than they did now.

"Hi everyone." I glanced around for Chester, still not understanding the mood everyone was in.

Marisa came out of the kitchen carrying a plate of sandwiches and put them on the coffee table. Emily sat herself on Ricky's lap;

she kept touching his face. She could see that he was upset and she kissed his face a few times. He rested his head on her shoulder.

"Haven't you grown, Emily! Come into the kitchen with me and give me a hand." Marisa reached out for her.

Emily was about to protest. "Em, please go with Marisa," I told her when I noticed that my old bedroom door was closed. There was a feel of gloom about that door. Their bags sat unpacked just behind the lounge. I sat down next to Ricky.

"Where's Chester? What's wrong?" I asked, my voice cracking.

My heart sank into my stomach. Ricky tried to steady himself before speaking. His eyes were red. He took a breath and then spoke.

"It's Chester. He has…cancer…"

I wanted to scream. I wanted to say, *"Okay, that's a sick joke, stop it."* But the way Ricky said it, there was no joke.

"How long?" I finely spoke after a long pause.

"It could be weeks or it could be days." Ricky was finding it hard to say anything.

"Days?" The word left my lips like the world was about to end.

"I'm sorry Laura, we didn't tell you right away. This is not the type of thing you can say over the phone. Chester wanted to come home. We had to wait until he could handle the flight back. The flight almost killed him, but he didn't want to die overseas. The doctors wanted him in hospital. He has to go into hospital tomorrow. We were waiting for a bed."

"Ricky, don't worry about saying sorry to me." I reached out for his hand.

Instead of taking my hand, Ricky grabbed me and hugged me. His body shook as he sobbed quietly. Wrapping my arms around him, I rocked him back and forth.

"What's wrong, Mummy?"

Ricky sat up and wiped his face to look up at Emily. Marisa stood there wiping her eyes.

"Chester is really sick, Em," Ricky replied.

"Can I go and see him?" She was worried; she seemed to understand what was happening to Chester. "I think it's best you stay here, Em. I will tell him hello for you." I kissed Ricky on the cheek before letting him go.

Emily took in a breath as I went to my old bedroom. She was about to plead to go in with me, but I shook my head at her; this wasn't the time.

"Can you tell me all about school and what you have been doing? Marisa and I have missed you and I bet you have lots to tell us," Ricky said, putting his hands out to Emily. She hurried over and climbed back onto his lap. A box on the table had Emily's name on it. Ricky pointed it out to her.

"We brought you some things from England." Emily began chatting about herself as she unwrapped her present. Ricky leant his head on her shoulder to watch her unwrap her gift.

I softly opened the door, the bedroom was dark. Standing in the blackness for a moment to let my eyes adjust. The bed finally came into view, on the bed was a heap of blankets. I wouldn't have known anyone was under them, but they shifted slowly up and down. Moving around the bed, I saw that Chester's face was chalky white, his eyelids red, and his lips pale; they moved in and out slowly as he breathed. A tuft of hair poked out of the blankets wrapped around his head; his hair was like straw. A feeding tube came out of his nose. I choked back a few quick sobs as I sucked in my breath. Kneeling beside his bed, I gradually reached out for Chester's hand. It felt like ice; the sense of him just holding on lingered in the air. Feeling my touch, Chester sluggishly opened his eyes. A smile crossed his face when he realised who was sitting in front of him.

"Hi," I said softly.

Chester blinked to say hello to me. I leant in to kiss him. His icy hand came to my face; he was trying to hug me. In his weakened state it seemed like he was trying to fly.

I pulled away to see him better. "You know, this is not the way to get attention. Emily is outside; she said to say hello."

"Oh, my sweet baby. I had to do something to get everyone's attention," he said in a weakened voice.

I moved in to give him another kiss on the forehead. "I've missed you. Work hasn't been the same without you," I told him.

"When you are a legend no one can follow you, and if they do they are only copying." I laughed, a little tear begun rolling down my face. Chester's cold hand reached over and wiped it away. "I need to thank you," Chester said. I didn't understand what he was saying. He went on. "When my family turned their backs on me, you were there; you and your family took me in. You don't know what it means to know that you and Marisa are there for me."

I shrugged it off. "That's what friends are for. You would have done it for me."

"Yes I would. By the way, Ricky and I are going to take Em from you."

"I knew it," I scolded him, then grinned.

Soon after, Chester's brain seemed to nod off. His eyes kept watching me, but he appeared half asleep. I kissed him softly before leaving.

We stayed a little longer with my friends. I didn't care where Paul was; it didn't matter anymore. Emily loved Chester and Ricky; when they did come to the house, Emily would have them play dress ups. They babysat her one day and by the time I picked her up, Chester had Em dressed in designer clothes. I didn't like

185

him doing that, as it wasn't good for her, but Chester wouldn't listen.

I knew that Ricky was not going to leave Chester's side, but Marisa and I could help. Ricky had told me there was nothing they could do; by the time they saw the doctor it was too late. The cancer had started in the liver and because they were travelling so much, Chester thought he had picked up a bug that he couldn't shake. If they had seen a doctor earlier, they could have done something; now the cancer had journeyed to other parts of Chester's body.

I rang Mum and Dad to tell them what had happened. Mum was happy to help with Em while I travelled back and forth to the hospital. Later that night when I arrived home, Paul wasn't there. I wanted to talk to him. I wanted him to put his arms around me and tell me it would be fine.

What was wrong with Paul? I didn't know. I was going to have to deal with his problem later. I didn't bother cooking him dinner, as his last night's dinner was still in the fridge. About two in the morning, I stood in the doorway of the bedroom after he had arrived home. He came into the hallway and stopped dead when he saw me.

"I didn't cook for you; your dinner from the night before is still in the fridge. That's if you're hungry. If you are going to have a shower again, use the other bathroom. I will not be around much. Chester has cancer. Ricky needs Marisa's and my help. Mum is going to care for Emily for me. My friends need me." I did not wait for him to answer. "I'm not sure what's happening with us right now. I don't want to think about it. I think it's best that you use the spare room." It hurt saying that to him, but I had to do it, it was time to be back with the people who care for me. They needed me to be there for them.

I turned and closed the bedroom door, curling into a ball on the bed. My hand reached for my necklace. The scarab necklace had hung around my neck for years; I hadn't had a dream like that since that night. Paul had never asked about it or stated that he owned it.

My dark figure was what I wanted now, the feeling of his arms around me. I let out a silent sob as I closed my eyes.

"O my heart of my different ages! O not stand up as a witness against me, do not be opposed to me in the tribunal. Do not be hostile to me in the presence of the Keeper of the Balance. For you are my ka which was in me, the protector who made my members hale. Go forth to the happy place whereto we speed; do not make my name stink to the Entourage who make men. Do not tell lies about me in the presence of the god; it is indeed well that you should hear."

The next day, once Paul had gone to work, I hurried around the house cleaning up. I was planning to spend my days at the hospital, as I had been given time off from work. After dropping Emily off at Mum and Dad's I hurried to do a few things before going to the hospital. I made Mum promise not to leave Emily alone; I told her that I would be ringing to check on her.

Marisa and I thought that Chester would like to make his hospital room a little homier. Mum gave me a quilt that Chester seemed to like. Chester had seen it and said that he would steal it if Mum didn't watch it, she was happy to give it to Chester.

I also stopped by one of Chester's favourite clothing shops, as he needed some clothes to wear in the hospital. I knew Chester would hate for everyone to see him with his hair dry and almost falling out.

When I told the shop assistant about Chester, he was shocked. He knew Chester and Ricky well and was more than helpful. He knew Chester's taste as well as Chester did. I didn't want to get anything that Chester wouldn't wear, so the shop assistant helped me find skullcaps, light jumpers, shirts, and track pants that Chester could sleep in.

187

My arms were full of gifts when I met Marisa outside Chester's room. She gave me a kiss on the cheek.

"How is he?" I asked.

"The same." Marisa took a few things out of my arms.

I didn't want to cry again. I gave myself a moment to pull myself together before I entered the room. The nurse walked out and held the door for both of us.

The room was different from a normal hospital room. This part of the hospital was where people came to die. A large window with heavy hospital-green curtains stood on one side of the room. The walls had been papered with pink and yellow poppies. A print of Dorothea Tanning's *A Little Night Music* hung over Chester's bed, as did a print of Gustav Klimt's *The Kiss*.

Chester was sitting under the blanket on the bed; he looked like a little old man. The mood in the room of a dying person is something you don't quickly forget. Chester seemed a little brighter than yesterday. Ricky reached over to Chester's hand before speaking. "We have had a lot of drugs today."

"I'm ready to do my workout, Laura…I'm really stoned." Chester grinned, waving his hands around, his voice soft and breathy.

"No Chester, we are not doing a workout today." Ricky shook his head at him.

"How about some gifts instead?" I piped up.

Chester clapped quietly and grinned. "Come on Laura, show me the booty. I can't do any gift vouches…I'm a bit stuck…with the *death thing*." Ricky drew in his breath at Chester's joke; he was not finding it funny. Marisa took Ricky's hand to help reassure him.

First I flung out Mum's quilt on the bed. Chester's eyes lit up as his fingers glided over the square patterns. Mum had made it during the first year she was married to Dad; it had a lot of purples and greens in it.

Chester always said. *"Eve I'm going to jump into your window at night and take your quilt."* It was the "sick quilt." When we were sick, Mum would bring it out. It always made me feel better.

"Over my dead body, Chester," Mum would say to him.

"It's your mums'…and…it's over my almost…dead body," Chester said with a grin.

"Not nice, but yes. You're the sicky and you need the quilt."

Ricky sighed. Chester heard his discontent. He reached out and took hold of Ricky's hand, then kissed it. "Sorry," Chester said with his lips on Ricky's hand. He kissed it one more time, then turned his attention to the bags. "What's in…the baggies? I know them bags…I haven't seen them…in a long time."

The expression on Ricky's face said it all as Chester examined the bags' contents. Ricky was trying to hold on; he was finding it hard. Slowly Chester pulled out the clothes. The shop assistant had added free socks, a wool/cotton blend. When Chester saw the skull caps, he looked relieved.

"Thank you, Laura," Ricky said. He must have been thinking about what to do with Chester's hair as well.

Chester laid the articles of clothing, one by one, on the bed in front of him to see what matched the best.

Chester turned to Ricky and said, "Which caps do you…like the best?"

Ricky pointed to a blue cap with a tribal design on it. "I like this one."

Chester smiled. "Yes, I like this one, too…Laura, who helped you?"

"Vincent."

"Good, he has a....good sense of fashion." He nodded.

Chester wanted to wear his new clothes. Marisa and I thought it would be good to put flowers in some water and leave the boys to it. Ricky also seemed as though he hadn't eaten today. By the time we came back, Chester had changed into his new clothes. It had tired him out. He was laying back in the bed and falling asleep, but he seemed happier. Marisa put a plate of sandwiches and a glass of juice in front of Ricky. While Chester fell asleep, Ricky picked at his food, protectively watching over Chester.

For the rest of the day we sat around talking quietly. Chester fell in and out of sleep. Ricky sat on a large grey chair. His hand lay near Chester's hand. Any time Chester moved or winced, Ricky jumped to his feet to assist him. Chester awoke only once that day for meds.

"I hope you are not all staying?" a nurse inquired later that day.

"No, Ricky is the only one staying," Marisa answered her.

"Very well, I'll get a fold-out bed for you, Ricky. Save you sleeping in a chair."

Emily had already eaten and finished her homework by the time I picked her up from Mum and Dad's house. Her brown eyes watched me in the dark as we drove home. "How's Uncle Chester?"

"He's the same."

"Can I see him soon?"

I was tired; it had been a long day. "This weekend, baby."

The house was dark when we walked in from the garage. Paul was not home. He was even later than he had been the night before. I didn't wait up for him. Sitting around the hospital all day had taken a lot out of me, but the stress of watching a friend dying sapped everything I had.

The next day, Chester's mum came to see him. Marisa and I hadn't seen her in years. I called her to tell her that Chester was dying. His mother was a round woman; she was short, with badly dyed hair pushed back into a bun. She always wore shirts with large prints on them. She didn't like me or Marisa; Mrs. Reed blamed us for the way Chester was.

"I'm sorry," I mouthed to Chester as she came in the door.

"It's…okay," Chester answered softly in my ear as I kissed him hello.

Ricky stood back, holding up the wall. Marisa and I stood beside Ricky as Mrs. Reed glared around the room at him.

"Is this HIV? I told you this lifestyle would kill you." She waved her hand up and down his body.

"I have…cancer…Mum. Not…HIV…" Chester answered her weakly.

"Fine. I'm sorry to hear that. Your dad said to say hi. He had to work, you know how it is. Your brother, well, he said…um…I have to go, hope you get better soon." Chester's mother stood up and kissed him on the forehead. "Laura, Marisa, could you talk to me outside please?" We followed her into the corridor.

"Who's that boy Chester is with?" Chester's mum asked quietly. She waved her hand towards the room, then put her hands to her eyes as she let out a sigh. "Oh, I don't care, we will not let that boy at the funeral anyway. We may let you, that's all. His *other* friends will not be allowed. I'm not sitting around here watching him kill himself. That's if he doesn't get better first. Does he have *H…I…V*? Is he just telling me he has cancer to make it easier on me?"

"No...how can you do this? He is your son," I said, trying to keep my voice down.

"He's my son; when this madness stops I'll be happy. This gayness is just insanity, a thing. He read about it in a magazine and

191

then tells everyone...*he likes boys*. In front of the *whole* family... on his father's birthday of all things."

"Yes, we know what your family did to him," Marisa snapped at her.

Mrs. Reed waved off Marisa, then went on. "That so-called boyfriend of his is not getting anything of Chester's. That's all they're after, you know. You never see a poor gay man. As soon as my son is dead, that leech is out the door. I don't want to upset Chester now, so I'm not going to say anything."

"I think you better go. You can pick over his bones when he is dead," Marisa growled at her.

Marisa and I were holding each other. "You kicked him out on the streets. Marisa and I have been his family. We cared for him like a real family should have. You have no right to him."

CHAPTER 13

We told Chester about what his mother had said. He amended his will later that week so that Ricky would get all of his money. Ricky didn't want to hear it; he became angry at Chester and left the room. Chester lay back on the bed and let out a breath. He didn't want to fight with Ricky, either.

"Don't worry, Chester, I'll go after him," I reassured him.

After a few moments of searching, I found Ricky sitting on a bench seat in a round garden walled by the hospital's windows. The garden was used for patients who needed a quiet place to sit. A water feature sat in the middle, with daisies planted around it. Other benches lined the wall, and furry shrubs sprouted between the seats. Ricky's head sat in his hands; he was sobbing. I put my arms around him. Ricky leant into my shoulder and let out a breath.

"You can't make me go back, Laura. I can't do this anymore." He let the words out hopelessly. He was tired; he hadn't slept or looked after himself in months. He had once been well-dressed, but now his lustre was gone.

"When I first met Chester, he sat himself down next to Marisa and me and said, 'We are going to be lifelong friends," I told Ricky, who let out a quick laugh.

"When I first met Chester, he came up to the counter and said, 'You are going to take me out and I don't care if you are dating anyone,'" Ricky said. "How can you forget someone like him? How can I live without him? Why give me someone like Chester and then take him away?" Ricky sat up, grabbed a stone and threw it into the fountain. The pebble plonked into the water.

I thought about it for a moment, trying to put together the right words. "I don't know. I heard something the other day. People like Marilyn Monroe, James Dean and Princess Diana are like comets. They all come into our lives to lighten them up, to take our breath away. The payoff is that they can't stay here for long. However, they stay forever young. John Dean, our professor, told us about soul mates. When you meet your true soul mate, you'll have a payoff there as well. You lose them early or you meet them late—there is always something. You might not be able to have a child with them, or they might be married. There is always a slight heartache. "

Ricky glanced up at me. I handed him a small packet of tissues from my pocket. I had been keeping them handy since I started coming to the hospital. I shouldn't have phoned Chester's mum. I had been hoping it would bring them together somehow. I hated the thought of my friends hurting.

"I think you're right. He is my soul mate. I hate it when he talks like that; he just blows off the fact that he is dying." Ricky wiped his eyes, then blew his nose. "His mother is no one new; so many of my other friends have lost family that way." As he tucked his tissue into his sleeve, I noticed that Ricky had well-formed hands; he could have been a hand model. It's strange what you see when you shouldn't.

"When I found Chester on the side of the road that first week at university, he just blew off the fact that he was homeless," I said. "He told me that Yul Brynner had sent a car for him; he was staying in the penthouse. His family had kicked him out and didn't want anything to do with him. He just blew it all off. It hurt him deeply, but I know that he hated even more to see *you* hurting. That's why he's blowing it off now." I kissed Ricky on the cheek. He wrapped his arms around me and we held each other for the longest time.

When Chester had first arrived at the hospital, he could slowly walk up the corridor to the canteen. The next week he couldn't walk that far; he had to go to the canteen in a wheelchair. During his last week, all Chester could do was sit in his bed. Ricky was dutiful; he would turn Chester every hour and attend to his every need. Later that week, Chester had become like a rag doll. He had been put on oxygen because his breathing had become laboured.

Marisa and I took turns caring for Ricky; while one helped him out, the other stayed with Chester. We drove Ricky home so that he could shower and change. Every time, as soon as Ricky was finished, he wanted to go back to the hospital. He was like a robot; he had no emotions. I didn't blame him, this was not time for emotions. Marisa and I kept a very close eye on Ricky. He was acting strong in front of Chester, but we were not sure how long he could keep it up.

During Chester's last days, Mum and Emily came to see him, but they didn't stay long. Chester could not hold a conversation like he used to. It was unfair to make him try, so Mum said her goodbyes knowing that this would be the last time she would see him. Emily didn't like it; she wanted her Chester better again. She had drawn butterflies for him, and he stuck them near his bed.

As we had done the first night we began caring for Chester, Emily and I came home to an empty house. I hadn't seen Paul in three weeks. Unsurprisingly, a stream of people came to see Chester, but it still amazed me to see how many people wanted to say their goodbyes. The last time we saw any of Chester's family was when his mother had come to see him a few weeks ago.

Four weeks after Chester entered the hospital, the doctor told the nurse to up his morphine. Ricky swallowed hard as the nurse injected the morphine into Chester's bag. It was later in the night when we were told that he was heading into his final hours.

"Why are there mushrooms...growing out of the walls?" Chester asked twenty minutes later. He feebly swotted at something as he spoke. "I wish these butterflies...would leave me alone. They...want to land in my ears. Emily...draws...good butterflies. Laura?" Chester met my eyes, half-heartedly swatting the butterflies away. The morphine was doing this to him.

"Yes," I answered. Chester weakly wiggled his finger at me to come closer.

"Don't…lose…my…Emily…because these butterflies…they will follow…you," he said, grinning.

I didn't understand what he was saying. "Okay," I answered to humour him.

"I'll be…watching." Chester rolled his head over to Marisa. "Tick tock…Marisa, you'll be…late, please don't wait." Marisa seemed confused by what he was saying.

Hours later, Chester lay on his bed, just breathing. Every part of what we knew as Chester was slowly slipping away. The spark that was him was being used up. He was slowly being taken away from us.

"I think this is it," the nurse told us softly as Chester drew in a long breath, some moments later.

Marisa and I left Ricky alone with Chester to give them a chance to say their goodbyes. With no more to say, Marisa and I sat silently in the hallway of the hospital. I stared into space while Marisa began turning a bracelet on her arm.

I don't know how long we sat there. Ricky came to the door and let out a breath. "It's time."

As we entered the room, I could feel death near. A cloud had come over the room; a window was open, and a steady breeze was blowing. The curtains were moving a little, as though someone were playing with them. The open window was an old tradition, one that ensured the soul would not be trapped in a room. I had read this years ago, but had never expected to see it acted out.

In the middle of the room, my friend lay nearly lifeless. His eyes slowly opened as we moved closer to the bed. Chester breathed in; it was a long second before he let out the breath. When he breathed, his whole body rattled, but not from the cold; life was leaving him.

I sat at Chester's feet. Ricky was on Chester's left side, as he had been for weeks. Marisa was at his right. The nurses were coming in every ten minutes. They studied his charts and wrote notes before taking his obis and leaving without a word. There was nothing they could do for Chester; these were his last moments.

Chester took his last breath at 10 p.m. "It was fun," were his last words.

Ricky put his face into Chester's shoulder. He could cry now. Ricky didn't have to be strong in front of Chester anymore. Chester's lifeless body lay in front of us.

"Thank you, Chester, for making me laugh," I said through my tears.

"Thank you, Chester, for driving me crazy," Marisa added, half smiling.

"Thank you, Chester…for being my lover. My soul mate." Ricky stood and kissed Chester on the lips. "It's okay now; you can go. We will miss you, but now, my love, you are as free as you ever wanted to be."

That night I once again came home to a darkened house. It felt empty, as though no one lived there anymore. Emily was staying with Mum and Dad. Slowly I flipped on the lights to prove to myself that no one was there. I felt as hollow as the house; every part of me had drained away. I had nothing left.

Every morning before going to the hospital, I had cleaned the house. I ensured that our clothes were washed and in the dryer before Emily and I left. However, tonight I noticed that, in the dining room, a chair had been moved. We didn't use that side of the table. In the kitchen, the dishwasher contained an extra coffee cup as well as two wine glasses. In the kitchen's bin was a wine bottle. We had wine in the house, but this was not the brand we normally drank. Plus, Paul usually drank beer. Who would he drink wine with? The thought bewildered me.

I followed the trail into the lounge room. The TV remotes were on the floor, but I had set them on the coffee table that morning. Paul insisted that the house always be immaculate; anything out of place stuck out like a sore thumb. I went into the bedroom. Nothing was amiss there or in the en-suite bathroom. However, in the main bathroom, the shower floor was wet and puddles were on the tiles. In the laundry, two dirty towels lay in the hamper. My good sheets were rolling around in the dryer; they were almost finished. I took in a breath and my legs went out from under me. I had taken only a step into the hallway. My face was wet; I must have been crying. My mind didn't want to think. I knew everything, but I didn't want to hear it. "Chester. Oh God, Chester. It's so unfair."

A few weeks later, Chester and Ricky's friends stood under the Harbour Bridge at the Rocks side. It was about ten minutes to 10, the hour when Chester had died. Emily held my hand while Dad and Mum stood next to me. Marisa and her family were there as well. Chester had been cremated a few weeks ago. Most of his ashes went to his family, but we were able to get some and say goodbye in our own way. His family made a fuss about it, but Chester's lawyer had helped us out. In the end, they gave in.

Now, under the Harbour Bridge, Ricky stood at the water's edge with Chester's ashes in his hands, which were shaking from grief. The number of people who had come to say goodbye to Chester was amazing. Music from *The King and I* played, just barely audible over the sound of sobbing. The group of moaners contained a mixture of female and male couples, drag queens dressed in bright colours, work mates from the museum and University, and people I didn't know. The colours of their clothing reminded me of an abstract painting.

Ricky closed his eyes and drew the urn to his lips. His mouth moved swiftly as he silently spoke to the urn. He glanced at the sky. As he opened the urn's lid, he peered down at Chester's ashes and sighed.

"We're here tonight to say goodbye to our friend. Chester Reed." Ricky's voice came out of him as though he wasn't there. "Thank you, everyone, for being here tonight to show how much we loved Chester. He would have loved this. It's all about him." Everyone laughed.

"He was given to us for a short time to show us how to shine. He is now forever young." Ricky smiled at me.

"Hear, hear," the crowd added.

"We love you, Chester," a voice said from behind us.

Marisa and I stood behind Ricky as we moved onto a jetty. A light wind stirred up around us. After a moment of hushed silence, Ricky leant over the railing and tipped the contents of the urn into Sydney's Harbour. As Chester's ashes tumbled free, people from the crowd placed paper boats with tea candles into the water to help on his journey. Individuals in the crowd spoke in whispers, saying their last goodbyes to Chester. Emily came over to help with my boat. Then she turned to Ricky and hugged him. He melted a little in her embrace.

Chester's ashes seemed to linger in the air as though they were watching the lights of the little boats. The vessels unhurriedly floated into the dark water of the harbour. The lights seemed as though they were heading into their next journey. In a carefree manner they slipped away from us and out of our lives, as Chester had done.

For the last month, Paul hadn't called to find out where Emily and I were. Em told me that he did see her the other day when he picked her up from school. After Chester's memorial, I went back to Paul's place. The kitchen clock slipped onto 2 a.m. as I waited for him to come home. It was time to talk, to find out what was really going on. Emily was staying at Mum and Dad's place.

About twenty minutes later I heard Paul's Ute pull into the garage. He stopped mid-stride as he came into the kitchen and saw me sitting at the breakfast bar. Paul was dressed in a good shirt and pants; he looked like he had been drinking.

"Hello," Paul said. "You're still up? You didn't have to wait for me. I'll be in soon. I just want to have a shower first."

I let out a laugh. "It's time to talk. I haven't slept here in weeks."

"How's your friend? Is he better yet?" Paul asked as though the words didn't mean anything.

"No, he died two weeks ago. Tonight, my family and my friends said goodbye to him." I held back the tears.

"I didn't know. I'm sorry. I've been so busy. I had to work away. You know how it is." The lies kept tumbling out of him. I had been blind for so long, but that was over.

"Is your old friend still around, the one you like to drink with?"

Paul rubbed his face in frustration. "Yeah, I'm sorry. He wants to go for a drink and I lose track of time." Paul crossed his arms, his mood changed.

"What does this friend of yours drink, Paul?"

"What all men drink, beer," he said through his teeth.

"You sure?" I asked, moving in my seat.

"Yes." He was now looking intently at me as though I had done something wrong. I was about to step over the line; I wasn't supposed to ask too many questions about his actions.

"I think you should go to bed; it's late." That was my first warning. I ignored it. Normally I would back down and play the blind wife. Not tonight. It was time to fix the mess I had gotten

200

myself into. My friends had tried to stop me six years ago. I didn't listen then, but I was listening now.

"You know," I went on. "When a woman lives in a house, she notices things that men don't. She knows how she left things. She knows if...*you*, say, stay home all day. I can walk around this house and know what *you* have done that day."

"No, I didn't know that. I think you need to go to bed, Laura." Paul was getting angry, which was my second warning to drop it. Paul's eyes hardened and his nose flared like a mad bull's.

Time was running out. I went on, my heart pounding in my ears. "The other week, after Chester died, I came back here." I took a deep breath as Chester's name came to my ears. "I was hoping that you would be here. I needed you. I had just watched a friend die. You were not here. That's when I noticed the chairs sitting out from the dining table—that was my first clue. Now stop me when I get this wrong. You and your guest had a coffee in the dining room. Then you went into the lounge room and watched TV while drinking wine." I swallowed quickly before going on. "You and your guest went to the spare bedroom; from the state of the mattress it was for quite a while. Then you and your drinking mate moved to the bathroom. From the mess on the bathroom floor, I could tell you were not alone. Then I came back tonight, and I saw that, once again, you have had someone here since then. I haven't been here since that night. This time you have been using our bed. I'm guessing that I'm right. I want to know who it is. I'll leave and then you can do what you want to do without me in your way."

"It just happened," Paul said coldly. His phone rang.

"Don't answer that, Paul," I said sharply.

Paul took his phone out of his pocket, then looked at it before placing it face down on the kitchen bench.

"Who is she, Paul? I have the right to know how much of a mug I am. How much shit I have believed from you."

201

The phone rang again. I jumped to grab it before he could. Not looking at the number, I answered it.

"It's nothing to do with you." Paul tried to take the phone off me.

I moved it away from him. "I'm speaking to my ex-husband right now. You're welcome to him when I'm finished talking."

I hung up before whoever it was could answer. I threw the phone onto the bench, looking sharply into Paul's eyes. "I have a right to know who it is. How much of a fool am I? Was it since we were together? The first time you asked me out? Did you count on Emily?"

Time was up; I knew he would kill me if I didn't finish soon. I was scared of Paul; I didn't want any more games.

"Who is she, Paul? Or should I ring back and find out that way? Who?!" I yelled.

"I'm sorry that I haven't been there for you the last couple of months. I should have been here for you," Paul said in a mocking voice.

"Who?!"

"I'm sorry, Laura," Paul said, half-smiling.

"With all of this stalling she must be someone I know. Am I right?"

Once again I could feel the tears flowing down my face. I was sick of crying.

"Jennifer," he said, glaring at me.

"Goodbye, Paul. Here, these might fit her better." I took off my rings and slammed them on the kitchen bench.

Paul came around the bench to stop me. "You're not going anywhere." He seized my arms and shook me so hard, my teeth rattled as my body moved back and forth.

"Get off me, you asshole. Go back to your whore; she's waiting for you."

I swung my knee up between his legs as hard as I could. Paul fell to the ground in a heap, knocking me off my feet. We hit the floor hard. The air in my lungs rushed out of my body, leaving me stunned for a moment. Paul rolled around, groaning in pain. Shaking off my stupor, I took my chance to escape. I pushed off the floor while trying to breathe air into my lungs. Paul gained a moment of comprehension. He lashed out his hand to seize my ankle. With one rapid yank, my legs flew out from under me. My body slammed to the floor, just missing the corner of the kitchen bench and the stools.

Holding one hand between his legs, Paul looked at me, his face turning to fury. He knocked the stools out of the way as he crawled over to me. He swung his hand in the air to hit me across the face. My body was shaking. Gasping for air, I twisted my body around to dodge the blow of Paul's hand as it swung back. He was stronger than I was. I had hurt his pride and the anger was in his eyes. I managed to kick one last blow to his head. His hands flew to his face.

"You're not going anywhere, bitch!" Paul yelled as I stumbled to my feet.

"The hell I'm not," I answered him.

Crawling commando-style across the floor, Paul ankle-tapped me, making me stumble a little. I swung out my leg. My foot landed on the side of Paul's face as I held onto the kitchen door frame. Pushing off it, I hurried out of Paul's house for the last time and ran to my car, which was just down the road.

I was breathing hard as I fumbled with my keys, which slipped through my fingers. I tried to find the car key. Paul was nowhere to be seen, but it was early in the morning and no one would see if he hit me on the head and dragged me back inside the house.

Once in the car, I locked the door to give myself a chance to settle down before driving away. My mouth was dry. I sat in the four-wheel drive, trying to swallow while gasping for air. Not wasting any more time, I started the car and began to drive. All of a sudden, a hard thump hit the back of the car; it felt like a rock. I jumped, making the car jerk as it moved forward. In the rear-view mirror I could see Paul standing in the street; he was about to throw something else. For a split second I thought about backing over him, but then I thought better of it and drove off, leaving him behind. He yelled something I couldn't hear over the engine.

The day I went back to Paul when I learned that I was having Emily, my heart had known that I was lying to myself. All this time I had kept the mess growing. He continued lying to me. I swallowed his lies like an addicted fool with the idea that Emily needed a father.

Jennifer would be happy that she had upset me once more; she would enjoy knowing that she had taken Paul away from me. She was to blame as much as Paul, as he was a married man. She knew that he was out of bounds. Any decent woman who found out would walk away. That wasn't Jennifer; she would devour anyone who was in her way. I'm sure she would walk over her own mother to get what she wanted.

It was still early when I pulled up at Mum and Dad's house. Luckily, there was no damage to the back of my car. Silently, I made my way to my old bedroom, pausing to check on Emily, who was sleeping securely in Bess's room. Knowing that she was unharmed after all that had happened, I made my way to my room. My face and body hurt, but I felt free for the first time in a long time.

I didn't need to turn on a light; I knew this space well and my body fell onto the bed. I let out a long breath to calm myself. The pain could wait. Paul wouldn't come after me here; there were too many witnesses.

Taking my necklace in my hands, I held it tight and closed my eyes.

In the dark, a strong but tender hand came to my face, I knew this touch; I had felt it before. It had been six years since I had encountered him. I hadn't dreamed of him or sung to him. I had been closed down all this time. But now, in my hour of need, my Dark Figure lay next to me and his lips came to my cheek. The warmth of his breath lingered on my skin. It felt good. I reached out my hand, but nothing was there. Understanding this, I could feel his arms tighten around me as I let out a hushed sob. I could feel him on my skin, but I was alone in the dark. His body pressed against mine. My heart felt a little hurt from my inability to respond to his touch. I gave up and enjoyed whatever was happening. I rolled onto my side while he kept holding me with his face nestled in my shoulder.

"It's over," I said as I closed my eyes. I felt safe in his arms; it felt like the place where I belonged.

A few weeks later, I hired Chester's lawyer to help me with the divorce. He was good and wasn't going to let Paul get away with anything. To my surprise, I found out that Paul owned the house outright, as well as the unit that Jennifer and the twins were living in. I had hidden my bruises with makeup. Marisa saw through it, but to her credit she didn't ask any questions. She was just happy that I had left Paul.

The night before Paul and I were to meet in the lawyer's office, Emily had gone to bed and I had a quiet moment to look over the papers.

"You should go and talk to Paul."

I jumped a little. Mum was reading the papers over my shoulder.

"Mum, it's over; he's seeing Jennifer."

She brushed aside what I had said. "Oh, don't worry about that. Married couples go through this all the time. That's nothing; go and talk to him before you do anything that will end your marriage."

"It's not nothing, Mum, it's over." I couldn't understand what Mum had just said. I remembered that she had been like this when Paul and I first broke up. Now I wasn't sure what she was doing. Something was bothering her; she had been acting strange ever since Em and I had come back. Every time she had a chance, she would tell me to go and see Paul, or she would ring him herself.

The next day, Dad and Marisa came with me to provide support. Paul sat on the other side of the table, with Jennifer beside him.

Jennifer's hand didn't stop touching Paul. She glanced up to see my reaction. It was one thing to know about this, but another to see it. She sat there like the cat that had gotten the cream. Marisa was ready to slap her, and I think I would have jumped in and held down Jennifer if Marisa needed me to. Instead, I controlled myself.

Dad was disappointed in Paul; he peered up at him with disapproval. Paul, on the other hand, gazed out the window; to him, this all seemed like a waste of time. He yawned a few times, sat back on his seat with his hands on his head, and swung the chair back and forth. We were sitting at a long, polished brown table with black high-back leather chairs. I hadn't said anything to Marisa or Dad about the night I talked with Paul. Every now and then, Jennifer whispered into Paul's ear; he just shook his head or nodded to answer her. The lawyers finally came into the room; we were in there for half the day.

Eventually, it was determined that Paul would pay money to help with Emily, while I was to be given enough to set up a new life for myself. This meant that half the money from the property sales would go to me. Paul was to have Emily on weekends. I didn't want the house or the unit; they had been discoloured with what Paul had done. I wanted a new life with an unpolluted environment in which to raise Emily.

Paul and Jennifer stood in the hallway after we had finished; we hung back to let them leave. However, when we came out, they were still there. Paul had his back to me. Jennifer smiled a little and turned to Paul to kiss him passionately on the lips. With a growl, Marisa seized my arm. Dad moved in front of me as though to guard me. Marisa hissed at Jennifer as we passed.

Later that week, I decided to talk to Emily about what was happening. I had kept it from her until now. I detested having to do this. I was hurting Emily, and there was no easy way to do this. Mum and Dad were out the day I spoke to her. Emily was playing with her dolls on the floor of my parents' lounge room. Sitting next to her, I picked up one of her dolls to comb its hair. I needed to put this right.

"Mummy?" Emily jumped in before I could speak.

"Yes, Em."

"Why don't we live at our house anymore?"

"Em, you know how things change?"

She paused to listen, tilting her head at my question. "What do you mean?"

"Well." I stopped for a moment. How was I going to do this? No one had given me a handbook about it. *How to Hurt Your Child One-O-One.* How to tell your child that her father didn't love her mother any more. Children think that mothers and fathers are always meant to be together. Letting out a breath, I quickly said, "Mummy and Daddy will not be living in the same house anymore."

"Where am I going to live?" Emily asked.

"With me."

"Can't Dad live with us?"

"No, your dad does not want to live in the same house with me anymore."

"Where are we going to live?" Her little eyes moved from side to side as she thought about what I had said.

"Well, we're going to live here for a while. I'm not sure what we will be doing next."

Emily went back to her dolls. "Mummy, why doesn't Daddy want to live with you anymore?"

"Because we don't love each other anymore."

Emily leant over and hugged me. "It's okay, Mummy, I still love you."

I smiled and said, "Thanks, Em. I love you, too."

CHAPTER 14

The next weekend, Emily and I returned from house hunting. Houses on the North Shore of Sydney were expensive. The houses in my price range were either too far from Emily's school, or were in need of renovation, which cost money that I didn't have.

As I walked into my parents' house, Mum handed me a plate of sandwiches for Dad. He was working in his shed, which meant that he was cleaning his gardening tools while watching sports on TV and having a few beers.

Emily ran into her room. Paul was taking her that night and she wanted to be ready when he arrived.

"Mum said that you haven't eaten." I announced as I placed the plate on Dad's little table.

He turned down the TV's volume and grinned at me. "How did you go?"

I pulled a face and rolled my eyes. "Same thing."

Dad turned off the TV and headed for the backyard; he paused to wait for me. Not sure what he was doing, I followed him to where he stood with his hands on his hips.

"I hate mowing this lawn. I'm too old," he told me, waving his hand over the backyard.

"Don't say that, Dad. You're as young as you feel."

He put his arm around my shoulders. "It's true, however. The house is a corner block; it's a good size. If I sold you this back part, you would still have the money you need to build a small house."

"Really?" I couldn't believe it. This would be just right. If I had to, I could sell the house later, but for now it would be mine and no one could take it from me.

"Yeah, really. Your sister can't complain because you're going to buy it. Besides, I need something to help out with my retirement." Dad grinned.

I understood that if Dad helped me out, he would have to help out Bess. Instead, if I bought the back part of the yard, it would be better all around.

Eight months later, my little home was ready. Mum and Dad seemed happy to have their house back. My home had three bedrooms, and all the rooms were a good size. The exterior had two types of coloured bricks, with light ones around the doors and windows, which I loved.

Emily and I spent our spare time going to junk shops and yard sales to find things to go in or on the house. The house had a Georgian look. Inside was a mix of old and new furniture. Emily seemed happy; she had the best of both worlds. From Mum and Dad's house, a gate led into our backyard. It was becoming a well-walked path, as Emily and Mum used it daily. No one seemed to use the front door. Everyone who knew us used the sliding door that led into the dining room and the kitchen.

Shortly after I moved into my home, Ricky couldn't face living in Sydney anymore. It reminded him too much of Chester. He was a shell of himself. Marisa, Emily, and I stood in Sydney Airport, holding onto Ricky as his plane to America was called. Ricky and Chester had always talked about moving to San Francisco. I think Ricky needed to be by the sea, but not too close to what he had lost.

"Thanks everyone, for everything. If you visit San Francisco, come and see me."

Emily gazed up at Ricky. "Please don't go. Who's going to play dress ups with me?"

Ricky bent down and took Emily's face. "Are you still my best girl?"

"Yes."

"You need to look after your mum. I still love you." A tear fell down Emily's face. Ricky was trying not to cry as he wiped it away with the back of his finger.

"You're my one and only, Em. I love you, but I need to go."

"I'll be good. When you come back we have to play Barbie," Emily said, trying to be brave.

Ricky smiled. "Good. Look after my Doctor Barbie; she's my favourite."

Emily nodded.

Ricky kissed Emily again. His plane was being announced once more. He put his arms around Marisa and me for a last hug.

"God, I'm sick of good-byes. This will be good. I need this," he said as he moved away from us.

"Bye, Ricky."

Ricky ran to his gate, gave us a quick wave, and was gone. Ricky's departure confirmed the fact that our lives had unwillingly changed.

The museum seemed hollow without Chester. Out of habit, my eyes turned to his office as I passed it. I had to check myself when the sensation of his loss came to my heart. At times it took my breath away. Plenty of people wanted to take his job, but Dr Colman, to his credit, left the position open before making a commitment to anyone.

The diaries I had found with the necklace were in a box in my office. I had forgotten about them and they had laid there for years. I had studied them a few times, but mostly I had left them overlooked and hidden away—until a week after I went back to work following Chester's death.

The office needed a good cleaning. My mind still hadn't settled after leaving Paul, so I decided to burn off my unneeded energy.

211

The diaries sat under the finds table in a shoe box, waiting for me to read them again.

Once more, I read the handwritten notes about a dig in Egypt in the 1970s. Dr Dixson and Dr Kaplan had found the tomb of a nobleman, an overseer of the Pharaoh's horses. The Pharaoh was Hatshepsut, a woman who ruled during the 18th dynasty. Females didn't become Pharaohs every day; it was a big thing back then, and when her brother came of age, he bullied her off the throne. Hatshepsut had built an obelisk that stood in front of Karnak Temple and the Temple of Horus, near the King's Valley. In Ancient Greek, the word "obelisk" means "roasting prod," and I often giggled about its meaning.

Upon reading the diaries again, I remembered that Dr John Dean had talked about a Dr Dixson when I was at University. Dr Dixson was an American Egyptologist who worked during the 1970s and 1980s. A lot of finds were credited to him, and he was quite important in the history field. I emailed Dr Dean about the diaries to learn whether the Dr Dixson they mentioned was the same one Dr Dean had talked about. Egyptologists formed a small community, and Dr Dean talked about Dr Dixson as though he was a legendary individual.

The phone rang late one night in my new home. I had just sat down after putting Emily to bed.

"Hey Laura, good to hear from you. How's Marisa?" Dr Dean's muddled accent came over the phone.

"I'm good. Marisa is doing well. Did you get the scanned copies of the diaries?"

"Yes, I've been doing some digging for you. I found that most of his finds are still in our storerooms here at the college and the Met." Dr Dean was head of the Ancient Egyptian History department at Columbia University and the Metropolitan Museum of Art in New York City.

"Is there any chance that my museum can display some of the artefacts? I've been doing some digging of my own and I think I've found the nobleman's mummy and a few of his artefacts at Sydney University, as well." I said, hoping that he would agree to the loan. Hearing his uncertain groan, I realised that he couldn't agree over the phone, so I continued. "Marisa isn't seeing anyone at the moment. I think she's been wanting to call you." Marisa needed to fall in love again, so I thought I would give them a little help along.

I heard a breathy laugh over the phone. "I've been meaning to come home to see my family. I think we can work something out." He paused, then added, "I'm sorry to hear about Chester."

I went quiet before answering him. "Thanks, Dr Dean."

After a few months of phone conversations and countless emails, we were given the exhibition. Dr Colman had jumped all over it. The way he talked, one would think that he had found the diaries and put together the exhibition himself. Marisa, was overjoyed, as her professor would be coming with the exhibition. The Metropolitan Museum of Art is one of the biggest museums in the world, and this was a big coup for Sydney.

I had to laugh when Dr Dean arrived at the museum. Marisa acted surprised to see him. Dr Dean was now close to his late 40s, and his hair had turned to salt and pepper. However, his skin was just as tan, and his eyes still crinkled when he smiled. His smile grew wider when he laid eyes on Marisa. It was all an act; they had spent the previous night together. It was good to see that Marisa had something to smile about, as it had been a long time.

"Marisa, I haven't seen you in years. It's nice to see you again," Dr Dean said. They hugged and kissed each other. Dr Dean slowly let go of Marisa. A big smile came across his face when he saw me. I had seen him the previous night while we unloaded the artefacts into the loading dock. Marisa hadn't stayed to help; she didn't want to create any fodder for the museum's gossips and Dr Colman.

213

"Laura, it's nice to see you again." Dr Dean flung out his arms as he approached for a hug.

"Hello, Professor. It's been a long time since last night." I shook my head at him.

"Oh Laura, I think you can call me John." He kissed me on the cheek as he let me go.

"Good to see you again, John," Dr Colman said, standing behind us.

John turned and shook Dr Colman's hand. "It's Dr Dean, Bill. You should know that," John corrected him.

"Oh, sorry. Dr Dean. Nice to see you again. I did a good job, don't you think? To get all this together."

"Oh yes, Laura did a wonderful job. I could always count on her in class to add a little extra. She should be doing more." John gave me a nudge; his nose was out of joint that Dr Colman had not given me a better job until now.

"I'm sorry that your colleague couldn't make it," Dr Colman added smugly.

John let air out of his nose. "He'll live." A colleague of John's was supposed to come with him, but the man had been turned back at the airport. I wasn't sure why. Because of the way John had answered Dr Colman, I felt it was not right to ask questions. When John arrived at the museum, he had not been in the mood to talk about what had happened. It had made him over an hour late to unload the artefacts, and it seemed that his opinion on the subject had not gotten any better.

It was good to see Marisa had something to smile about it had been a long time.

The week before the exhibition opened to the public, we worked together to set up the artefacts. "What's that song?" John asked one day.

214

I snapped out of the trance I had been in. "What? Oh…um…it's just something I hum sometimes."

John half-laughed. "You know, that's uncanny. I heard someone humming the same song the other day. I can't remember who it was."

Before I could say anything more, Dr Colman arrived to take over what I was doing. He tried to muscle his way in and take over the exhibition, but John wouldn't let him. There was a lot to do, and Dr Colman's assistance would have been helpful, but there was no time for a power play. John knew Dr Colman well, as they had worked together during their younger years. There had been some upset between the two of them, and it seemed that they had not gotten over it.

Each artefact had to be unpacked and placed in its showcase. The paperwork for each artefact had to be checked and double-checked. The condition of the artefact had to be graded, then the item itself had to be photographed. That photo had to be compared to the photo that came with the paperwork to ensure that the item had not been stolen or damaged.

Slowly, as the week passed, the Special Exhibition room came together. The centrepieces were the treasures of the nobleman Hepra's tomb, which Dr Dixson and Dr Kaplan had found. One of the nicest pieces, I thought, was a golden bridle and whip, which had been given to Hepra for his service to the Pharaoh. The mummy of the nobleman Hepra had laid in Sydney University's basement, but now he had come to life once more. He was sitting in a place of pride in our exhibition room.

Black-and-white photos of Dr Dixson and Dr Kaplan lined the walls of the room. Enlarged text from the diary was posted on the wall near the photos. The rooms curved into separate areas to highlight all the artefacts. The notebooks I had found at Paul's house six years ago stood in their own case next to the mummy. Dr Kaplan had once owned Paul's house, but had died years ago. Dr Dixson had died a year before John went to New York.

215

I didn't tell anyone about the necklace. I had read the two diaries from cover to cover, but found no mention of it. The tomb inventory made no mention of a scarab, either. It had been made into a necklace, and no one was going to miss it. No one even knew about it, so I didn't feel too guilty.

On the night of the opening, Marisa couldn't stop beaming. We were holding a preview to wine and dine our guest from New York, and also to thank the museum's stockholders, thereby ensuring that the money would keep flowing. Dr Colman lived for these events; he stalked around the museum all night. Holding his glass just so, he told the same jokes to different groups of people. He brought out his Hawaiian shirt for these events, and his stomach stuck out over his white pants. His booming laugh could be heard over the crowd's chatter.

In his suit jacket and dress pants, John was a strange sight, as he usually wore button-down shirts and daggy cotton pants. John and Marisa kept giving each other glances and standing close all night. Without thinking, Marisa wiped dip off his face. One wouldn't know that they had been apart for so long. I made a vow to myself that I would get the two of them together. I knew it wouldn't be hard. After what I had gone through with Paul, I couldn't stand the fact that the two of them didn't see what they really had together.

Attending these types of parties by myself was difficult. Paul had never come to such events, as he was always away. Now, however, I had an excuse as to why I was alone; it was because I was no longer married.

"Mummy, you look good," Em had told me earlier that evening while bouncing on the bed.

"Thanks, baby." I kissed her good night in my old bedroom in Mum and Dad's house.

I had to be at the museum, sucking up my pride and keeping a smile on my face. It was my job to butter up all the stockholders and benefactors so that they knew why they had spent their money to bring all these artefacts to the museum. They seemed happy; there were smiles all around and everyone was content.

"How are you doing?" Judith asked. She rubbed my arm, seeming concerned.

"Good, Judith."

"That's good." She nodded before moving off into the crowd. It had been a hollow concern, but I was acting happy tonight, so what did it matter? Then I thought about the way Chester had lit up on nights like this, and my heart turned.

As the night progressed, everyone mingled in their own groups. I stood at the back of the room, drinking a glass of red wine next to a bust of Ra. I finished my last mouthful and got ready to leave. My job was done and fresh air sounded good. Backing away and walking out the back door, I made my way out of the museum. No one noticed.

Sandringham Garden is in Hyde Park, across the road from the museum. It looked like a Roman ruin and wasn't the best place to be at night. Homeless people slept in the bushes and the dark part of the park. Lately, I had found myself walking off in a daze, deep in thought. This place was just as good as any for walking and nursing my broken heart.

For Marisa, the month that John was in town was over all too soon. Though she wouldn't say much, I knew she didn't like the fact that John was leaving. I half expected that Marisa would go with him, but she didn't. I think she was holding out for the following year, when our museum would be sending us to New York with the same exhibition we had just shown. John had ensured that Dr Colman would put me in charge, with Marisa assisting. We would be staying for one month, just like John had, and Emily would stay with Mum and Dad while I was gone. This was hard for me, as I still didn't fully trust Mum.

The night after John left, I sat at my dining table. It was small, but I had just enough room to catch up on my work and read

217

emails. I received a message from the museum, seeking employees who wanted to go to Egypt to work during the digging season. I read the details and looked at photos of the previous trip.

"You should go."

I jumped and turned around. "Dad!"

"Sorry love, I didn't mean to scare you. Your mother wanted me to return your dish. I used my key." Dad read over my shoulder again. "You should go."

"I can't," I said, taking the dish off him and placing it in the dishwasher. "Do you want a coffee? Tea?"

"Why not? No, wait, your mother has apple pie cooking. I'm not staying." Dad stretched his body and dropped his hands, rubbing his belly to show his satisfaction about the treat he would be receiving.

"Because I'm going to New York next year for a month." I pointed at the hallway that led to Emily's bedroom.

"So?" Dad crossed his arms and frowned at me.

"It's not fair on you and Mum. It's only a few months away, and I'll be in Egypt for three weeks."

"So?"

I looked at Dad. "You don't mind if I go?"

"Don't mind? Go! I know this is what you've always wanted to do, and who knows; you might have fun. Put your name down." He paused. "I should get back. Good night. Put your name down."

"Night, Dad." He kissed me good night then pointed at the computer.

That night in my dreams:

This time I was sitting in a wing-back chair, watching the fire in the large fireplace in front of me. The fire was the only colourful thing. The fireplace was black and white. The walls were black, as was the background. The fire was the only light in the room. It highlighted My Dark Figure, who was sitting in a chair on the other side of me.

"I've missed you," I said.

"I have missed you as well. Things are changing," My Dark Figure said.

"Yes, I know. Why are we doing this?"

"Do you ever wonder?"

"All the time." I sighed.

"The path always goes somewhere, but not always to the ending we want. That's the game we have to play. The soul has to play this game of endless starts and endings to get to the finish."

I rose from my chair and walked over to My Dark Figure. I sat down next to him and put my head onto his lap. He stroked my hair softly; it felt good.

"Life goes on. It always needs to keep moving. It can't stand still," My Dark Figure continued. "Look."

I lifted my head slowly, keeping my chin in his lap, to see where he was pointing. The back wall had fallen away. I could see the bank of the Nile and, on the river, the triangle-shaped sails of the boats. An ibis walked into the room. The light from outside dazzled my eyes. It was hard to focus. The ibis came close to us and tapped its beak on the floor.

"I want to go, but Emily needs me." Tears rolled down my face. My Dark Figure wiped them away gently. The overwhelming need to be in Egypt overpowered me.

"I'm here," My Dark Figure said. "You need to go; you need to find yourself again. Our souls are ready now. I need you; come to me."

The alarm clock screamed, pulling me out of my dream. I rolled onto my back and wiped my eyes, which were wet from tears. I hated waking from these dreams; it hurt too much.

That morning, I took Emily to school, then took the train to work. I was still a little spaced out, and my thoughts drifted back to my dream. I couldn't help it. The words spoken—the words of My Dark Figure—echoed in my mind.

A man sat down heavily next to me and woke me from my daydream. He took a magazine from his bag and began flicking through it. He stopped at an article about Nefertiti's Temple and what it would have looked like in ancient times. John and Dr. Dixson had found this temple some years back; it was a big thing in the world of Egyptian archaeology.

I turned my head and looked out the window. The train had stopped at a station where a billboard stood, advertising perfume. The sticker on the perfume bottle looked like a pyramid, and the model in the ad sat next to palm trees.

The train started moving slowly. A wall covered in graffiti passed my window. One of the drawings was a cartoon of King Tut. It had something written underneath it.

"You go girl."

When the train arrived at my stop, I was happy to leave. I started walking and kept my head down, as I didn't want to see any more signs.

"You okay?" Marisa asked later that morning. Marisa was in the North Basement, looking at hummingbirds. She frowned when I almost dropped a pot.

"What are you doing a few months from now?" I asked, carefully putting away the pot.

"Nothing. Why?"

"Do you want to go to Egypt?"

220

She grinned. "I thought you would never ask."

"Do you want to go or not?"

"John's heading this one and I was going to drag you kicking and screaming," Marisa said, narrowing her eyes. She seemed more pleased that John would be there, not me.

I shook my head. "Like I'm going to see you; you're going to be *busy*." Then I changed the subject. "Do you want to go shopping at lunch? We need something to wear. All my old digging clothes died long ago."

"Also, we need something to wear when we go out. And you'll see me; I have to work and we have to eat." She grinned.

As soon as I got back to my office, I replied to the email. Later, while shopping, Marisa and I chatted as we looked for everyday clothes to wear during our trip. Our destination being Egypt, we needed to ensure that our clothes were appropriate for the country.

"Marisa?"

"Yes?"

"Did Dad talk to you about taking me to Egypt?"

A guilty expression crossed Marisa's face.

"Well?" I asked again as she looked down. "Go on. Say what you need to say."

"Your dad had something to do with it, but that's not it. Since you married Paul…no, since you met Paul…you've forgotten how to be you."

"Be me?" I asked.

"Yeah. You seem not to be you anymore. It's as though you've forgotten how to be you. You don't sing anymore. I don't think I've seen you space out in years. Also, the way you dress…"

"What's wrong with the way I dress?" I looked down at myself.

"You were more relaxed, but now you dress the way he wanted you to. It's like 'Snobby Mum.' When we lost Chester, and with you leaving Paul, you seemed to lose yourself even more. Your dad was hoping that if you go, you might find yourself again. Don't get angry with him."

"'Snobby Mum,' that hurts. I have a daughter now. Being a mum, things have to change."

"Yeah, I know. But that spark you had…you lost it somewhere. I think Paul slowly sucked it out of you. When was the last time you sang with The Band? Laura, you can have a spark and still be a mum. That's why I was going to make you go. You never went back to University to study archaeology; something always came up. Your dad is worried about you. And I'm sorry about the 'Snobby Mum' thing."

"It's alright; I think the universe wants me to go."

"What do you mean?" Marisa stopped what she was doing to watch my expression.

"It's nothing, just a dream I had last night." I had been thinking that this trip would make Marisa happy, but everyone was conspiring to make me happy instead.

"Oh goody, a dream! I love weird dreams. Tell me everything."

I waved it off. "Don't worry, I know what it means."

"Spoilsport." Marisa grumbled.

I didn't want to tell Marisa about My Dark Figure. She would see it as a bad omen, and that was the last thing everyone needed to know. The Figure didn't have any bad vibes. Everything boiled down to the fact that I needed a holiday and I was going nuts. Besides, My Dark Figure was mine; I didn't want to share him.

That night, Emily stood in the kitchen, her arms crossed and a frown on her face. "Why can't I go, Mummy?" she pouted. This had lasted for half an hour. Emily was not letting it go. She thought she could wear me down, but it wasn't working.

"Because this is a work thing and you need to stay here."

"I can come and help with the digging. I helped Grandma and Grandpa Gibson last time I was at their farm. I helped dig a hole for the tree they were planting."

"This is a different type of digging, Em. I need you to stay here and care for Grandma and Grandpa Sinclair."

Emily plonked herself onto a chair in the dining room and crossed her arms for a second time. She was trying to hold her breath. I walked over to her and poked her cheeks; a rush of air came out of her mouth.

"This is so unfair. I want to go." She scowled at me, her brown eyes burning so much I could almost feel the heat. I waited for her head to spin around and for her to start talking in tongues. Kids know just where to hit you. You feel guilty for leaving them in the first place, and they know how to make you feel even worse.

Throughout the next few days, when I least expected it, Emily tried to convince me to take her to Egypt. "Mum, I'm willing to give up school for three weeks. My teacher thinks it will be good for me and I can show photos and slides to my class when I come back," she told me one day after school.

"I'm the adult and you can't come with me. I'll bring you home something nice."

Paul wouldn't have let me take her for so long. At least I had peace of mind that Dad would be caring for her. However, I knew how Mum could be, and that worried me. I tried to get Mum to reinsure me but it was useless, she was not listening.

223

CHAPTER 15

Before long, I was leaving. Marisa and I had a non-stop 14-hour flight to Cairo. Because we were traveling for work, we were able to fly business class, I slept a little on the plane.

The next morning we arrived in Cairo, were we would be staying for two days. The next night, we would travel to Luxor by train. After our 12-hour train ride, we would travel across the Nile to Thebes and join up with John's team.

Walking out of the airport, we were hit with the busyness and smell, of Egypt. It was a mixture of dust, herbs and petrol fumes. High-pitched horns blew as traffic hurried by. A minibus waited to take Marisa and me to the Sphinx Hotel, where students and professors stayed while in Cairo. After we boarded, the bus driver gave us a white-knuckle ride to the hotel. He seemed to be attached to the car horn, using it as a driving aid as he wove through the hectic streets.

Marissa and I were sharing a room, which was fine. The room had two double beds and a bathroom. Marisa hurried to the bed on the far side of the room and threw her bags beside it. I flopped down on the other bed, my body still rattling from travel. The minibus ride still playing in my head; it seemed that everyone drove the same way here.

The bed slumped in the middle; this was no five-star hotel. However, the room was clean and the bed was soft. A large wooden fan dangled from the ceiling. The walls were painted white, and wood panelling wrapped around the room. A mini-fridge sat opposite the beds, as did a counter where one could make coffee or tea.

"Coffee?" I asked Marisa.

She was taking clothes out of her bag. "I'm going to have a quick shower. You go ahead; I'll make something after I'm finish."

Once alone the urge to see the city over whelmed me. Wanting a bird's eye view I stepped onto the balcony, with my drink in hand. The noise and herbal smell of the street rose to greet me. The balcony was in the shade, it felt cool. A light fog sat across the city, giving everything a grey glow. This time of year was much cooler; most excavations were done during the early part of the year.

I could see the Pyramids from the balcony, and the sight took my breath away. They lay across the Nile from where we were, but were still massive. I tried to take it all in so that I could remember everything. Many people of history has seen these buildings, I had a theory that most large ancient buildings like Stone Henge were built because of them.

"Wow, that's worth it," Marisa said from behind me.

I nodded and looked around, I was smiling as I let out a sigh. We had only a few days in Cairo, so we had to see all the sights today and tomorrow. Marisa handed me the camera. I could have stood there all day.

"See, I knew it was going to put a smile on your face. It's nice to see you smiling again," Marisa said.

I grinned, then quickly took a photo of her. I took another one of the view. "The Pyramids are bigger then you think. You see them in pictures, but seeing them for real is a different story."

"So, what do we do? Eat or go to the museum?" Marisa asked.

"We eat, then go to the museum."

"Good idea."

The waiter handed us menus as we sat at one of the tables in the hotel dining room. He was dressed in a white gallibaya and a black waistcoat and turban. He smiled as he waited for us to order. The dining room was large and set up with round tables that had white tablecloths. Pillars dotted the room, and the wallpaper was decorated with Islamic designs. The floors were covered with

225

sandstone-coloured tiles, while thick curtains dressed the arched windows.

"Salaam aleikuum," I said to the waiter, giving him the formal Arabic greeting.

"Aleikuum salaam," he replied.

I looked at Marisa. "Do you want tea first? Then we can order something to eat."

"Yes, that's a good idea."

"Itneen shay afwaan." *"Two teas, please."*

Contented after eating, we made our way through the streets, where the madness had not quieted down. Cars were not the only form of transportation on the streets; a few horses and carts passed as we headed to the museum.

The black iron gates that wrapped around the front of the museum greeted us. I felt like I was walking into a church as I stepped into the outside courtyard. Excited, I began taking photos. The museum's limestone steps stopped me. My heart was racing and I felt a little scared, as though something were about to happen. To calm myself, I ran my hand over the white blocks to feel their power. I had seen this museum so many times on the Internet, and now I was here.

Inside the museum, a large pool of water sat in the middle of the ground floor; its purpose was to maintain moisture levels so that the artefacts didn't dry out. Islamic designs were set into the museum's tiles and the pool floor. The top-level glass roof allowed dull sunlight to float through and highlight dust particles. Light flooded the main area, giving the museum a magical feel.

The place was busy. People moved around, breaking the dusty light every now and then as they walked through the building. A cloud of women in black burqas glided past me as my eyes adjusted. I blinked, just beyond the women, I was sure I had seen My Dark Figure.

226

"Come on, you. If you're going to do that every time, we aren't going to see anything." Marisa tugged on my sleeve to snap me out of my daydream. "You were humming. You okay?" She seemed smug that I had been humming.

"I'm fine." I flashed Marisa a guilty smile as she dragged me away. We gradually made our way through the large square rooms, examining the artefacts in their glass cases. I felt like a kid in a candy shop. I kept having "wow" moments when I saw in real life things that I had previously seen only in books, or on TV or the Internet.

My heart began pounding when we entered the room with Tutankhamen's treasures. I saw a few things that were in the book I had found a lifetime ago at the school fair. Marisa understood why I was acting the way I was, and left me to have my moment. Something in a small case had caught her eye.

I went over to Tut's death mask, which stood in the middle of the room. People crowded around it, but I managed to get close. My eyes ran over its details. I admired the workmanship and the blue stone on its headdress. It was a lot brighter than it had been in any photo I had seen; the gold gleamed brightly. Tut's kingly beard sat a little to one side, not dead straight. 'If you were about three thousand years old, you wouldn't sit so straight either,' I told myself.

A feeling came over me, the sensation that someone was watching me from beyond the display cabinet. To my surprise, a pair of blue eyes was studying me from the other side of the case. My heart skipped a beat as I met the eyes, which belonged to a tall man.

He seemed younger than I was, but I wasn't sure how young. His eyes were shining and his mouth was trying not to smile. He was western and, I think, an American. His dark blond hair was cut short, and it looked like he hadn't shaved in a few days. He was very handsome.

227

His eyes were playful. It seemed he was enjoying watching me, which unnerved me a little. My heart beat faster. I didn't know why, I took a breath to steady myself. Then I realised: I had never acted this way before, which is why I was unsettled.

To calm myself down, I turned my eyes away from him. I tried to focus on the mask, but my mind was racing, screaming at me, "WHO IS HE?!" I fought the question. I could still feel his eyes watching me. My cheeks had gone red. I was about to shift my eyes back to see if he was still there, but I stopped myself. I lowered my eyes and turned to another case.

Marisa hadn't finished looking in the room and was contentedly spending time reading the information on the artefacts. I slowly moved to another tall case in the corner of the room. Inside was a golden fan, one of Tut's. It once had feathers, but they had rotted away.

I took a quick glance over my shoulder to see if the man was still there. My heart sank a little, as he was nowhere to be seen. I feared that I would never see him again. Not using my head, I hurried out of the room. I saw no sign of him in the walkway.

I sighed and touched my cheek, trying to rub away the blush while I walked into another room. It had been a long day and I was being silly.

A large statue stood at the far wall of the room. It had large thighs, and its arms were thin and weak-looking, a style not typical for this time. The limestone statue was of Akhenaton. He towered over me, the expression in his eyes intense. Akhenaton was Tutankhamen's father.

"It's a statue of Akhenaton." A voice came from just behind me.

My whole body shuddered at the sound, as though I were being turned on for the first time. Steadying myself, I nonchalantly glanced over to see who was talking to me. It was the man from the other room. He seemed taller and he stood just near me, as though he had always been there, just waiting for me to turn around.

I felt as though every moment of my life had been leading up to this. I tried to shake it off, for the thought unnerved me. Who was this man?

"Yes, that's what the sign said," I said teasingly, pointing and trying to sound calm.

He gave a little laugh at my answer and nodded; the smile hadn't left his lips. "His wife was Nefertiti. They changed Egypt when he came to rule," he said, pointing to the statue.

"Oh, I've heard of Nefertiti. I don't see the bust that they show on TV and books." I looked around, trying to play along.

"It's not here. That's in Berlin's museum," he said as though trying to teach me.

"Oh, silly me. I'm in the wrong country," I said, slapping my forehead. I knew what country the bust was in, and he seemed to be enjoying our game. He smirked at my joke.

"I hope you don't leave this country yet. We've just met." He was still smiling at me.

"So, why is this statue different from the others? It's all deformed." I knew the answer to that one as well.

The man gave me a double look before answering. "Well, as I said, Akhenaton changed a lot of things when he came to rule. He changed the art as well as the religion. He also changed from many gods to one god."

I knew all these things, but being on holidays, I wanted to have some fun. If a handsome 20-something was going to flirt with me, I wasn't going to stop him. His voice sounded like that of My Dark Figure; I tried to push the thought out of my head.

"What hotel are you staying at?" he asked.

"They say that we Australians are to the point, but you Americans are more so," I murmured.

"What did you say?" he asked.

I shook my head, not wanting to repeat myself. I knew he had heard me. "You're not going to wine and dine me? Just right to the hotel for some holiday sex, then we're over. Anyway, what's not saying you're some type of mass murderer on holidays looking for your next victim?"

He chuckled. "Okay, at least leave me with a name. I need to know."

"I've only been in the country for a few hours." I put my hands on my hips. "No."

He threw his hand to his heart, acting as though I had hurt him. "I've just given you a free history lesson; you can't give me a name?"

He moved closer. I could feel his breath on my face, and my shoulder could feel the heat from his body. Oh God, I wished he hadn't done that. My knees felt as though they were about to go out from underneath me.

"You know, Mr. American History Teacher, you're too young for me," I said softly.

He studied my face and his head moved a little at my words. It seemed as though he had been lost in a dream. "If I wasn't too young for you, which I don't think I am, Miss No Name Australian, would you have dinner with me?"

He lifted his hand to touch my face, but stopped himself. It seemed as though he was going to say something, but didn't know how to say it. He smiled sweetly. An unseen force seemed to be holding us in this spot. The world didn't matter anymore. If this had been the end of the world, I would have been perfectly fine.

He continued. "Because you've only just gotten off the plane, I'll go easy on you. I think you need a good wining and dining, but only with me," he said in a playful tone.

"If I had met you after being here for a few days, then maybe I would have dinner with you," I said.

His eyes sparkled as he took a breath through his nose. He pulled himself up to his full height of over six feet. I grinned at him, not knowing what he was doing.

"Another chance meeting. Mmm, I like that. If you're feeling the way I feel at this moment, then I'll take that chance. If we meet up in a few days, I'm going to take you out for dinner. You're not going to say no. Then you're going to have to tell me your name." He watched me for a moment. I felt myself smiling.

He took my hand and kissed it. My whole body screamed at the feel of his lips on my skin. I kept telling myself, 'I don't know this man.'

Somehow, he seemed to understand what was in my mind. He raised his hand once more, and this time tenderly stroked my cheek with the back of it. We remained there a lot longer then we should have. It was as though I knew him, as though he were an old friend. I think people were moving past us, but I wasn't sure.

"Goodbye, Mr. American History Teacher," I said softly, finally able to say something as I looked into his soft blue eyes.

He took a moment, as though trying to understand what I had just said. "I'll see you in a few days. Good-bye 'till then, Miss No Name Australian," he said as softly as I had spoken.

He let go of my hand, turned, and left the room. I tried to stop myself from running after him.

"Crap," I said under my breath, my head was still spinning. I wanted to go after him. I wanted to tell him my name, my phone number, my home address, what hotel I was staying at, and where I was going in a few days. I felt as though I wouldn't see him again.

However, I stopped myself. I let out my breath slowly. My heart was pounding in my ears.

I glanced up to see Marisa, who was looking over her shoulder to where my mystery man had gone. She came up to me with a stunned expression. "Who was that?" she asked.

"Um…um…um…I don't know. I didn't get his name. But if he finds me in the next few days, we're going on a date…I guess."

Marisa slapped me on the shoulder; the sound echoed throughout the room. "We've been here in Cairo for only a few hours and you're getting picked up by younger guys. You cougar."

"Marisa, stop it. In a few days we'll be in Thebes; he'll never find me. Come on, let's go and see the rest of the museum before it closes."

"You mean before you go running after him and tell him where we're staying?" Marisa grinned at me.

I snarled at her and pulled her out of the room. "Marisa, I hate it when you're right," I groaned.

The next morning we were still jet-lagged, so we took our time before going anywhere. That afternoon we travelled to the Pyramids via the hotel bus, which stopped at a few other hotels on the way. By the time we drove up the tarred road to the Pyramids, my ears were ringing from having listened to a British mother and father trying to calm down their kid, who had been running up and down the bus the entire way. Marisa rolled her eyes at me when the little boy screamed as his father dragged him off the bus.

Pleased to get away from the family, we hurried to the Sphinx and Cheops Temple.

Your mind conjures an idea of how big something is, but when you see it for real, it's either much bigger or much smaller. The Sphinx was larger than I thought it would be; its watchful face towered over us. I laid my hands on its paws to feel the sensation. I thought I could feel a slight tingles in my fingers.

232

As we walked around, the hawkers played their parts as though performing in a well-rehearsed production. Throughout the open-air museum, they jostled trinkets we didn't need, at us.

Out of the blue, a man hurried up to us. "This you will love." He had a badly carved Shabti. "It's real, it's old, you buy." He shoved it in my face.

I pushed it back, shaking my head at him. "It's not real," I replied, trying to move away.

He nodded, shoving it back. "You buy, you buy. It's real…lot of money."

Marisa gave me a sideways glance; she could see that it wasn't real.

"I'm an archaeologist; I should tell the museum what you have," I told the man.

Without a word, he hurried away, thinking that we were going to get him into trouble. My words didn't stop the other hawkers, who got pushy. As we walked around, I found myself saying "no" in English and Arabic.

A few times throughout the day, Marisa caught me humming. "This is the most I've heard you humming," she said.

I just grinned at her. I was having a good time. I was happy, the time the light show on the Pyramids started, we had managed to see everything. A set of stone steps had been made up for people to sit on while they watched the show. The large crowd contained a mixture of cultures. Everyone sat shoulder to shoulder on the stone steps waiting for the show to begin.

"You know what?" Marisa asked as she took two bottles of water and a package of crackers from her bag. She handed me one of the bottles.

"Thanks," I said. "And what?"

"Chester would have loved this."

233

"Chester didn't like sand," I said as I opened my bottle of water.

Marisa giggled. "No, I'm not talking about being here. I'm talking about what happened yesterday." She chewed on a cracker, waiting for my reaction.

"Oh. He wouldn't have let that go, wouldn't he?" I smiled.

"He would have loved the fact that you've been looking over your shoulder since then."

"I've lost the plot, haven't I?" I was feeling a little childish.

"No, you're just having fun. It's good to see, for a little while anyway. And tomorrow we'll be in Thebes working with John and I'll have a secret smile on my face, too."

"Ooh, lucky you." I teased.

"That's none of your business." Marisa smiled.
We both snickered as the lights started on the Pyramids.

CHAPTER 16

The next day, our bags waited in the car that the hotel had sent to take us to the train station, which was a little way from the Pyramids. Inside, Ramses train station looked like a church and reminded me of Central Station in Sydney. The different platforms were packed with people, and I found myself searching the crowd as I had done yesterday. Women dressed in burqas seemed to float by me; they reminded me of a group of nuns.

his was everyday life in Cairo. Some of the men dressed in the Western style – shirts and long pants. Others wore turbans and gallibayas, which were white pants and long shirts that fell to the knees. They always looked washed and pressed, and I was impressed at how white they were. I had many articles of white clothing that I had given up on because they had stopped being so white. Many women wore the latest fashions, but there were no outrageous clothing styles here. Marisa and I were dressed the same way; we were Western women and didn't want to create unnecessary upset because of what we wore.

Our train to Luxor was called, first in Arabic, then in French, then in English. Marisa and I hurried down the platform. The luggage cars carried a mixture of boxes, luggage, and livestock – chickens, ducks in crates, some goats, even a young donkey. In the cheaper cars I saw a few people carrying goats and other livestock with them. I smiled when I saw a little black goat lying like a baby, asleep in a woman's arms as she climbed aboard. Egypt, like India, was never short of people.

In our first-class carriage, a conductor met us just inside the entrance. He smiled as we handed over our tickets. The museum had paid for second-class fare, but when Marisa and I saw what it looked like on the Internet, we paid the extra for a first-class sleeper for both ways.

"Very good; this way." The conductor pointed down the train's walkway.

We lumbered our bags to our cabin. Once we had settled in, we relaxed in our seats, waiting for the train to leave on its overnight journey to Thebes. After the final warning over the loudspeaker, the train roared to life. As it moved, it rocked from side to side. Then, with a final jerk, the train began its journey.

Later that night we left our cabin to find the dinner car. It was romantic; the first-class cars had their own dining car, with white tablecloths and fine china. The tables each had four chairs and ran down either side of the car. A small bar sat in the corner. The scene reminded me of an old black-and-white movie.

Eating dinner and sipping wine, we watched the lights of Cairo fade away. I was excited; this would be the best time I had had in a while. However, I also felt a little sad that I hadn't seen *him* again. *He* would forever be just a moment in the museum, one that had happened a long time ago.

After dinner, we changed for bed. I had drunk a few wines with dinner and had a light buzz. The cabin was small. A three-seater sat along the wall, hiding our beds. The carpet and curtain were beige. Our beds had been pulled out for us, and we climbed to the top bunk, giggling like schoolgirls. We had been chatting like old hens since we had come back from dinner.

I was digging in my bag when my hand brushed something cold. I pulled it out and showed it to Marisa. She grinned. It was the duty-free bottle of scotch that I was saving for Dad. Marisa dug into her own bag and pulled out novelty coffee cups with prints of Isis on them.

"I'll have to buy Dad another bottle. Once it's open, we'll have to finish it. It's going to die a good death," I said as I poured first Marisa, then myself, a glass.

"Aunt May won't mind that I'm using her coffee cups," Marisa said.

After the third glass, the giggling wouldn't stop. We became chattier as I poured us each another glass.

"Here's to Chester. We miss you and love you." Marisa held her cup in the air.

"Here's to Chester. And here's to Paul. Hopefully Jennifer shows her true colours and Paul sees what she is really like…and versa- vicer," I said, kneeling on the bed with my cup in the air. I knocked back my drink as the train jerked to one side.

"Isn't it 'vice versa'? I'm sure that's what we learnt at school or something. Anyway…yes, Jennifer, you home-wrecking hussy. Also to that not-so-good-in-bed ex-husband of yours. Chester was right, wasn't he? Paul was never good in bed, was he?" Marisa swallowed her drink, her voice slurred. She watched me for a moment, then drunkenly waved away the question, as I hadn't answered it. She filled our glasses again, pointed her finger at me, and smiled. "Here's to your Mystery Man; here's hoping he finds you again." Marisa smiled wider. "Yes, she needs to get some. After having Paul for six years, you need a good shag."

"Marisa, we're in a conservative country. You can't say that." I slapped at her and missed.

"Oh come on, Laura, we're drunk in a conservative country, you know you want him. Who wouldn't want that tall, attractive, mysterious stranger? Everything a woman wants. Shove a woman's brain in there like they do in books and he would be perfect. Some women lay there at night and dream about men like that. He was about to do you right there in the museum. If you don't want him, I'll have him." Marisa swayed her hips from side to side. The train jolted and she fell in a heap on the bed, though she managed to save her cup. She burst out laughing.

"Greed is a sin, Marisa," I said. "Well, here's to John. Hopefully he's as good as you don't say he is. Here's hoping you two finally realise that you're made for each other. Bloody well get married."

237

Marisa opened one eye; she seemed shocked at what I had said. "I've never said anything about him."

"That's my point. He must be good if you don't want to share the details. And get married you belong to each other."

I was right. Marisa moved onto her knees and sat back on her feet. Filling her cup, she let out a sigh. I giggled at her and she glanced up at me.

"We're drunk," I continued. "It's okay, you're back together. Don't let him go." I began to sing, a little louder than I should have. Marisa nodded; she knew that I was right.

We finally wore ourselves out and slept well. Sleeping on a train is an art; it feels as though you're sleeping upside down.

The next morning, the sun was bright. We moved slowly as we departed at Luxor. I needed my sunglasses when we stepped off the train.

A driver met us at the Luxor station and once again madly drove us to a car ferry that would take us across the Nile to Thebes. My head was spinning. I wanted so much to enjoy this part, if only my head would let me.

After another bone-crunching ride along and down the side of the Nile, we pulled into the hotel car park just before lunch. I was happy to get out, as my head was rattling from the constant horn blowing. The way Marisa twisted in her seat, I knew that John must have been waiting for us. My stomach was turning on me too much to care. I needed more sleep and something to eat; in which order, I didn't know.

Marisa leaped out of the four-wheel drive and ran into John's arms. I slid out slowly from the other side, taking my time to give John and Marisa a chance to say hello.

When I reached John, he lifted my sunglasses and smiled. He shook his head and made a clicking sound. He was too bright and noisy; his teeth seemed to gleam.

"You don't look well. You look like you need to sleep more. Trains are not that bad to sleep on," he joked.

"Thanks, John. It's nice to see you, too."

John hugged me with one arm; he hadn't let go of Marisa. "Good to see you, Laura." When he let go of me, I saw who was standing behind him and took in a quick breath.

A few feet behind John was my Mystery Man, who had a playful, smug expression on his face. Marisa had seen him too. She grinned behind her hand before taking a swift glance back at him. She made a sly face at me. If I were closer to her, I would have hit her.

"Crap," I said under my breath. I wasn't ready for this. I was hungover. Oh well, he would take a second look now and leave me alone. He was too young for me anyway.

I lowered my head so that I could hide behind my cap and sunglasses. I wanted to make a run for it, but I didn't know where I was. I remembered my bags and turned back to the four- wheel drive. The driver had dumped them on the ground behind the car, leaving us to carry them into the hotel.

I began fumbling with my bags; as I dropped my carry-on, a hand reached out from nowhere to grab it.

"Here, I'll give you a hand, *Laura.*"

I jumped. My Mystery Man was standing a lot closer than I had thought he was. I liked the way he said my name. Over the top of my sunglasses, we made eye contact. It seemed like only a moment that we had been apart.

"Um, thank you. That would be nice," I said, standing back and breaking our eye contact so that he could pick up my bags.

I was trapped, with the Nile on one side and the desert on the other. The driver was nowhere to be seen. No way could I run for it. My Mystery Man knew that I was cornered; without another

239

word, he moved toward the hotel. Defeated, I trailed behind him, taking a backward glance at Marisa and John. They were talking rapidly, probably updating each other about my Mystery Man.

My Mystery Man held the door and waited for me to catch up. Once I was in the lobby, he swiftly moved past me. This was the Kings Valley Hotel. It and the Lotus Hotel next door were set up for students and professors. It was close to – and a good centre point for – most digs.

It was also in need of renovation it seem like it was in its original state. I noticed that I was standing on a cracked floor tile, but everything looked clean and the staff seemed friendly. There were a few students in the lobby, standing around and talking to each other. A few of the girls looked at my Mystery Man, then at me. They put their heads together to talk as they went into another room. I didn't blame them; he was handsome. He put down my bags to check me in. I stood back and looked around.

The floor was covered with reddish ochre tiles. The male hotel staff wore white gallibayas, red fezzes, and red waistcoats. The long front desk was made from the same dark wood that covered the back wall, which held brass hooks for keys and square mailboxes for mail. White pillars held up the roof. A row of phones stood on the far wall, which, like the other walls, was painted white. Two large wooden doors led to the dining room, which was busy with people coming and going. My stomach rumbled at the thought of food. On the other side of the lobby was an elevator. I watched it all as my Mystery Man booked me in.

This way," he said when he finished. He ushered me to the elevator. "Your room is 273. It's the woman student's area. Male staff are not allowed up there, but since you're not feeling well, I'll take you up." He moved the keys around in his hand.

"Thanks." I wanted to tell him that it was just a hangover. Students glanced at me as they passed. For some reason, it seemed to be a big deal that he was talking to me. He didn't take any notice of it.

After a few awkward moments during which we waited near the elevator, the door slid open. My Mystery Man held out his hand, indicating that I should enter first. I nodded in gratitude as he followed me in. The doors glided shut, we were alone and out of ear shot of others.

He was being nice, and I was out of practice in terms of flirting so. I decided to, as the Americans said, "take the bull by the horns," and turned to him.

"Are you going to tell me your name, since you know mine?"

"Nope." He was enjoying this; the smirk on his face.

Sluggishly, my mind began to work. "If you're working with John, does that mean you're an archaeologist?"

"Yes." He wasn't adding anything.

I went on. "You now know my name *and* where I'm staying, but you're still not going to tell me your name." My head was too cloudy for this.

"That's right." He crossed his arms and pulled himself up to his full height.

I sighed. He heard me and glanced down at me for a moment before turning his eyes back to the elevator door. He was still smirking.

"Can I call you 'Doctor,' then?" I asked

He made a chuckling sound. "If you like."

We stood quietly for a moment before a thought came to my mind. "You're the one who couldn't come to Australia."

He nodded; that was the only time he stopped smiling.

I nodded slowly. Before coming to Australia, John had said his colleague's name once on the phone. It had slipped my mind. This was annoying me.

The elevator stopped. The doors seemed to stick a little as they opened, breaking my chain of thought. My Mystery Man walked ahead to show me to my room. The floor had a lot of rooms and, like the rest of the hotel, was also in need of renovation. The carpet was green with little palm trees. The walls had white wallpaper with gold pyramids.

Before I knew it, my Mystery Man had unlocked my door and placed my bags just inside it. Then he turned and held out his hand to give me the key. To my surprise, as I reached for it, he took hold of my hand.

"Thank you for bringing my bags to my room," I said softly, leaning against the door frame. His hand felt strong. That tingle I had felt in the museum came back; my skin was alive at his touch.

"You're welcome, Laura. I will say, this wasn't much of a challenge. Two days later, I find you. Anyway, what are you doing Wednesday night?"

I swallowed hard. "Going out on a date with you. A deal is a deal," I answered in a mousy voice.

He nodded, his thumb moving over the back of my hand. "A deal is a deal, then."

"You can't say that I go back on my word. Where are we going, since you're not a mass murderer?" I wanted to kiss him, pull him into my room, make passionate love to him, but I pushed these foolish thoughts out of my head.

He studied my hand in his. "I'll pick you up in the lobby at 7:30 Wednesday night," he said softly, grinning.

"I can't say 'no,' can I?"

"No. A deal's a deal." He looked deep into my eyes. My knees were about to give out. It was a good thing we were alone in the hallway.

"At least give me your first name, Doc."

242

"What's the fun in that?" he asked.

"You're driving me crazy." I frowned at him, sounding a little hurt.

He studied my eyes; it looked like he was trying to find something in what I had said. There was something there something more to his story. For his young age it had seemed he had seen a lot more and this I think accounted for his maturity. I was sure he had his fair share of flings, but he seemed like a nice guy. There was something about him; something was telling me not to stop this, to let it run. I was sure that I was flushing red.

He smiled at me again. I felt like a little girl, even though he was younger than I was. He shouldn't have known how to do this stuff; he was only in his 20s.

"Well, you're not going to forget me then, will you?" He raised one eyebrow.

I swallowed again. "No, I don't think I can."

He lifted my hand to kiss it. "You need some rest. I'll see you soon."

"Bye."

He slowly let go of my hand and walked away. I waited until he got into the elevator, then fell into my room, out of breath.

"Why am I letting him do this?" My heart was racing like a train once more. I threw my hands into the air. "Great, now he has me talking to myself." This man was too young for me.

I tossed my bag on the table, then collapsed onto the single bed next to the far wall. The room had a small bathroom with a shower, sink, and toilet. Next to the bed was a small window from which I could see the Nile. I had a small plywood cupboard in which to hang my things, as well as a desk in one corner. The desk would come in handy when we began digging, as I would have to write reports for Dr Colman. But not today. I closed my eyes for a few minutes to let my heart slow down. After a while, I heard a knock on the door.

My heart began beating faster again. "Shit, no more; I need sleep," I grumbled to myself. He must have come back for some reason.

Another knock pounded on my door.

"Yes!" I answered, keeping my eyes closed.

"Laura, it's me." Marisa's voice met my ears.

I groaned and rolled off the bed. "Coming!"

"How are you feeling?" Marisa asked as she stalked into my room and began inspecting it. It seemed as though she thought she'd find something interesting; she looked a little disappointed when she didn't find it.

"Hungry and tired. Thank John for the room."

She nodded and sat down carefully on the room's only chair, which was on its last legs. I sat back down on the bed and pulled my hand luggage beside me to look for my bottle of water.

"Did your Mystery Man tell you his name?" Marisa asked.

"No. We're going on a date on Wednesday. Did John tell you his name?"

"I'm not allowed to tell you. *However*, they work together at the Met and at the college in the Egyptian department. John did say that your man was very happy to see you. You have to learn his name yourself. Sorry I can't help."

I lay back on my bed and pulled the pillow over my face. *"Men! Why do they do that? Drive you crazy,"* I muffled into the pillow.

"That's the fun of it, remember? You're a little out of practice, that's all. Being with Paul all this time, you've forgotten. What it's like to be with a real man, I mean."

244

I peeked out from under the pillow to make a face at Marisa. She smacked my foot.

"He's too young for me."

"Age is just a number," Marisa said, then added, "How are you feeling?"

"I'm fine. But now my foot hurts. How about you?" I sat up.

"Don't be a baby. But I'm fine. John is here, and that always makes me feel better." She grinned, then continued. "You said you're hungry. Let's go and eat. John and your man are busy. We'll be meeting with them later."

"Where are you staying?" I asked, swinging my legs to the floor, a little swifter then I should have.

"With John. Don't worry, I'll come up for air to see you. I think you're not going to be alone for too long."

I stuck out my tongue at Marisa.

"That's not very nice coming from someone your age, and a mum, too," Marisa said, following me out the door.

The dining room was large, and it contained the same palm tree carpet that was in my room. Dining tables and chairs were on one side of the room; there was a bar in the back, and a buffet on the far wall. On one side of the buffet, two doors led to the kitchen. On the other side, a door led to the professors' hotel rooms. The dining room also contained a stage along one wall, near the tables and chairs. In the corner sat a group of old lounge chairs, which were filled with students from various colleges.

My eyes quickly glanced around the room.

"He's working with John."

I turned back to Marisa, trying to act as though I hadn't been doing anything. "Who?" I asked, though I didn't wait for her to say anything. Instead, I made my way to the buffet.

245

Food was part of the package deal, and it was a mixture of Western and Egyptian fare, with plenty of flatbread. The burgers looked like they had been sitting there a little too long, so I opted for the vegetable curry.

Marisa and I sat down at one of the spare tables. A group of female students watched us, they begun talking behind their hands as Marisa and I ate.

"Are we back at school again?" I asked Marisa. She followed my line of sight. One of the girls seemed to have taken a dislike to me, as she was glaring at me.

"I guess so," she said loudly enough for them to hear. They turned their heads as Marisa spoke.

After we finished, I left Marisa, planning to return to my room for a nap. It was just before 1:00 in the afternoon, which meant that in Sydney it would be about 11:00 at night. Mum and Dad should be awake; they needed to know that we were okay. The lobby had a row of landline phones that I could use.

To my surprise, Emily answered the phone. She had been waiting on my call.

"Hello." Her excited voice came over the line.

"What are you doing up?"

"My legs are quicker than Grandma's."

I let out a laugh. I was too far away to be angry at her. "How are you?"

"I could still come if you want me to."

I sighed. "Em, my room is too small."

"It's okay, I'll sleep on the floor."

"You can't fly by yourself. We don't need to go over this again."

I finally managed to get Em off the line, then spoke to Mum and Dad for a while. I was happy to hear from them and to know that everyone was okay. Now I could sleep.

As I hung up the phone, I noticed a paper cutting framed on the wall. The paper talked about a cache of mummified cats that had been found at Karnak Temple. It also contained a photo of John and *him*.

I smiled. *'Matt Dixson,'* I mouthed. "Dr Matt Dixson was the grandson of Dr Jack Dixson."

Jack Dixson was one of the owners of the diaries I had found in Paul's house. I looked down at my necklace. Dr Dixson was no longer alive, but now I felt guilty about keeping it. I would give it back to Matt when I saw him again.

Contented that I had found his name I made my way back to my room. The rusty springs squeaked as I fell onto the narrow bed. I kicked my shoes onto the floor and pulled the covers over me.

CHAPTER 17

When my eyes opened again, the sun was still up, but the light was different. My side hurt; I hadn't moved while I was sleeping. I didn't know if it was the next morning or the same afternoon. I sat up to look out the window. It seemed like morning, but I wasn't sure. A mist covered the Nile, and the light was still low. My stomach grumbled. I must have slept all night; my watch said it was 6:30.

When I was ready, I went to the dining room to eat. There were a few students already awake, they were lazily lounging in the recreation area. We wouldn't start the dig until tomorrow, so I had the day to myself. There was no sign of Marisa, John, or Matt, but I was too hungry to wait. I was also looking forward to not having to think about anyone but myself, at least for one day. I slowly ate some breakfast, enjoying the quiet. I noticed the hotel supplied bottles of water, so I filled my canvas bag before leaving the lobby.

The car park was empty of people. Since I hadn't had a chance to look outside the day before, I did so now. Karnak Temple stood on the other bank, visible through the row of palm trees that stood in front of it. The bank of the Nile was just beyond the car park. A dock for the Nile ferry perched down from where I was standing. Groups of people were waiting for the boat, which was spluttering over to them. This ancient land was slowly coming awake.

I stopped at the bank. It was a little like the dream I had just before Em was born. A mist swayed through the air off the water. A light breeze slowly moved the reeds, which made a rustling noise. A large boulder rested a few feet away from me; it looked like a good spot to sit and take in the morning. As I took a seat, a white water bird looked at me; it was searching for frogs in the reeds. Once it realised that I wasn't going to hurt it, it carried on with its mission.

248

The greenness of the palm trees and the reeds looked strange against the desert sand. Sand had been everywhere in Cairo, and Thebes was the same. It blew across the road, covering parts of it.

The sun was still casting long shadows. It felt warm on my back. The weather wasn't hot; it seemed that it might be a nice day.

After taking a few photos, I pulled a notepad out of my bag. Contentedly, I drew the local people at the dock, with Karnak in the background. I could have taken photos, but it seemed right to draw the scene instead. The scent of spice was everywhere; the breeze always had a hint of it. I felt a lot better. Breakfast this morning had made me feel human again.

"Good morning, Laura."

My heart skipped a beat as I looked down from my boulder to see Matt's smiling face looking up at me.

"Good morning," I replied.

"Did you sleep well?" Matt asked.

I straightened my back and nodded. "Yes, I did, thanks. How did you sleep?"

"Quite well, thank you. May I join you?"

"Sure." I moved over a little as he climbed onto the boulder.

"Not a bad spot; I like sitting here sometimes." He stood for a moment, taking in the view.

"Do you come here often?"

Matt sat next to me and studied my drawing before answering. "You found my thinking spot." He grinned.

"You don't mind me using it?"

"No, I'm happy to share it." He pointed at my drawing. "That's good; I like it."

"Thank you. Do you want it?"

He frowned. "Don't you want to keep it?"

"Just think of it as a 'thank you' for helping with my bags yesterday." I ripped the drawing out of the pad and handed it to him.

"Thanks." He began comparing it to the actual scene, then handed it back to me. For a second, I thought he didn't want it. Then he smiled and said, "Can you leave it in the pad until later? I want it back."

"Sure." I placed the pad and drawing back into my bag.

We sat there taking in the view for a while. It was nice. There was no need to make conversation or nervous chatter. It felt natural to be together, not like it had been with Paul, when I felt as though I needed to know everything was okay all the time.

'What the hell am I doing? He's younger than me' was the thought that repeated in my mind. The age difference troubled me, but Matt was a gentleman, a rare trait among guys his age. Finally, I thought, *'This is a holiday thing; don't read too much into it. I'm not going to marry him.'*

Matt broke the silence. "You weren't at dinner last night. Marisa went up to your room to get you, but you didn't answer."

I gave him a timid expression. "I didn't hear her; it would have been like waking the dead."

"Wow, you must not have been feeling well. You know not to drink the water, don't you? Are you okay now?" He seemed genuinely concerned.

"I'm fine. Yes, I know about the water and the ice. It was just jet lag and a hangover," I said, smiling coyly at him.

He let out a laugh. "You had a hangover yesterday?"

"Yes," I answered. "The driver didn't help. Marisa and I drank my dad's duty-free scotch on the train. It was a big bottle." Taking

250

a deep breath, I rushed the next part. "You took me by surprise yesterday. I never thought I would…I mean, that you would be here. And don't laugh at me. You've been doing that a lot."

"Sorry. I liked my surprise. I was happy to see you again. Don't you drink?" Matt looked at my face, trying to understand.

I was feeling foolish now. "When you have a child, you don't get the time to drink as much as you did BC."

"BC?" he asked.

"Before Children."

Matt's expression changed; his body slumped a little. "Are you married?" he asked.

I put my hand out to touch his arm. "No. Not anymore. I have a daughter," I said, trying to reassure him. I was a single mum, and that was a fact I couldn't change. I realised that some men considered it a problem.

"What's her name?" Matt asked quietly.

"Emily," I said with a big smile. "She's a real handful. She's upset that I didn't let her come here."

Matt let out a slow breath. It seemed as though he was trying to phrase the next question correctly.

I butted in before he could ask. "You've been really nice to me. I'm a single mum. If you don't want to be caught up with that type of thing, that's okay."

Matt met my eyes; they were hypnotic, I couldn't look away.

"You being a single mom doesn't worry me. I was worried at first that you were still married."

"Oh, sorry. I was divorced some months ago. Are you single?"

"Yes," he answered quickly. "Have we ever met before? I feel like I know you." We looked at each other. I took a breath to clear my mind.

251

"Yes, we met in Cairo's museum a few days ago." I giggled.

"You know that's not what I'm talking about." He shook his head at me.

"No, I would remember if I had met you before."

He nodded as he looked out over the Nile. "Do you know that the goddess of the Nile was a lioness? She was the giver of life."

"Really."

Matt smiled a playful smile that I was growing to like. "Have you seen the Tombs yet?" he asked.

"No, not yet. This is my first time in Egypt."

"Well, I'll fix that." Matt jumped to his feet and climbed down from the boulder. He waited for me at the bottom, holding out his hand to help me down. "Come on, I'll show you."

"Thank you, Matt Dixson," I said as I climbed down.

"Very good. Nice to hear you say my name. It sounds nice the way you say it."

"Are you hassling my Australian accent?" I asked him playfully.

"No. I like your accent."

We took a short walk near the dock, just under some sandstone hills, was where we found the ticket booth for the Tombs. A large, rusted sign leant against the booth; it contained a list of the tombs, written in English and Arabic. I tried to pay for my ticket, but before I could take out my money, Matt had ordered both of ours in Arabic and paid for them.

"Do you want to walk? Or we can take the bus," he said.

I glanced over at the bus that was ready to leave. One of the windows looked like it had a bullet hole in it. A large group of people who had just gotten off the ferry were lining up to board the vehicle. It was filling up quickly, and people were beginning to fall out. I was not in the mood for another white-knuckle ride today.

"How long does it take to walk?" I asked.

"Only half an hour."

"I'm happy to walk. It would be nice to be away from the crowds."

Matt nodded in agreement.

A narrow, well-trodden, sandy track led behind the ticket booth and between the hills. On one side were sandstone rocks that ranged in colour from deep brown to grey, yellow to white. Some parts of the rock face fell into a rocky gully. On the other side of the track, some of the land sloped up into rocky cliffs against which long shadows were cast. In Ancient Egypt, one's shadow was important to one's soul, and should never be lost.

Matt ambled beside me, never trying to hurry me as we walked. It was nice.

"I know your name and which country you're from. Now tell me more about you," I said as we wandered along. We had bumped arms a few times when the track became narrow.

"All right. But you have to tell me about yourself when I'm finished."

I nodded.

"Mom and Dad were Harry and Lisa," Matt began. "I grew up in Birdbe, Kentucky, but now I live in New York." He hesitated; it seemed as though he wanted to tell me more about them, but he stopped. "I would come here to Egypt with my grandpa. He was an archaeologist."

"Yes, I've heard of him. Are your father and mother archaeologists as well?"

"No...they were teachers."

253

"Were? Are they retired?" I asked.

Matt took a breath, then answered. "They passed away when I was nine." He kept eye contact as though to see how I would respond.

I lowered my voice. "Oh, I'm sorry. That's sad."

"It's okay." He brushed it off.

It felt like we were taking our time. "Dr Jack Dixson was your grandfather?"

"Yes."

You should have his diaries back. I have something else that might have been his. I'm sorry I didn't tell anyone about it." I stopped walking and pulled out the necklace I was wearing. Matt held it in his fingers. I began to take it off so that I could give it to him.

"I remember this. Where did you find it?" he asked as he put the necklace back around my neck.

"I found it with the diaries, under a floor in a house I once lived in." I didn't want to say that it had been Paul's house; he didn't rate in this.

"It belonged to a woman named Mary," Matt said. "Grandpa Jack gave it to her. It was a sad story; I'll have to tell you about it one day." He smiled a little and rubbed his thumb over the necklace. "Keep it. He would love the fact that you have it."

"Thank you. I'm sorry about your family."

He shook his head as he let go of the necklace. "It's okay. Your turn." He smiled.

"Well, you know about Emily; she's six. I live in Mum and Dad's backyard in Sydney. Mum is Eve and Dad is Dan. They're looking after Emily while I'm here." I grinned, trying to lighten his mood.

"I like it when you talk about Emily. Your face lights up."

"Your face lights up just as much when you speak about your family."

He nodded as we began walking quietly side by side once more. Matt took my hand; this time I didn't want to pull it away.

"Are you worried about the age thing?" Matt asked after a few moments.

"Yes," I answered softly.

He stopped again to look at me. He placed his free hand on my face. I moved my cheek closer into it.

"I've been wanting to do that for a while," Matt muttered softly.

I smiled, enjoying the feel of his hand on my skin. "The way I look at it, the world doesn't matter right now. Let's just live for today."

"I like that," he said gently.

Matt ran the back of his hand softly on my cheek. I didn't stop him. I looked back into his eyes and said, "It's nice to meet someone who doesn't care if I was married or not. I guess I'm a little gun-shy. Did John tell you anything about me?"

"The other day at the museum I didn't know who you were. John said Marisa was coming with a friend she worked with. The one who had set up the exhibit for the diaries – that was all he told me. When I saw you in Cairo you didn't have a ring on, but that didn't mean much. You could have taken it off before coming to Egypt. I do care if you're married. It's something I'm not into – dating married women."

"But why me?" I wanted to understand what was happening here. I had never felt like this before.

"Man, your ex-husband must have done a number on you."

didn't know why, but a tear ran down my cheek. Matt gently wiped it away with the back of his finger. I looked at him and a shiver ran down my spine. He was acting like My Dark Figure. Was that who this man was? I put my hand to his chest; his heart was pounding a little fast. He had been acting like Mr Cool, so it was nice to know that I was doing the same thing to him that he was doing to me.

"When I saw you through the case, it was the look in your eyes. Do you know that you wear everything in your eyes? The way you were looking at the mask…it was like you were seeing it for the first time. Was it?" he asked.

"Yes it was. They say that your eyes are the window to your soul. I was drinking it into my soul."

Matt's hand came up to meet my hand on his chest; he held it there.

"They also say that blue is the colour of the soul," he said. "I could see the power it was giving you. It fascinated me. 'The magic,' Grandpa Jack would call it. I was enjoying watching you drink it all in, and that's why I wanted to talk to you. Not only that, I felt that I knew you or that I had to know who you were."

"I feel the same, as though I've known you before. It's still…all this is stupid." I wished I had my hat to hide under; I was going red again. He was watching me. I continued. "Was he a good man? Grandpa Jack, I mean."

He smiled. "*This* is not stupid. And they were all good people."

I wanted to kiss him. The world around us didn't matter. My head was spinning and it felt good.

"What did your ex-husband do?" Matt continued. "I know I shouldn't ask, but I want to know."

"No, it's fine. I don't know. Marisa put it best. He took me away from myself. I lost how to be me. He also had an affair." I said the last part quickly.

256

Matt shook his head. "The man is a fool. Lucky for me, though. Well, we have to find you, then. "I had given him the basics he did not need to know everything. How could you not like him. His lips moved closer to mine. I closed my eyes ready to kiss him.

All of a sudden, voices bounced off the cliffs; people were walking up the path. Our lips brushed for a brief moment, then we pulled away. Egyptians didn't like people doing this type of thing in public. We were visitors in the country, and our moment was gone.

Matt softly brushed his hand on my cheek once more. He quickly squeezed my hand as we both sighed. My heart pounded in my ears.

"Let's go see the Tombs." Matt's voice was a little out of breath.

"Tomb 62 has to be the last one?" Tomb 62 belonged to Tutankhamen.

Matt smiled; his eyes were playful again. "Yes."

We finally turned the corner into the Valley. The yellowness of the high sandstone walls was remarkable. The sun made them glow. I didn't know that my feet had stopped moving. My eyes tried to drink in everything. There were no words for how I was feeling. It was one thing to see the Valley in books and on TV, but this was surreal.

Matt moved next to me, snapping me out of the moment. I looked at him sheepishly and smiled. "You must think I'm ludicrous," I said, looking up at him.

"No, I understand how you feel. I did the same thing when I was six."

"Oh, that makes me feel much better." I playfully slapped him on the arm.

Matt chuckled. I looked at him and frowned. "Not nice." I slapped him again, but he caught my hand to stop me.

"All right, I'll be good. I'm not laughing at you. Come on." He was enjoying himself, but I wasn't. He held onto my arm, and I tried to pull away from him. He let me go after I struggled a little. Then he looked me in the eyes. "I'm sorry," he said gently, waiting for me to respond.

I nodded. He tried to take my hand, but I playfully slapped him as I walked away.

Matt quickly caught up to me. "My name is Ozymandias, King of Kings, Look on my works, ye Mighty and despair," he said.

"Oh, I like that." I was impressed.

"Percy Bysshe Shelley wrote it." Matt seemed kind of chuffed that he had impressed me.

The Valley contained the tombs of the Pharaohs and noblemen; it was an area where they could sleep in peace. In ancient times, Egyptians believed that Ra came to take people to the underworld. At sun, they would rise and return to their tombs until the night. One's afterlife was the same as his or her life on earth, but a lot easier. If a person was a fisherman in life, he would be a fisherman in the underworld, but the fish would jump into his nets.

The Valley's high cliffs were perfect for hiding the Kings from the outside world, but now too many people knew where they were. There were a lot of people around, and at times we had to step to one side to avoid being trampled. Buses arrived at the bottom of the hill; some were small, others were large coaches. The local sellers commenced their dances with the tourists, trying to get the visitors to part with as much money as they could.

We walked around the first two tombs. Matt took pleasure in testing me to see how much I knew. It was like having my own personal guide. I liked listening to him. Some Americans could be over the top, but Matt wasn't. I hadn't laughed so much in ages; he had an evil sense of humour that I enjoyed.

"Have you been on a dig before?" Matt asked while we walked to Tut's tomb.

"No. However, I found a Shabti a few years ago. An alabaster one. It was with a house lot that came to the museum, I didn't get to dig it up."

"Really? Who did it belong to?" Matt seemed interested; he had stopped walking.

"It didn't say; the name had been cut out. It belonged to someone's wife."

"What happened to it?" he asked a little too eagerly.

I let out a sigh. "Dr Colman wanted to research it. I haven't seen it since. It was about seven years ago now."

"Oh, Dr Colman. John told me about him. A real pain in the ass." Matt shook his head, then quickly changed the subject. "I'm guessing I don't have to tell you anything about Tut."

"No, I'm good. I've read Howard Carter's book on Tut." I grinned at Matt as we lined up to enter the tomb.

"Really? I'm impressed. I have a hard time getting my students to read anything."

"I didn't read 63 volumes. I read the cut-down versions."

"Why aren't you an archaeologist?" Matt asked as we moved forward in the line. I hesitated to answer him and bought time by pulling out two bottles of water. I took a drink from one and gave the other to Matt. He drank a few mouthfuls, waiting for me to answer.

"I like the research side," I began. "I did go to University, but I had to leave after the first year. I had money problems. I got a job at the museum to help with that. John got me the job there. I was about to go back to school when I fell pregnant, then got married.

Somehow, being an archaeologist fell behind. What about you?" I pushed the question back at him.

"Oh, it's in my blood, Anyway, Grandpa Jack would have haunted me from his grave if I didn't."

I chuckled. "I know John worked for your grandpa; he would go on about him in class. How did you get your job at the college?"

"John and a cache of cats' mummies. Grandpa Jack had been looking for them for years. They're part of Nefertiti's temple. I proved to the college that they couldn't live without me, so here I am."

We moved down the stairs into the tomb's passageway. Only ten people at a time could enter, and we could stay only ten minutes. When Carter found the tomb, the passageway had been filled with sand and contained a few jars and pots left behind by robbers who had entered the tomb in ancient times.

The artefacts we saw bore the names of Tutankhamen's father, Akhenaten, and an unknown Pharaoh, Smenkhkare. We travelled down a walkway. I loved this. My heart was pounding and I lightly ran my hand along the wall.

The light that filled the first small room was bright, but my eyes adjusted. I stopped. I couldn't help myself.

I see wonderest things," I said as we entered. This was what Howard Carter had said to Lord Carnarvon when the latter asked, "What do you see?"

Matt chuckled and rolled his eyes.

I ran my hand along the white wall of the antechamber, which was just over three meters by eight meters. I wanted to feel its power. A woman rushed past me, bumping into me as she hurried into the tomb. I sighed; she glared back at me. Matt shook his head and reached out his hand to show me the other room.

The tomb had four rooms. The annex was two meters by four meters and rested behind a sealed wall that was closed to the public. A room just off the shrine was known as the storage room; it was where Tut's stillborn babies had been found. It was sad. The babies had lain in their own tiny coffins, buried under their father's things and forgotten. I thought that this tomb was made for his children and he died before they could start a new tomb for him.

We couldn't go into the shrine room, which is where Tut laid in his gold sarcophagus. We stood in the antechamber, looking down at him. Matt stood close behind me. He was quietly reading to me the text that was on the pink granite outer sarcophagus.

The other tourists pushed in to see. Matt wrapped his arms around my body to protect me. I felt that this was where I belonged.

Looking up at the picture on the back wall. It was an image of Aye and King Tut as a mummy. Aye was opening Tut's mouth so that he could speak his name in the afterlife.

Matt had stopped reading. I followed his gaze to the corner of the room. His eyes moved from side to side as though he were watching something.

He sighed, I spoke softly. "They say that if you speak their name, they come back to life. It refills their soul. I think they like to hear their names. It lets them know that you still love them, and they live on in a way."

Matt looked down at me. "That's a good way to think." There was something about this tomb. He seemed sad. "It's been a long time since I've been in here," he said.

We made our way back into the hotel lobby, some hours later. I didn't mind giving up my day to spend a day with Matt. Matt had stopped holding my hand. I didn't worry, as his students were around, watching his every move. It wasn't a good impression to set.

261

"I'll see you at dinner tonight. You're not going to have another nap again, are you?" Matt asked.

"No, I have a report to start and I have some emails to send. I'll be wide awake for dinner." I shook my head and smiled at him near the elevator. I dug into my canvas bag to return the picture.

"Thank you." Matt gave me a quick, playful look. "I'll see you at dinner, Laura."

"Thank you for today, Matt Dixson."

He nodded at me, then walked off into the dining room.

I let out a breath. I gave him a few moments before I went into the dining room to take something back to my room to snack on.

We had stayed at the Tombs longer than I thought we had. It was after lunch, and I didn't realise how hungry I was. Dinner was at 7:30, so I had time to kill.

My head was still spinning. It was hard to focus on my report because my mind kept floating back to Matt. I sat in my hotel room, drinking water. Matt was ten years younger than I was, but one would never know that from the way we interacted. Somehow, Matt and I met in the middle.

I found an email from Dr Colman that changed my thoughts.

Hi Laura,

Hope you are having a nice time. Don't forget, you are on a Working Holiday. You need to write and send back your reports and photos. I don't need to see your and Marisa's drunken parties, but I do need updated photos of Egypt's sites. I know that you'll see this email before Marisa does. Could you remind her that she is also on a Working Holiday? I do not need to remind you that I will need the same photos and reports from the dig that you and Marisa are on.

Dr B Colman.

Dr Colman hadn't gotten over the way John behaved while in Sydney. Dr Colman would be a fool not to see how John and Marisa felt about each other.

I spent the afternoon laying on my bed doing some light reading and watching the roof, which had water marks on it. One of the stains looked like a frog. My mind happily drifted, looking for more shapes.

It was a little after 7:30 when I finally made my way to the dining room. I didn't want to look too eager. I had washed away the sand from earlier, and dressed a little neater.

Marisa, John, and Matt were already at a table, waiting for me. Both men stood up when I approached. It was the type of behaviour a girl could get used to. Matt pulled out the chair next to him for me to sit in. The dining room was full, but we had a table to ourselves, just off one side near the back of the room.

"Thank you." I smiled at Matt. He also had dressed a little nicer.

"You're welcome, Laura."

I said my hellos to everyone. Marisa gave me a glance. I could see that she had questions for me.

"Nice to see you awake. It was like waking a mummy last night." She was enjoying ribbing me.

"Well, this mummy was really tired last night," I joked back.

"I didn't see you two today. What did you get up to?" John asked.

"Laura and I went to see the Tombs," Matt said, looking a little unsure about what Marisa and I were doing.

"So you two enjoyed the day, then?" Marisa asked.

"Yes, Matt is really good at getting you to see things in a different way."

"Really." Marisa was trying to make my words sound dirtier than I had intended. The two men began to look worried. I had to bring her down a bit.

"So, I was reading my emails before, Marisa, and Dr Colman would like to remind you that he has not seen any reports from you and that this is a *working holiday*."

"Well, this is going to be an interesting three weeks." John was shaking his head at the two of us.

We both looked at John and let out a laugh. "We'll behave ourselves." I smiled at John, then back at Marisa.

"Don't look so worried, Matt. We go on like this all the time." Marisa waved me off.

Matt raised one eyebrow. I smirked.

"Just laugh it off, Matt. Don't try and work us out," I said. He shook his head in disbelief.

With everyone talking at once, the room was noisy. We had a bottle of wine on the table; once we finished our first drinks, Matt and John stood up. I was about to stand up, too, when Matt placed his hand on my shoulder to keep me in my seat.

"Laura, would you like me to get you a plate of food? What would you like?"

I glanced over at the buffet. "Yes, that would be nice of you, Matt. I'll have whatever you're having."

"Okay, I'll surprise you then." Matt smiled.

"Now, you two behave yourselves while we're gone. We don't want to see two girls fighting." John mocked our behaviour, pointing his finger at both of us.

"We'll try not to, sir," Marisa and I responded like school kids.

As soon as the men were out of earshot, I took my chance to hassle Marisa. "So, you two have come up for air, have you?"

She waved me off. "Come on, Laura, I'm dying to know what happened today."

I shrugged. "I told you, we went to the Tombs. We have a date on Wednesday night. He's been a gentleman all day. And no, I didn't *bore* him with the Egyptian stuff because he likes the Egyptian stuff."

Marisa seemed despondent about what I had told her. She looked over to John and Matt.

"You know they're talking about us," I said.

"Of course they are. Men gossip just as much as women do," Marisa replied. "See that group of girls?" She nudged her head towards a table near the stage.

"Yes."

"Well, Matt teaches a few classes at the college. When they knew that Matt was coming to Egypt, there were more signups for this trip. I overheard some of those girls talking this morning and…" Marisa put on a big smile.

"And?" I asked.

"They don't like us being here."

"This *thing* with Matt is only going to be a holiday *thing*, so they can have him back after three weeks."

"Laura, the way he's looking at you, I don't think he wants it to be a holiday thing."

I shook my head. "We talked about that today…" I couldn't finish what I was saying, as Matt and John had come back.

Matt was a really nice guy, and if we had more time I would let things play out, but three weeks was all we had.

After dinner, the students performed a comedy skit that they had made up about Mark Antony and Cleopatra. The lights went down. The male students played the female roles, and the female students played the male roles. I had never laughed so hard. Poor Cleopatra's breasts were enormous.

Marisa and I were on our second bottle of wine, while Matt and John drank beer. When I leant back from pouring Marisa another glass, I felt Matt's arm resting on the back of my chair.

He leant over to me and whispered, "I hope you don't drink too much tonight. I would hate for you to miss out on your first day of work tomorrow."

I just gave him a look.

After the play, Egyptian musicians came up on stage and started to play. They clapped as belly dancers followed them on stage, wiggling their hips. The musicians wore white shirts, black waistcoats, black pants, and red turbans. The women wore flowing, brightly coloured belly dancing outfits. They swirled around the stage as the musicians played. Once they had finished, the women wanted people from the crowd to join them. Marisa jumped up and grabbed me.

"Come on Laura, let show these college kids how it's done."

There were quite a few of us onstage; a young girl ran around giving everyone scarves. The dancers showed us a few moves and we copied them as the band played slowly.

The music built up in tempo and the dancers picked up the beat with their hips. We followed. There were a few howls of laughter from the audience. Some of the students trying to dance fell over themselves as they jiggled around the stage. They looked as though they were swinging hula hoops.

Marisa and I had received a few lessons in belly dancing from Aunt May when we were in high school. I think we were keeping up. John and Matt seemed to like what we were doing, as they weren't laughing. On the contrary, John and Matt were calling out and cat whistling us. The men gave us a standing ovation when we left the stage. I wrapped my scarf around Matt's neck as we reached the table.

He flipped the scarf around his neck. "I'm not giving this back." He jiggled one of the ends at me.

I grabbed the other end and wiggled it back in his face. "Maybe I don't want it back."

"Good, because I'm keeping it."

The night was over too soon. I was hoping that after today and tonight I would stay in Matt's room, but instead he escorted me to the elevator that led up to my room. Without a word, he pressed the button. When the door opened, Matt took my hand and kissed the back of it.

"Good night. Sleep well. I'll see you in the morning." His lips felt soft on the back of my hand. The sensation could have kept me going for months.

"Good night, Matt. I enjoyed tonight. Thank you." With my head spinning, I managed to get the words out. I thought it sounded okay.

His playful smile came across his face. "Sweet dreams, Laura." He slowly let go of my hand, but it seemed for a moment that he didn't want to.

CHAPTER 18

The next morning Matt's smile was large, as I made my way to the table. Mine was just as big.

"Good morning, Laura. How did you sleep?" Matt asked as he stood to pull out my chair.

"I slept really well, thanks. You?"

"I slept well, thank you."

"Morning everyone." I nodded at Marisa and John. Marisa had her head in her hand and was fluttering her eyes at me, mocking the way Matt and I were acting. Throughout breakfast she kept giving me glances; in return, I gave her a swift kick under the table.

When we had finished eating, we made our way to the car park. A group of students and Egyptian workers were waiting to go to the dig site, which was south of the Nile, about an hour-and-a-half drive away. Some of the students were running late. One of them came crashing out of the hotel doors while pulling on a shoe. Another followed, eating flat bread and washing it down with a bottle of water. He began choking on the bread and drank more water to clear his throat. With a sigh, John paused to make sure the student was okay, slapping him on the back to assist him. Once the student had stopped choking, John continued organising the rest of the students and workers.

John was in charge of 15 students, while Matt was in charge of the other half. The Egyptian workers were spread over the two groups; they were a valuable part of the dig team.

"Come on you lot, we're not on holidays now. Be on time. If you don't show up in the mornings, we're not waiting for you."

John stood in front of a large truck, marking off the names of students and workers as they got on.

Marisa and I waited by the four-wheel drive for John and Matt to finish. It was better that we hung back to let them get on with it.

"John's driving." Marisa pushed me into the backseat. "Shotgun," she informed me.

"What if I want to sit in the front seat?"

Marisa glared at me; I was trying to ruffle her.

Once the men were finished, they boarded the four-wheel drive. John was to drive ahead of the trucks. It was still early, and I was enjoying the ride down to the site. We were travelling alongside the Nile. It was nice to have a smooth driver for a change. The road was sealed, with high cliffs finally giving way to open farmland. People had worked this land for thousands of years. The tombs that we had seen the day before contained images of people working their fields; things had not changed.

Because donkeys were a cheap way for people to get around, every so often we would pass a donkey and cart. John had to convert to Egyptian driving to move a few over. I craned my neck when we drove past men ploughing their fields with cows; it was just like the images on the tomb walls. I was loving it all.

Egypt rolled by us. People outside the car window went about their business—a woman carrying clothes in a big bag on her head, a man herding his goats, another man with a donkey and a cart containing a few children who were going to school. This land was timeless; history was everywhere.

Every now and then, the Nile came into view. The greenery and palm trees slid past my window. Matt had been watching me for a while.

"Where are you?" Matt asked softly in my ear.

I snapped myself out of my thoughts. "Just something I do on long trips in the car or train."

"What's that?" He looked intrigued.

"I'm imagining that I'm sailing down the Nile and that the boat is following the car."

"You can't do that if there's no river." Matt seemed confused about what I was doing.

I smiled. "You can think whatever takes your fancy. Boat, train, horse or cart. You also can pretend that there's a river. It breaks up the trip and gives you something to do."

Matt thought about this for a moment. "I like that. Can I sail with you? Is it an Egyptian boat?"

"Yes and yes."

Matt and I sat quietly as the landscape passed us. John kept his hand on the horn, periodically breaking our quiet. Eventually he began to slow the Jeep. I straightened to look out the window on Matt's side. John turned the four-wheel drive onto a dirt road. A family that was working in its fields stopped to watch us drive down the pothole-ridden track. They were clearing a channel to water their crops. The truck was having an easier time than we were; I held onto the seat as John tried his best to miss the potholes.

We finally came to a stop at a flat, unfarmed area. There were high cliffs in the distance. Palm trees lined a river that came up from the Nile. This sandy area had once been a village with shops, craftsmen's workshops and people's homes. One side had been excavated the year before by a different group; our group was there to finish the site. It needed to be documented before it became farmland.

Two men in black uniforms and head scarves were waiting for us in a rusty Mazda. Without a word, John jumped out of the four-wheel drive. He went over to them with paperwork in hand. John

270

shook their hands before handing over the papers. He appeared to know them, as they greeted him warmly. One man lit a cigarette and offered another to John, who politely refused as the other man examined the paperwork.

"They're local police, just ensuring that we have the right paperwork to be here. The local tribes like to know that everything is above board. Nothing to worry about. Just make sure you keep your heads and extra body parts covered while we're down here. It's a requirement for women in this part of Egypt," Matt informed us. I nodded.

Once the officers were satisfied that the paperwork was correct, they said their goodbyes. Matt went over to help John. We followed him to where the students and workers were waiting near the truck. Matt repeated to the female students what he had said to us in the four-wheel drive. Marisa and I stood back while Matt and John told us where we would be working for the day. We needed to unload the finds table, tent and sifting trays.

"Is everything going okay with you and Matt, then?" Marisa asked while we carried one of the finds tables over to the work area.

"I guess so." I didn't want to say much, as there were too many ears around.

"You know what the strange thing is? I think you two were made for each other," Marisa told me as she adjusted her scarf over her head.

"What are you talking about, Marisa? I've only known him for a few days."

"I know, but after a few days you're happy to share with him the travel thing that you do. You told me about it only a few years ago. You didn't even tell it to Chester."

"Leave it, Marisa. It's a holiday thing, that's all. What does it matter what I tell him?"

"Does he know that?" Marisa was holding up one end of the table as I pulled out its legs.

"Yes, we talked about it yesterday. I told you that." I couldn't add more, as a few students had come over near us.

"Okay." She shook her head at me.

Once we had finished setting up, Marisa and I made our way back to the four-wheel drive. I needed to get away from Marisa's questions. I made my way to the back of the four-wheel drive to play around with my digging tools. They were wrapped in cloth with pockets. It contained a trowel, hard brush, soft brush, hand shovel and two smaller paintbrushes. I once used it on a day trip during my first year; it had been sitting in my office gathering dust since then. It felt good to use the tools again.

"Are you ready?" Matt asked as he came around the back of the four-wheel drive. I jumped a little. He laughed as he briefly touched my arm to steady me.

"Sure am." I handed him his tools. I was looking forward to this, like it was my birthday.

Matt squeezed my hand, then let it go. "This way."

I followed Matt to a row of mud-brick walls. They had once been small houses, though if you didn't know what you were looking at, you wouldn't have given them a second thought. Sand had piled against the walls, turning them into sand mounds. The desert always covered things, which was good because it preserved history.

The houses were in five rows, divided by a narrow lane. They lay in an uneven grid pattern. Matt placed his students and the Egyptian workers into various groups spread throughout the houses. There were ten houses in each row—a lot to get through.

Matt and I were working together. After twenty minutes, Matt appeared to be impressed with how I was digging. I had found my first artefact after a few moments of clearing sand. It was thrilling

272

to see something that had not been seen for thousands of years. Instinctively, Matt sat up to assist me, but stopped when he realised I didn't need his help. I gradually brushed the sand away with my large paintbrush.

"What do you think?" Matt asked, still watching me after I had uncovered the item.

"It's a lamp." I made a face at him.

He shook his head. "Yes, I know you know that, but how old do you think it is?"

I picked it up and rested it in the palm of my hand. It looked like an ashtray that a child would make in art class. Matt didn't want a light answer, and I wanted to impress him with what I knew.

"The olive oil would go into the well and then cloth would be put in the pitted part, here. I'm not sure how old it is, but with the pots that were pulled out in the last dig, it could be Roman."

Matt nodded, then raised one eyebrow at me. "But."

"But there were a lot of pieces of pots from the Fourth Dynasty here as well. So the house may have been used in the Fourth Dynasty, which was between 2500 and 2400 B.C., the time of Kufu, who built the great Pyramids. Nothing in between then until the Roman times after 30 B.C."

Matt looked impressed. "Very good. I know who Kufu is, but very good."

"Thank you. I meant 'Before Christ,' not 'Before Children.'"

"I got that."

We finished the first house within an hour, then catalogued what we had found. We mapped the room; Matt and I worked well together.

"Dr Dixson, can I have your help *please*?" This was one of the students whom Marisa and I had seen talking about us in the dining room. She had a round face and dark brown hair, and was shorter than I was. She was young and pretty.

Matt didn't say anything, just nodded; he seemed a little wearied by her, but was trying to hide it. I didn't know how to read his behaviour. "Can you go on to the next room? I'll be back," he said.

"Sure." I looked at Matt, then to his student. I was getting the impression that Matt wanted me to say it wasn't all right for him to leave, but it wasn't my place to say so.

I sat for a moment and watched them walk away. Letting out a sigh, I knelt in the doorway of the next house. I scraped away the sand with my trowel. The walls of the houses were only about five feet tall at their highest. The rooms were about six feet by six feet in size. People were smaller in ancient times, but it still amazed me how small these houses were. This room had a lot more sand in it than the last one. I took my time clearing it out.

Looking up to see what Matt was doing, I noticed that he and the student were in an intense argument near one of the highest walls. The student seemed to want to talk about something other than work. She kept grabbing at Matt, who kept pulling his arms away from her. I was the only one who could see them, as a wall blocked everyone else's view. I couldn't hear what they were saying, but I could see the pleading look on her face. Matt had crossed his arms and his back was stiff. He took a swift glance my way, so I ducked my head to brush away some sand. When I peered up again, Matt had walked away and so had the student. He had gone over to the other students who needed his help.

Sitting back, I knew that what I had seen was not just a student-and-professor thing. I knew that I shouldn't care about it, but I also didn't want to start something if Matt was involved with someone else. I slipped off my scarf to fix my hair and wipe sweat from my forehead. Letting out a sigh, I went back to work.

About a foot from the front door, I unearthed some cloth with my trowel. I switched to a large brush. Gently I brushed away sand to find what I assumed would be the end of the cloth. Instead, I found a foot, the bone of which was sticking through the dried flesh. I paused.

Egypt was an Islamic country, and no one who was Islamic could be dug up. I needed to stop, but I was not experienced enough to make that call. I needed Matt to look at the foot and give me the go ahead. He was still helping the students. Not wanting to interrupt him, I went over to the meals area for a drink.

To waste more time, I took my finds to the finds tent and handed in the records for the first room. The tables in the tents were set up to give us a snapshot of how the ancient people lived in this village. Glancing over the tables, I saw a lot of pottery, beer pots, lamps and bowls that people used and threw away when they broke. There was a good mixture of business artefacts as well. Fishermen, farmers, potters—their tools that made the pots and bowls lay next to the artefacts. The table for my finds was half full. I labelled my finds from the first house, then laid them on the surface.

Matt hadn't finished with the students by the time I came out of the tent, but he needed to know what I had found. It seemed that they were digging up oil jars. Made of clay, the jars were large; the bottoms weren't flat, so they could only sit on their sides. I thought I would tell him about the second room, then maybe help the students or do something else.

Matt had his back to me and was holding one of the jars as a student dug it out. "Matt?" I said.

"What the *hell* do you want? Get the *hell* away from me! Can't you work without me looking over your *damn* shoulder?" Matt yelled so loud that his voice echoed off the cliffs.

275

He hadn't looked up at me, but everyone had heard him. The force and anger in his voice made my stomach drop. I took a few steps back; my heart had gone into my throat.

The student stopped digging. With a stunned expression on his face, he watched me back away. Matt glanced at the student; his head twitched before he quickly turned to see who he had yelled at.

This was not the Matt I had been working with all morning, or the one I had spent the day with yesterday. I continued backing away from him, then hurried back to the trucks and out of sight behind them. My breath came hard and I was trying to hold back tears while walking in circles.

"*Laura?*" Matt's voice sounded concerned as he called for me. "*Laura?*" His voice was getting closer.

I wanted to run, but this wasn't the place. "Bloody desert," I muttered.

"*Laura?*" Matt came around behind the trucks. The look on his face had changed; it matched his voice. He walked up to me with his hands out.

"Don't touch me!" I moved backwards, trying to get away.

Matt paused. "I'm sorry, Laura. I shouldn't have talked to you like that. I apologise. Please don't be like this. I'm so sorry." Matt attempted to take a step closer to me. I took one back.

"My ex-husband thought it was all right to talk to me like that. I'm not getting mixed up with someone like that again. I don't give a *shit* who you are."

"I'm sorry." He took another step toward me.

My back hit the truck. "I don't know you," I breathed. I wiped my face, realising that it was wet. The sand mixed with my tears, scratching my cheek.

"Don't say that," Matt said softly, moving a little closer. "I'm sorry."

276

"I don't need to get mixed up with more problems." I shouldn't have acted like that, but the way he had spoken to me was as though I were a stray dog. He had been so nice to me, so tender, but *that*—it scared me.

"I'm sorry, I wasn't thinking about what I was saying. I apologise, Laura." Matt put his hand on my shoulder. I flinched. "Oh hell, look what I've done to you…Laura, you're trembling. I'm sorry. Please understand, that wasn't me. I would never treat you like your ex-husband did. I'm sorry." He ran his hand down my face and I leant my face into his hand. He gently wiped away my tears with his thumb.

"I should just leave. I think me being here isn't a good idea. If you're dating someone else, I don't want to get in the middle," I croaked out.

Matt frowned, then closed his eyes, realising what I had seen. "Laura, don't say that. Please…I wasn't thinking. I don't talk to people like that. I don't know what came over me. I'm sorry. Please forgive me…please don't leave. I said I wasn't dating anyone and that's the truth, please believe me." His hand lingered on my face; he held it there so that I would have to look at him. "The guy you were with this morning and yesterday, that's me— not what you just saw. The one who talked to you like that isn't me. Please believe me, Laura, I don't want to hurt you. I don't ever want to hurt you. Please believe me, Laura."

I couldn't meet his eyes. Matt lifted my face so that I would look at him.

"Please don't leave, Laura. I'm sorry, Laura, please believe me. That student—she's young and a little mixed up. That's all."

I still couldn't speak. I sighed to clear my head and I closed my eyes. When I opened them again, I studied Matt for a moment. His eyes were telling the truth, but there was more.

"I just don't understand what that was," he said softly. "You don't have to forgive me now, just understand that it's not me. I'm sorry."

I began to suck my bottom lip, holding back tears. Matt's lips came close to mine. He paused; I didn't turn away. He brushed his lips on mine. A tingle went down my spine and flushed my body as I let go of my bottom lip. He began kissing me gradually, slow and gentle. It was as though he was trying to show how sorry he was.

As quickly as we had begun, a coughing sound made us break away.

"Is everything all right here? Matt, can I see you?" John had a displeased expression on his face. Marisa was standing beside him.

I hid my face a little behind Matt. He glanced down at me to see if I was okay.

I nodded. "Just give us a second, John. Everything's okay."

"You all right, Laura?" John asked.

"Yes John, I'm fine."

"All right, then." John and Marisa walked to the other side of the truck to wait for Matt.

"I need a minute and then I'll go back to work," I said, looking up at Matt. He touched my face.

"Are you sure?" Matt asked. He sound anxious.

"Yes, I'm fine," I answered.

"I'm sorry," he said as he gently kissed my forehead.

"I know you are."

Once Matt was out of sight, I slid to the ground. My head was a mess. I didn't understand these emotions. I shouldn't be feeling this, not now, not yet. My body was thumping from that kiss and my head was twisted from him yelling at me.

Marisa scuttled over and squatted next to me.

"What happened?"

I looked at her in a daze. "I don't know...he yelled at me."

"Then he kissed you?" She sat down.

"Yes...I know." It had felt good, too.

Marisa handed me a bottle of water. I drank it quickly, almost finishing it.

"Marisa, I just don't understand what's happening. He seems like a nice guy, but that outburst...he was arguing with one of the students. Then he snapped at me. I don't want to get mixed up with someone like that again."

"Did he explain about the student?" she questioned.

"He said that he wasn't dating anyone. He told me she was mixed up. I know he isn't telling me the full truth there. I'm going to ask him about it again. If he lies, that's it."

"He doesn't look very happy with himself."

"I know."

"Did he apologise?"

"Yes, more than once. Did John say anything to you about him?" I had begun moving the bottle around in the sand. My thoughts were a mess.

"He said that Matt's a nice guy, a little mixed up at times, but a good person. John said that this is the happiest he has seen Matt in a long time. They've known each other for years and he said that Matt would never do anything like that."

I let out a slow breath. "I met him only yesterday. It's a holiday thing. Crap, Marisa, what am I doing?"

"You can always go home," Marisa said.

"True."

279

"It's not like he's your soul mate or anything." Marisa was trying to joke. I just let out a breathy laugh.

I leant my head back onto the truck and looked out at the greenness of the palm trees that ran along the riverbank. The wind was blowing through the trees, moving them from side to side. I let the movement wash over me; it was calming me down.

"Are you going to be all right?" Marisa asked. She could see that I was tuning out.

I nodded. "Yes, just give me a minute."

Marisa put her hand on my knee. "All right. I'll give you a moment." She left me without another word.

I went back to the palm trees. They were doing the trick, calming me down. I let what had happened play back through my mind. At the same time, I let what was said drift into my thoughts. I think the power of Egypt was helping me.

"Too much too soon," I said to myself.

I could let this thing between Matt and me play out, or I could walk away. Deep down, I was telling myself not to walk away from Matt. He was my Dark Figure; I had known that when he first spoke to me. I never understood the dreams. *What if he was my soul mate?* A long time ago John had talked about twins' souls, or soul mates. What was happening between us was a classic case. At the end of three weeks I had to walk away from Matt. When that idea came into my mind, my soul began to hurt. I couldn't walk away, not yet. Immaturity was not the factor here; in fact, Matt was more mature than any man I had ever known. Somehow, we met in the middle. Something was telling me that Matt needed me. I liked what this voice was saying. Matt was upset that he had hurt me. Paul, on the other hand, never cared whether he distressed me. The expression on Matt's face showed that he was concerned that he had hurt me; that was what was stopping me from walking away. What would I do?

"I'll play it out," I said so that I could hear the words aloud.

With that, I put my sunglasses and scarf back on and hid my face as I marched around the truck. I peeped around; some of the students and the workers looked up when I came into view. Marisa and John were waiting. Without a word I went back to where I had been working.

Matt had gone back to work with his students. His young female friend peered at me as I passed; she didn't seem too pleased. Matt glanced up and for a split second I thought he was going to come over to me, but he appeared to think better of it.

Back at the house, the foot was still uncovered. I covered it again before going to the next house. After working alone for a while, I heard the sound of footsteps in the sand behind me. I didn't look up until a hand rested on my back. I knew who it was; we locked eyes for a moment. Matt frowned. An expression of confusion crossed his face, then changed to concern. I had been humming. We maintained eye contact, saying nothing. There were too many eyes and ears around. Matt knelt next to me. I ran my hand down his unshaven cheek and smiled. Matt closed his eyes for a moment and nodded before I went back to work. Without a word he began working alongside me.

We worked in a near silence that was broken only when I asked occasional questions. John finally called for everyone to stop for lunch. We found a shady area near the trucks in which to eat. Marisa and John joined us. Food had been set up in a tent by Egyptian employees of our hotel. Throughout lunch, Marisa kept watching me to see if I was okay. She was also studying Matt; it seemed that her feelings about him had changed. Matt and John did most of the talking; I was still not in much of a talkative mood. I was content to hear about the pot pieces that had been found. John and Matt were happy to discover that this site had been in use in the Fourth Dynasty, in the age of the Pyramids.

"It looks like the site has been used on and off since Kufu," John said.

Matt looked around. "It's good farming down here. Also, it's a good rest stop before going down to the Nile and into Africa."

After I ate, I felt a lot better. Matt finally turned to me. "Why did you skip that house?"

"I found bones," I answered him.

Matt looked toward the room. "We'll leave it until tomorrow."

This was fine by me, as I wanted to take photos around the dig site. Matt needed to help the students. John did the same, so Marisa took photos near where she had been working at the other side of the village.

On our way back to the hotel, Matt and I sat in the backseat, our silence continuing. In the stillness, I watched the country slide by me. I could feel Matt looking at me every now and then. We still needed to talk, but not now.

We had work to do once we arrived back at the hotel. The finds had to be put in the research room, which was essentially a big shed just off the side of the hotel. There were quite a few finds to be put away. We spent an hour unloading the trucks, then storing and recording the finds. They had to be placed under lock and key.

Once we finished, I wanted to go up to my room. However, Matt had other plans. He took hold of my arm and towed me towards the rock.

He examined my face before speaking. "Laura, I need to know if you are all right."

I put my finger on his lips. "Matt, stop. Listen to me. You scared me today. I never expected you to act like that." He tried to stop me by shaking his head, but I went on. "However, until then you had been nothing but a gentleman to me."

He pulled my finger off his lips. "Laura, that wasn't me. As I said, I don't know what came over me. I told you yesterday, and I mean it today—I don't treat anyone like that. I shouldn't have kissed you before, but I wanted to show you that I didn't mean to hurt you."

"I know. I'm still standing here. I had two choices—walk away or stay."

Hurt crossed his face. "Please don't go."

"That's why I'm standing here talking to you, Matt. I don't want to leave. But I don't want to interfere with your friend."

"My friend?" he questioned.

"The student who came over for help. I saw you fighting. If I have misunderstood anything, I'll stay out of the way. I know there's something more. Please tell me the truth." I needed to push this; there was more there, and I couldn't leave it.

Matt looked at the ground and let out a sigh. "I dated her last year. She has this crazy idea that we're still dating. It's been over for quite some time. There's nothing going on; she wasn't meant to be here. Laura, can we start this again? Please."

Matt was panicking, thinking that I was about to leave. I had to do something to let him know that I wasn't going to walk away. I had to make him understand that I knew he was sorry. I needed to be sure about his student friend. Matt was holding onto my shoulders, waiting for me to talk. I was pretty sure that I was okay with the situation, but that student wasn't going to let it go, and this worried me.

Now I was acting according to my heart and not my brain. "We have a date on Wednesday night, don't we?" I asked, looking Matt in the eye.

He sighed.

"The kiss before—well, it was nice. You can do that again; I won't stop you. But if you're playing me, I'll go home and you'll never see me again."

Matt sighed in relief again. I slipped my arms around his neck. He leant his forehead against mine. "Yes, we have a date on Wednesday. I'm still very sorry. I'm not playing you, Laura."

"You're not telling me where we're going. *Are you?*" I asked to lighten the mood.

He smiled for the first time since this morning. "No, I'm not telling you."

Matt's hand hovered under my chin to lift my head for a kiss. It was gentle and tender. I could have kept going, as that tingling sensation travelled back down my spine. It journeyed around my body, which was crying out for more. It had been a long time since I had enjoyed this.

When I came out to the carpark the next day after breakfast, John and Matt were intently talking to each other. John jabbed Matt in the chest a few times it was as if he was trying to prove a point. However when they saw me they broke off their conversation. I was intrigued about what they had been talking about but it was not my business. It was not hard to have an inkling that it was to do with what happened the day before.

That day Matt and I began working on the room that I had missed the day before. We were still not back to where we had begun, but maybe it was better that way. A new start was the right thing.

The mummy's head was fragile; I had to lie on my stomach to hold it. Matt was also on his stomach, brushing away the sand to free the skull with his trowel and brush. It was a fine balance— damage the skull, or save it. The smell from the mummy wasn't too pleasant; it surprised me how the sand still held the smell of death. Yet Carter had noted that Tut's mummy still smelt of herbs and spices when they opened his coffin over two thousand years later.

Matt seemed better at managing the smell then I was. My head was pressed against his shoulder. I could feel the mummy's hair and dry skin; the tip of my fingers held the bottom of its jaw.

Matt seemed to be enjoying the fact that I was so close. He smelt like a mixture of masculine sweat and deodorant. I was humming.

"I remember the first time I did this. I think I was acting like you. You get over the smell the more you do it." As Matt spoke his voice vibrated in his body.

"When was that, when you were six again? I'm just out of practice," I joked back at him.

"No…I was nine. It was the first time I worked with John. I'll have to get you to do the next one so that you get into practice again."

"No worries," I said. I looked over his shoulder. Matt was shaking his head at me. He went back to work, then stopped when I began to hum again.

"Is that the Billie Holiday version or Janis Joplin?" He said this in a strange voice.

"Do you want me to stop?"

"No, it's funny; I used to have dreams of that song. It's kind of reassuring."

"Really. I had a dream of someone telling me to come here to Egypt. I don't know, but I would just hum that song without knowing. Do you believe in soul connections?" I couldn't help it; I said the last part without thinking. I was talking nonsense. Now he would think that I was mad.

"Sort of. I don't believe in New-Age mumbo jumbo," he said. I didn't believe him.

"I'll be careful with the humming. I'll also do the next mummy. You seemed happier where I am right now," I said, changing the subject.

"I'll hold you to the next mummy. You're right, I can't argue where you are." It felt like Matt was smiling, but I wasn't sure. "I like your humming. Don't stop."

The moment passed slowly. My arms were hurting, so to take my mind off it, I needed to talk. "I know this is the wrong time to ask, but since it's just you, me and the mummy here, can I ask a few questions?"

Matt chuckled. "Go ahead."

"How long did you date your student?" I needed to know.

"Um, it was a couple of months. It was just pure arr…" He stopped.

"Okay, I get it. You don't need to finish. Have you dated anyone a little longer term than that?" I shouldn't have asked these questions; my mouth was running away with me.

"I dated a girl while I was in college. I wanted to marry her and have a family, but she didn't. She left me for another guy."

"I'm sorry. That's hard."

"Tell me something; would you get married again?"

I lay quiet for a moment. He was waiting, I couldn't take too long to tell him what I was thinking. "Right now, if someone asked me I would say no. However, in a few years and if I was in love, I would say yes."

"I understand that. I think I would have given the same answer. What's the other question?"

"How did you know there was another question?" I joked.

"Oh, I don't know. I could just feel that there was something else. Go ahead."

286

"He said he doesn't believe in New-Age mumbo jumbo, but he's a mind reader," I muttered at him.

"Har har. Go on. I have a comedian on my hands."

I sighed to give myself a moment. "How old are you?"

"If I tell you how old I am, will you tell me how old you are?"

"Yes…I'll give you an average," I said nervously.

"Well then, you first." Matt knew he had me. I could drop it or keep going.

"Thirty-six," I said quickly. I was going to lie, but it slipped out faster than I had wanted it to. "Now you," I said.

Matt chuckled at me; I was still speaking quickly. "Twenty-six." He answered a lot easier than I had.

I think I took in a breath. I wasn't sure, but he stopped working to look back at me. "Are you alright?" he asked.

"Yes," I answered, trying to keep my voice even. "Since you aren't going to tell me where we're going tomorrow night, you have to tell me if I should dress up or down."

Suddenly, Matt sat up. He pointed with his trowel. I was holding the skull in my hands; it was free from its resting place.

"Don't move." Matt gingerly leant over to pick up a box for the skull. I lay still, trying not to move. The sand around the mummy was about to fall in. Matt put the box next to the skull. I could still see the man's eyes; they were half open and the iris was still intact. It felt as though I could crush the skull if I pushed too hard.

"It's nice to see that he didn't die in pain," I said, trying not to think too much about what I was doing.

Matt looked at the mummy's face and nodded. "I never noticed that before. I've seen it on the Screaming Mummy, maybe, but I haven't noticed with others," The Screaming Mummy was a man who died in about the Fourth Dynasty; no one knew why he looked

287

like he was screaming. "Gently," Matt said as I slowly moved the skull into the box. His hands hovered over the skull, ready to catch it if I dropped it. We still had the rest of the body to do. "How did you work the faces out?" Matt asked while placing padding in the tray around the skull.

"I had to research mummies last year for Dr Colman. After hours of looking at endless pictures, I started noticing that you could tell how they died."

Matt stopped for a moment. He tilted his head to one side as though he were watching a film. He made a face. "You're right, amazing. Why was Dr Colman having you look at mummies?"

"He had a talk at the University and I had to ensure that he had his facts right," I said, annoyed.

"I never worked with Dr Colman, but he seems like a real ass."

We started removing other parts of the body. The mummy needed to be removed because it could have been stolen. It had a few artefacts intact, and they could fetch a high price on the black market. A few wooden Shabtis lay next to the man. Some of his wrapping had rotted away over time so that we now had a mixture of wrapping and body to remove. It was sad because the mummy had been there for so long. Throughout the morning everyone came over to view the mummy, so working on the body became slow going.

"So?" I asked when we had a quiet moment. I had begun working on the other side of the body.

"So what?" Matt asked. He seemed to have forgotten my question.

"Matt, please, if you don't want to tell me where we're going, that's fine. One way to stress a girl out is to not tell her what type of clothing she should wear. Which way, Matt—up or down?"

He smirked; there was an evil look in his eyes. "Something black and silky would be nice. What do you mean 'up or down?'" he asked, grinning at me. He was lucky that I couldn't hit him.

"You know what I mean. Dressy or non-dressy." I pulled a pleading face.

"Oh, all right. Dressy will be fine."

"Now I'll be thinking that there's more to it." I looked at him, pleading for him to understand women's ways.

"Okay, I'll dress up too, but not too dressy. We're not going to a ball. Is that better?" Matt went back to work, but he was still smirking.

"Yes, thank you. Then I'll dress down. Are my work boots all right?"

Matt quickly raised his head to look at me. I was smirking at him while I scraped away more sand.

"I'm joking," I snickered.

"Har har, very funny. Women. Really, sometimes I don't know. Why do men bother?" Matt teased back.

"Because we're worth it."

It was good to have the Matt back whom I had been with the other day. It was nice to laugh again. I had caught him looking anxiously at me throughout the day. That morning when I went out to the car park, I had seen John and Matt speaking. It looked as though Matt was trying to reassure John that everything was fine. All day I reassured him through the way I talked and acted. By the end of the day I thought it was working, though I wasn't sure. Matt's student friend tried to talk to him, but he kept walking away from her. She was now working with John's group on the other side of the site.

That afternoon we lifted the mummy out of the ground, then placed it onto wooden boards. A sheet was placed over the body to help protect it; also, this was a human and he needed respect. The mummy was placed in the back of the four-wheel drive; he was going to be stored in the finds room at first, then would be studied, recorded, and placed into storage with other mummies in Luxor. At that point, hopefully he would rest in peace. All of this was to keep him safe because once he was found he needed protection. Not only that, he had a lot of information to tell us about his life.

That night at the hotel, I came down to dinner after washing the sand off me. Once again, Matt pulled out my chair. A few of the male students had jumped on stage; there were instruments left for people to play, and they weren't doing too badly. However, no one could sing. Marisa kept looking at me to go up there.

After the last student butchered one of the latest hits, I went over to the stage. "Do you know how to play anything other than the latest hits?"

"Yes, if you can do better, we can."

I nodded and jumped onstage. "How about 'Little Boy Girl Blue,' do you know that one?"

The guy who was playing guitar smiled. "Hell yeah."

The rest of the night they weren't going to let me go. I had had a long day and wanted to sleep, but everyone in the dining room seemed to come back to life after a few songs. Matt had a look of amazement on his face when I came back to the table. I wanted to eat, but the students wanted me to sing more.

Later that night, after one last drink, John and Marisa left us. Matt once again walked me back to the elevator that led up to my room.

CHAPTER 19

It had reached the night of the secret date. We started the day early, like we had done all week. Matt seemed happier, almost back to the Matt I had come to know.

Around mid-morning one of John's students found a box of clay tablets. We stood around the finds table as John and the student opened the wooden box. It contained what looked like about a hundred small hand-sized tablets. Matt picked one out of the box. Running his fingers down the cuneiform, he read it out loud.

"High counsellor, may the Nile give you a good harvest."

"The Great Royal Wife would like to give you the blessing of Bassett," I added over his shoulder.

Matt looked up at me in surprise. John slapped Matt on the shoulder. "Laura reads cuneiform as well as you."

"Really." Matt was impressed.

"She was at the top of my class. Just like you, Laura knew how to read it before she came to my class," John added.

"Tone it down, John," I said, going red.

"Wow, impressive. Do you want to help with the cataloguing of the box?" Matt asked me.

"Sure," I said, looking around at the students sheepishly.

"Here Brad, you do rubbings of the scripts and Laura, you can write a basic translation. We'll do a full one later." Brad was the student who had found the box. John nodded in agreement at Matt's decision,

Some of the tablets had to do with disputes; one was over someone's wife running off with a slave, while another involved someone who had stolen goats from another person. There were taxes that needed to be paid to the Pharaoh Kufu, a shipment the Pharaoh was waiting for but that he had not received. Brad helped me number the tablets; it would take weeks to decipher them fully.

Matt came back over just before our morning break to see what I had found out about the tablets. He stood and read as I told him what I had found.

"Flawless. Why you aren't…keep up the good work," he said.

"Thank you, Doc." I tried not to watch him walk away, but I couldn't help myself.

"Laura," Marisa murmured as she came hurrying over. She had been watching us and Brad had gone for a break.

"What is it, Marisa?" I said, trying to read. She had a tray of finds and was making out that she was doing something with them.

"Do you know what you're wearing tonight?" she asked out of the side of her mouth.

There were a few students around. "No." Now I was talking out of the side of my mouth as well.

"That's not good. You should be thinking about it."

"I did bring a dress to go out in." I didn't want to think about it. I had been nervous all day; thinking about it now would make things worse.

"What if you don't like what you have?"

"Marisa, there are no malls around here. What do you want me to do?" I asked, looking around. I had said that too loud and students were looking at us.

"Do you need to borrow anything?"

"No, Mum, I'm fine. Thank you." We had gone back to talking out of the sides of our mouths.

"What if he *wants to*…you know?"

292

"Marisa!" I said loudly. Then, "Marisa," I said a little softer, making a face at her.

"Well, what *if?*"

"Marisa, do I ask what you do with John? No."

"I know, but when was the last time you went on a *real* date?" Marisa asked in a hushed voice.

"I do remember how to go on a date and *it's none of your business.*"

"That's my point. The last time you went out was with Paul. Wait, I don't think so, Dylan maybe. I'm sure Paul was like dating a dead fish."

Just then, John and Matt walked up to the table. I think they had heard the last part. The students had heard everything and were now talking behind their hands, looking at Matt and me. I had been feeling okay up until then.

"What are you two up to?" John looked at us and then at the students.

"Nothing," we both said, smiling at them.

"It's time for a break, or do you two need a little more 'girl time?'" John seemed to have suspected that we were up to something. Matt was clueless about what was going on; he glanced back and forth at both of us.

I jumped to my feet. "No, we're fine. After all that reading, I need a break. Matt, what do you want to drink, coffee or tea? How do you have it?"

"Coffee, white, one sugar. Thanks." Matt looked at me, unsure of what he had missed. On the other hand, I had the impression that John was upset with Marisa, as if he was worried she had done something wrong. I brushed it off. I didn't want to care anymore; my nerves were getting the better of me.

293

Later in the afternoon, when we arrived back at the hotel, we unloaded the finds that had been discovered that day. My stomach was doing flip-flops. Matt seemed cool; he strolled up to me after we had finished. He took me to one side. We hadn't had much time to be with each other all day.

"I'll meet you in the lobby at seven-thirty," Matt said.

"Yes, all right."

"All righty, then." Matt kissed me on the cheek as he left.

To calm my nerves, I had to do something before seven-thirty. I couldn't call home, as it was midnight in Australia.

Sitting up in my room, I slowly read through my emails. I tried to read Em's email, but after reading a line for the third time, I stopped and looked around the room.

"Crap, what am I doing?" It was only six o'clock.

Now the panic that I had been trying to hold off all day began seeping in. Looking around the room, I sucked my bottom lip. I threw my suitcase onto the bed, which squeaked under the weight. Flicking open my case, I saw that my dress was folded under one of my shirts. I took it out and laid it on the bed. After my talk with Marisa today, I didn't know whether the dress was right. After a moment spent picking up the dress, then setting it back down, I gave up and headed for the shower. Under the warm water, I felt good, as though I had been at the beach all day, minus the salt water. My nerves had paused and somewhat slipped away, though not completely.

I took my time drying my hair; I didn't have perfectly straight hair, so I needed to be careful that I didn't end up looking like a poodle. My makeup was just right. I was about to add a bit more eyeliner when I heard a knock on my door. My heart leaped. It was just before seven; he had said that he would meet me in the lobby.

"Who is it?" I called from the bathroom. My voice sounded out of breath.

"Laura, it's alright. It's just me, Marisa."

I sighed. "I'm coming." I rushed to the door with a towel around me. I opened it before rushing back to the bathroom.

"How are you doing?" Marisa called.

"Hanging in." I answered as I peeked out of the bathroom.

Marisa was near my dress. "This one?" She asked pointing at it.

"Yeah, I was thinking of putting the blue and gold shawl with it." I moved a clump of hair over my shoulder.

"Here." Marisa held out a bottle of perfume.

"Oh, I like this one. Thank you," I said as I smelt it.

Marisa made me a cup of tea to calm me down, and to waist that last half hour.

"Are you still okay about me dating Matt?" I asked out of the blue. Maybe John had told her something I needed to know.

"Why do you ask?"

"Yesterday…I saw John and Matt in the car park. John didn't seem to be happy with Matt."

Marisa put down her cup. "John has to make sure that no one is doing anything that could get the college into trouble. An English college was almost kicked out of Egypt for publishing research that the Egypt Antiquity department deemed wrong. They have stricter laws here, you know that. We have to be careful about what we do. This isn't our country. And besides, John was looking out for you as he always has. I'm fine."

"Okay, just me being silly." I drank the last mouthful of my tea.

Time had run out. My butterflies were now doing the rumba in my stomach. Marisa handed me my dress. In the bathroom, I awkwardly stepped into it. My fingers couldn't zip it up; I was all thumbs.

295

I came out for help. Marisa smiled. "Oh. Nice."

"Thanks. Zip me up, please." I gave myself one last look in the mirror before leaving. Marisa didn't come down with me.

The door of my elevator slipped open, revealing Matt in the lobby. My heart skipped a beat when I saw him. I enjoyed watching Matt's eyes pop a little as I moved to his side. "You look breathtaking," Matt said, looking into my eyes as he took in a breath.

Normally Matt wore a New York cap, jeans, and a t-shirt. Now he was wearing a black dress shirt, dark brown dress pants, and a dinner jacket with no tie. He looked and smelt good; he had shaven off his three days of stubble.

"You look really good, too," I said with a smile in my voice. I was glad that it hadn't come out in a squeak.

A playful smile came to his lips. "Ready to go?" he asked.

"Yes, let's go. Still not telling me where we're going?"

"No." He chuckled.

Matt took my hand and escorted me into the car park. Thinking that there would be a car waiting for us, I glanced around as he led me past the vehicles. He gently guided me to the wharf. We must be going on a ferry was my first thought however, we paused in front of a boat. It was rusty and old; one of the workers stood smiling at us. As with most things in Egypt, the boat had an art deco look to it.

"Salaam aleikuum." *"Hello."* The worker greeted both of us.

"Aleikuum as-salaam," we answered him.

Matt stepped onto the gangplank, then offered his hand to help me on board. The gangplank moved; I didn't like the feeling, as though it could fall at any time.

"Shukran." *"Thank you,"* I said to Matt. He looked into my eyes and smiled.

296

We made our way to the back of the boat. I stopped. The boat had once been painted white, but now it was rusty and peeling. It looked like it had once been a fishing trawler.

The boat owner smiled at us. He bowed a little as he walked to the front of the boat. The back was draped with brandy-coloured see-through curtains hanging on a frame. A table and chairs stood in the middle of the deck, while a large lounge sat near the back railings. All of it reminded me of an Arabic tent. I smiled.

"You like?" Matt asked.

"Yes. Very much. Worth the surprise."

"Good." He puffed out his chest and grinned.

The boat began to rumble under my feet. Matt held out his hand to show me to the couch. We both fell into our seats as the boat jerked forward. I let out a giggle.

The boat slowly spluttered down the Nile to the south, passing the dig site on the way. Matt opened a bottle of wine and poured me a glass.

I looked around and smiled. "Very nice."

"I did ask if I could sail with you down the Nile."

"You did."

We sat watching the palm trees, ancient sites, and people on the shore glide past us; it was as though we were in a dream. The sun was going down and everything had a golden, bright glow to it. Matt wrapped his arms around me.

"Tell me something about yourself," I asked Matt quietly.

I didn't think he was going to answer me. He kissed my hand. "My mom would always have to watch my pockets. Grandpa Jack would encourage me. I kept bones in a tin in my pocket. One summer I found a dead mouse; mice have the same bones we do. I buried it in a little rock grave so that I could dig it up the next summer. Grandpa Jack was going to have me write a report about

297

what the mouse looked like and other things I noticed had changed. The next summer the mouse was just bones, and I carried it around in the tin. When I had nothing to do, I would put the bones together. When Mom did my washing, if she started to scream I knew that I had left my tin in my pocket. '*Mathew Ryan, come and get this tin before I throw it in the trash*!' Mom didn't like mice." He grinned at the memory. A softness came to his eyes. I liked it.

"I don't blame her," I laughed.

"Your turn."

"There was a poem that I had to recite when I was a kid, in front of the school. Do you want to hear it?"

He smiled. "I'm all ears. I enjoyed your singing the other night; I should enjoy this."

"All right. I'm glad you enjoyed it." I sat up and took a sip from my glass, then cleared my throat. "*Wilt thou love me sweet when my hair is grey, and my cheeks have lost their hue? When the charm of youth shall have passed away, will you love as of old prove true? For the look may have change, the heart may range, and the love be no long fond; wilt thou love with truth in the years of youth and away to the years beyond? Oh, I love you, sweet, for your locks of brown and the blush on your cheek that lie, but I love you most for your kindly heart, that I see in your sweet blue eyes, for the eyes are the signs of the soul within. Of the heart that is real and true, and mine own sweetheart, I shall love you still, just as long as your eyes are blue. For the locks may bleach, and the cheeks of peach may be reft of their golden hue; But mine own heart, I shall love you still, just as long as your eyes are blue.*"

I continued. "It was written by Banjo Patterson; he was a famous Australian poet." I sat back and sucked my lip. I shouldn't have told him that poem. It was a love poem.

Matt sat quietly for a moment before answering. "I love that poem."

298

The boat began to slow down as it pulled over to one side of the bank at a small dock. I sat up, thinking that we were going to get off. Matt stayed in his seat. The boat owner appeared from the top cabin upstairs. He hurried around to the ropes to tie up the boat. A woman who must have been his wife came out of the lower cabin. She was carrying a tray of food that she placed on the table, smiling at both of us.

Matt got up. "Shukran." *"Thank you."* Matt tipped the boat owner.

"Ma'a salaama," they said to us.

"Ma'a salaama." *Good bye."* We watched the owner and his wife as they left the boat and made their way to a waiting car.

"I'm driving the boat back when we're finished," Matt said. He watched as a look of shock developed on my face as I realised that we were going to be alone on the Nile. There was nothing but desert on both sides. We were past the dig site, and papyrus reeds stood tall near the boat.

"Oh, okay," I answered, sounding worried.

Matt pulled out a chair at the table for me to sit in. He went to a gramophone that was sitting in the corner; after a few moments, the voice of Billie Holiday came winding out.

"Very fitting. It's like we're in an old black-and-white movie."

Matt smiled and poured me another glass of red wine.

I looked around, still feeling a little worried. "Are we safe here?"

"Yes, very safe, don't worry. We'll be fine," Matt replied as he watched me drink my wine quickly. "I don't want you getting too drunk now," he teased me.

I held out my glass so that he would fill it again. The sun was turning the light to a golden colour around us. I served our plates.

"Cheers." Matt lifted his glass to mine.

"Cheers."

I enjoyed the sounds of the oncoming night as we ate. Once again, there was no need to talk. My nerves were almost gone, but they were just waiting to come back.

"You said you dug up your first mummy when you were nine?" I asked as we finished eating. I sat back, sipping my wine.

"Yeah, it was my second time coming to Egypt with Grandpa Jack. He wanted me to work with John's team that day. I was given a square. I had gone down only a few layers when I found it."

"The photo in the lobby. When was that taken?"

Matt let out a laugh. "That's how you found out my name."

I smiled and nodded. "Yes."

"Very good. Seven years ago I had just found out that I was working for the college. Grandpa Jack wanted to find Nefertiti's second temple. He had found the first one, you have the diaries on that. It was like his Holy Grail. We found the cache of mummified cats that belonged to her temple. We haven't found the second temple; we're still searching for it. When I became an archaeologist, John kept harping on the fact that he wanted to find it, so we spent a season looking for it and found the cats."

I remembered reading about it, but never put two and two together. "Sounds like your grandpa would be happy that you found it. Must be a buzz to find something like that."

"He would have been. '*That's my boy.*'" Matt's face lit up when he talked about his grandpa. "That Shabti—did you ever find out anything about it?"

"No. I knew it was important. I think Dr Colman has it locked away in his office."

"Mmm." Matt didn't seem happy about this. "What about your daughter?" He changed the subject.

300

I smiled. "What about her?"

"What's she like?"

"She's headstrong, loving, caring, smart, and beautiful. She was upset that she couldn't come."

"Just like her mom. She should come next time; I'll show her around."

"So, do you get to use your bullwhip when you run through the tombs?" We moved over to the couch; Matt had opened another bottle of wine.

Matt smiled. "No, I'd rather fight crocs."

"Oh no, you're not to fight them. You need to jump on them and say silly catchphrases. I'm Australian, I should know."

Matt let out a laugh. "True. The other day…" He looked at his glass. I took a sip from mine. I didn't want to go over this again, not tonight. "I need to know if you're all right," he asked as he looked up from his glass. "I never meant to hurt you. You must know. I'm sorry about that."

"I know you are. You keep watching me to see if I'm alright. I'm fine, please believe me. As I said, if I didn't believe you, I wouldn't be here."

"The last time I dated Piper was the middle of last year. I don't know why she came to Egypt. I had to end it; she can be a little too much."

It was the first time I had heard her name, but we were going over old ground. To stop him, I kissed him. He looked at me. His hand came up to my cheek. He was about to kiss me again when the record stopped.

"Do you want to hear another record?" Matt asked.

"Yes please," I said, a little breathless.

"Do you like the blues?"

"I like a lot of music. I love the blues."

The night air was getting colder. Once Matt replaced the record, he began lighting candles. They had an odd smell to them. Wrapping my shawl tighter around myself, I strolled around the back of the deck, which had a soft glow. It was as though we were in our own world.

"What's behind this door?" I asked, pointing at the door the boatman's wife had come out of.

Matt looked at the door. He paused, then pulled a face before answering. "A bedroom." Quickly he pointed upstairs. "There's a galley up there."

"Does someone live here?" I asked, thinking we weren't alone.

"No, it's a holiday boat."

"Oh." I studied the door, rubbing my arms to get warm.

"We can always go back to the hotel," Matt said. He closed his eyes and shook his head, realising what he had just said. "Um…"

I smirked. "No. Let's dance." I smiled at Matt; it was nice to know that he could get a little rattled.

"I can do that," he said softly.

We slow danced to the sound of John Lee's guitar weaving in the air. I rested my head on Matt's chest as he wrapped his arms around me. I felt warm and safe, as though this was where I belonged. When the next song began, Matt's hand came under my chin to kiss me. His other hand slid slowly down my back. He paused, giving me a chance to say no. I shook my head a little as I brushed my lips on his.

This kiss was a lot stronger, more breathtaking. My hand moved up into Matt's hair. His arms enclosed me and he tried to guide us backwards toward the door to the bedroom. My shawl fell to the floor as I slipped off Matt's jacket.

We missed the door; I let out a grunt as we smashed into the wall.

"You okay?" Matt asked, looking worried that he had hurt me.

"Mmm," I said, finding his lips again.

I think he tried to say something else, but I wasn't listening. My body had stopped tingling and was now burning. Matt's lips left mine and rapidly moved down my neck to my chest. His hand went down the side of my body, over my hips and down my thigh. He stopped at the back of my knee and pulled my leg up over his hip. I took in a yearning breath, which made Matt's hip push into mine.

Our breathing became harder as our actions became more intense. "We should move," Matt said, breathing into my ear.

"Yeah," I said as I looked up at the roof, trying to stop.

It didn't work; our lips found each other once more. However, in the middle of our yearning for each other, I managed to free my hand to try and find the door. Matt's hand reached out and found it before I did. He peeled us off the wall and into the cabin without our lips leaving each other.

Our lovemaking was like nothing I had ever experienced; it was as though we had always known how to please each other. At different times that night, we woke each other up to make love again. Finally, in the early hours I fell asleep in his arms with the feeling of Matt running his hand through my hair.

The next morning, when I woke alone in the white brass bed, the walls of the cabin were bathed in light, highlighting every piece of flaking white paint. Closing my eyes, I tried to decide whether I should get out of bed. My body and mind were as one; the feeling of pure pleasure bathed my cells. I felt as though I had fallen back asleep; the previous night drifted into my dreams.

Finally my stomach won out when the smell of breakfast reached my nose, I opened my eyes to see that my shawl had been placed at the bottom of the bed. Wrapping it around myself, I noticed that there was another door near the bed. The smell was coming through it. I opened the door to find steel steps going up. With another grumble of my stomach, I followed the smell.

At the top of the stairs, I found Matt cooking over a one-ring gas burner that sat on a narrow bench with a round sink next to it. Matt was shirtless, cooking eggs. I stood quietly to enjoy the view. He turned his back a little; to my surprise, a part of his back was deeply scarred. I remembered feeling something the previous night, but didn't realise what it was. The scar went from his left shoulder, half way down and along his spine. My heart sank at the thought of how it had gotten there.

Matt began to dish out the eggs. "Good morning," I said as he finished.

He turned and smiled, stopped what he was doing, and came over. He studied me for a moment. "Good morning. You okay?" He ran his hand on my cheek.

"Yes, I'm fine."

"Are you hungry?" Matt asked as he kissed me.

"Yes," I answered, kissing him back. "It's going to get cold."

"Yes, it'll get cold," he answered as we kept kissing each other. "How did you sleep?"

"Not bad. You?"

"I had a good night." He grinned, then continued kissing me. I was trying to kiss him too, but I was smiling too much. My stomach growled. Matt stopped. "I better feed you or I might lose you."

The table was a plank of wood with four legs attached to it. The chairs were old and mismatched. It seemed that every part of the boat badly needed a coat of paint.

"You're a good cook," I said. Matt had cooked the eggs just right; there were no slimy bits.

"No hangover?" he asked.

"No, my head is fine."

Matt finished eating, then sat back. His eyes had watched my shawl as he ate. He had a playful look on his face as he took in what I was wearing. "We should head back soon. I have to have the boat back by sundown," he finally said, reaching over to run his fingers on my shawl, feeling its texture.

"That's too bad, I'm enjoying myself," I said, looking down at what he was doing.

"Mmmm, I heard." He raised one eyebrow at me.

I stood and went around to his side of the table. He sat me down on his lap and his hand found its way under my shawl. His lips moved softly over my shoulder as I dragged him to the floor.

When we finally pulled away from each other, we needed to get back, as we had missed a day of the dig. I was sure that John wouldn't allow us to have much more time off.

We showered and changed. "Do you think they missed us?" I asked. I leaned on the wall, watching Matt drive the boat. We were almost back to the hotel.

A playful smile crossed Matt's face. "I think they'll live."

"We could keep going and cruise the Mediterranean."

He looked around the wheelhouse. "I don't think the old girl could take it."

"I think this old girl could." I grinned at him.

He gave me a side glance. "Stop that. There's nothing old about you." I leant over and kissed him on the neck. "You better behave; I might crash the boat." Matt chuckled as he took hold of my body and kept hold of it.

My other hand came to rest on his left shoulder. My fingers could feel the scar under his shirt. I needed to know what had hurt him; the thought of it really upset me.

"How did you get this scar?"

Matt's head turned to my hand. He sighed a little before turning his attention to the front of the boat. I saw his eyes close a little longer than a blink.

"I was in a car accident when I was fifteen. I don't remember much of it," Matt said quietly.

"That must have hurt." I ran my fingers over the scar. "Was that when your mother and father died?"

"No, they died in a house fire well before that."

"I'm sorry to hear that. I'm sorry if it upset you." I kissed his shoulder.

"No, it's fine. I'm okay with you knowing it. Yeah, it hurt; I was in the hospital for quite a while because of it."

Matt went quiet. His hand came up to my wrist and he dragged it around to kiss the palm of my hand. I had hit a painful memory. I held him a little tighter. It seemed that he had had a hard life, and if he didn't say more, that was okay. His temper the other day almost made sense now, but still wasn't excusable.

"Is John going to be upset that we missed the day?"

"I thought he would be, but he seems to be okay about it."

"Marisa must have had a hand in it."

"Yeah, the old boy is a little softer when she's around."

"When the two of them get married, my job is done."

Matt nodded agreeing with my statement.

Everyone was still at the dig site, which gave us time to change. I felt like I was in a dream. I was happy. We spent the afternoon in the finds room looking over the mummy that I had found the day before. It needed to be recorded before being shipped over the Nile to Luxor. We finished with photos of the mummy; you wouldn't have known that we had had a night together. We had gone back to our act, as though nothing had happened.

I had enjoyed our quiet afternoon together, but it came to an end with the sound of trucks and the four-wheel drive pulling up outside. Our time alone was over. Matt gave me a quick kiss before the door opened.

The quietness shattered with the sounds of talking, laughing, and joking. Matt held the door for everyone, Marisa dashed past him.

She glanced at Matt and grinned. "Hello, Matt," she said as she breezed past him, quick but friendly.

Shaking his head, Matt gave me a quick look before going outside to help the others.

Marisa yanked me off my stool and dragged me to a quiet part of the room. She wanted to grill me quickly. "So, you two finally came home. Did you have fun? Was it a nice place?"

"Yes, *yes*, and none of your *business*." I grinned; the students were filing into the room.

"Ooh, that good?" Marisa had to stop grilling me, but what I wasn't saying gave her a grin from ear to ear.

Matt and I stayed in the research room with some of the students, working until dinnertime. Matt went around helping the students with the artefacts. Marisa had taken over his side of the dig that day. John seemed pleased that Matt was working late to make up for lost time.

Over dinner, while Matt and John got drinks, Marisa managed to get out of me where we had gone, but that was it; she guessed the rest. Piper and her friends kept looking at us and then talking. Piper did try to talk to Matt again, but he was having none of it. I was a little worried, but Matt said he had no interest in her. I had to trust him. This was a holiday thing and I didn't want to worry about it. However, my stomach turned every time I thought of going home. I gulped my last mouthful of wine, trying to push away that feeling.

After dinner we sat and talked for a while. Finally I needed to say good night to everyone; I needed sleep. Matt stood. His hand found its way into mine and he held it tight, not letting go.

I wasn't going back to my room, not that night. Matt led the way. We walked past the buffet and up to the staff hotel rooms. We ascended a flight of wooden stairs and walked through a heavy door. We saw a long corridor with rooms running off one side of it. The carpet was red with little, faded gold pyramids. Wood panelling lined the walls. It was dark up here; the only light flickered in the corridor. Matt kept hold of my hand as we made our way to room 116. The numbers of the hotel rooms didn't make sense, as the room before had been 114.

Matt's room was lined with the same wood panelling as that in the corridor, and the same red carpet. A bench ran along the wall near the door. Matt had a laptop on it and paperwork spread all over it. The room was bigger than mine, though his bathroom was the same size. Matt's double bed was only a few feet from the door and was flanked by two bedside tables with lamps. The bed sagged in the middle.

Matt closed the door. He came up to me and I turned to him. Matt's hands flew to my face. He kissed me tenderly once, then stopped. "Do you want to hear some music?" he asked.

"Sure." I sat on his bed.

In the corner was a CD Walkman with small speakers wired to it. It sat on the floor next to a pile of Matt's clothes, which were falling out of a trunk. He had a booklet filled with CDs.

"Do you want to hear more blues?" he asked as he twisted a CD around his finger.

"Sure. No iPod?"

"No, I like CDs."

I noticed that on the bedside table, my drawing leant on the wall. The scarf hung off the bed. I lay back. Matt lay next to me; he had put on Muddy Waters. My hand came up to his face.

"So, what do you want to do?" Matt asked playfully as he held onto me.

I looked up at him; he was trying not to smile. "Do you want me to go? I need sleep," I said, playing with him as I tried to get out of bed.

Matt's arm tightened around me; he wasn't going to let me out of bed. "No you don't; come back here."

My hand came back to touch his face. He hadn't shaved since last night, and I liked it. Matt kissed my lips slowly.

"Do you want me to go?" I asked again.

"No…I…think you…can…stay." He had begun kissing my neck. I wasn't going anywhere.

CHAPTER 20

Early the next morning, I had to untangle my way out of Matt's arms, as he had them wrapped tightly around me. I smirked as he made a snoring noise and rolled to the other side of the bed. As I was about to leave, something caught my eye out the window. I could see the boulder. It was kind of sweet to know that he must have been watching me.

I needed a shower and a change of clothes. When I finally came down from my room, Matt was waiting for me in the dining room. He had coffee and food waiting for me. The dining room was almost empty, though there were a few students having breakfast.

"Couldn't you sleep?" Matt teased as he sat down.

"No, some guy kept me up all night. How many days can you go without sleep?"

"I'll have to have a word with him. And ten days," Matt said smugly.

"Oh, don't worry. I don't mind so much, as he has really nice things to say. Plus, if he gets to be too much, I know how to handle him."

Matt reached over and took my hand, rubbing his thumb over it. "I bet you do," he mumbled.

That morning, Matt drove the four-wheel drive to give John a break. Marisa and I talked casually in the back. Three more houses had been cleared; there was one more house on my side left to do. I went to work on the next house. When Matt finished with his students, he came over to work with me.

A nagging feeling of what to do when the three weeks were up kept dancing in my head. It was what had woken me up that morning. The anticipation of Wednesday night was over, and I had to consider what would happen now. I had a feeling that Matt didn't want this to end, though I wasn't sure whether he had thought about it. I was kicking myself for telling him that poem on the Nile. I think I had been swept up in the romance of it all. If I was being honest with myself, I didn't think I was ready to give him up. When I was around Matt, I felt happier; I felt that I could do anything. This was wrong; I shouldn't be having those types of feelings for someone else so quickly and so early. After three weeks, I had to give up Matt and go back to my life. Emily needed me; I was her mother.

I sighed. Matt looked over at me. "You alright? You look worried."

"No, I'm fine. Just concentrating on what I'm doing."

Matt sat up and watched me for a moment; it seemed as though he was trying to read my thoughts.

"I was just thinking that you haven't shown me any of the sites yet, or where you found the cats," I said, trying to stop him from thinking that anything was wrong.

"No, I've been busy." Matt grinned and a playful look came across his face. "Well, I'll have to make us unbusy and take you this weekend."

"Do you think you can handle it?"

"Sure, easy."

That night we lay on the bed entwined. It was hard to tell where either one of us began or ended. We had just finished making love intently, and I was falling asleep in Matt's arms.

"I haven't given you anything," Matt said tenderly in my ear.

My eyes opened. He was studying my drawing. "It's nothing," I said. "I didn't spent money on anything. You liked the drawing so I gave it to you. You liked the way I danced and the scarf was a token of my thanks. Besides, you gave me the necklace."

311

He picked up my necklace and examined it for a moment. "No, you found that. Still, I should give you something because you're not getting these things back."

I wanted to go to sleep. He didn't need to give me anything; in fact, I wished he wouldn't. It would make everything so much harder if he did.

Matt's arms pulled away from me. Making a grumbling sound, I pulled my pillow over my head as he left the bed. I tightened the pillow over my ears as he opened his trunk and noisily went through it. I bounced my foot on the mattress to make him stop as I groaned at him again.

Matt began throwing things at me. I rolled into a ball while pushing the pillow harder into my ears. He began snickering. Out of nowhere his arms dragged me closer to him. He snickered once more as I grumbled at him again. Then he untangled me from the sheets and pillow.

"What are you up to? I'm going back to my room," I said, glaring up at him. He had a grin on his face. I tried to heave away from him; whatever he was doing was scaring me and he needed to stop. I didn't want to end up married or something.

"No, you're not going back to your room. I'm not doing anything," Matt said, a smug expression on his face.

I sighed before turning around to sit up. "Mathew Ryan Dixson, what are you up to?"

"Well, I was thinking that since I haven't given you anything, I should give you something." Matt lifted his hand, which he held in a fist. "Put your hand out."

I stared at his hand, not sure what he was doing. He needed to stop, as he shouldn't have been giving me anything.

"Go on, put your hand out. You don't trust me, do you?"

"Matt, that's one thing I do. I do trust you." I put my hand to his face; he was looking hurt.

"Do you?" Matt asked, seeming surprised. "Really?"

"Yes." I sighed as I put out my hand. Matt slowly opened his fist and let what was in it fall into my hand. It was a ring—a small ring that would fit only on my little finger. It was heavy and yellow.

"Matt," I said in a hush. My hand flew over my mouth as I stared at the ring. It was a snake eating its tail—the sign for eternity. I looked at him in surprise, then swallowed. "Matt, that looks…" I looked at the ring closer.

"It's very old and…" Matt cut in.

"….and it's twenty-four carats."

"…and twenty-four carats." Matt chuckled at how I was acting.

"You can't give me this," I said, trying to hand it back.

Matt pushed my hand away. "Yes I can. It's mine. I didn't pay for it; I found it."

I swallowed hard. "Where did you find something like this?"

"It was Grandpa Jack's. He gave it to me after I found it in his office. It's the symbol of rebirth. Do you like it?"

"Yes I do. But Matt, it was your grandpa's; you can't give me this."

"Wear it. It's not like I'm asking you to marry me or something. It's just…" Matt stopped. He wasn't smiling.

"Just what?" I asked, trying to understand his mood. It seemed that he had been about to tell me something, but had stopped. "Matt, what?" I put my hand on his chest; his heart was beating fast.

He reached out and placed his hand over the ring. "Laura, for the first time I feel I can trust someone. I don't normally. I kinda

313

trust John. But you…it's like I can tell you anything. You would understand, not judge me. So I want you to see it as a thanks, that's all. Don't make too much of it. It's alright, really."

A guy had never said that to me before—that he could trust me. I didn't know what to say. I leant over and kissed Matt on the lips.

"I'll wear it. I should thank you."

"What for?" he asked.

"For helping me find me again."

"Apart from me yelling at you." Darkness crossed his eyes again.

I let out a long breath. "You've made up for that."

Matt half smiled. He took the ring out of my hand and slipped it onto my little finger.

"Thank you," Matt said. He pulled me on top of him and gently kissed me.

The next morning was the weekend, so we were able to sleep in a little later. Matt went downstairs so that we could have breakfast in bed.

"John and Marisa want to come with us today," Matt told me when he returned, setting down a tray of food.

"That sounds good. I'm sure Marisa wants to grill me some more about what's been going on," I said, taking a sip of coffee as Matt sat at the foot of the bed.

He chewed the inside of his mouth for a moment. "How much detail do women go into?" Matt asked finally.

"I shouldn't tell you."

"Why not?" Matt asked.

"It'll betray the sisterhood code of conduct. That's why not." I grinned at him.

314

"Go on, I won't tell. I promise." Matt put one hand over his heart and held up his other hand, which was holding a piece of toast.

I took another sip of coffee. Matt gave me a pleading look. I rolled my eyes at him and swallowed what I was drinking. "Well, friends—I mean, the ones we trust, not the friends who tell other people everything. Our trusted close friends, we tell them everything. Chester would have told everyone and Marisa wouldn't."

"Chester?" Matt looked a little worried.

"I didn't tell you about Chester, did I?"

"No you didn't."

I took a deep breath. Since the day I had seen Matt in the car park, I hadn't once thought about Chester. I didn't know whether or not that was good. "Chester, well, he was good friends with both Marisa and me. He worked with us. We all met at Uni."

"Uni?"

"College."

"Right, okay, got you. Go on." Matt waved his toast at me.

"He died. A few months ago, from cancer. He and Ricky, his boyfriend, are like family."

"I'm sorry; you've been through a rough few months." Matt rubbed my leg to reinsure me..

"Yeah, but I'm getting there. It's okay." I was trying to sound brave, but Matt wasn't having it.

"Chester would have told everyone else?" Matt asked.

"Oh yes, and if I had let anything slip, he would have ensured that it slipped out when you were around just to get a rise out of you. Don't get me wrong, it wouldn't have been anything important; he kept those things to himself. But with Marisa…I tell her more things."

"What sort of things do you tell your friends?"

"I don't know. Things that women find important but that you men don't."

"Like what?"

"Stuff." I grinned.

"That isn't telling me anything."

"I know. Because I'm trying to stop you from asking these types of questions." I took another sip of coffee. I didn't want to say anymore, but Matt was playing now. He enjoyed watching me trying to wiggle out of this.

"What else?" he asked.

I looked at him for a second, trying to think of a way to stop this. "Well…we sometimes compare notes."

"Compare notes?" He tried to sound cool, but now he was worried. This was more fun.

"Yes, compare notes. Oh come on, you men do it too. We just do different types of comparing, that's all."

"You and Marisa compare *notes* about me and John?"

"Maybe. Worried?"

"Yes," Matt answered.

"Don't be. I'm not having a mad affair with John." I was happy that he was sweating a little.

"Thank goodness for that because I'd be very lonely." Matt picked up the tray and put it on the floor. I snickered at him. Matt crawled over to me, making growling sounds. He pinned me down and tried to kiss me.

I pushed him back. "Male ego." I shook my head at him. "Rule One—thou shalt not lose face. Rule Two—thou shalt not bruise a male ego. Rule Three—thou must stroke the ego when Rules One and Two have been broken."

"I like that," Matt said.

I tried to get off the bed. "We're going out today. I need to get dressed." Matt pinned me back down; he was about to kiss me. I moved my head. "I need to get dressed."

"Come here, babe; I need my ego stroked. You damaged me." Matt leant down and moved his lips on my neck.

"Liar," I mumbled through my giggles.

Later that morning we met John and Marisa at the ferry dock. We were going to Luxor Temple. John and Matt were eager to show off Nefertiti's temple and where they had found the mummies.

I still hadn't gotten anything for Emily, Mum, or Dad yet; I thought this would be a good chance. I could see that Marisa wanted to know what was going on. After telling Matt all that stuff, I had to be careful.

The ferry putted across the green water. We were packed in like cattle. One side of the ferry was open, with hard wooden and metal seats. The choice of where to sit was limited. A man sat near us with a small herd of goats on string tethers that he kept a tight hold of. Marisa was sitting on John's lap, while Matt and I were shoved against a wall next to them. I held Marisa's legs over my lap to make more room for the goats. If this had been midsummer, it would have been unbearable, but now I thought it was kind of fun. The goats smelt like goats, and the little ones were cute, though the males could be evil looking.

My hand moved on Marisa's leg; her eyes narrowed to my ring. "Ooh, I like that," she said, grabbing my hand and trying to talk as quietly as possible. We weren't on a tourist boat, so Marisa needed to keep her voice down. She knew how many carats the ring was and what it meant. There were endless stories of women who lost their fingers to people wanting jewellery from tourists, so we needed to be careful.

"I like it. Matt gave it to me last night," I said.

Marisa looked at me and then at Matt. I grinned at him and he rubbed my arm.

"Lucky you." Marisa nodded. There it was again; she was hiding something.

Matt was listening, so I couldn't say more. "I like it," I said quietly.

We were almost to shore when one of the goats broke its tether. Matt reached out to grab it. He kept hold of it, stopping it from jumping overboard. Marisa gave me a quick look and mouthed, *"We need to talk."*

"We'll talk later," I mouthed back at her.

Matt carried the goat off the ferry. I held onto another goat as Matt and the local man restrained the other animals. "Shukran. *Thank you.*" The man patted Matt's hand before he bowed at me, then led his unruly herd away.

Matt took my hand as we strolled up to Luxor Temple from the dock. In front of the Temple was a small boy. He sat in a squat with a blanket in front of him. On the blanket was a pile of leather-platted bracelets. Emily would have loved one. I let go of Matt's hand.

I bent down to look at the bracelets. "Ahlam," I said to the boy.

"Ahlam. *Hello*," the boy said back to me.

"Bikaam? *How much?*" I asked.

"Hamsa LE. *Five dollars*." He put one finger up, indicating one bracelet.

I picked up a purple and green bracelet that I thought Emily would like. Then I picked up a black one.

"Hamsa LE. *Five for two*." I held out the two bracelets.

"La. *No*," the boy said.

"Itneen LE. *Two dollars*," I said

"Itneen?" he said in surprise.

"Nam. *Yes*," I said, still holding out the two. Then I smiled at him.

"Nam." He smiled at me.

"Shukran. *Thank you*," I said as I handed over the money.

Matt grinned as he watched me. He took my hand as soon as I was close to him.

"Khoaga. *Tourist*," Matt said to me playfully.

"Thank you. Today that's what I am—a tourist. You need to be nice or I won't give you this." I wiggled the black bracelet in front of his nose.

Marisa and John had gone ahead. I picked up Matt's arm to tie the bracelet around his wrist. I slowly let go before walking away from him.

"Shukran," Matt said as he hurried after me and grabbed hold of my hand. With the other, he took me around the waist. He rubbed the tip of his nose on my neck as I let out a giggle. There was no one around to upset.

We spent most of the morning walking around the temples. We didn't need a tour guide, as Matt and John had all the facts. The two men took us around Nefertiti's temple to show us where they had found the cats.

"This consumed most of Grandpa Jack's career, looking for this temple," Matt said as he moved around. It was as though he were at home.

319

"I can see why. It's impressive—or it would have been at one time. It's worth the hunt," I said. The temple looked as though, in a previous time, it would have been all white. In the sun it would have been remarkable to see. Now there were some tall walls and pillars with which the Ancient Egyptians had covered it up.

"It was hiding out in the open, just behind Karnak Temple all this time. They covered it over once. Amarna had ended. No one knew it was here, but Grandpa had a hunch."

Matt was excited that he had finally impressed me. I hovered my hand over one of the white walls. I didn't want to touch the paintings; they were old and demanded respect. There were damaged paintings of Nefertiti and her family praying. The image I was studying was of the offering of the mummified cats.

"It was worth *the hunt*. That's what gave me the idea to search for them. That picture," Matt said.

John and Marisa were wandering around hand in hand as John pointed out different parts of the temple. Not many people knew it was here. Tourists wanted to see the bigger temples, so we had the place to ourselves. Matt showed me to the front of the temple and unlocked a metal hatch in the floor. We slowly opened it. Matt took a small torch out of his pocket and moved the light around in the darkness.

My eyes took a moment to adjust to the light. The smell of sand and dried flesh rose from the hole. I had smelt it before, while digging up the mummy the other day. I began to see little faces. Laying side by side, piled up on one another, were small bodies— more than one hundred. Matt leant into the hole and gently lifted one of them. He quickly glanced at John, who was still showing Marisa the wall paintings.

In Matt's hand was a grey, neatly wrapped body—one of the cats. "This one Grandpa and I found when I was ten. I hid it in here so that no one could take it," Matt said in a hush. I reached out my hand to touch it. I smiled; it felt as though it could break.

Matt glanced over my shoulder. John and Marisa were approaching us. Matt slowly lowered the mummy into the hole. He gave me a quick wink just as John and Marisa came to see the cache of cats.

The rest of the morning we packed in as much sightseeing as possible. As lunchtime approached, we wandered over to the bazaar that had been set up for tourists. Matt and John left us to buy lunch. Marisa and I found a table to sit at.

"I'm getting used to all this service; it'll be hard when we go home," I said, watching Matt walk away.

"What are you doing, Laura?" Marisa asked.

I let out a breath before I said, "I don't know."

"Have you two talked about what's going to happen?"

I was about to answer Marisa but I was stopped. An old woman came rushing up to us, her eyes fixed on me. She startled me. The Arab people have a way of looking at you, as though they can see into your soul. I sat back in my seat.

That's when I realised who I was looking at. It was the woman I had met in the museum when I was a child. My jaw dropped as she stood over me.

"I have message for you, child," she said in broken English.

"Cleo?" I breathed. She still looked the same age she had been years earlier. She wore the same clothes and carried the same bag.

"You don't see what's in front of you. The both of you. Soul-bound...twisted... Une connexion ame. Heureux, malheure endehors. You see...you see." She pulled my necklace out of my shirt and wiggled it in my face. "Une connexion ame. Heureux, malheure endehors." She pointed at Matt and then me. "Yes, see? It all lead to this."

"Hey!" I could hear Matt's voice yelling behind us, but I couldn't see anything but her.

Matt yelled once more. My eyes stayed on Cleo. She let me go, backed away, and hurried off into the crowd. Matt came rushing up to me. I think Marisa had tried to pull her off me, but I wasn't sure.

"Who was that?" John asked as he hurried behind Matt.

"I don't know," Marisa answered.

I couldn't speak; all noises sounded as though they were coming through a tunnel. It was as though I were having a dream.

"Laura, are you all right? What did she say to you? Laura, you look white as a ghost. Are you alright?" Matt touched my face and rapidly rubbed my cheek to get me to look at him.

I shook my head to clear it. "A ghost? It was nothing. Don't worry about it. Silly fortune tellers; you never know when to believe them."

"She must have said something to worry you. Did she say her name?" Matt asked, still holding my face.

Trying to process what had happened, I answered him. "No…she didn't. I'm fine…um…Matt. Don't worry." I felt like every part of my energy had been pulled from me, like I was stoned. My head was light. Matt tapped my face to try and bring me around.

"Matt, we better take her back. She's a bit green around the gills," John said from beside me.

"Laura, can you walk, or do you want me to carry you?" Matt tried to pick me up.

I slapped him on the shoulder as I sluggishly moved away from him. "I don't…like to be…carried. I'll walk. I'm fine. I just feel like…I need a nap." I felt silly.

That afternoon, back at the hotel, I curled into a ball and slept until dinnertime, when I opened my eyes again. Matt was fussing over me like a mother hen. I felt the back of his hand touch my cheek softly as I opened my eyes. "What time is it?" I asked.

"It's about seven o'clock. How you feeling?"

"I'm fine...I'm sorry." My voice was gravelly.

"What for? You didn't do anything."

"It was all silly. She was trying to get a reaction out of me. I shouldn't have slapped you. It just upset me that she kept pushing it."

Matt frowned. "What did she say?"

"She said that I was bound to something. I really didn't understand it; her English wasn't good. It sounded like it was French, which I don't speak."

The next morning when Matt and I went down for breakfast Marisa was waiting for me.

"Laura, I'm going for a walk. I want you to come with me. John's going to be working this morning and we haven't had much girl time since Cairo."

"You didn't want to do anything, did you?" I asked Matt.

"No, it's okay. I have a few reports to write. You and Marisa go have some *girl time*."

I gave him a double look; he was enjoying the words "girl time." I wished I hadn't told him; some men are happier when they have no clue.

Matt left for the finds shed. I wasn't too happy that Piper tried to talk to him as he left the dining room. However, to his credit, he waved her off.

I came to a stop at a pile of rocks; there was a sandy path that led down to the Nile just away from the hotel. A little way down, near papyrus reeds that stood tall on both sides of the path. I stopped to look out over the river.

Marisa walked past me before stopping. She crossed her arms while facing the Nile. "Laura, what's going on with the two of you? I mean, I don't care if you're going to carry this on, but…"

"Yeah. The *but*. That's what's worrying me. Marisa, how do you do this? You like John more than you're letting on, but the three weeks are going to end. There's something more there." She was still hiding something.

"No, there's nothing. You like Matt a lot more than *you're* letting on. What John and I have is different, Laura. We know where we're going and what we're doing."

"Are you sure about that? I've seen the way John looks at you. The man is mad about you, but you just let him slip through your fingers." I wasn't irate at Marisa for whatever she was hiding; it must be for a good reason.

"This is about you, not me," Marisa snapped.

"Is it really?" I snapped back, letting out a breath to calm myself. I carried on. "This isn't going to be easy. I don't want to hurt Matt. I have the feeling he has had a lot of hurt in his life, and there's a lot more. I also know he doesn't want to hurt me. Oh crap, I don't know." I sat down and put my hands over my head.

"Why did he give you the ring?" Marisa asked.

"Because he wanted to let me know that he trusts me."

"Is that all it means?" she asked me harshly.

"I don't know." I picked up a handful of sand and let it fall out of my fingers. It was time to tell her a few things. I didn't know how she was going to take it. "Marisa, don't laugh, please."

Marisa sat next to me. "What is it? I won't laugh. We've been friends since school. We tell each other everything, don't we? Tell me."

I didn't look at her. I let the last specks of sand fall from my hand. "You see, I haven't told anyone this."

324

"Tell me, Laura."

"All right. You'll now know that I have lost the plot. When I found out that I was having Emily, I had a dream of here, of Egypt. There was a figure in this dream. This Dark Figure. The humming is connected to this as well."

Marisa was now looking troubled. "Go on."

"I didn't think much of it. It was just a dream, right? Before I came here, I had the same sort of dream again, but not entirely the same. The same figure was there. It was saying that I needed *to find myself again* and come here to Egypt. That's what I meant that day when I said, *'I think the universe wants me to come here.'* Marisa, the dark figure was Matt. All the humming I have done over the years it's about meeting him. "

Marisa's expression hadn't changed. She watched me for a moment. "Laura, what are you doing?"

"That woman yesterday and the dreams." I was trying to explain, but it wasn't coming out as it should have. It was getting muddled.

Marisa was now thinking that I was losing the plot. I could see it on her face and I wanted her to understand.

"Laura, you don't dream of dark figures like that; they're bad omens."

"No…you see, not this one. The figure talked like Matt and also touched me like he does. The woman yesterday, she was..."

Marisa talked over me. "You were holding hands with Matt all day yesterday; the woman was watching you." I was glad I was sitting down, as I didn't understand any of it.

"When I'm with Matt, it's different than when I've been with anyone else. I feel like I'm alive again. It's as though he breathes life into me. Paul never did that for me, and not even the other guys I've dated. I feel like I can take on the world when Matt's around. He's ten years younger than I am, but I don't care. In few weeks I have to go home. It's the most unbearable feeling that I've felt so far in my life. I need to go home to Emily. Crap."

"What are you going to do, Laura? You have to talk to him. The thing with you, Laura, is that you don't just walk away from things that easily. What are you going to do?"

"I don't know. I know. It's a holiday romance and nothing else." I was trying to sound brave and to convince myself. It wasn't working.

I held the little finger with the ring on it in the air. I didn't know whether Marisa believed me about the dreams, but at least she understood what my heart and head were saying, even if she didn't like the dream side of things.

Once back at the hotel, I needed to have some time to myself. I didn't want Matt to know I was confused. It all boiled down to the fact that I had to talk to him about how he was feeling. However, that wasn't hard to guess. I needed some time to settle myself down. I went up to my hotel room and told Marisa that I had reports to write and emails to send. It had been a long week, and it had been only *one week* since I had really met Matt, but it seemed like years. How would I get a man like Matt out of my system? If I just walked away, he would end up being the person I thought about on cold, dark, lonely nights. He would become those endless questions. Where are you now? Should you have been? Do you think of me? Maybe he was the one.

I didn't write any emails or reports. I transferred my photos from my camera to my laptop. Then I flopped on my bed and lay there looking at the ceiling. The way Marisa had been acting played in my mind. She was hiding something. What I had said to Matt about Marisa the other morning came back to me. If John had told her something and told her to keep it to herself, she would. I made a promise to myself to not make it hard on her.

In the end, Matt and I had to say goodbye to each other at the end of three weeks. Not a problem. Right.

Matt and I had two weeks left together; he could grow to not want me around in those two weeks. Problem solved. I sighed when I thought that.

"I don't think that's going to happen," I said to myself. I wasn't going to ruin our last two weeks together.

The day had slipped away from me. I hadn't realised how late it was. I had missed dinner. The dining room was almost empty, with only a few students sitting around and talking. Others were playing games. I made my way up to Matt's room. I had a key, so I let myself in.

Matt was at his laptop, typing out research notes. The blues was playing softly in the background on his CD player. It felt like I was coming home.

"Hi," I said quietly.

Matt's face lit up when he saw me. "I was starting to think you fell in the Nile. You missed dinner."

"Yeah, I know. I'm sorry."

Matt sat back. He put his arm out and pulled me onto his lap. "You all right?"

"Yes." I rested my head on his shoulder.

He held me tighter. "You sure?"

"Yes. You know, I was thinking that we haven't been to Amarna yet," I said, playing with his shirt.

"You haven't. I've been there a few times," Matt said, looking smug. "You're a good diversion, do you know that?"

"I am. And don't rub it in about Amarna. Do you think you're going to take me next weekend?"

"Yes, you're very good at it. All right, I'll take you next weekend. It's a date. I can't resist a woman who is playing with my shirt like that." He kissed my forehead.

Matt knew something was up, but he wasn't going to drag it out of me. I was in the mood to just be cuddled. He ran the back of his hand on my cheek. I closed my eyes. Opening them, I ran my fingers over his unshaven face. He was back to three-day growth again.

"Do you want me to shave?"

"No, I like it. It suits you."

"Yeah, it makes me look older," Matt said in a macho voice.

I smiled. "I didn't think that the age thing was worrying you."

"Is that what's upsetting you?" Matt sounded concerned.

"No." I still had my head on his shoulder.

"I'll get it out of you. I have ways of making you talk." Matt said it in a funny German voice. He lifted my face gently so that he could kiss me. This kiss was going to lead to more. Matt stopped and sighed.

"I'll tell you anything if you're going to do that to me. I'll even tell you a few lies to make it more interesting if you want," I said playfully.

"I really need to finish this report. Your dinner is on the bed."

Sighing, I tried to stand up. Matt tightened his arm around me and looked me in the eyes. "Whatever it is, you can talk to me about it. You know that, don't you?"

"I know and I will. Don't worry about it now. You have a report to write and I have dinner to eat. The CD needs to be changed and maybe a shower." I was trying to lighten his mood.

Matt wasn't playing. "Will you?"

I kissed him once. "I will."

I went over to the bed to eat. The CD ended just as I finished. I went over to change it. Flicking through his CDs, I saw that Matt had a good selection—Green Day, AC/DC, Powder Finger, The Doors, Muddy Waters, John Lennon, and Janis Joplin were just some of the artists on a few of his burned discs. I put on a mixed disc; it was nice to know we had the same taste in music.

In his trunk he had some archaeology magazines. I moved them around. In addition to a few dirty shirts and socks, I found a photo of a couple. I pulled it out to look at it.

"This, your mum and dad?" They stood smiling at the camera. It looked like they were at a country fair, with a young kid eating an ice cream. It was Matt as a young boy.

Matt stopped typing and looked around. He nodded.

"You look like your mum, I think. They look like a loving couple."

"Thanks, they were." He didn't seem upset. I put the photo back and picked up a magazine that looked interesting. I lay on the bed to read and turned my back to him.

I was halfway through an article about a statue that had been found in the sea at Alexandria when I felt the bed sag down. Matt's hand found its way under my blouse. He slid his hand over my shoulder to reveal the skin. His warm lips tenderly kissed it. I rolled over and we looked at each other for a moment. There was no need for talking; it was as though everything had been said, for this moment anyway.

My need for him was matched in his eyes. Matt lay down next to me and his lips found their way to my neck. My hand went through his hair. I enjoyed the sensation of Matt touching me and the fire that was pulsating through my body. His three-day growth on my skin intensified my breathing. Matt pulled himself up a little so that I could unbutton his shirt. My fingers glided over his chest, and his eyes closed at the pleasure of my touch.

When his eyes opened, they were hungry. Matt turned his attention to my stomach. I took a deep breath as he softly bit my skin. Matt's lips obsessively moved up my body as he slipped off my blouse.

My hands began exploring his body. He stopped me by taking hold of my hands and placing them over my head. He wanted to take his time. Every time I tried to move he would stop me by either kissing me or moving my hands slowly back over my head.

Finally giving in, I closed my eyes to enjoy the sensation of his lips moving over my skin. My body arched as I drew in a deep breath. His arm tightened around me; he was breathing as hard as I was. My whole body was on fire at every touch; my breath became harder and faster. I was having trouble staying still, which excited him more. He gently kept hold of my arms to stop them from moving. Matt's breath was just as hard and hot on my skin; he stopped to catch his breath.

In one movement, Matt rolled me over so that I was on top of him. Sitting up, my body arched back. His hands skimmed up to bring our bodies closer.

"Oh babe, do you know how beautiful you are?" Matt breathed as his lips found mine.

Later that night I lay there, watching the darkness. We had sealed the deal. We hadn't said it, but it was there. It had been there ever since the moment we had laid eyes on each other. It had been only a week and it shouldn't have happened like this. But we were in love. I finally fell asleep.

Matt woke me up for work by touching my face and kissing me, the next morning. When I opened my eyes to see him smiling at me, I smiled back.

He ran his finger along my hairline, waking me gently. "I meant what I said last night. You are beautiful," Matt said quietly.

I placed my hand on his chest to feel his heart. "Do you mean that?" I was still half-asleep and this wasn't the time to have this type of conversation. It was really unfair.

"Yes," Matt said softly.

"The way you treat me and what I feel when I'm with you…no one is going to compare to you after this."

Matt's smile turned into a frown. "Apart from the day when I yelled at you and terrified you to the point that you wanted to run away from me."

I sighed, then kissed him. "Matt, please, not again. We've gone over this already."

"I know. But still, I'm sorry."

CHAPTER 21

The next week moved along faster than I wanted it to. Matt was still trying to get out of me what was wrong. I hated it. I didn't want to kill our remaining time together. We spent the week working at the dig site, and I acted as though it were our first week.

Luckily, Marisa and John didn't want to go to Amarna with us the following weekend. We travelled north by Jeep, up the Nile from Thebes, then took a ferry to the east side of the river. Matt paid for a day hire of an old VW van. The back part of the van had been cut out and wooden seats placed in the back. The doors on the sides didn't open, so we had to get in through the back. The front seats were falling apart, and a few springs poked out of them.

The drive to Amarna from the dock was bumpy. There were no seatbelts in the van, so I had to hold on as we climbed the side of the hill. I didn't know if the old van would make it. The gears groaned as Matt geared up to reach the top of the slope. At least it wasn't that far if we broke down.

Finally we made it to the makeshift gateway to the site. The two men at the gate seemed to know Matt, as they greeted him warmly. Matt paid entry to the site, then we drove up to a large, flat plateau. From where we were, we could see palm trees lining the Nile.

Matt stopped. From the back of the van, on the flat plateau, we could see mounds of sand. It was quiet up here. After the busyness of the ferry and ferry docks, we were alone. We could have been the only people left on earth. The city was laid out in front of us under the piles of sand.

Hand in hand, we walked around the old city. From years of study, I knew the layout well. I had read about it and knew its history. This was where Akhenaten and Nefertiti moved the capital from Thebes. It was where Akhenaten changed the religion and where he almost killed Egypt's greatness. This was the birthplace of Tutankhamen. It's where his mystery had begun. It was where I was going to talk to Matt about our future.

Some say that Akhenaten and Nefertiti were so in love that they hid away from the world. It was kind of fitting; the history here involved two lovers who had changed their world to make it better for themselves. It didn't work, sadly.

We went through the tombs, which were located in the hills that lined the outskirts of the city. I let Matt do all the talking while we walked through them. He went through the history of the tombs. He showed me one of Nefertiti's famous images, of her racing her chariots. A local man sat alone at the tombs, watching them. He greeted us as he opened the tombs for us. I felt sad for him. He looked like he would be happier doing something else, but this was paid work. Some people in Egypt lived on a lot less than we did.

All day I put on a brave face. I think I acted well. I smiled when it was needed and even cracked jokes, but my body felt numb. It was as though I were going to my death.

We stood in Akhenaton's tomb. Matt watched me walk around it with his hands in his pockets. He was standing on a wooden platform. I noticed him examining the floor. He seemed happy about something before going back to watching me.

"You know, the Egyptians were good at hiding things. You could be standing on top of something and not know it," Matt said out of the blue.

Akhenaton's tomb was just a rock-cut cave now; they had smashed everything after he died, and the reliefs were hard to read and see. Wood flooring had been placed inside to help protect the tomb. Where Matt was standing, Queen Tiy—Akhenaton's mother—was said to be placed after her death.

Around lunchtime, we had a picnic in the back of the van. I chewed listlessly on my sandwich and drank more than I normally would have. Luckily, Matt hadn't noticed that anything was wrong.

If Matt had asked me to run away with him, I would. The thought of talking to him was getting overwhelming. I was glad when my bladder got to be too much for me and I had to take a moment.

Matt showed me the hut where Nefertiti's bust had been found. I had joked to him about the bust the first day we met. "If we dug, do you think we would find more?" I asked, trying to sound light-hearted.

"It's over-dug; we'd be lucky." Matt grinned. It was just a pile of mud bricks. The bust had been found in the sand by a German archaeologist before World War II. Egypt wanted it back in the 1940s, but Hitler stated that, *"Something so beautiful must be German, so therefore it must stay German."* That's why it was in Germany.

I let my mind run as we walked around the Aton Temple. I was going to kick myself later for not enjoying this more.

Hand in hand, we walked to the North Palace. It was our last stop. I stood and looked at where Nefertiti herself had walked in her garden and swam in her pool. Her own world where nothing could hurt her—a protected place.

Matt took hold of me; I could feel his breath on my neck. *"Beautiful of face it pleases me to look on her face. When I hear her voice, my heart rejoices. When she is away from me, I will not speak her name as she may not come back to me,"* he said. "I didn't have to say it in front of a class; Grandpa Jack made me read the poems on my summer vacations. Mostly he would make me translate things he sent to me; then he would correct them." I turned to look in Matt's eyes. "Akhenaten wrote that for Nefertiti," he continued, looking at me and trying to determine what I was thinking.

"He was a good poet, but not good at running a country." It slipped out of my mouth.

"Mmm." Matt brushed the hair away from my neck.

334

"Matt."

"Yes," Matt answered as he slowly began kissing my neck. He wasn't listening.

I gave him a moment; what he was doing felt good. "We need to talk," I finally said.

Matt stopped before sighing. "Yes, I know."

We held each other tightly. "I have to go home next Sunday," I spoke into his shoulder.

"I can't come with you. Is that what you and Marisa were talking about the other day?" Matt wasn't angry; he pulled me back to see me better.

"Sort of."

He let me go and took a few steps away. "I need to tell you something about me, Laura. When I had the car crash, I…" Matt turned away and hung his head. "Laura, I killed some people."

I stood frozen to the spot. I hadn't seen that coming, not at all. I let him finish.

"I was driving the truck, I was drunk, and I was only fifteen. I was in the hospital, then I went to…prison. John found me. He worked with my grandpa, as you know. He found me while I was in jail. John helped me get into college, then helped me get my job as a professor. I was in for second-degree murder. I was let off for good behaviour after seven years. I went to college, but had to report to my parole officer every week. I'm allowed to come to Egypt only because the old head of the Egyptian Museum in Cairo vouched for me; he was friends with Grandpa Jack. That's what I was doing when I first met you—reporting to the Cairo Museum, which I have to do every time I come here. The week before coming to Australia, I was busted again for drunk driving; that's why I was turned back at the border. Also, when Australia found out about the jail time, I was given a one-way ticket home. My college girlfriend left me when she found out about my past."

335

He hadn't looked at me yet. My knees went out from under me. *"He's not like Paul"* kept running through my head.

Matt turned around, hurried over to me, and wrapped his arms around me. "I'm sorry. I'm sorry. I'm sorry," he kept saying.

"Paul will stop Emily from leaving," was all I could breathe out. Tears streamed down my face. I looked back at Matt, who wiped my tears gently. His face had aged and his eyes had gone dark.

"Laura, I love you. I loved you the first time I saw you. You've taken my heart and my soul. They belong to you and no one else. I don't want them back."

I sucked on my bottom lip before I spoke. "Matt." I should have lied, but it was impossible. I couldn't, not about this. "I...I...I love you, too." Matt held me tighter.

Returning to my thoughts, I pushed away from him and staggered to my feet, taking a few uneasy steps. Then I turned to look at him. Helpless, he sat where I had left him; this was hurting him just as much as it was me. I couldn't stand the pain in his eyes; I had to turn away from him. The sound of his hand hitting his leg echoed in the air and made me jump. It was followed shortly afterward by the sound of him getting to his feet.

The dreams and Cleo didn't need to be spoken about here. He would have understood; none of this mattered anymore. This was going to hurt, no matter what happened. *We couldn't be together*. I felt that my soul was about to die.

"You're not that person anymore. But..." I said, trying to hold my voice. "We can't be together. No matter how we feel, I'm a mother. I have to think of Emily. She's more important than *us*. This was only to be a holiday thing. That's all. Not this."

Matt rushed over, grabbed my shoulders, and spun me around. "What if we just leave? We could go from here right now. We could be with each other, Laura, anywhere in the world you want."

I placed my hand on his chest; his heart was beating as fast as mine. "Matt, we can't...we can't. Emily, Matt, she's my baby. Matt, I can't. Paul would never let her out of the country. We can't do this long distance; it'll never work. I didn't want this to happen. I've never done this before, Matt. We fell in love. And...I...don't know what to do here."

Matt dropped his hands from my shoulders. "I don't know either," he said softly.

I closed my eyes to say this next part. "When I leave Egypt, we have to say goodbye. That's all we can do." Matt pulled me close to him and held me. I didn't want to be let go.

That night at dinner, John and Marisa guessed what was going on. Neither Matt nor I had talked much throughout the meal. After we had eaten, I wanted to go back to my room, as I needed to do some work. When I stood, Matt took my hand and wouldn't let go. That night in the dark, we held each other. I didn't sleep much; I felt numb.

The next morning the numb feeling remained. I sat in the backseat. Matt was driving and Marisa sat in the back with me. John tried to speak to Matt a few times, but Matt was just as terse as I was; he spoke when spoken to, but nothing more. At the dig site, John and Matt left as they did every morning to set up.

Marisa hung back to talk to me. "What's happening, Laura?"

With ice in my heart and throat, I answered her. "We're going to say goodbye on Sunday. We can't be together; it won't work. He can't leave to come to Australia, and I know I can't go to America."

"Did you tell him about our trip to the U.S.?"

"Shit." I had forgotten about it. "No Marisa, I didn't. It's best that he doesn't know. Tell John not to tell him. We need to have a clean break. We should have each other out of our systems by then." I hated the words I was saying, but it had to be like this.

Not wanting to talk anymore, I left to go over to the houses that we were clearing out. After a few moments I uncovered bone again. I shook my head. "I found bone."

Matt had been standing behind me, watching. I could feel him standing there. I looked up at him. He nodded before kneeling to assist me.

We sat there all day unearthing the mummy quietly. It was only shop talk now; our happy chatter and ribbing were gone. It wasn't right any more. The mummy was that of a woman, and it took all day to unearth her.

After that, we began sleeping in our own rooms. Matt acted polite to me. We stopped touching each other; that was the hardest part, but it was for the best. I sat at the same dinner table, and Matt still pulled out the chair for me. I felt like a china doll—any wrong step and I would break.

We still worked together a few times, and I caught myself looking at him. When I realised what I was doing, I looked away quickly. Matt did the same thing, and we would lock eyes. I could see that the pain in his eyes matched the pain in mine. A few times Matt's mouth moved as though he was about to say something, but I glanced away to stop him. The most difficult part was the lonely nights; the bed was hard and cold. I wrapped my arms around my shoulders and tried to feel something.

On the last morning at the dig site, I came down late. I couldn't bear sitting across the table from him. I tried to time everything so that I would be in time when they were ready to leave. Matt wasn't there, but Marisa and John were waiting for me.

"Where's Matt?"

"He's not coming today. Come on, we're late. I'm not playing around with his shit today," John said as he started the four-wheel drive. He was mumbling under his breath; he wasn't happy. "It's like working with Jack again. I should have known better. Nothing but trouble." Marisa crossed her arms and sat back in her seat. She

338

didn't look at me. *'Marisa is stuck between John and me,'* I thought.

I worked on my own that day. I didn't talk much to anyone. An uneasy feeling that Matt wasn't right kept dogging me. I wished for the day to end; it was driving me crazy that he was hurting. Piper was watching me; John had kept her working with his team. It was as though she was waiting for me to leave.

After an eternity we packed up. This was our last day at the dig site. It was sad to see it for the last time, but it was over.

My heart was hammering rapidly as we came to a halt in the car park. I needed to help with the finds and other things from the dig site. This being the last day, everyone was in a party mood. I wasn't. All afternoon my heart hadn't stopped pounding. I couldn't make the time go any faster.

When I went out to the truck finally, it was empty. They didn't need me anymore. I closed my eyes. *"He needs me,"* I breathed to myself. Opening my eyes, I turned to hurry into the hotel.

"Laura?"

I turned. John grabbed my arm.

"Laura, leave it, please."

"John, I'm sorry. I should have never come here." I let out a slow breath. "I'm sorry you and Marisa are in the middle of this."

"Don't say that. There's a lot about Matt you don't understand."

"He told me about his record."

John sighed. "I don't want to see you getting hurt. That's all."

I didn't want to go into everything. "Thanks, John. You're always looking after me, but I'm a big girl. I know what I'm doing," I lied to him.

"All right." He let me go slowly. I swiftly disappeared into the hotel.

339

I hurried upstairs to Matt's room. The door was locked, but I still had the key. The room was dark and clothes were everywhere. It smelt of beer. Making my way to Matt's bed, I could just see him in the dark. He had his back to me. Taking off my boots and pants, I slipped under the covers, running my fingers gently along his scar. Matt's body moved at my touch. My hand found its way through his arm before I buried my face into his back. His body moved slowly. He took hold of my hand and placed it on his face. He deeply inhaled as though to breathe me in. He rolled over to face me. His eyes were red from drinking and I could smell the alcohol on his skin.

"I'm here," I said softly. I gently kissed him on the lips.

We lay there looking at each other. Matt tenderly skimmed his fingers on my face. We held onto each other, not wanting to make love. I was glad of it; if we had made love, it would have been harder.

We fell asleep holding onto each other. Throughout the night I woke up periodically to watch him sleep. It was an uneasy night. We both could feel the hurt that this parting would create. His eyes opened as his hand came up to my face. He lightly kissed my lips. We repeated this a few times throughout the night and ended by entwining into a tight hold, to fall into more uneasy sleep.

The light of day began crawling up the wall; time was running out. If only time could stand still. I wanted to hold on to these last moments. His smell, his touch, the way we made love. The way we laughed, his playful smile—they weren't mine any more. He had given me his love, but I had no right to keep it.

Watching the light on the wall, I found my heart and soul hurting, I didn't want to leave. Matt was awake; I could tell because his breathing had changed. I looked over and swallowed hard; he was watching me. He didn't let me say anything, just pulled me close to passionately kiss me. We tried to hold each other back, but ended up in a frantic, yearning kiss. It was time to say goodbye, but we didn't seem to know how.

340

I was the one to pull away from him. He rolled onto his back and covered his eyes with his arm. "I'm not going to go to the airport with you. I can't do it," he said hoarsely.

Putting my face on his shoulder, I let out a breathless sob. "I think that's the best." I meant to sound cold, but it wasn't working.

"I love you, Laura," Matt said through his arm. He sounded easier than I did.

I pulled away from him; I didn't want to do it, but I had to go. Unsteadily, I put on my clothes, then placed the room key on the bench. My breath was shaky. I made the mistake of not holding my breath and took in an uneven gasp as I tried to leave the room.

Matt's hand came from nowhere and grasped my arm. He turned me around and looked at my face, which was wet. He wiped my face before kissing me. I had to stop this; I had to go. I pulled my face down to stop him, and Matt's head went back. Sucking the bottom of my lip, I laid my face into his chest.

Muttering. "Goodbye,"

He stepped back and we stood looking at each other uneasily. My hand moved to the doorknob. I had to get out of there.

Matt closed his eyes and crossed his arms. "Goodbye, Laura."

I opened the door and began to hurry out. Matt breathed my name. "Laura?" I stopped in the doorway, though I didn't look at him. "I love you. I always have, you know that. I've seen you in my dreams for most of my life. I've known you for a long time."

I closed my eyes and swallowed. "Yes, I've been watching you all this time as well. No more, please, this is killing me." I said the last part quietly and hurried out the door.

"I'm already dead," Matt replied.

"I love you," I breathed.

Marisa came to my room later that night. I had been hiding from Matt, who was on the other side of the hotel. I smiled, trying to look brave. She had a tray of food with her, I picked at it as we talked.

"He told me about him being in prison. It's all right that you didn't tell me."

"John told me not to. I'm sorry. I'll see you at five in the morning," Marisa said as she left.

"Yeah, okay. It's all right, don't worry about it. I get it; it's cool."

"I don't say her name as she may not come back to me." Came to my mine this was part of the poem *he* told me at Amarna.

The next morning was like seeing everything in reverse. I had packed my bags the night before and they were sitting at the door. I went down to the main lobby to hand in my key. I paid whatever money I owed. It was still dark outside. There was no sign of *him*. I half expected to see *him*. John was there to say goodbye to us. Once he finished kissing Marisa, he came over to me.

"Laura, it's been nice to see you again."

I half smiled. "Thanks John. Good to see you, too."

"We named the mummy after you."

"Thanks. Hopefully the female one. Look after *him*, John, for me. Please. Don't be hard on *him*."

"I'm sorry. He's made of tough stuff; he'll be okay. I'll kick his arse a few times to get him going. He'll be right as rain in a few days." John made a face. I didn't believe him.

"Thanks."

I should've dropped my bags, gone running up to his room, and not left his side. Instead, I gave John one last hug and left Marisa and John to say their last goodbyes.

We were driven to Luxor's airport, which was a short flight from Cairo. I didn't say much, though Marisa and I chatted a little.

342

The last two nights I hadn't had much sleep. On the flight home, Marisa gave me the window seat, as I had been in the aisle on the way there.

When the plane took off, I felt as though I was leaving part of myself behind. The plane levelled out and I pushed back my seat and curled into a ball. I must have fallen asleep, because the next thing I knew I was being told we were about to land.

"Marisa, I'm sorry," I said hoarsely.

"What for?" she asked.

"I meant to go to Egypt to forget about my problems, not to make more." I felt silly about the way I was acting.

"Laura, to see how happy you've been over the past few weeks and then to have it taken away from you—that really sucks."

I shook it off; I needed to control myself. I let out a breath. I wasn't to think of *him* anymore. "What are you and John going to do, then?"

"I may have to get him to marry me." She half-smiled.

"Good. Don't waste it."

I was met at the airport by Emily, Mum, and Dad. Emily jumped into my arms. She had gotten bigger and she was who I wanted right now. Her arms around me reassured me that I was right in what I was doing.

"Mummy, Mummy. I missed you." She was kissing me over and over.

"I missed you too," I said as I kissed her back.

Once back at the house, Mum wanted me to have a coffee. I wasn't going to say no.

"Mummy, what did you get me?" Emily asked as soon as I had sat down in Mum and Dad's lounge room. I pulled a bag from my carry-on and gave it to her.

343

"Some things are for Grandma and Grandpa, too."

Mum came in and set down a tray with coffee. Dad sat back in his chair, watching Emily.

"You look tired, Laura. Are you not feeling well? I heard about Egypt; you can get sick."

"It was a long flight, that's all." I was about to pick up my coffee cup.

Mum's eyes quickly narrowed onto my ring. "Where did you get that? It looks old."

I looked at the snake ring. "I bought it in Cairo." The lie fell from my lips too quickly and easily.

That night, I sang Emily to sleep. Thinking she was finally asleep, I left her to get ready for bed. When I came out of my bathroom, I found my bedroom light on and two brown eyes watching me. Emily had gotten in my bed. I wanted time on my own, but it wasn't meant to be.

"Just for tonight, okay?" I sighed before getting in next to her. "Move over. You must have missed me."

She nodded. Emily gave me a big smile. The camel that I had brought her lay next to her. I closed my eyes. My head was still racing, but I finally fell asleep. I had to work the next day.

That night in my dreams, *I found myself in the room again, a fire creating its only light. I could see him now; he was no longer my Dark Figure. I hoped that he would sit and speak to me, but he was slumped in his chair. His head rested in one hand, while a bottle fell from his other hand. It was a beer bottle, and it rolled across the floor. I went over to him and pulled his head back. He didn't say anything to me, just looked past me.*

I sat beside him. He slowly ran his fingers through my hair as I hummed to him.

"Why are you doing this?" I said finally.

344

"You left me."

The alarm woke me; he was gone again. Emily was still in my bed. I wiped my face, for I had been crying.

Time had its own rhythm in Sydney, and it was as though I was missing the ticks of everyone's clocks. A notice came home with Emily later that week. She had a play coming up. It was *Swan Lake* and the girls in her class wanted to wear tutus.

The next afternoon Emily sat next to me at the sewing machine, chatting away. A knock sounded at the front door. Emily took a breath.

"Go and get that Em, please." Emily jumped up and ran to the door, slapping her feet on the wooden surface as she ran.

"Em, don't run in the house. And pick up your feet," I said as I stuck my finger with a pin.

The feeling of something brushing my cheek made me glance around. The same feeling came to my face just as Emily returned with Marisa. Emily was dancing in front of her. I was half out of my seat, glancing around the room and trying to see who was here.

"Hi Marisa. How are you?" I greeted her as I sat back down uneasily.

"You all right?" she asked with a concerned expression on her face.

"Yeah, how are you?" I looked at Emily, then back to Marisa.

"I'm fine." she answered, sitting at the table.

The feeling came to my face again; my eyes widened as I gasped.

"You sure you're okay?" Marisa asked.

"Mummy, you've gone red in the face."

I was unsure about what was going on. "Do you want a coffee?" I asked while putting down the tutu.

345

"I'll get it. Here are some photos of the trip," Marisa said.

She put them down beside me. Emily came over and sat down. I hadn't printed my own photos off the work laptop yet. I flipped through Marisa's pictures, giving them to Emily to look at when I had finished. As I handed them to her, I told her what each photo was about.

"Who gave you these?" I asked.

I handed the next one to Emily, then stopped. I held a photo of me and *him*. It had been taken at Luxor Temple. He was holding me and we were both smiling happily at the camera.

"John sent them by email today." Marisa could see the look on my face as she sat down. I had gone quiet.

"Ooh, Mummy who's that?" Emily asked, her eyes lighting up. She was still looking at the photos. I had forgotten she was there. "Do you have a boyfriend?"

"No. Stop it, Em."

I flipped the photo over and put it on my lap. Quickly I skimmed through the rest to see if there were any more, but to my relief there were not. Handing Emily the rest of the photos, I stood with the photo of *him* and I. Without a word, I left the room.

"Sorry Laura, I didn't know. I didn't look at them," Marisa called after me.

I just nodded at Marisa.

Once in my room, I closed the door. I sat on my bed and looked at the photo. *"Laura?"*... *"I love you."* His voice came to me as clear as it had that morning.

"No more Matt, please; this is killing me."

"I'm already dead." The words echoed in my mind along with images of the dream I had had the night I came home.

The book that Cleo had given me years ago lay in my drawer. I opened it and placed us between the pages. I needed to show everyone that I was okay. It was time to forget Egypt.

"So, how was your first day back at work?" I asked as I returned to the dining room.

"Good." Marisa frowned at the way I was acting. "They've hired someone new for Chester's job."

"Yes, I heard. I haven't met him yet." I was carrying on as though nothing had happened.

Marisa was waiting for me to get off this subject; I could hear it in her voice. I wasn't going there.

"His name is Scott," she finally said. "I didn't see him either. He was down at the Rocks. There's a set of 1970s units that have been pulled down. They had found something older under them. It looks like it was a school or something."

"Anything good?" I asked. Emily had finished looking at the photos and handed them back to me.

"No, not yet," Marisa said, taking a sip of her coffee.

I knew I had to go to New York in a few months, but by then *he* should no longer be mine.

Heart of the soul

My eyes kept gliding back to John and Marisa, they had their backs to me as they spoke to Piper. I could not move, my feet felt like jelly. A waiter walked past Piper with a tray of glasses an arm came past her to the tray, that's when I saw *Him*.

My heart was thumping fast, I couldn't hear over the pounding of my heart in my ears, my legs still couldn't move. I had seen *Him* in my dreams this was the first time in months I had seen *Him* in the flesh. *His* eyes looked over to me as he took the glass off the tray. *He* looked good I felt my eyes soften,

He was clean-shaven my mind was telling me to run, but my body didn't want to act. I had to hold myself I wanted to go to *Him*, I was trying to tell myself no I needed to run.

"No I can't do this." I muttered unknowingly to myself.

He had frozen it was as if he didn't understand it was me. That was my chance, I had to move but I still couldn't. Piper turned to see what *He* was looking at, she frowned when she saw me. John and Marisa turned around to see what they were looking at. John swiftly flung out to seize His arm, *He* threw John off. Marisa had a concerned look on her face as she looked at me then to *Him*.

His eyes slowly begun to understand it was me, now it was time to move I had to go He was about to pounce. Piper was trying to talk quickly to *Him*, *He* wasn't listening, the expression on *His* face was of confusion and anger.

"I can't do this." I said a little louder, He begun to shake his head as if to tell me different

My Texan friend was still talking to me, a group of people walked between *He* and I. It had broken our trance, my body could move. I quickly disappeared into the crowd, I glanced back he was trying to find me. *His* mouth was moving, I think he was saying it under *His* breath it was getting louder as I ran for the door.

"Laura?" I couldn't listen my mind was telling me to stay.

"Laura stop! LAURA!"

www.ingramcontent.com/pod-product-compliance
Lightning Source LLC
Chambersburg PA
CBHW062012170626
46813CB00001B/122